By Beatriz Williams

Husbands & Lovers
The Beach at Summerly
The Wicked Widow
Our Woman in Moscow
Her Last Flight
The Wicked Redhead
The Golden Hour
The Summer Wives
Cocoa Beach
The Wicked City
A Certain Age
Along the Infinite Sea
Tiny Little Thing
The Secret Life of Violet Grant
A Hundred Summers
Overseas

HUSBANDS
& LOVERS

HUSBANDS & LOVERS

A NOVEL

BEATRIZ WILLIAMS

BALLANTINE BOOKS

NEW YORK

Published in the United States by Ballantine Books, an imprint of Random House, a division of Penguin Random House LLC, New York.

BALLANTINE BOOKS & colophon are registered trademarks of Penguin Random House LLC.

LIBRARY OF CONGRESS CATALOGING-IN-PUBLICATION DATA

Names: Williams, Beatriz, author.
Title: Husbands & lovers: a novel / Beatriz Williams.
Other titles: Husbands and lovers
Description: New York: Ballantine Books, 2024.
Identifiers: LCCN 2023040323 (print) | LCCN 2023040324 (ebook) | ISBN 9780593724224 (hardcover; acid-free paper) | ISBN 9780593724231 (e-book)
Subjects: LCSH: Women—Fiction. | LCGFT: Novels.
Classification: LCC PS3623.I55643 H88 2024 (print) | LCC PS3623.I55643 (ebook) | DDC 813/.6—dc23/eng/20230919
LC record available at https://lccn.loc.gov/2023040323
LC ebook record available at https://lccn.loc.gov/2023040324

Printed in the United States of America on acid-free paper

randomhousebooks.com

2 4 6 8 9 7 5 3 1

First Edition

Book design by Erich Hobbing
Sunrise art: Allison/stock.adobe.com

With gratitude to my kids,
who never ate the wrong mushroom

HUSBANDS
& LOVERS

Mallory

June 2019
Mystic, Connecticut

I kissed Sam goodbye on a Saturday morning toward the end of June, and the call that changed my life came the following Friday afternoon.

Actually, the call came in twice. I'd stepped away from my desk to do some gardening. I remember the tomatoes were growing like crazy that summer, the roses exploding on their bushes. Everything so abundant. Sometimes, when I'm stuck on an idea, I find it helps to walk away for a bit and do something else, something with your hands, something useful, and that knot in your mind will loosen and unwind into the bread dough or the soapsuds or the stacks of folded clothes.

Or the soft, rich loam of a vegetable bed.

It still fills me with terror, to look at that patch of earth and remember how I knelt there, staking the rampant new vines, humming to myself while a new pattern took shape in my head—a trailing creeper in a pristine shade of spring green, not too dark or too light, the color of promise, delicate shoots and leaves curling from the parent vine.

At a few minutes to three, I stood up, dusted my jeans, shucked off my gloves, and went into the house for a glass of water and my sketch pad.

I remember my phone lay on the kitchen counter, because I hadn't carried it outdoors with me. You know how it is. I meant to step out for a few minutes to pull some weeds, maybe water the tomatoes, breathe some fresh air, but one thing led to another, and it was a beautiful day, eighty degrees and not as humid as it gets later in the summer. A breeze came in from the Mystic River, tinged with brine. Tourists would be swarming the drawbridge for ice cream. Over at the aquarium, kids would be screaming with joy as the belugas hurtled past on the other side of the plexiglass. Anyway, my phone sat alone on the counter, so I picked it up to check for messages and startling news alerts, maybe a little light scrolling, and instead I saw that I'd missed two calls from Camp Winnipesaukee.

You know that feeling. Every parent knows that feeling.

Probably nothing, you think, *probably just some missed paperwork or an impulsive, inappropriate exclamation.* Maybe a fistfight, God forbid. Kids could get scrappy at that age.

But your body's not so logical, is it? Your body's evolved for catastrophe. Your body leaps straight to the worst scenario. Your stomach turns sick, your trembling hand picks up the phone. Your heart cracks against your breastbone.

You swipe the number to call back.

You say, in your voice of fake buoyance, *Hi! This is Mallory Dunne. Sam's mom? You were trying to reach me.*

And you hear the tiny silence, the fraction of a sigh as the person on the other end gathers courage for the task before her.

Then the dreaded words:

Mrs. Dunne, I'm afraid I have some difficult news.

I think I must have driven the entire three hours to New Hampshire in a state of shock. *Now, don't panic,* I told myself, over and over. *This is not really happening. This is just a movie you're watching, a script you're acting out. Kind of like the metaverse!* Whatever that was.

Not *real,* anyway.

Not your real son, the love of your life.

I remember how I rinsed out my coffee cup and put it in the dishwasher before I left. I mean, you can't just leave a cup of coffee on the kitchen counter when you lark off to New Hampshire for

God knows how long! I swiped on a little lipstick, even though my hand shook so badly I looked like one of those Instagram people who color over the edges of their lips to make them look bigger. I started to throw a few things in an overnight bag and then thought, *What if he dies and I'm not there in time to say goodbye?*

I dropped the overnight bag and ran out the door to the car. I made it all the way to Springfield before I realized I wasn't wearing any shoes, so I had to pull over at a gas station and buy flip-flops. And gas. And three Kind bars and a bottle of water, because I was about to pass out.

He's not going to die, I told myself. A perfectly healthy boy doesn't die from eating a bad mushroom.

Unless it's too late.

Unless said boy ate said mushroom on a dare the day before and didn't mention this fact because he didn't want his friends to get in trouble, so he spent the night and the morning in the infirmary with so-called stomach trouble because the nurse had no idea she was dealing with a case of mushroom poisoning.

Unless the damage was already done.

Unless they were keeping him alive only so I could say goodbye and give permission for organ donation.

Could you donate a kid's organs if he'd ingested a poisonous mushroom?

A Range Rover zoomed past, New York plates. I looked at the speedometer and saw I was going only sixty-four, like it was no hurry, no emergency, don't want to get a speeding ticket or anything.

I pressed the accelerator.

He's not going to die, I said aloud.

My shining, beautiful boy.

Who loved to play soccer in the fall and baseball in the spring.

Whose favorite food was s'mores.

Who went boogie-boarding last week with his cousins at his aunt's house on the Cape and pretended to get attacked by a shark. (*Not funny,* I told him, after I fished him out of the water.)

Who filled an old jam jar with fireflies the night before he left for camp and told me he figured the lights came from all your ancestors in heaven, keeping watch over you.

I pounded the steering wheel. So where were all the fucking fire-flies yesterday?

Just as I reached White River Junction and turned off the interstate, it started to rain. A couple of fat drops, a couple more, and the next thing you know—monsoon. I turned on the windshield wipers. Three seconds later, I turned them on high. Wildly they pumped across the glass and still I couldn't see a thing. Sheets cascading before me. Like trying to look through a waterfall.

What happened next is a true story.

I'm tearing down this road through the New Hampshire woods toward the hospital, right? Every second counts. But I can't see ten feet in front of me. So I'm straining my eyes, not even blinking, and this dark shape flashes into view and *whoomph!* Smacks into the windshield and the jaws of the wipers.

Probably I scream, I don't know.

Just a few inches long, this poor creature, this bird. Whisking back and forth, back and forth, feathers everywhere, and I'm crying now, screaming and crying, begging God to free the bird because I can't pull over, I need to reach my son before he dies.

But the poor thing remains stuck in the wipers, smearing blood across my windshield that the rain washes away. I can't even tell what kind of bird it is. I just keep on driving, and praying, and crying.

The rain was thinning out as I swerved into the parking lot of the Dartmouth Hitchcock Medical Center, where they'd airlifted Sam a little after noon today.

(Later, when I saw *that* line item on the explanation of benefits notice from Blue Cross, I would get up to pour myself a glass of bourbon.)

But at this point, I wasn't thinking about how much any of this would cost. Save my son, that was all I cared about. I found a miraculous space near the emergency room and slammed the brakes and got out. A man stood nearby smoking a cigarette. He stared at the bird on the windshield of my old Volvo station wagon, handed down from my sister.

"Is it dead?" I demanded.

He looked at me. I still have the image of him in my head—this young, smart, hardscrabble kid in green scrubs. I remember thinking he might have been a resident or a medical student, by the look of him—a kid who got in the hard way, no fancy private schools, no tutors or pushy parents. Job after school bagging groceries to save up money. He just wanted to be a doctor.

"That's an owl," he said. "A baby owl."

"Is it dead? Just tell me, is it dead?"

"Of course it's dead," he said.

At the ER reception, I fumbled out some explanation about summer camp and mushrooms to the nurse on duty. He was used to hysterical parents and interrupted me to ask, in a voice that was neither kind nor unkind, for the patient's name.

I took a deep breath. "Sam Dunne."

"Date of birth?"

"May tenth, oh-nine."

"Relationship to patient?"

"I'm his mother, for God's sake!"

He tapped away on his computer keyboard, staring at the screen. "Name?"

"*My* name?"

"Yes, ma'am."

I stared at the part in his hair. Light brown waves. Pink scalp.

The nurse looked up. "Ma'am? Your name?"

Starts with an M, I thought. *You can do this.*

He waved his hand slowly in front of my face. "Ma'am? Do you need to sit down?"

"Mallory!" I sagged in relief. "Mallory Dunne."

The nurse turned back to his computer and resumed the tapping. "I'll need your ID and insurance card, please, Mrs. Dunne."

"My what?"

"ID and insurance, please."

I gripped the edge of the counter and leaned over. "My son is dying and you want to see my *identification?*"

"Mrs. Dunne, I need to ask you to calm down—"

"Calm *down?* I just drove three hours to get here! I don't even know if he's alive! He's ten years old! He's surrounded by strangers! He needs his mom!"

"Mrs. Dunne—"

"I want—to see—my *son!*"

The nurse closed his eyes, filled his lungs with patience, and said, in a nice slow kindergarten voice, "I understand. And I'm still going to have to ask for identification. For security reasons. If Sam's father—"

"Sam's father," I said, "is not in the picture."

"Irregardless—"

"That's not a word, damn it!"

The nurse picked up the phone. "I'm going to call security now."

"Call *security?* Are you kidding me? My *son* is in there! I need to see my son and you're going to call security?"

"Mrs. Dunne, you need to calm down—"

I pointed my finger at his chest. "Don't *ever* tell a woman to calm down! Especially a *mother* whose *child* is in the *emergency room!* And some *man* is trying to keep her from *seeing* him! And I am not a *missus,* by the way!"

The nurse rose from his chair, telephone in one hand. "And I'm telling *you,* Ms. Dunne, you need to start practicing calm right now. For your son's sake. Because you're going to need it."

Half an hour later, my sister arrived at the waiting room they set aside for hysterical parents. I jumped from the chair.

"Paige? What the hell are you doing here?"

"I'm the emergency contact, remember? I got here as fast as I could. Oh, Mallory." She stepped forward and pulled me into her arms. She smelled of gardenia soap and responsibility. "You're such a screwup, honey. Only *you* could end up in hospital jail."

"Have you seen him? Is he okay?"

"I talked to the doctor. He's stable. Critical but stable—"

"Critical? What does that mean?"

Paige pulled back and held me by the shoulders. "Let's go see the doctor together, okay?"

Dr. Stephens was a slight, intense, blond-ponytail woman of the type who runs eight miles at dawn before she goes to work. She looked up from her clipboard and delivered a searing gaze as I approached with Paige.

"Mrs. Dunne," she said.

I opened my mouth to correct her, then slammed it shut.

"Doctor?" I said meekly. "I'm Sam's mother."

"Yes. I'm very sorry about what's happened. We treat a certain number of mushroom cases each year, but it's rarely so serious as this."

"How serious?"

"The next forty-eight hours will be critical. Your son has ingested a basidiomycete fungus known as *Amanita phalloides*—"

"I'm sorry, what?"

Again, her eyes impaled me. "A death cap mushroom."

"Oh, shit," I said.

"I thought you were already informed."

"They said *mushroom*. Not fucking death cap."

You could almost hear her bristles arranging themselves. Her eyes weren't clear blue but opaque, like a cloudy sky at dawn, and I couldn't tell if she objected to my attitude or my language or both.

Paige gripped my elbow. "Excuse her, Doctor. It slips out when she's emotional."

"Of course," said Dr. Stephens. "The death cap contains two primary types of toxins—amatoxin and phallotoxin. In the initial period, which begins several hours after ingestion, the patient will experience the common symptoms of gastrointestinal distress—vomiting, diarrhea. So in these early stages, unless we know the patient consumed a mushroom, it's easily dismissed or misdiagnosed as a norovirus."

"Stomach flu," Paige said knowledgeably.

"Exactly. Especially in the case of children, and *especially* when they're reluctant to tell adults what they've been up to." Dr. Stephens clicked the end of her ballpoint pen. "However, during this time, the toxins have already begun to attack the patient's organs—"

"Oh, shit," I said. "Oh, shit."

"—principally the liver and kidneys, in the worst cases leading to organ failure and death."

I was acting in a movie, I reminded myself. This wasn't really happening.

"But you can treat it, right? This is modern medicine. You can give him something."

She looked at her clipboard. "The immediate concern is dehydration. He's been on an IV drip, replenishing fluids, electrolytes. There are a couple of different antibiotics that have shown efficacy in counteracting the toxin—"

"And you're giving him those?"

"Yes, along with intravenous silibinin—that's an extract of what's commonly known as the milk thistle—which helps the liver fight the damage caused by both toxins."

"What else?"

She shrugged. "We treat the symptoms. The rest is up to his body. How much he ingested, when exactly he ingested it."

"Is he in pain?"

"He's in a coma, Mrs. Dunne. That's common, in these cases."

"Can I see him?"

Her face softened. "Of course. Come with me."

She started past us. I touched the elbow of her white lab coat to stop her.

"Dr. Stephens? It's *Ms.* Dunne. Not Mrs."

The doctor made a note on her clipboard. "And his father?"

This time it was Paige who spoke up. "His father's not in the picture."

Against the white pillow, Sam's face was the color of a Dorito. I might have gasped.

"That's the jaundice," said the nurse.

I dropped into the chair next to the bed. Not because I wanted to, but because I couldn't hold myself up any longer. "Shit," I whispered.

"You can touch him. Talk to him. Let him know you're here."

Around him, the machines beeped and burped. Sam had always been big for his age, robust like his father. Radiant. Energy bursting from his skin. Too much, sometimes. So much that I would collapse in bed at night and cry because I was so exhausted, because there was nobody else to keep this ball of fire from hurtling into space, because Sam was all up to me.

The shrunken, yellowed body on the bed couldn't be Sam. It wasn't him. There was some mistake.

Then I looked at his face. A curl of damp gold hair on his forehead, the same color as his skin. I brushed it back. Behind me, Paige put her hand on my shoulder.

"Hey, buddy," I croaked. "It's Mom. Sorry it took me a while. Traffic."

The monitors beeped back.

"Anyway, I made it. I'm here. We'll get you all better in no time. And when you wake up, so help me—"

Paige snorted back a laugh.

"A mushroom, for God's sake. A goddamn mushroom."

"Mallory, don't swear in front of the kid."

"Sorry, buddy. *Darn* mushroom."

The nurse finished checking all the monitors and turned to us. Back and forth, me and Paige. "So . . . you're the parents?"

Paige snatched her hand from my shoulder. "Oh, Jesus, no. I'm her sister. She's the mother."

"Gotcha. Well, you've got one tough kid there, I'll say that much."

"You think so?" I said.

"For sure. Kinda cute under all that yellow, right? He looks like that singer."

"Oh?" Paige said innocently. "Which singer?"

"You know. Sits on a stool and plays his guitar? That new song about the birds flying south, not looking back." She hummed a few bars. "You know who I mean. He was on the cover of *People* a couple weeks ago. Dead ringer, this kid."

I turned back to Sam and sandwiched his limp hand between mine. I was so dizzy, I thought I might throw up.

"I don't know," I said. "I haven't heard that one."

Later, when I looked back on that first week in the hospital, I wouldn't be able to remember much. They say it's a blur, experiences like that, and maybe it's a cliché but it turned out to be true, the way clichés sometimes are. I would like to say there was a single moment of revelation, a turning point after which we knew Sam would survive, and we had joy and resolution and a happy ending in which we thanked all the doctors for saving his life and drove back home in that fragile moment of late afternoon when the air is washed with gold. Like in the movies.

But life isn't a movie, and that moment never came.

We kept time by the beep of the monitors and the rising and setting of the sun on the other side of the window, out there in that world where ordinary people got on with their lives, went on vacation, enjoyed the summer. Paige brought her kids and booked one of those extended stay hotels, and nobody complained about missing the summer on the ocean or the scarcity of fried clams in the New Hampshire hills. Her husband drove up on weekends to join us. Nice guy, Jake.

Paige delivered me coffee and sandwiches and made sure I brushed my teeth and changed clothes.

Day by day Sam went on living, breathing, existing, and the fear of his death was replaced by fear for the future ahead of us.

What was to come in this new world in which my ten-year-old son did not own a functioning pair of kidneys.

One discrete moment I do remember. I remember walking out of the hospital to drive to the hotel room Paige had booked for us, not because I wanted to leave but because she insisted. This would have been the second day, after I spent that first night sleeping—or not sleeping—on the chair in Sam's hospital room.

You need to sleep in a bed, Paige told me. *Sam needs you to sleep in a bed.*

So I trudged out to the parking lot and found my car. The hour was late, and because it was the end of June and this was New Hampshire, the sky had only begun to darken. The air was heavy with shadow. Would have been spooky if anything was left in this world to scare me.

I got to the car and stared at the lump of feathers stuck at the base of the windshield wipers.

I had forgotten about the bird.

A baby owl, said the man with the cigarette, and he was right. I didn't know much about woodland birds, but you could tell it was an owl by the shape of its head and its dead glass eyes. A small, juvenile owl. Probably just left its nest. Had flown out into the wide world and run smack into my panicked windshield and died, and the mother owl and the father owl never knew what happened to him.

In my ears, I still heard the relentless beep of the monitors. The tick of Sam's life.

"I'm sorry," I whispered to the baby owl. "I'm so sorry."

I sat down on the curb and opened my palms.

On my right wrist, my mother's bracelet had slipped around the wrong way, so the ends pinched the tender skin on the inside of my arm. She'd left it to me when she died, and I still felt a shock to see it wrapped around my own wrist instead of my mother's—a golden cobra, its hood arched to strike, two tiny emerald eyes and a tiny ruby tongue reaching eternally for the tip of its tail. Her own mother had given this bracelet to her, she'd told us when we were little, and I had never seen Mom's arm without it.

Until her funeral, a year and a half ago.

The snake's eyes glittered at me, the same color as my mother's.

"I need her so much," I whispered. "Why did you take her?"

But the cobra didn't say a word.

CHAPTER ONE

Hannah

August 1951
Cairo, Egypt

The cobra probably took refuge in the pavilion when the sun fell behind the hotel roof. Now it flared its hood indignantly at Hannah. Its eyes were like beads of oil. It flicked its tongue to taste the air and struck.

Hannah couldn't blame the cobra. How do you condemn a snake for being a snake?

Alistair had warned her about the cobras when they first arrived in Cairo. He'd been posted there during the war, so he felt himself a real expert. *Your Egyptian cobra grows to about four or five feet in length*—in his voice of empire, holding two pompous arms apart—*and venomous as the devil. Bugger'll crawl directly into your house or tent or trouser leg, so you'd bloody well better watch your step.*

Hannah had listened attentively and watched her step. When she and Alistair had taken that trip to Luxor last week, she'd seen them among the rocks from time to time, scorpions too, but they always slithered away. Alistair was probably disappointed. All day he'd carried a machete at his belt and cherished the idea of lopping off some cobra's head at the vital instant. What a capital story *that* would be!

Hannah didn't have a machete now. She didn't have so much as a nail file—she'd simply picked up her pocketbook and left the table. An impulse, that was all. Alistair holding forth about Indian partition, the Beverleys nodding along numbly, Alistair's smothering remark when she tried to interject a light observation—*Don't be silly, Hannah.*

She'd mumbled something about a cigarette and stalked through the packed, yammering dining room, through the Arab Hall to the gardens.

The air still hung thick and warm from the late-summer sun. The mosquitoes stirred. The smell of jasmine made her drunk. She'd heard some laughter near the loggia and crept into the shelter of the pavilion, surprising a cobra who was just settling down for a nice quiet nap.

Of all the places to die! When you thought about it, it was almost funny. All those ways she might have met her end—those accidents and objects that might have killed her, the waves of bombs, the German soldiers followed by the Soviet soldiers, to say nothing of weather and germs and a hundred other things—all those fatal moments she'd survived by miracle or force of will or some capricious God she no longer believed in—and now this?

The back garden of Shepheard's Hotel in Cairo. A dull, predictable evening in August.

What a joke, a colossal joke.

Who would have thought it would end like this, when she'd woken this morning in the plump, narrow bed in the bedroom she shared with her husband? When the soft-footed servant knocked on the door with Alistair's tea and the first of several cups of sweet, strong Turkish coffee that would punctuate Hannah's hours until lunch—why, who would have told Hannah to enjoy those coffees to the utmost, because they were her last on earth?

Who would have thought she would be dead by midnight, as she read aloud to Alistair from the newspaper while they ate the breakfast that was brought up on the tray?

When this morning, as usual, she'd straightened Alistair's necktie and pecked his dry cheek goodbye? When she'd taken the papers he had left on the corner of the desk the night before and typed them up on the typewriter, correcting the mistakes as she went along? (Alistair was a careless speller.) When, precisely as usual, she'd allowed herself the cigarette during the drive to the club, followed by the lunch, followed by the tennis with the Foreign Office wives, followed by the gin and tonic, followed by the drive home and the long bath and the second cigarette?

Who would have thought she would never experience those things again?

And when Alistair had returned from the consulate and taken up his books and his pen, as he always did, while she settled on the sofa to read the English novel and stopped to watch a lizard scurry this way and that across the floor and up the wall to disappear into the crack near the ceiling? Who would imagine she would never learn what happened to the man who loved the woman who was married to the other man?

When six o'clock struck and she rose from the sofa and poured her husband the Scotch and soda and helped him dress for dinner?

When she put on the long black dress that suited her figure and the pearls and the elbow gloves?

When she drank the second gin and tonic with lime?

Then the silent drive across the river to the hotel. The champagne cocktail. The second champagne cocktail. The prawn cocktail followed by the chilled tomato soup.

The conversation about the king—that ass Farouk, Alistair had called him.

The orchestra that had slid into the waltz as the waiters whisked away the soup and served the fish. Then the meat and vegetables. Then the salad. Then the dessert and the cheese and the nice Yquem and Indian partition and *Don't be silly, Hannah.*

Who would have whispered in her ear—when she leaned back in her seat and finished the Yquem and thought, *I shall scream—Well, don't worry, old Hannah, you've only got fifteen minutes left to live?*

That her final seconds were ticking down as Hannah rose from her chair, mumbled about the cigarette, and stumbled her way from the dining room through the Arab Hall to the doors that opened to the gardens, where Mr. Beck, the assistant hotel manager, appeared out of thin air and asked her if she required anything.

* * *

Oh, Mr. Beck. What a shame about him! Now she'd never see Mr. Beck again.

He was Swiss, according to one of the other Foreign Office wives. All the hoteliers abroad were Swiss. Somehow the profession was bred into them, the woman didn't understand how. Maybe it was something to do with neutrality. Or a tradition of mountain hospitality. To Hannah, though, the only thing Swiss about Mr. Beck was his surname. He had large, cool green eyes below straight black eyebrows, and long black eyelashes for good measure. His features were almost delicate, except for the strong jaw anchoring the bottom of his face. Like any good hotel manager, he was invisible, voiceless, except when you needed him.

Then he appeared like a djinn.

Is there anything you require, Mrs. Ainsworth? he'd asked her, not five minutes ago, and stupidly she had said *No, thank you* and continued on her way.

Haughty, they called her. She'd overheard that once. *Haughty bitch, that wife of Ainsie's. You know how he found her. God knows where she came from. Who her people are. Damned lucky old Ainsie took a fancy to her.*

Oh, she'd overheard them, all right. As they intended. The English were so polite—they'd never say these things to her face.

No, thank you, she'd said to Mr. Beck, the hotel manager with the green eyes, and continued into the gardens, alone, a little drunk, but then she was always a little drunk by evening—that was the only way you got through the day without picking up one of those slim, elegant silver knives they laid out in the dining room and murdering somebody.

Or yourself.

Now this damn cobra.

In Egypt, the cobra was sometimes called an asp, which made you think of Cleopatra. According to legend, she had her servants smuggle an asp inside a basket to her private chambers, where she was confined by Caesar or somebody.

Hannah doubted this story. An Egyptian cobra was a large snake and would almost certainly object to being stuffed inside a basket—

especially a basket small enough to smuggle into Cleopatra's chambers without raising anyone's suspicions. But Ptolemy said so; therefore, it must be true. Anyway, did it really matter how Cleopatra got the snake into her bedchamber? The point was, she died of snakebite. Unless the whole incident was a metaphor—the snake in the lady's bedchamber administering the lethal dose of venom. You get the idea.

Hannah's snake—cobra, asp, whatever you wanted to call it— was certainly real. Its tiny scales were speckled brown and its hood made a perfect arc. It lay along the railing so that when she'd sat down, a second ago, her face was only a yard away from the cobra's face—close enough, anyway, so that in the light that spilled from the hotel windows behind her, every detail was sharp.

They say time slows down at the moment of danger, and Hannah would have agreed. She'd had all the time in the world to admire the snake's beauty, the perfect hood, the infinite brown-speckled scales. All the time in the world to smell the jasmine, to hear the faint lilt of the orchestra that would sing her to sleep.

She noticed the exquisite pattern of mosaic tiles in the pavilion.

She imagined Alistair's red face, pinched in horror—what a shock this would be, who on earth would pour his Scotch and soda the way he liked it. But this lasted only an instant. Another face replaced Alistair's red, pinched one; then more faces, each one by itself yet all at once, hitting her in the gut so she couldn't breathe.

Rage.

Grief.

All this commotion she hadn't been able to feel in years. All this in the oil-drop eyes of the cobra that lunged for her neck. How stupid.

Hannah flung up her arm. The fangs sank into the back of her hand. As she fell, the world turned white, too bright to bear. The pair of arms that caught her was part of the dream.

Is there anything you require, Mrs. Ainsworth?

Yes, Mr. Beck. I require everything. I require you.

CHAPTER TWO

Mallory

June 2022
Cape Cod, Massachusetts

Paige calls me on the way home from dialysis.

"Can you talk?" she asks.

I glance at Sam in the seat next to me. He's got his AirPods in, delivering music. For his twelfth birthday I broke down and gave him a phone, because I needed to be able to contact him in an emergency, right? His hair flops over his forehead now, a few shades darker than when he was little. I can't pick out his expression as he watches the dunes go by. Sometimes it hurts, the way he's growing up, turning into somebody else. I used to understand every thought that crossed his face.

"I'm listening," I tell Paige.

She gathers herself up in a sigh. "So, it's about Mom," she says.

It's about Mom.

As it happens, those were the exact words she used to break the news when Mom died, four and a half years ago. I remember it was October because I was making Sam's Halloween costume. He was eight years old and wanted to be a space alien. I designed the whole thing myself. I was just finishing up the hands—kind of a cut-and-stitch of this puke-green satin I'd found among the fabric remainders and a pair of rubber household gloves—so I was a little irritated that she'd interrupted me with her damn phone call.

I sighed and said *What about Mom?* You know, expecting another thorough sister-to-sister discussion about Viljo, Mom's latest lover. Viljo was this blond Finnish god about seven feet tall with whom Mom was apparently having the best sex of her life, so naturally Paige disapproved of him. Blah, blah, he's too young for her. Blah, blah, he wants her for her money.

To which I might reply something like, *What money?*

To which Paige might reply something like, *Grandma and Grandpa were loaded, right?*

To which I never replied because Paige didn't know what I knew, which was that Mom considered that money tainted and gave away every dollar to the Appalachian Mountain Club for hut refurbishment as soon as she inherited it. God knows Paige would have fainted if she knew *that.* She always hated those hikes in the White Mountains where Mom hauled us every summer. *Literally the worst weather in the world,* she'd remind us. *It says so on the brochure.* So I would redirect the conversation, and it was kind of a shock for Paige when the lawyer read out Mom's will, which left Paige the little house in Provincetown and me the leftover cash in a trust for Sam's education.

But I digress.

Paige told me to sit down, and I told her I was sitting down already, could she get to the point, and Paige said, *All right. The point is, Mom's gone.*

I said I already knew Mom was gone. Gone to Peru with Viljo.

Honey, I mean the forever gone, said Paige. *I mean she's dead.*

She and Viljo—Paige called him *Dildo*—had been climbing the terraces at Machu Picchu and Mom had lost her footing. I don't know if you've ever visited Machu Picchu, or seen the photographs, but those terraces are steep, apparently. She fell some way and hit her head on the stones. By the time they got her airlifted to a hospital, she was in a coma with a brain bleed. She died in Viljo's arms the next day.

Honestly, you can't make this stuff up.

I'll spare you the drama of flying out to Peru to arrange for Mom's body to be flown home. The memorial, the cremation, the scattering of ashes off the Cape Cod shoreline at sunset. Tracking down Dad on the backstretch at Santa Anita, from which he sent his condolences but refused to attend the services, on the grounds that funerals were a drag and the Breeders' Cup was around the corner.

I'll spare you the stages of grief and the way I still find myself reaching for the phone to tell her something, only to realize she's not there. You've heard all that before, and if you've experienced it firsthand, I'm so sorry.

The point of this story is that Paige called *me* to break the news of Mom's death, instead of the other way around. I mean, Mom and I were peas in a pod, right? She told me everything, things she probably shouldn't, like where she lost her virginity and how often Viljo went down on her. She told me the whole story with Dad, and about the year she dragged her cello to Paris and busked in a Metro station to pay for food. She called me up when she got a bad Pap smear, or found some terrific new cheese at the farmers market, or had to take the cat to the vet.

She called Paige to tell her what she ought to get me for Christmas.

So how come Paige knew about Mom's death before I did?

Because she listed me as her emergency contact, Paige said, a little bashfully.

Well, that made sense. Paige is everybody's emergency contact. She's *my* emergency contact. If you're having an emergency, you want Paige on the other end of the line. Paige will answer the phone, she'll drop everything, she'll donate her own blood. (Paige is O negative, as you would expect.) When disaster strikes, you want Paige making sure there's toothpaste in the overnight bag and that specialist in Dallas is flying in for a consult.

You sure as hell don't rely on Mallory to fix things.

I understood. I understood just fine.

But that doesn't mean it didn't hurt.

Oh, and what happened to Viljo? He was so shattered about Mom's death, he went home to Finland and took orders at a monastery just inside the Arctic Circle. He still sends us Christmas cards every year.

Like I said, you can't make this stuff up.

* * *

The hand-me-down Volvo is just young enough to have a Bluetooth connection to my cellphone, and Paige's voice blares through the speakers.

"Mallory? Are you still there?"

I glance at Sam, who's still staring out the window. His finger taps his knee to the beat of whatever's coming out of his earbuds. I turn down the volume on the car's speakers.

"I'm still here. What about Mom?" I ask warily.

"So, I have a confession to make," she begins.

"Oh, crap."

"*Well?* If *you're* not going to start this thing yourself, I don't have a choice, do I? I mean, we could sit around waiting for our asshole father to change his mind and give his grandson a kidney—"

"Paige, for God's sake. Don't swear in front of the kid."

"What, Sam's listening?"

"He's in the car with me. He's got his AirPods in."

Paige makes a noise of frustration. "Mallory, this is important. This is . . . this is big."

"Then why couldn't you wait for me to get there in person?"

"How far away are you?"

"I don't know. Half an hour, no traffic? Just passed the Orleans exit."

She makes another noise. "Fine. I'll pour the vodka Spindrifts."

Since Mom left Paige the house in Provincetown, at the tip of the scorpion's tail that is Cape Cod, Paige and her husband Jake have done a lot of work to it.

I don't know how to say this delicately, so I'll just come out with it: Jake makes a lot of money. He's in some kind of finance partnership with a couple of Yale buddies, and apparently he's good at it, although you wouldn't know this to bump into him in a crosswalk. He would apologize and ask if you were okay and pick up that thing you dropped, and you would go on your way, crossing the street, never imagining that the spindly guy in the slim fit khakis and the Red Sox hat and the navy L.L. Bean fleece vest with the embroidered East Rock Partners crest on the left side made five million bucks last year. (I'm just throwing a number out there. I have no idea how much bread Jake makes—Paige scrupulously never talks about money.) He is six foot two with dark, wispy hair and a face so bland as to defy description. Paige met him at Yale, junior year, and they got married twelve years ago at the Catholic church here in Provincetown, reception on the beach at Mom's house.

In those days, we used the word *quirky* to describe our childhood home. It was nine hundred square feet of stone and cedar shingles that had survived a hundred years of nor'easters, plus the occasional hurricane, without much alteration to the original plan, except to add electricity and hot water. I remember it had a bedroom for Mom and a bedroom I shared with Paige and a bathroom down the hall that groaned when you filled the tub and groaned when you emptied it again. The kitchen was a lean-to and the parlor also served as a dining room and library, with great big windows that faced the ocean and had to be battened down with sheets of plywood before every storm.

To her credit, Paige, who is respectful of history, did not tear down this house when she and Jake undertook renovations. It now serves as their master suite, in fact, and the pipes no longer groan when you fill the tub, maybe because Paige knocked down a couple of walls to enlarge the bathroom into a haven of marble and reclaimed driftwood that smells of spa.

Then they built on to our original house a whole other house, a coastal grandmother type house, which Sam calls a vibe. (Paige and Jake call it Summersalt—get it?) We stay here for several weeks every summer, trying not to spill anything, while Sam and I make the thrice-weekly trek to Barnstaple for dialysis, as we did today, and back again. We park our car next to the garage and walk across the gravel to the exemplary mudroom where everybody has his own cubby, like at preschool. In the snowy kitchen, Paige talks on the phone to someone who's sourcing new wallpaper, by the sound of it. She spies us and tells this person she has to go now, they'll talk later.

"So!" She looks at Sam. "How'd it go, buddy?"

Sam gives her a strange look. "Great. Thanks. Is Ollie around?"

"They're down at the beach with Brittani, sweetie. You want to go down and join them?"

"Sure." Sam turns back to the mudroom.

"Remember not to drink too much water!" I call after him. At the new bathhouse on the edge of the lawn, right before you get to the causeway over the inlet that leads to the dunes, Paige has installed a drinks station, which is, I have to admit, pretty handy. Ice and water and a fridge full of Spindrift.

"He's okay, right?" asks Paige. "He's so hard to read now."

"He's fine. So what's up?"

She's still staring at the mudroom entrance, brow knit. "Did the doctors say anything? I've been reading up on the effects of renal failure and long-term dialysis—"

"Look, I know what you're trying to say, all right? Yes, my son needs a new kidney. Yes, he is on the donor registry. Yes, we have tested all our known relatives for a good match. Yes, you know how that went."

"Fucking Dad."

I shrug. "It wasn't an ideal tissue match anyway. Three out of six. And it's not like Dad's taken the greatest care of himself all these years."

"A shitty kidney is better than no kidney."

"Plus, he's in his seventies. It's a stale kidney. And it's his decision, right? Organ donation is not for everybody."

"Just so you know," she says, "I no longer consider him my father."

"And I appreciate your loyalty. Now, where's my drink?"

"Oh, shoot! I forgot. Decorator called. Wallpaper drama. Hold on a second."

"No drama like wallpaper drama, I always say."

She scurries to the booze cabinet. "Seriously, you're going to need this. I'm still kind of shaking."

"Shaking? What are you talking about?"

Paige sets the vodka on the pristine quartz and opens the beverage fridge, not to be confused with the industrial Sub-Zero on the opposite wall that requires its own Eversource substation. "You want to slice up some lime? Cutting board's in the cabinet just below you."

I bend to open the cabinet door and retrieve the wooden board.

In this kitchen of immaculate stone and stainless steel and appliances from outer space, the cutting board is a relic from childhood. I love the stains and scars, the familiar grain of the wood. I can picture Mom slicing up onions, tomatoes, eggplant, zucchini, basil. I reach for a lime from the citrus arrangement in the middle of the island.

"It used to freak me out," I say, "the way you could even think about wallpaper or limes when you're upset about something. You know, making sure everyone has an afternoon cocktail in tasteful surroundings."

"Wait, what? What's that supposed to mean?"

I slice the lime into halves, and the halves into quarters. "Then I realized that's how you cope with shit."

"It's better than denial."

"Who's in denial?"

"It ain't just a river in Egypt, right?"

I wait for her to finish pouring the Spindrift and pop a lime quarter into each glass. "I'm not in denial, okay? I live with this thing every day. No french fries, no bananas. Every day I look at my son and I hear the clock ticking, right? So don't tell me I'm in denial."

She sips from her drink and I note that her hand is, in fact, shaking.

"Look, we tried the family members, okay? We just don't have that many of them. Mom's dead. Her parents are dead. Dad doesn't give a shit. You *do* give a shit, for which I'm eternally grateful, more than I can say, but you're not a good match. Your kids are too young."

"Honey," she says, "I know all this. We've been over this."

"So we're stuck waiting for our turn on the transplant list. Which, thanks to Covid, and thanks to Sam's rare tissue type, isn't exactly moving fast."

"We are not stuck waiting on the damn kidney list, okay? There are *options*."

I set down my glass. "No."

"Mallory."

"*That* is not an option, Paige. That has *never* been an option."

"Not even to save your son's life?"

"So, let's unpack that for a second—"

"There's nothing to *unpack*, Mallory." Paige lifts her fingers to form quote marks around the word. "He's Sam's father. Biological fact. He has kidneys. Also a biological fact."

"Number one, if you think it's possible for me to even start that conversation with, like, a man in his position, you're delusional."

"Delusional? All you have to do is email him. It's not like he doesn't know your name."

"If Monk Adams reads his own email, then I'm Beyoncé. His handlers probably get ten emails a day from women claiming to have given birth to his love child. Or wanting to."

Paige points a finger at me. "Do you know what you are? You're a coward."

"Are you fucking kidding me?"

"You're so scared of getting hurt, you'll sacrifice your own son."

"That is total bullshit. Total. I'm doing Sam a favor. I'm *sparing* him."

"Sparing him from what, exactly? From having a father? A working kidney?"

"Do you think—do you *honestly* think—I could just walk up to one of the most famous men in the world and say, 'Hi, Monk. I gave birth to your son thirteen years ago, and by the way, could you spare him a kidney?'"

Paige folds her arms. "Yep. That's exactly what I think you should do."

"What if he *rejects* Sam? There's not enough therapy in the world for that, Paige. Or worse, what if he sucks Sam into that life of his, that whole music world celebrity bullshit?"

"You have to *try*, Mallory."

"He's not even a good match."

"How do you know that?"

"Odds are."

"Odds *are*? Are you serious?"

I look down at the cutting board and the two remaining wedges of lime, reclined on their sides. The paring knife sits between them, one of those German brands with the deadly black handle. For the first time, I notice the music piping in from the magical speakers. Some piano piece, probably Chopin. Mom used to play Chopin when we were babies to settle us down. Since Paige never leaves a single detail to chance, I imagine the choice of music is no accident.

"Paige. Leave it alone, okay?"

"I'm just saying that if he were *my* child—"

"Well, he's *not* your child, okay? You don't know. You don't know what it's like to raise a kid without a dad—"

"That's your *choice,* Mallory—"

"You don't *know!* You have no idea what it's like to do this alone."

Paige picks up her vodka Spindrift and jiggles the ice. A ponytail holds back her blond-streaked hair; some pink balm tints her lips. She's wearing navy Lululemon capris and a navy V-neck tee. Everything about her is burnished and symmetrical.

"You know what?" she says. "You're right. I have absolutely no idea what it's like to shut the father of your child out of his life. I have no idea in the world why you would do such a thing to yourself and to Sam. And do you know why that is?"

"Because you have no fucking imagination?"

"Because you've never *told* me, Mallory. You won't say a single word about what happened that summer. How you ended up pregnant. I mean, Monk *Adams.* Of all people. So, yeah. Don't blame me if I fill in the blanks myself."

"Let's all remember he wasn't famous back then, right? He was a college student. He was nobody."

"He was somebody to you."

"He was a mistake, that's all. A big fat fucking mistake for which I've paid every single day of my life since, believe me."

Because I'm saying this into my glass, as I reach for the Spindrift can to top myself up, I miss the look of horror on my sister's face until I notice she's made no reply.

I look up. Paige stares over my shoulder at the mudroom entrance.

I knock over my glass as I spin around. Booze everywhere. Paige grabs a dishtowel.

"Mom?" says Sam. "I forgot my swimsuit in the wash."

"To be clear," I say, rummaging through the laundry pile, "*you* are not the mistake, okay?"

"Mom, stop."

"*You* are not what I regret. I don't regret you for a second and never have. These aren't yours, are they?"

I pull out a pair of pink trunks, spangled with small blue whales. Sam shakes his head.

"Those are Uncle Jake's," he says.

"Gawd, it's like a Vineyard Vines fever dream. What color are yours?"

"Blue. Like, dark blue."

"Anyway, my point is—you know, I love you and all that. I wouldn't trade having you for anything."

"Mom, *stop,* okay? I know what you meant."

I uncover a pair of skinny dark blue trunks with a neon green waistband. "These look familiar?"

He swipes it. "Thanks."

"So what do you *think* I meant?" I ask.

Sam sighs. He's wearing shorts and a T-shirt that says Bear Lake Campground—there's no such place, I think the shirt is from J.Crew Factory—and it hangs so loosely on his skinny frame, I want to feed him a hamburger. He's been growing out his hair and the curls spill over his forehead. He pushes them back and says, "You mean it sucks raising me all by yourself."

"What about you? Does it suck for you? Not having a dad?"

He shrugs.

"What about Uncle Jake? He's like a dad, right?"

"Kind of."

"Do you ever think about your real dad?"

"Kind of."

"Do you ever wonder why he isn't around?"

"I *know* why he isn't around."

"Why's that?"

"Mom, stop."

"Stop what?"

"Stop trying to be my therapist."

"But you don't have a therapist."

"Duh."

"Do you think you *need* a therapist?"

"Mom, you are so *bad* at this."

"I'm sorry, okay? I just want you to be all right. I hate that you don't have a dad like the other kids. I mean, even the divorce kids have dads, even if they're not around as much. So I feel bad. That's what I meant about paying for my mistake. My mistake was not giving you a real dad."

"Mom, I know."

"Know what?"

He sighs at me, the way only a thirteen-year-old boy can sigh at his mother. Sighs and pushes his sand-colored hair back out of his face again, and for a second the gesture feels so exactly like a similar gesture, fourteen summers ago, I can't breathe.

"I know who he is, all right? My dad."

"What?"

"I said I know who he is."

"Who? Who do you think he is?"

"That singer guy."

"Which singer guy?"

"Monk," he says. "Monk Adams."

I laugh like a maniac. "That's just silly. Monk Adams. What makes you think that?"

"One, I have ears, okay?"

"Oh, *that*? You mean down there in the kitchen just now?"

"Mom, please. Like all the time. You and Aunt Paige. Aunt Paige and Uncle Jake. The girl who cuts my hair who's like, *Dude, you look just like Monk Adams.*" Sam rolls his eyes. "Plus, it makes sense, right? I mean, I know how to use Google. You went to the same prep school and everything. He lives on that island where you used to work."

I sit down and lean back against the clothes dryer. "All right, Sherlock. So what else?"

"What do you mean, what else?"

"What else makes you think you're Monk Adams's love child? Other than your otherworldly handsomeness and universe-exploding charisma, I mean."

Sam wads up the trunks in his hand and turns to walk out of the room.

"Because you never play any of his songs."

* * *

The words flash back into my head as I close the dishwasher door and press the Start button.

It's about Mom.

I turn to Paige, who stands at the kitchen island, refilling her glass of rosé. We've been dancing carefully around each other since the afternoon—prepping dinner, managing kid traffic, every word pitched half an octave higher than usual. Paige hires a local college kid to keep her three girls on track with all the tennis lessons and swimming practice and Khan Academy and what she calls *beach time,* which is now the official name for the way we spent all our summers when we were kids, just messing around under minimal adult supervision, but Brittani goes home at five to get ready for her waitress shift at the Black Sheep and Jake, of course, spends the weekdays working in the city.

So with one thing and another, I've been distracted.

I reach for the wine bottle. "Hold on a second. What *about* Mom?"

"Mom?"

"In the car. On the phone. Something about Mom."

She sets down the glass and claps a hand over her mouth. "Oh my God. I can't believe I forgot to tell you."

Paige's office sits off the kitchen, like a pantry except it holds all the family admin in exquisitely organized shelves and file drawers that slide in and out on their soundless tracks. The wallpaper is kind of a mod paisley on a sea-colored background. There is a stack of art books on the window seat. Her laptop lies shut on the built-in desk. Next to it, a glossy file folder of madras plaid coordinates with the wallpaper colors in some indefinable way.

She picks up the folder and opens it.

"So, I decided to do a little research," she says.

"What kind of research?"

"Family research."

"Oh, Paige. Come on. Do you really think some third cousin twice removed is going to donate a kidney to Sam?"

"Mallory," she says, "I have to do *something*."

"Because *I* won't. Is that what you're saying?"

"The baby daddy situation is what it is. I'm not going to change your mind." She nudges the folder against my chest. "But maybe this will."

Some reflex causes me to grab the folder. I hold it between my fingers like you might hold Yorick's skull. "What do you mean by that?"

"I mean I went through all those boxes of files Mom left in the attic. Stuff she kept from our childhood, stuff she kept from her parents."

"And?"

Paige folds her arms. "Look at that first page."

I look down.

Certificate of Adoption, it says.

"Holy shit. We were *adopted*?"

"Not *us,* stupid. Her. Mom. Look at the date. Twenty-seventh of June, 1952."

My brain feels like it's spinning on a wheel. The old typescript blurs together. I can't comprehend this; I can't even read it. *Adopted.*

I think of my grandparents. Elderly, formal. Having us to dinner at their house in Brookline, the smell of lemon polish. Mom lighting up a cigarette after we left.

I look back up at Paige. "What the fuck? Why didn't she tell us?"

"Who knows? I mean, I guess it explains why she's an only child. Grandma and Grandpa adopted her out of a Catholic orphanage near Galway—"

"Wait, *Ireland*? You're saying Mom was born in an Irish orphanage?"

"And that's not the really weird thing. The weird thing is that the mother wasn't some unwed teenager—"

"Wow, thanks."

"Shut up and listen." Paige snatches back the folder and rifles through a few more pages. "Look at this. There's no name, right, because it's supposed to be anonymous. But where it lists the description of the birth mother, it says—right here—it says she's white, English, thirty-four years old . . ."

She plucks the paper out of the stack and dangles it in front of me.

". . . and married."

CHAPTER THREE

Hannah

September 1951
Cairo, Egypt

The flowers stood in their vase on the corner of Hannah's desk—white stargazer lilies with delicate pink centers, pink English roses, purpling phlox. The nurse had carried them to her room nine days ago, when Hannah arrived home from the hospital.

Miss Britton had been referred by Mr. Beck, the assistant manager at Shepheard's Hotel, who seemed to have the solution to any dilemma you might pose to him. She was an elderly British woman, like a great-aunt, with short bluish-white hair and a narrow, lined, no-nonsense face. She and Hannah had had a pleasant conversation about snakes on the second day, when Hannah was feeling better. Miss Britton had propped her up on some pillows and fetched more coffee and cataloged all the snakebites she'd known. This took some time. *You're lucky you was wearing them gloves,* she'd told Hannah, in conclusion, *and the serpent didn't have the chance to bite deep. That's the difference, mind you. How much venom gets into you. How on earth did you manage to save yourself like that?*

Hannah had explained how she hadn't saved herself at all. How the hotel's assistant manager had happened by the pavilion at the vital instant.

Well, then, you've got a guardian angel, that's what, Miss Britton had said.

A guardian angel. The words recoiled in Hannah's head as she gazed at the extravagant flowers in their vase, smelled the extravagant scent of them. Inside her desk drawer, she kept the card that had arrived with the flowers.

At the top, the words *Shepheard's Hotel* in raised black ink. Underneath, some quick, small handwriting—

> *Wishing you the speediest possible recovery, so that we may once more enjoy the charm of your company here at Shepheard's.*
> J. Beck

The irony was, they'd come to Egypt for Alistair's health.

A bad bout of pneumonia one winter, followed by a flare-up of the rheumatism that had plagued him since the war—that's how it went, for a man of Alistair's age, who'd devoted himself to the service of empire, long hours in beastly climates, two world wars and all the dustups and crises and economic depressions in between. Summer in the English countryside hadn't helped—one gray, drizzling day after another. Another dreary London winter of coal smoke seasoned with bitter damp and labor strikes would have just about done him in.

What you require is a hot, dry climate, Mr. Ainsworth, the doctor said sternly, removing his stethoscope, *or I can't answer for the consequences.*

So Alistair had spoken to the foreign secretary, an old friend, and arranged for a secondment as a kind of political liaison to the ambassador in Cairo, nothing too strenuous, a desk in the consulate and a pleasant apartment in a British neighborhood.

He'd told Hannah the news at the beginning of July, once it was all arranged. They were in the bedroom. Hannah remembered how Alistair sat in his armchair with the footstool and the lap blanket of Scotch plaid, while Hannah stood in the middle of the rug with the tea tray and tried to gather her thoughts around the idea, the word even—*Egypt.*

She didn't know much about the political situation there, except that the Egyptians weren't amused by the new state of Israel and even less pleased by the British, whom they'd been trying for years to boot out of Egypt altogether—the Suez Canal included. Well, that was for Alistair to worry about, wasn't it? Hannah did not concern herself with politics, not anymore. She'd set down the tea tray and picked up the teapot.

Alistair said, *You'll be happy to make all the arrangements and so on, won't you, darling?*

Hannah had handed Alistair his tea and said that sounded splendid.

Alistair had sipped his tea and leaned back in his armchair. *Do you know what I think I'll do,* he said. *I think I'll start that book I've been talking about. What do you think? You can help with the typing and research and so on. Give you something to do with yourself, won't it?*

He'd reached for a cucumber sandwich. Hannah had stared at his hand—pale, long-fingered.

Yes, dear, she'd said.

The apartment building overlooked the vast green polo fields of the Gezira Sporting Club, so you could pretend you had never left England at all, except for the heat and the bawab, the Egyptian porter. His name was Salah and he had a wife and three children who lived across the river in the Bulaq district. The oldest was a boy of nineteen who had attended the Royal Military Academy and had just been commissioned second lieutenant. Salah was anxiously awaiting news of his first posting.

"Good day, Mrs. Ainsworth," said Salah. "Do you need the car this morning?"

"No, thank you. I think I'll walk today. Have you heard from Abdel lately?"

Salah's face burst into sunshine. "He's at the barracks in Ismailia, a very prestigious assignment."

"That sounds wonderful. Ismailia's in the east, isn't it?"

"Yes, along the canal. So if the bloody Jews try to cross the Sinai, he'll be right there to stop them, inshallah."

Hannah's hand closed around her handbag. "Well," she said, "I certainly hope it doesn't come to that."

Already the air was growing hot, the dusty pandemonium of Cairo's streets was building to its daily crescendo. When they arrived here five weeks ago, Hannah had taken in this spectacle and felt something overturn in her middle. It wasn't just the crowds—the men in their robes, the donkeys pulling their carts, the beggars, the prayers, the smell of fruit and spice and sunshine and dirt and excrement. It was the edge of chaos. It was the misery existing alongside the indifferent affluence. It was the rage you felt roiling beneath the skin of everything—buildings, streets, people—until you thought it must certainly burst.

Cairo was as unlike England as it could be—as unlike her married life as she could fathom—the tall, narrow house on Cheyne Place; the chill, damp Lincolnshire countryside where Alistair's family home brooded over a moor. And yet everywhere you looked in this hot, mad city, you saw the stamp of Western civilization. The sporting club with its polo fields and racetrack and clubhouse. The orderly neighborhoods and suburbs of Cairo, embellished like the arrondissements of Paris. The cafés, the hotels, the Turf Club. The men and women in their fashionable clothes, their hats, speaking French and Italian and English as you walked past on your way to eat ice cream at Groppi's.

You sometimes had the feeling that the ordinary Egyptians themselves were only spectators to all this, the throbbing civic life of Cairo and of Egypt itself—their own country.

Like me, Hannah thought, as she crossed the bridge into downtown Cairo. *A spectator to my own life.*

The perspiration streamed down Hannah's back and arms and through her white gloves. She hurried along the sidewalks, down the bustling streets, not catching a single eye, closing her ears to the voices that clamored around her. Some days, walking or driving through the city, she had to stop and sit somewhere—anywhere, a café or a department store—and swallow back the panic in her throat, force back this blackness like a spill of oil in her head.

Some days she could simply block it all out, like a woman with no past at all, no past and no future.

Keep walking, she thought.

She walked and walked, heels clacking the sidewalk, hot traffic streaming around her, until the veranda of Shepheard's Hotel appeared around the corner.

Shepheard's, the most British establishment of all.

Hannah walked past the front doors and the porters, through the lobby, and right up to the front desk, where she asked for Mr. Beck, the assistant manager.

The clerk gave her a knowing look and picked up the house telephone.

Hannah was introduced to Mr. Beck in the dining room at Shepheard's, over a month ago.

She'd been in Cairo for four days, and a few of the Foreign Office wives had invited her to join them for tea. Three of them stood waiting in the lobby when she'd swept inside, six minutes late, flushed and frazzled, having taken a wrong turn and wound up in some street she couldn't discover on her map. Everyone wore pale colors and pearls and the kind of gaze that searched out imperfections. Hannah always felt she should straighten her hat or her hair or her skirt. They were women who inhabited their lives as the wife of somebody—Mrs. Bertrand Beverley, Mrs. Colin Hill, Mrs. Stanley Marlow—so Hannah sometimes had trouble remembering their first names.

The tea salon was ornate and lofty, full of fluttering women and the clink of china and the perfume of orange pekoe. At first Hannah hadn't taken much note of the man who came to stand by the maître d' at his desk. He wore a suit of pale linen and bent over the desk, presumably to consult the reservation book. He was trim and perhaps a touch above medium height—an inch or two below six feet—and really not that remarkable, until he turned his head to consider some table a few yards to the right of Hannah, and the movement caught her notice for some reason. She couldn't say why. She was in the middle of an exchange with Helen Hill and simply lost the thread.

Hannah had jerked her gaze back. "I beg your pardon, what did you say?"

"I *said*"—Helen laid a smile on the word *said*—"it's a shame you weren't in Cairo during the war. Parties every night. Everybody passed through at some point. Do you remember, Lillian?"

Lillian Beverley shook her head. "We didn't arrive until '48."

"Shame. Were *you* in Cairo during the war, Mr. Beck?"

Hannah startled. A man stood at her shoulder, between her and Lillian.

"Naturally," he said.

He was, of course, the man in the linen suit who had been speaking to the maître d'. He had a slight accent, possibly French, though you couldn't say for certain. He smiled at each one of them—a table of four ladies, Hannah and Helen and the other two—and came to Hannah last. Turned his face toward her and the two of them stared at each other, starstruck.

Those eyes, she remembered thinking. *The color of hope.*

"This is our newcomer," said Lillian. "Mrs. Ainsworth. You've seen Alistair Ainsworth around the place, haven't you? With my Bertie? Back in Cairo from England? His wife."

Mr. Beck picked up Hannah's hand and kissed it. "Welcome to Cairo, Mrs. Ainsworth."

She must have looked amazed, because Helen had laughed. "Mr. Beck takes a personal interest in all his guests. It's his job. Isn't it, Lucien?"

"It is my pleasure," he said, making a small bow.

After he left, Helen leaned forward and lowered her voice. "They *say* he had to do with special operations, during the war."

"Special operations?"

"Intelligence and that kind of thing. Sabotage. Can you imagine?"

Over at the next table, Mr. Beck shared a friendly chuckle with a pair of women in white dresses, one about forty and beautifully polished, one a long-limbed teenager hunched over her plate—a mother and daughter, maybe.

Helen continued. "I asked him about it once, point-blank, but he just laughed at me and changed the subject. They're not allowed to say anything about it, you know. Official Secrets Act."

Hannah had allowed a last glance at Mr. Beck, who had stepped away from the other table and now walked briskly toward the french doors at the side of the dining room. She'd thought what it might be like, if you had once lived in the desert engaged in perilous sabotage operations against a ruthless enemy, to manage the dining room of an elegant hotel.

Flirting with the wives of British diplomats who came to take tea and gossip in the afternoon.

Mr. Beck's office was small and tidy. Not a stray paper existed anywhere, not a scrap of the usual flotsam. Everything in its place. He left the door decorously ajar and pulled out a chair for Hannah. She sat and arranged herself, handbag on her lap.

"You are well, Mrs. Ainsworth?" he asked.

"Yes."

"Your hand?"

"It's healing well. The snake wasn't able to inject much venom, the doctors say."

"It's true—the less venom, the better."

Hannah had all these phrases planned. Eloquent, polished, just the right degree of careless élan. She'd worked out the whole conversation, so she didn't have time to think—just to speak. She'd rehearsed it in her head a hundred times, lying in her hospital bed, in her bed at home. Now she tried to remember some scrap of this dialogue.

"Thank you so much for the lovely flowers," she said. "And the card."

He waved his hand. "That was nothing. The nurse who looked after you at home—the one we recommended—she took proper care of you?"

"Very much. In the end she attended more to Alistair than to me, really."

A quiver came and went at the corner of his lips. "Then we shall have to ensure she remains at her post, won't we?"

Hannah looked down at her lap. "I came to thank you."

"Thank me?"

"You saved my life."

"But this was nothing. In Egypt, the snakebite is a regular misfortune. Shepheard's keeps its own stock of antivenom."

"If you hadn't taken such quick action—the bite could have been much worse—the way you flung the snake—the last instant—"

"Mrs. Ainsworth, you are not to give this incident another

thought, I assure you. It was my honor to have been fortunate enough to perform this service for you."

All this time, she'd been staring at the handbag on her lap. Now she looked up. "But why?"

"Why?"

"Why were you there? You should have been attending to the dinner guests."

At last, he sat on the corner of the desk. The leg of his trouser stretched tight.

The office had no windows, like a cell in a prison. Behind the desk, some volumes crammed the shelves of a small bookcase. Hannah smelled the leather of the books, the tobacco of an earlier cigarette. A fan circled the ceiling over their heads. The room was so tiny, his shoe nearly brushed her shin.

"I think you understand the answer to that question, Mrs. Ainsworth," he said softly, sliding into French.

"You followed me."

"Yes. I was concerned for you. I thought perhaps you were unhappy, and an unhappy woman . . ." His voice trailed away.

"Yes? An unhappy woman is what?"

How strange it was, to speak to Mr. Beck in French. Because Shepheard's was so resolutely English, you mostly conversed in English there. But outside the walls of establishments like this, educated Egyptians spoke French. They preferred French culture to British. They read French books, watched French movies, admired French fashion and decoration. As for Hannah, she spoke French as fluently as English. So when Mr. Beck spoke to her in French, she opened her mouth and the French words came out, and somehow this changed the air between them. In English they were hotel manager and guest; in French they became something else.

Mr. Beck tapped one finger against his knee. "Is unhappy," he said.

"And this is a problem for you? My unhappiness?"

"For me? For *you*, madame. For you it is a terrible problem. It's a travesty. It makes me angry."

"You should call me Hannah," she said.

"Hannah." He held out his hand to her. "Lucien."

She clasped his palm and tasted the word on her tongue. "Lucien."

Instead of releasing her hand, he removed the glove and examined the scar near her wrist. "Forgive me," he said.

"Forgive you?"

"For not arriving an instant sooner."

He kissed the two small livid marks and replaced the glove on her hand. It seemed to Hannah that the wound burned more than it did when the snake's fangs were inside her, but that was just her imagination, naturally.

When he looked up, his eyes shone briefly as the light caught them. "Have you visited the pyramids across the river, Hannah?"

"No. We were supposed to go, but with one thing and another—Alistair's already seen them, during the war, so he wasn't that keen—and then the snake."

"What if I said I should like to take you there myself?"

Hannah imagined what it would have been like if she had toured Giza with her husband. They would probably have hired a dragoman with a pair of camels and spent a couple of hours riding around the plateau, viewing the pyramids and the Sphinx from various angles while the dragoman supplied them with facts. At one point she would have asked if she could climb down from the camel and explore on her own. The dragoman would have been shocked. He would have looked helplessly at Alistair and Alistair would have spoken to her in a conciliatory voice. *It isn't suitable, Hannah.*

"Do you think that's wise?" Hannah said.

Lucien shrugged. "I don't especially care if it's wise or not."

Hannah met his gaze. The fatal blow, those eyes of his. A startling true green. He must have seen the capitulation in her face because he rose from the desk and opened his palm to her.

"Let's go," he said.

CHAPTER FOUR

Mallory

June 2022
Cape Cod, Massachusetts

It's no secret that I have an embarrassing amount of trouble recalling the names of the other moms on the PTA committee or what time I'm supposed to pick up Sam from soccer practice. But I can still picture the exact expression on Paige's face when the lawyer read Mom's will.

Not the part about the money. Like I said, Paige already has plenty of that. She might have been surprised about the Appalachian Mountain Club thing, but she wasn't *disappointed,* per se.

Not until he came to the paragraph about the bracelet.

To begin with, we were both amazed Mom had made a will at all. Probably Paige had nagged her into it. Still, even Paige couldn't quite believe that Mom went through with the whole process, found a lawyer and everything, witnessed and notarized and all that. We sat there in his office in Provincetown overlooking Cape Cod Bay— a foggy, miserable day—kind of numb and stiff, not quite believing what we were hearing. The house, blah blah. The remainder of cash on hand, blah blah. Personal effects, blah blah. Paige got the Royal Doulton handed down from Grandma, and good luck to her.

My gold bracelet in the shape of a cobra, set with two emeralds of approximately ¼ carat weight each and one ruby of approximately ½ carat weight, has great personal meaning to me as it was given to me by my mother at my birth. I leave this bracelet to my daughter Mallory Rose, because she always wanted to try it on when she was a little girl, and I told her the bracelet could be removed only after my death.

Paige, it's fair to say, was not expecting that.

Eldest daughter and everything, right? She naturally assumed that Mom's heirloom bracelet would fall to her, like a royal title. And when that bracelet first arrived in its small brown package to my house in Mystic, I couldn't even think of wearing it. I felt like a thief.

I remember how I used to stare at it for long, silent minutes, turning it this way and that, as autumn crept into winter. At night, I would take the cobra from the drawer in the bedside table and run my thumb along the scales. Sometimes, if I rubbed it long enough, it seemed to me that the cobra stirred to life between my fingers, like a genie from a lamp. A trick of lighting or mood, I guess. I would glimpse the warmth of my mother's green eyes simmering inside the emeralds and think, *Oh, I know you.*

One night in January, restless and a little drunk, I slid the bracelet over my hand and settled it in place.

You'd think it might feel strange, this hard new object on my arm. But the funny thing about Mom's bracelet, it has a way of spiraling itself to fit the anatomy of your wrist. The coils clasp you right where your skin thins to a tissue. Where your pulse beats. Where your lover kisses you. I remember I lay there staring at this snake wound around me, like a vine that had grown there, returning the thud of my heart, and for the first time I thought I understood why my mother wouldn't take it off, never, not once, not even to let her little girl try it on.

Now I lie in my bed in the blue-and-white guest bedroom at Summersalt and watch another dawn pour over the gold scales and the curving hood. The emerald eyes glitter to life and this feeling smacks me—my brain's beating to a strange rhythm, I've hardly slept all night—like I've never seen this bracelet before in my life.

Given to me by my mother at my birth, she wrote.

But which mother?

You'd be surprised just how many foods contain potassium. It's a real pain in the neck because most of them are the kinds of foods kids live on—french fries, orange juice, bananas, anything with tomatoes.

And don't get me started on phosphorus. Think anything dairy—milk, yogurt, ice cream. Then there's salt. If your kidneys don't work, you don't pee much, so you have to limit fluid intake. Salt makes you thirsty, ergo no potato chips.

Of course, you weren't eating the potato chips anyway because of potassium.

And I used to think the parents of the allergy kids had it bad.

Anyway, even though Sam's pretty good about self-policing his diet, I like to keep an eye on mealtimes when we're staying with Paige and her girls. Most females are big on rules, at least until they hit puberty, but Ida's the youngest and kind of an anarchist. She used to sneak Sam bananas at breakfast until Paige found out and tossed them in the trash bin. This morning the gang's just horsing around with the Cheerios, but while I love Ida to death and she's secretly my favorite—I have a weakness for anarchy—you would never, ever turn your back on her.

As a result, I almost miss the story in the paper about Monk Adams's wedding.

I first googled his name when Sam was about a year old.

It was an impulse. I told myself I'd never look up Monk again—I'd made a clean break, no looking back. Anyway, I was busy! I had a new job, a new life, a newborn. I spent my days in a fog of baby care and block prints, my nights—well, in a fog of baby care and block prints. In between Sam and work, I shopped for groceries and washed the dishes. That was all. No books, no television, no movies, no news. I had no idea what was happening in the wide world until Paige called me up one day—she'd been working in Singapore that summer when Sam was conceived, so she hadn't yet pieced together any details—and said, *Did you happen to know a guy named Monk Adams in your year at Nobles?*

My heart stopped. *Kind of,* I said. *Why?*

Because I heard he's got some music album coming out. The first song just dropped and it's already number one on iTunes.

I remember this feeling like a car accident. The impact hit my chest and started waves of shock down my arms and legs and up my neck into my head. Even if I could think of something to say, I couldn't move my neck or my jaw to form the words.

Mallie? Are you there? asked Paige.

I mumbled something along the lines of *Oh yeah. I think he was into that stuff.*

To which she answered—this I remember clearly, it was so typical of Paige—*Well, you should try to get back in touch. You never know, he might remember you.*

After I hung up the phone, I poured myself a glass of wine and entered *Monk Adams* in the Google search field.

Well, you already know what turned up in the results—Monk Adams and his debut album, *Sunrise,* which launched him into orbit around this ordinary earth that mortals walk. By now, you've seen his photograph a thousand times, so I don't have to attempt to describe that smile, that jaw, those arctic eyes. You've hung your dreams on those cheekbones, you've imagined your arms around those shoulders. You've laughed and cried with him, you've cheered and screamed. Admit it, you bawled like a baby when he dedicated the Grammy Award to his aunt who died of ovarian cancer and urged all women watching tonight to make their appointments for that yearly exam, in memory of Aunt Barbara.

Trust me when I tell you that Aunt Barbara was worth it.

I must have spent a couple of hours reading all the stories—at that point, they were all giddy newcomer profiles, you remember them, like that fresh-faced photo shoot for *Men's Health* with all the adorable anecdotes—while I finished the bottle of wine, a choice I regretted the next morning when I woke up to this new universe in which everybody knew who Monk Adams was, everybody worshipped Monk—a world not so different from the one before it, true, but this time it wasn't just our circle of friends under his spell. It was all the people in the world. People who heard his music and saw his picture and went to his concerts.

Everybody.

I told myself I was happy for Monk. Of course I was! He'd done exactly what he said he wanted, as we burrowed together in the sand that summer, trading our secrets, beat-up guitar plucking out music from the drowsy air, except he'd succeeded beyond anything either of us dreamed of. But how could you expect that Monk Adams, wanting to defy his father and write songs for a living, wanting to bring stories to life in music, would do anything less than dazzle the whole world?

I mean, I could hardly blame Monk for being Monk, could I?

Anyway, I never searched Google for Monk's name after that, but I hardly needed to. I kept track of him against my will, because you can't exactly help reading the tabloid headlines as you stand in line at the supermarket, next to your son, who bears a startling resemblance to the man beaming off the cover of *People* magazine.

Or *this* photo. Black and white on the front page of the Lifestyle section of the *Boston Globe.*

You should understand that Boston takes what I'd call a proprietary interest in Monk Adams. He's a local son, after all—born and raised in Brookline, prepped at Nobles and Greenough, college over the Maine border at Colby. To be fair, this is not exactly what you'd call a typical Boston upbringing, but for a guy who could walk his pedigree back to the *Mayflower,* he maintains a fairly convincing regular-guy persona. He wears a Red Sox hat at concerts, for God's sake. Sitting there on his barstool as he croons into your soul.

Anyway, the *Globe*'s gossip page is freaking out over unconfirmed reports that Adams is marrying his longtime girlfriend in a hush-hush affair on Winthrop Island, at the eastern end of Long Island Sound, where his family spends the summer. Rumors suggest a ceremony at St. Ann's Episcopal Church, reception at the Winthrop Island Club, a flotilla of vintage Gar Wood runabouts to ferry the guests to and from the island, which famously doesn't have any public overnight accommodation except for a few leaky bedrooms above the bar at the Mohegan Inn.

When contacted by the *Globe,* the story continues, Adams's spokesperson refused to comment.

But you all know what *that* means.

Paige bounds into the kitchen. I flip over the newspaper and lay it on the counter.

"Holy beans," she says, mindful of the kids even in her excitement. "Did you hear about Monk Adams getting married on Winthrop this summer?"

At the edge of my peripheral vision, Sam looks up from his bowl of Cheerios and oat milk.

Paige glances at Sam and back to me. She's wearing a pair of navy stretch capris and a Lululemon tank. Her face is bare, her skin's flushed, her hair's scraped back in a damp ponytail at the back of her head. She likes to do Pilates on the beach each morning while she's reading the news on her phone. Don't ask me how that works.

"Hey, do you mind giving me a hand covering the furniture on the patio?" she chirps. "I think it's going to rain."

The bougie new patio at Summersalt used to be our vegetable garden, back when we were kids. Now a saltwater pool flickers in the sunshine. There is an outdoor fireplace, flanked by a sectional sofa and chairs and side tables, all cushioned in shades of coral and blue. Paige sets about pulling the fitted waterproof furniture covers from the storage closet in the pool house.

"I have this idea," Paige says.

"Absolutely not."

"You don't even know what it is!"

"I can guess. You want me to crash Monk Adams's wedding to that supermodel. Whatever her name is."

"First of all, her name is Lennox. Lennox Lassiter. *Secondly,* she is not a supermodel. What is this, 1999? She's a lifestyle influencer, as you would know if you pulled your head out of the ground once in a while."

"Paige, I don't even know what that *means.*"

"*Thirdly,*" Paige says, handing me one end to spread over the sectional, "I'm not talking about crashing the wedding. That would be stupid and counterproductive. He would hate you forever."

"News flash. He already does."

"*What?* Why?"

I adjust the corner a final time and straighten from the sectional. Paige stares at me with her inquisitive fox eyes. I turn away and pull another furniture cover from the stack on the coffee table. "What's this one for?"

"Dining set."

I walk toward the long teak table under the awning, wrapped with fairy lights. "So what's your big idea?" I ask over my shoulder.

"DNA test," she says.

"Are you serious? How am I supposed to get my hands on his DNA?"

"Not *Monk's* DNA." She lifts the two enormous lanterns from the middle of the table and sets them on the paving stones. "Yours. Or mine, if you won't cooperate."

"Wait, what are we talking about?"

"I'm talking about *Mom,* you screwup. You know, the fact that it turns out we don't know a single thing about where we came from? All we do is we send in our DNA to one of those ancestry websites and find out."

Together we drop the cover over the table and chairs like a tea cozy. "No. Nope. No fucking way."

"Mallory, come on. I don't know what your problem is with this stuff. Everyone's doing it."

"*You* haven't, or you wouldn't be asking me."

"Mallory, there's a story here. *Our* story. Where we *came* from. Don't you care? Don't you want to find out the truth?"

Before I can reply, she lifts the lanterns and marches back to the pool house. I stand there on the paving stones and follow the metronome swing of her ponytail.

"No," I call after her. "Not really."

Paige stops so fast, the lanterns swing from her hands. "*What?* How can you not want to know?"

"Ever heard of this chick called Pandora and her box?"

"For the love of God, Mallory. What are you scared of this time?"

"I don't know. Sending my genetic information to some corporation? My entire fucking *genome*?"

"Please. It's no big deal. They have privacy rules in place. It's all encrypted."

"Sure it is. Do they tell you that on the website? All our databases are encrypted and totally one hundred percent hacker-proof?"

She starts back toward the pool house. "Hackers are after *financial* information, Mallory. They don't know a double helix from confetti."

I trot after her. "You don't think this kind of information is valuable to somebody? The government? Pharmaceutical companies, maybe? Next thing you know, you get one of those *Update to our privacy policy* emails you can't be bothered to read through before you click OK, and presto, corporate profits are booming—"

"Oh, for God's sake. You and your Marxist bullshit."

"What the hell, Paige. I am *not* a Marxist. I mean, not since college. But I'm also not about to hand over my entire DNA sequence to the capitalist pigs."

Paige sets the second lantern on the shelf in the storage closet and closes the door. "You know what? This isn't about your stupid conspiracy theories. You're just scared."

"Me? Scared? Of what?"

"Of what it might tell you. Like maybe you have the breast cancer gene or a predisposition to macular degeneration. Admit it."

"Okay, fine. I've always subscribed to the ignorance is bliss philosophy. I think it's served me pretty well. Compared to you, anyway."

"Me?"

"Total mass of seething anxiety. Admit it."

"You're such a bitch, Mallory."

"You're such a bitch, Paige."

Paige's blue eyes drench me in loathing. A couple of drops smack the top of my head. The air smells warm and worried; a cloud rumbles offshore. She was right about the rain, like she's right about everything.

"Fine," she says. "*I'll* spit in the damn vial. Either way, we're going to find out what the story is with Mom. And do you know why?"

"Because you can't stand not knowing?"

"Because I love my nephew, that's why. And I want to find him a new kidney, like, *before* the next global pandemic."

To get to the ocean from Summersalt, you make your way past a long, shallow tidal inlet and through some tall grass to the dunes. When we were kids, Paige and I used to roll down them and scramble back up like a pair of human bulldozers. Now a pair of mesh fences marks out a narrow path. After the squall passes through, I follow Sam up this track and down the other side, where the ocean smashes on the sand and the world is nothing but sun and salt water. To watch your kid tuck his board under his arm and stride out into this pandemonium—just as Paige and I used to do, a million years ago—is to learn what faith really means.

Before the accident—I like to call it an accident for some reason—I would say a little prayer that went something like, *All right, God, just be gentle with him, okay? Gather him in your tender hands and give him back to me when you're done.* I don't know if I really believed in God, or whether I was just invoking his name because it was convenient to pray to something instead of nothing.

Either way, I don't pray anymore. I settle myself on one of Paige's sisal beach mats and watch my lithe, golden-skinned son dive like a porpoise through the breakers, as fearless of fate as Monk was. I close my eyes to the sun, and if I think anything at all, any articulate idea, it goes something like, *Dear Lord, haven't you fucked with me enough already?*

Paige plops down next to me in the sand and kicks off her flip-flops.

"Sent off my spit," she says. "Should get the ancestry report back in a few weeks."

"Sweet."

She nudges my foot with hers. "Still can't wrap my head around it. Why Mom would keep a thing like this from us. Do you think maybe she meant to tell us but died before she could? Out climbing ruins with Dildo?"

"You think *Mom* kept it from us? Please. That's all on Grandma and Grandpa. It's just the kind of thing they would do. Adopting a baby from Ireland and passing it off as theirs."

"She *was* theirs, Mallory. She was their *child*. They raised her and loved her, which is more than you can say of this woman who gave her up to the Irish nuns." She lifts her knees and hugs them. "Anyway, you don't know Grandma like I did. She would've told Mom."

"Disagree. If she'd told Mom, Mom would've told me."

"Oh, is that what it is? You're pissed because Mom didn't tell her precious soulmate *everything*?"

"Shut up, Paige."

She tosses a newspaper into my lap. I lift my sunglasses and peer into Monk Adams's grinning black-and-white face, tilted just a few degrees, like they caught him in the middle of a joke.

"Nice photo, right?" she says.

I pitch the paper into the sand next to the beach mat.

Paige leans back on her elbows and squints at the surf. "It doesn't matter how you tell him, okay? The fact is, he needs to know. He just does. And Sam needs him to know. And whatever happened back then, *you* need to put on your big-girl pants and get it done."

The ocean seems to be holding its breath. The surface twitches. Sam's head bobs impatiently between one slow wave and another. I push myself off my elbows and sit up.

"I guess you're not worried about sharks," says Paige.

"Sure, I worry about sharks."

I throw my gaze past the breakers, where a new wave rises. Higher and higher it climbs. Sam scrambles on his board, paddles his arms, poises just so at that delicate instant when the height of water above the surface reaches equilibrium with the height below the surface.

Paige springs to her feet and shouts, *Jesus Christ!*

The water crumples over itself and Sam sails true along the crest, arrow-perfect like Monk used to do, and for a second there it all comes back, so that I might be living it again—the summer, the surf, Monk grinning his way out of the waves to plop down on the sand beside me and shake the droplets from his hair into my lap.

Then he's gone.

Just Sam, popping up like a cork from the surf. Flinging the salt water from his shaggy gold hair.

I collapse backward, woozy with relief, and stare at the hot white sky.

I met Benjamin Monk Adams in a scene from a movie. I think the movie would be *Dead Poets Society* except that Nobles is coeducational and mostly day students, although a minority of us were what they call "five-day boarders" who went home on weekends. Every Friday Mom would drive to Dedham from Provincetown and collect me, and every Sunday she would drop me back off. Paige was four years older and starting Yale, so it was just the two of us in that car, blasting tunes, chattering like sisters.

One Sunday evening in the middle of October we pulled up outside the dorm just as Monk was climbing out of his grandparents' Mercedes station wagon.

Mom turned down the radio and let out a wolf whistle.

"Who the hell is *that*?" she asked me.

Six weeks into the school year, here was what I knew about Monk Adams: One, that he was a third former—like me—and already stood an inch over six feet tall. Two, that he took all the honors classes and played quarterback for the junior varsity football team. Three, that he was the handsomest boy I'd ever seen, like a movie star playing a high school student, so far out of my league he might have lived in another state.

Four, that his girlfriend was a blond day student named Sophie, who played forward on the girls' soccer team and had legs as long and tanned as the legs of a racehorse.

Because it was one of those October warm spells and the car was an old one—the cherry-red mid-nineties Toyota 4Runner that saw us through most of my childhood—the windows were rolled down and Mom's voice rang right out into the clear air.

Monk's head swiveled in our direction.

"Oh, shit," I muttered.

Mom gave the horn a toot and waved from the window.

"Yoohoo!" she called out. "Young man! Could you give us a hand?"

The Mercedes scooted off. Monk stood right near the streetlamp, so you could see the slow, quizzical smile spread across his face. He hoisted his duffel bag on his shoulder and walked toward us.

"I am going to kill you," I told my mother.

Mom leaned across me. "Hello there!"

Monk stuck out his hand. "Monk Adams, ma'am. Are you Mallory's mom?"

Up until now, the sum of my interaction with Monk Adams came to a few distant, furtive, smoldering glances on my part and a single, blank thought bubble of blissful inattention on his. I don't think I'd ventured within ten yards of him except that one time in the dining hall when I'd happened to fall in place behind Monk in the salad line, and even then he never noticed me because he was—as usual—surrounded by this crew who'd started Nobles together in the first form, while I was still attending the small public middle school in Provincetown.

I remember thinking, *Oh my God. Monk Adams knows my name.*

"That's right," Mom said. "Are you heading into the residence hall right now?"

"Yes, ma'am."

"Do you mind giving Mallory a hand with her bag? I packed her some boots and rain gear for the autumn weather and it's a little heavy."

"Mom, I can handle it," I said.

"Sure, no problem," said Monk.

He reached for the door handle and *opened the door for me.*

I climbed out. My legs were so rubbery, I had to grab the edge of the door to steady myself.

"Bag's in the back?" he asked. But he was already on his way to the battered rear of the 4Runner. He gave the window a little rap with his knuckles and Mom obligingly popped it open for him while I stood there a few feet away, mute and frozen. He reached inside and plucked out both duffel bags.

I lurched for one of them and mumbled, "I've got it."

"No worries. One in each hand," he said, lifting them both at once. "Balances me out."

I wanted to point out that he'd already slung his own duffel bag over one shoulder so he wasn't balanced out at all, but my mouth was too dry to dislodge my tongue, and anyway I was afraid the words would come out garbled, like I'd had a stroke or something.

Maybe I *had* had a stroke. I was absolutely feeling stroke-level disorientation at this point.

While I stood there like an idiot, Monk walked around to the driver's side. "Mallory's awesome, Mrs. Dunne. She's in my fifth-period art class? Serious talent."

"Why, thank you, Monk. It's *Ms.* Dunne, by the way."

Under the seedy glare of the streetlamp, I saw Monk's grin flash wider still, if such a thing were possible.

"*Ms.* Dunne," he said.

"Mallory's always loved art. You should have seen her drawings from preschool. She would line up all her My Little Ponies and sketch them perfectly. I mean, you could see the personality of each pony right there on its face."

"Love it. My Little Pony. My kid sister has those." He straightened and slapped the roof of the 4Runner, such that I was afraid it might crumple under his palm. "Nice to meet you, Ms. Dunne. I'll make sure Mallory makes it to her room okay."

"Why, thank you, Monk. You're such a gentleman. Have a great week!"

She craned back to me and winked. As she drove away, she waved her hand cheerfully from the window.

Monk looked at me, still smiling. "Cool mom."

"I'm so sorry about that. Seriously, I can carry my bags."

Monk started off toward the dorm entrance. "Naw, I got you. Mother raised me right."

"Are you sure?" I said, tagging after him.

"Actually, it was my aunt Barbara."

"What's that?"

"My aunt Barbara raised me. You're on the cross-country team, right?"

"Yes."

"We watch you guys doing those hill sprints from the football field. Brutal."

"Yeah, the coach is pretty tough."

"That senior girl out front, she's a freak."

"She's being recruited by Dartmouth."

"Oh yeah? Good for her. Only way to get in anymore, right?"

He opened the door for me, and for an instant we made eye contact. Sun blind.

Then we swooped into the commons, where a bunch of kids sprawled on the armchairs, watching TV. They looked up together like meerkats.

"Hey, guys," he said. "You all know Mallory, right?"

Nobody knew Mallory, but they all said hey.

Monk looked at me. "Where's your room?"

"Second floor. But I can totally take it from—"

Monk Adams was already heading for the stairs with my two duffels. We stopped to check in with the RA—they were still building the new dorm with the modern key cards and everything—and proceeded up to my room, where he set down my bags under the shocked gaze of Lindsay, my roommate. She mouthed something to me. I made one of those scared, bared-teeth smiles.

Monk turned to me. "You want to pop some popcorn?"

"Sure," I said.

Monk had a couple Costco boxes of microwave popcorn in his room on the boys' wing. We popped a bag in the microwave in the first-floor commons.

Then we sat on the sofa and talked until curfew.

I wish I could remember what we talked about that evening. It was probably just normal getting-to-know-you stuff, where are you from, how many siblings, how do you like Nobles—all the things I know about Monk without knowing how I know it. Maybe he told me then about how much he loved music, how he played guitar and piano and wrote songs in his head while he lay in bed, trying to sleep. But I can't say for certain.

I wish I could.

I wish I'd had the foresight to record those hours on my memory, to understand how often I would return to them as the years passed and Monk Adams no longer existed down the stairs from me, across the dining hall, dwarfing the desk next to me in AP Lit as we passed notes inside our battered paperback copies of *Hamlet* and tried not to laugh.

I wish I could remember every word we ever said to each other, like those people who can recall their entire lives like a gigantic library of video clips.

What I do remember is how it *felt* to talk to Monk Adams for three hours straight, like you were the most important, most fascinating person in the world. I remember the way his face tilted as he listened to me, his pale eyes, the dimple in his chin. I remember the size of his hands that could palm a basketball or spread across an octave and a half on a piano keyboard, and the scar on the right side of his jaw, which—I would later learn—had been split open by a lacrosse stick when he was eleven.

I remember dreaming, as I lay in bed that night, heart bouncing from my ribs, that maybe Monk Adams felt the same connection I did. Maybe he was the kind of boy you dreamed about, the unicorn boy, the boy who peered beneath your surface to marvel at the weirdness roiling within.

Maybe he might want to break up with Soccer Sophie of the Thoroughbred legs and hold me in his heart instead.

On the sisal beach mat next to mine, Paige settles back and folds her arms behind her head.

"Did I ever tell you about my Yale friend who summers on Winthrop Island?" she asks.

"You mean Lola? Only about a dozen times a year."

"We were just texting each other, and you're never going to believe this."

I reach for my straw hat and lay it over my face.

"It turns out, her family's house is just down the beach from Monk's place," says Paige. "Isn't that weird?"

"Fuck off, Paige."

"Just the day, Mal. Just one day, that's all I'm asking. It'll be fun."

I lift the hat and turn my head to face her.

"Fuck. Off."

Long story short, I'm huddled next to Paige in the cockpit of the Fjord, sipping artisan coffee from a Yeti mug as we kick across Buzzards Bay toward Point Judith. Half past seven in the morning. Sun glowing pink behind the eastern clouds. Kids raising hell in the seats behind us. A fragment of a sentence keeps repeating in my head, the one at the end of *Gatsby,* the one everybody knows so it's become one of those sad, pretentious clichés. But it's true.

Boats against the current.

I swallow back a mouthful of scalding coffee and stare through the sticky morning haze at the shore ahead on either side.

Boats against the current, my head beats on.

Borne back ceaselessly into the goddamn past.

CHAPTER FIVE

Hannah

September 1951
Outside Cairo, Egypt

Hannah had met Alistair six years earlier, at a displaced persons camp outside Vienna. Sometimes it seemed to her that it couldn't have happened so long ago, that six whole years couldn't have passed since the end of the war, but the calendar insisted.

She'd been living at the camp for about three weeks and had gained back a little weight, a little color. She spent her days caring for the sick in the infirmary—Hannah never seemed to come down with anything, her body had probably seen off every germ in Europe by then—and her nights reading the books sent to the camp by the Red Cross, in whatever language she could find. Sometimes she managed a few hours of deathlike sleep before startling awake, heart hammering, without any idea where she was or how she had arrived there.

So she'd had to remember, all over again.

Late one afternoon at the end of September, around the time the first cool winds whistled between the hills, smelling of autumn, word was passed for a Hungarian translator. Hannah rose from her bunk and followed the orderly down the rows of huts to the officers' quarters, where a couple of Englishmen—one tall and spare, about sixty years old, and the other one young and muscular—were attempting to question a Hungarian man who had recently made his way to the camp from the Soviet lines. The Englishmen were from the British Foreign Office and wanted to know about German atrocities. The older one seemed to be some sort of career diplomat and the younger was a lawyer who regarded Hannah as if she were empty space. Hannah's English was a little rusty, and she had little experience with legal or diplomatic jargon, but she managed all right.

Afterward, she asked to speak to the older one in private.

"This man was lying," she told him. "He's German by birth. Gestapo or SS, probably. I suspect he hid like a coward among the refugees when the Soviets came in and freed the prisons and camps."

The diplomat offered her a cigarette and lit them both up. Hannah hadn't smoked a real cigarette in months and it hit her head like a locomotive. "How do you know he was lying?" he asked.

She shrugged. "I can tell a German speaking Hungarian."

The man considered this for some time. In silence she watched him smoke. His suit hung from his spindly frame. He had graying brown hair, parted down the middle and combed straight back like a man from a previous decade. The style made his long face even narrower, his cheeks even more gaunt, papered by thin, pale skin. Only his eyes saved him from homeliness. They were a bright, icy blue that pierced you all the way through. When he finished the cigarette he offered Hannah a glass of Scotch, which she also accepted, and a permanent job as his translator.

As it turned out, Hannah was right about the prisoner. He was arrested for war crimes and prosecuted at Nuremberg, and Alistair Ainsworth received a commendation from Churchill himself for his keen assessment of the situation and adroit handling of the entire affair.

At the conclusion of the trials, Alistair asked Hannah to marry him.

All this she explained to Lucien as they drove west out of Cairo in his rattletrap Fiat, windows open to the hot breeze.

He passed her the cigarette they were sharing. "Did you love him?"

She dragged on the cigarette and handed it back to him. "I felt as much for him as I was capable of feeling for anyone."

"Not at all, then."

"No, I didn't love him. But I didn't dislike him. I respected his intellect, his integrity. I thought I could grow to love him, once my heart warmed up again. And he would take me away from Europe, which was the object."

"And he had money."

"You men," she said. "You're so quick to judge a woman who marries for money. But men are the same. A different kind of treasure, that's all."

"I didn't know there *was* another kind."

"Beauty." She took back the cigarette. "Men fall over themselves for a beautiful woman, women fall over themselves for a rich man. So who's the more greedy? At least money is useful. And it doesn't fade with time."

He laughed. "All right, I concede."

Hannah propped her elbow on the door and waited for him to ask what had brought her to the displaced persons camp in Austria.

What she'd had before she had nothing.

Lucien crushed out the cigarette in the overflowing ashtray and lit another while he steered the car with his knees. When he'd filled his lungs with fresh smoke, he asked her about the sea voyage from England.

Lucien parked the car near what seemed to be an encampment of souvenir sellers and dragomen and tossed some coins to a small boy who tucked the money inside his ragged shirt and touched his forehead. Taking Hannah's hand firmly in his, he led her through the throng. Hannah knew a little Arabic by now, but not enough to understand the chatter around her and it was a relief when they emerged into the open desert, flat except for the pyramids rising above the dun sand, the Sphinx gazing east toward the Nile.

Hannah unclasped his hand. "I don't want to ride any damn camel."

"We're not going to ride any camels, believe me."

The space around them was vast and monochrome. A yellowish haze coated the horizon and the hot white sun overhead. Lucien had a long, graceful stride, like an antelope. Hannah skipped to keep up. They skirted around the Sphinx temple and approached the beast from the south. Hannah held the brim of her hat in place as she gazed upward to its head.

"I suppose you've stood here a hundred times by now," she said to Lucien.

"Each time is like the first."

She turned her head. He was looking not at the Sphinx, but at her. Under the brim of his hat, his eyes were a dark arboreal green. She stepped away to examine the outstretched stone paws, as high as her own head.

"Were you born in Cairo?" she asked.

"No, I was born in Alexandria. My mother's family still lives there."

"Lillian said you were Swiss."

"Lillian?"

"Lillian Beverley."

"My father's Swiss. *Was* Swiss, I should say. He died some time ago." He paused to place a palm on the rough stone arm of the Sphinx. "They never married. He had a wife in Geneva."

"How modern."

"Modern? I would say this kind of arrangement is as old as civilization. But he took good care of us. I went to the American school in Alexandria. Then boarding school in Switzerland. A year of university in France before the war started."

"Your English and French are impeccable."

"So are yours."

"My father was a professor," she said, "and my mother was English."

He took her right hand by the wrist. "Go on, touch it."

"I don't dare."

"It's only stone, after all. One day it will be dust, like us."

Hannah allowed Lucien to lay her palm on the side of the paw. He moved his hand away and she closed her eyes.

"What do you see?" he asked.

"I don't know. Four thousand years. Winters, summers without end, again and again. Some man carving this under the sun. Brown skin. Perspiration. Chisel."

"I wonder how he died."

"Do you think he's dead? He's inside the stone yet. Don't you feel him? Pouring himself right through his tools and into the mineral, forever." She slapped the block with her hand. "Until it turns to dust. Even then."

"He was about twenty-five, I should guess," said Lucien. "He spent his entire life here. His father was a stonemason before him."

"What about his mother?"

"Would it be bad of me to suggest she worked in the laundry?" He nodded to one side. "There was a whole village here. An entire town of people who lived for nothing but to build these tombs."

"You seem to know a lot about it."

His hand fell away. "When I was a boy, I wanted to study these things. To dig them free from the sand."

"An archaeologist?"

"Yes. But my father died, and my mother insisted I study something practical, like the law. So the dream stayed where it was, in my head. Come." He took her hand and pulled her westward, toward the rear of the beast. Hannah supposed she should feel anxious or ashamed, walking like this in the hot, brazen daylight with a man who wasn't her husband. Hand in hand. But nobody gave them a second glance, or even a first. To the rest of the world, Hannah and Lucien were just another couple touring the pyramids, probably on an Egyptian honeymoon.

They rounded the corner at the beast's rear. To Hannah's surprise, there was nobody near. Lucien turned and pulled her against him. Silently they kissed. Hannah fell back against the stone. Lucien braced his forearms on either side of her face and moved his soft mouth on hers. How sweet he tasted, like childhood. All along her chest and stomach they met. Not one inch of her was left untouched. She was engulfed, suffused; everything else crushed out. Nothing in the world but a pair of bodies, a pair of hips to which she pressed her own. Lucien lifted his lips a little and stroked her hair, sighed against her mouth.

"Open your eyes," he said.

She opened her eyes.

The sun beat down from the high west. Into each other they sweated and stared. She thought she was falling. She thought she was waking from a dream. Where was she? The warm, soft eyes searching her.

János, she thought.

The name rose from her ribs to sting her throat. My God, where had it come from? For years, she hadn't said the word, hadn't even brought the five letters together in her head.

Her eyes hurt; her chest hurt. She couldn't move. Rough stone behind her back. *Pyramids,* she thought. *You're in Egypt. You're married. Married to an Englishman.*

János is gone.

Lucien Beck touched the notch at the top of her lips with his thumb.

"What's the matter?" he asked.

Hannah pushed him away. "Nothing. Let's keep walking."

They walked along the causeway to the northern pyramid and climbed the stones until all the monuments came into view, arranged perfectly in the sand. Lucien pulled her up to sit on a block and propped himself beside her. From his knapsack he took a canteen of water and shared it with her, then lit a cigarette, which they passed back and forth. The sun drenched them. Hannah lifted her arm and pointed to the three small pyramids at the base of the one they sat on.

"What are those for?" she asked.

"Nobody knows for certain. But those ones, over there? Next to the last pyramid?" He pointed to the south. "Those are the tombs of the pharaoh's queens. His mother and sister and wife."

"How do they know this?"

"The hieroglyphs, of course."

"Can you read them?"

"A little bit. I'm not an expert, though."

She found his hand and wrapped her fingers around his. "Would you build your wife a pyramid after she was dead?"

"I don't have a wife."

"Your lover, then."

"Ah, well. I suppose I would build her a throne next to the sun."

"Oh, you're a poet."

He laughed. "Me? Not at all. That's from an opera. *Aida,* you know it? *Ergerti un trono vicino al sol . . .* Radamès, the Egyptian warrior. Secretly in love with the handmaid of the pharaoh's daughter." He lifted her hand and examined the knuckles. "Did you know this opera was commissioned from Verdi to celebrate the opening of the Suez Canal?"

"I have to confess, I don't like opera."

"No?"

"It's so sentimental. Build her a throne next to the sun? How stupid."

Lucien released her hand and leaned back on his palms. He wore a fedora of pale, fine straw and the sun cut a diagonal line across his cheek. He seemed to be studying her, although she couldn't return his gaze. She stared across the sand at the three small pyramids.

"How funny, though, for the Egyptians to commission an Italian opera for their canal," she said.

Lucien replied obediently. "Ah, but Suez was never really Egypt's canal, was it? The French came up with the idea, the money came from elsewhere. Then the British bought up our share when Egypt went bankrupt from all these modernization projects. Canals, roads, opera houses. No, this commission proved all too apt. Egypt for the Europeans." He reached for the brim of her hat and plucked off some insect. "Still, it's a beautiful opera."

Hannah climbed to her feet. For an instant, the height made her dizzy. Lucien grabbed her elbow.

"Steady," he said.

"Enough of this," she told him. "I want to see the queens."

Each one stood about twenty meters high, made of the same heavy blocks as the giant pyramids. Hannah reached out to drag her fingers along the stone.

"By themselves, they would be colossal," she said. "They would be wondrous."

"I suppose one could move them out of the pharaoh's shadow."

She dropped her hand to her side. "No, you couldn't. This is the trouble. They're fixed here for eternity, as he intended."

The sand had begun to stir in the hot afternoon breeze. A dusty haze coated the horizon. The sun was dropping now; they'd spent the day. Lucien touched her shoulder and she turned and leaned back against the rough stone block. He rested one hand next to her face and bent to kiss her. Brief, gentle kisses.

"This is stupid," she said. "We should go back."

Lucien raised his head and looked earnest. "Right now?"

"Before we do something even more stupid."

"This is not stupid, Hannah. This is true." He reached for her hand against the stone and pulled it up to his chest. "You're here because you recognize how true it is."

"Then you don't understand me at all."

"I understand you better than you think. I know you're laboring under some great sorrow."

Hannah pulled her hand away. "Everybody's laboring under some great sorrow."

"You need someone to worship you." He leaned forward to rest his hands on either side of her head. "Someone to remind you of the joys of love."

"Adultery, you mean."

"When a woman is married to a man like that—"

"I chose to marry Alistair. I knew the bargain I made."

"Love is not a bargain, Hannah."

"Of course it is. Every exchange between human beings is a bargain of some kind. Actual treasure or moral treasure, it's all the same. You agree on your price and make the transaction."

"Then you've given yourself away much too cheap. You're worth a hundred of him. A thousand."

"My God, listen to you. You and your pretty words."

"But I mean them."

"No, you don't. You're saying these things to get me into bed, that's all. Paying me the necessary toll to tuck into the pocket of my conscience, so we can move on to more pleasant business."

"Would you rather I didn't say anything?"

"I don't really give a damn, one way or another."

He murmured in her ear. "Have you been to the Mena House, Hannah?"

"No."

"But you've heard of it, yes? Right on the edge of the Giza plain. You can see it from here. Look."

She turned her head in the direction he meant. A splash of green, some white buildings like sugar cubes.

Panic struck her.

My God, what was she doing here? What had she done? A noise came from her chest, a throttled sob. She gasped for breath.

"Hannah—" he began, and then, "You're shaking, darling. What's wrong?"

He reached again for her waist to draw her back. *Darling,* she thought.

She yanked away and staggered around the corner of the pyramid, where the sun burned a ferocious white hole in the sky. She realized she was crying, that tears ran down her cheeks and dripped from her jaw. She put out a hand and collapsed against the side of this pyramid, built in praise of a faithful wife, to last for eternity.

Hannah had had a list of sound reasons to marry Alistair, but she'd never really understood why he married her. He'd lived sixty-one years without a wife—why now? She'd had nothing to bring to the marriage—no name, no money, just herself.

But since he hadn't asked her any questions, she returned the favor.

The Anglican chaplain of a regiment of military police married them after a two-day engagement—long enough for Hannah to stitch some old parachute silk into a modest wedding dress. Alistair's colleagues threw them a rousing wedding party in the restaurant of the local hotel in Nuremberg. After she and Alistair left to a hail of confetti ripped from old legal dossiers—there was no rice to be had—the celebrations continued for some time without them. All night Hannah heard them downstairs, toasting the bride and groom—long after the groom himself was fast asleep.

You would think she might have been anxious about the wedding night, but she'd had no qualms at all, really. Her body had long since ceased to be a thing of wonder to her, a source of delight. She had sunk her old ideas—sex as a sacred mystery, as an act of love—in a deep well, or she could not have survived what came next. Your body was just a bag of bones and skin, sex was just an act performed on you. Your soul existed apart from all this, where it kept safe, untouched.

Not that she'd expected Alistair to make violent love to her, just because they were married. In fact, he'd remained formal, even bashful, which was both touching and strange—hadn't Alistair been the one to propose marriage? You would think he harbored some powerful sexual desire for her.

But while he was commanding enough in a Nuremberg courtroom or a prison interview cell, and while he'd certainly gone to bed with women before, he had never gone to bed with a lawfully married wife. For some reason this took him aback. He'd sent her to bathe while he answered the congratulatory telegrams—his sister back home in England was shocked, to say the least—and when she emerged in a dressing gown, fresh and pink, he'd walked straight past her to wash himself.

Not knowing what else to do, Hannah had removed the dressing gown and got into bed.

Some time later he'd emerged, switched off the light, climbed in beside her. She'd heard him breathing heavily a foot away. Just as she wondered whether she ought to kiss him or something, he'd turned on his side and reached for her. His wet mouth covered hers while his hands kneaded her breasts like a pair of dough balls. He said not a word. After a minute or two, she reached down to hurry him along. He groaned at her touch and started to mutter. *Oh God, oh God, that's it, there we are, oh God, harder, harder, there we are.* She wasn't sure if he was instructing her or congratulating himself. Maybe both. The harder she stroked, the harder he got. At last he creaked into position. He was more vigorous than she expected. He shoved away in mighty, almost spasmodic jerks of his hips, apologizing as he went. *Almost done, darling,* he panted. *Sorry, sorry, nearly there.* She felt him nearing the brink, harder and faster, iron determination— *Almost, almost, blast it all, sorry, hang on, hang on, blast it, almost got it, sorry, almost got it.* There was a kind of rhythm to it, she realized, like the chuffing of a train as it worked up a head of steam. She clutched his skinny buttocks to encourage him. Finally there was a triumphal bellow that rang from the walls—*Fuck, fuck, FUCK!* He arched his back and went stiff as a corpse, then fell on her chest and apologized for the unseemly outburst.

Heat of the moment, he'd gasped. *Forgot myself.*

Quite all right, darling, she'd said, patting his back.

Good, good, he'd muttered. *Good girl.*

Then he'd rolled away and fell to sleep.

When Hannah had woken at dawn, her new husband lay next to her in exactly the same position, as if in a coffin, perfectly white except for the pink tip of his nose, snoring in long, deep rumbles.

She remembered how she'd crawled out from beneath the covers and lit a cigarette and smoked it slowly, naked and unwashed, staring out the window at the distant mountains, and said to herself, *I wonder if I'm going to have another baby.*

Now her indifference was gone. Her body was no longer a bag of bones and skin. Her body wanted to live again, wanted to melt, wanted to love.

Lucien's arms settled around her.

"Hannah, I'm sorry," he said. "Don't cry."

She shook her head. What else could she do? She couldn't speak. To speak you had to harbor some hope, and she had none. Either she went on existing like a stone pyramid, a monument to fidelity, or she returned to life in mortal sin.

Somehow they were sitting on the dirt. She cried into his shirt. He stroked her hair.

"I'll drive you back to Cairo," said Lucien. "Everything will be all right."

CHAPTER SIX

Mallory

May 2008
Winthrop Island, New York

I first stepped onto Winthrop Island off the noon ferry from New London. It was the Thursday before Memorial Day weekend and Monk Adams's stepmother was supposed to pick me up at the dock. I stood alone in the drizzle for a solid half hour before a vintage wood-paneled Jeep Wagoneer tore around the corner and jolted to a stop before me. Monk Adams jumped out of the driver's seat and shook the rain from his hair. *I'm so sorry, Pinks,* he said. (That was his old nickname for me, Pinkie Pie being one of the My Little Ponies.) *Becca's under the weather.*

I remember the phrase rang an un-Monk-like note, a ladies' luncheon kind of note. I hopped onto the worn burgundy leather bench seat and buckled up while Monk threw my duffel bags into the back. *Under the weather?* I repeated. *What does that mean?*

Monk shoved the Jeep into gear and winked at me. *Means you're in no condition to drive,* he said.

Which turned out to be the first entry in my Winthrop dictionary that summer. To be *under the weather* means you're either drunk or hungover. I never found out what they call it when you're actually sick.

Monk got me the job. I mean, obviously. It was our junior year of college and he'd called me up at the end of March from his dorm room at Colby, where they were in the middle of something called *fake spring*. (He explained that fake spring was a Maine thing—the first wave of balmy weather that came in to melt down the snow-pack, sending everyone into a bout of spring fever that ended abruptly when the inevitable blizzard hit on the first of April.) He asked how I was doing, how was the boyfriend (*Oh, same,* I replied), whether I had any summer work lined up yet. I said not yet, couple of internships still hanging in the balance. He said, *Stop me if this sounds too weird, but my dad and stepmom need a summer nanny at their place on Winthrop Island. They like to hire college girls, and last year's nanny took another job. Was I interested?*

I said sure. I asked how much it paid.

He said good question, he could hook us up to discuss all that. He said, *It's a cool gig, decent hours, nice guest room with your own bath, yards away from the beach. Plus, I'm right next door at my mom's family's place if you need a hand.*

The way he tagged on those last words, so deliberately casual, released a rash of tingles from the top of my spine to the ends of my fingers and toes and everywhere in between. At that instant, drowning in a pool of dopamine on the cheap cocoon chair in my dorm room, there was no way I wasn't going to take this job nannying for Monk Adams's dad and stepmom, right next door to Monk Adams, *all summer long.*

Even though I had a fairly serious boyfriend at the time.

I asked (exact same nonchalance) why I would need a hand.

I remember he made this awkward chuckle, almost embarrassed. *I guess Chippy and Blue can be a bit of a handful,* he said. *And my stepmom is . . .*

Is?

Kind of a trip, he said. *But don't worry. I'm caddying at the Club all summer. I'll take care of you.*

The Wagoneer started forward. The windshield wipers were old and streaky; the humid air collected in patches of fog on the glass. I couldn't make out the harbor very well, other than an impression of two or three shabby storefronts and a fire station—not exactly the ritzy enclave I'd envisioned. Monk had rolled down the driver's window—air-conditioning was for spendthrifts and wimps, according to the Winthrop code—and his left elbow rested on the ledge. My nerves were shot through with the shock of seeing Monk again. He seemed wider and leaner at the same time. His right hand rested on the wheel at twelve o'clock, more rugged than I remembered, knuckles cracked, like he'd been working with his hands. He shot me a glance, flashed a little smile, and pointed the Wagoneer up a steep hill. The engine rumbled from its dirty throat.

Monk patted the dashboard. "Beast."

"The classic. How old is it?"

"Old. Eighties, I think? It's been our summer car since I can remember. We call her Bessie." He flashed me another smile. "It's good to see you, Pinks. How long has it been?"

"That pub crawl in Provincetown, I guess. Winter break a year and a half ago."

"Right. That was fun. The old Nobles crowd. Good get-together. We should plan another one."

"We should."

I didn't mention that the old Nobles crowd had been *his* crowd, not ours. That Monk was the one who called me up, out of the blue (there were times I thought Monk only ever called out of the blue) and said, *Hey, bunch of us getting together in Provincetown for a pub crawl the day after Christmas.* Did I want to join in? I said yes. Duh. His friends had treated me with the usual affable tolerance, asked me how RISD was going. They were all grinding through economics and finance classes in the Ivy League and various liberal arts colleges around the Northeast. I was the token artist, like a mascot, so they could point to me and say, *See? We're not all a bunch of aspiring investment bankers and lawyers and tech bros!* Anyway, their efforts at conversation had petered out after the first stop on the tour, so Monk had hung back with me and we'd ended up talking in the corner booth at the Black Sheep (Monk sitting across the table with his legs propped on the seat next to me, me creating abstract art with emptied Splenda packets) until the others had long left, until the bar was closing down, until it felt safely within the boundaries of the friend zone to invite him to crash on the sofa at my mom's place. To my surprise, his face lit up. *Seriously?* he said. *Would that be okay?*

I said, *Sure, the accommodations are not luxurious, but it's better than driving all the way back to Boston on a beer buzz, right?*

He grinned and said it sounded a hell of a lot better. He drove the five miles to my mom's house at a grandfatherly pace. I handed him a pillow and a few blankets (Mom always set the thermostat to Pleistocene at night) and a spare toothbrush. He said thanks. We stared at each other a second before I turned and fled for bed.

I remember I couldn't sleep that night, knowing Monk Adams lay on a sofa *mere yards* away from me, on the other side of a wall the width of a paper towel. *I could get up,* I thought. *What would happen if I got up?*

Next thing I knew, I woke to a shriek when my mother walked through the living room on her way to the coffee maker.

By the time I'd thrown on a bathrobe and rushed out to explain, Monk had already won her over. They were chatting in the kitchen. Mom brewed extra coffee, extra strong, and pulled bacon and eggs out of the fridge. Monk scrambled the eggs and did the dishes. He left after breakfast, dropping a casual goodbye kiss on my actual lips, and for a while after that we would talk regularly on the phone, exchange texts, make promises to meet up at the next break.

Until we didn't. Until the gap between calls and messages expanded to forever.

In order to fill the Monk-sized hole in my life, I started dating Dillon. Dillon was a senior at the University of Rhode Island, majoring in something called management science. Attractive, funny, decent in bed, could hold a conversation, returned messages promptly. Check check check. For a while, it worked great.

Then Monk Adams called me in the middle of Maine fake spring to ask if I wanted to spend the summer taking care of his brother and sister on Winthrop Island.

And I said I'd take it.

"So explain to me about your family," I said to Monk.

"I mean, you know the big stuff already. Mom and Dad divorced when I was ten. He married Becca right after the papers came through, so you work it out. Twins were born a year after that."

"What's she like? Your stepmom."

He squinted through the windshield and the streaks left behind by the wipers. The grin dimmed a notch or two. "So, I can't lie to you, Pinks. She's kind of difficult."

"Difficult how? And why didn't you mention difficult before?"

"I hinted. To be fair. But the truth is, I didn't want to put you off."

"Oh, subterfuge. Nice."

The grin sprang back. "See, that's what I love about you, Pinko. Nobody else I know springs words like *subterfuge* into everyday conversation."

"Can you just stick to the topic at hand? Evil stepmother?"

"She's not *evil*, Pinks. She's like everyone else, she's got shit she's dealing with. She just doesn't always deal with it in the healthiest way. She gets—you know, difficult. Especially with chicks like you, younger and prettier. But like I said, don't worry. I'm literally a hundred yards away. Got your back. Team Mallory, all the way."

The word *prettier* had thrown me off. I croaked out, "Promise?"

Monk held out his hand, little finger crooked. "Pinkie promise."

We crossed pinkies. (Our old thing, because of my nickname. Dumb, I know. But it was ours.)

"Anyway, you'll like my dad," Monk said. "Everyone does. The arts are his thing. He's on a couple of boards and stuff. That's how he met Becca? Her family's got this big art foundation. You should show him your work."

"I'm not going to show your dad my *artwork,* Monk. That's like . . . weird. And pushy."

"He'd love it. He's into the whole scene. He's got this kick he's on right now, about championing the work of women artists. Because, you know, the patriarchy. Actually, now that I think about it, the only arts he *doesn't* encourage are mine."

Monk said it like a joke, but I knew better.

"He's still being a dick about that?"

Monk shrugged. "You know how it is. Bragging rights. He wanted me to intern in New York this summer with the other scions."

"I don't know what's worse, a banking internship or hanging out with the scions."

"Well, except *this* one. Right?"

"You're the exception to every rule, Monkfish."

He lifted his hand for a fist bump. "Stuck to my guns, though, Pinks. You'd be proud of me. Told him nope, I was spending the summer on the island, working on my music. He told me that was bullshit, I needed a real job. So I said fine, I'll caddy at the Club."

"Was he pissed?"

His voice deepened. "Caddying is for the scholarship boys, son. You don't need a leg up into this world. You're already in it."

"Well, fuck him."

"Fuck him," Monk echoed.

The road flattened out. Bessie's ancient transmission gasped for a higher gear and found it at last. I turned my head to the window and peered through the layers of drizzle and fog.

"Pretty cool cliffs over there," Monk said. "You can see the lighthouse and everything. When the weather clears up, I'll show you the view."

When I walked into the family room at Seagrapes and met Mrs. Adams, I thought maybe Monk had exaggerated for effect. She didn't look drunk at all. She looked immaculate. She had honey-blond hair highlighted with streaks of lighter honey—Grade A honey, if you will—and honey skin to match, improbably taut. The whites of her eyes matched the whites of her teeth. She opened her glossy lips in a wide smile of greeting.

"You must be Mallory! We're so delighted to have you here. Monk, honey, could you put Mallory's luggage in the nanny suite?"

"On it." Monk disappeared around the corner with my two duffel bags—the same ones he had carried for me into the residence hall at Nobles, years ago.

"He's told us so much about you," said Mrs. Adams.

"Oh, heck. And you're still willing to take me on?"

She blinked, like she didn't get the joke. "He said you were terrific with kids."

This was news to me, as I hadn't had much to do with kids at all at that point in my life, let alone in Monk's company.

"Love kids," I said. "Love 'em. Speaking of which?"

"Chippy and Blue are upstairs with their math tutor between noon and two." A thump shook the ceiling above us. To her credit, Mrs. Adams continued without a pause. "So you've got a little time to rest and unpack and have a bite to eat. You're welcome to take whatever you like from the kitchen. Grace will give you a hand."

"Grace?"

"Our housekeeper," she said. "She's been with us for years. A member of the family, really."

Now I caught it—the ever-so-slight slurring of a word or two.

Monk popped back around the corner, adding several watts to the overcast air in the family room, surrounded on three sides by french windows that offered nothing but gray.

"Monk, honey," said Mrs. Adams, "would you mind sticking around to introduce Mallory to Chippy and Blue? They don't finish with Carson until two, and I'm due at the Club for the ladies' activities committee."

Monk sighed. "I guess I could make the sacrifice."

"Don't you have to babysit some golfers instead?" I asked.

"Not when it's raining, Pinks," he told me.

I guess Chippy and Blue can be a handful, Monk had said.

But the pair who came thundering down the stairs at exactly one minute past two o'clock and threw themselves at Monk, one on each side, seemed civilized enough. Chippy wore a pair of drawstring chino shorts the color of goose turd and a brown T-shirt that said Brunswick Soccer. Blue wore a sleeveless seersucker shift of pristine pink and white. Both were lightly tanned and had matching straw-gold hair, Chippy's cut short and Blue's gathered back in a luxurious ponytail.

"Guess what, monsters?" said Monk. "Mallory's here!"

The twins turned to me in unison, looked at each other, and broke away from Monk to run yelling into my arms—one on each side, just like they had with Monk a moment ago. My arms were full of fragrant kid limbs. My mouth was full of fragrant kid hair. *Maaaaallloreee!* they said, like they'd been waiting all their lives for me to appear.

I raised my gaze to Monk, who folded his arms and traded smiles with me.

This is going to be a piece of cake, I thought confidently.

Six hours later, I called up Monk on his cellphone. No answer. A minute later, he called back.

"They won't go to bed," I said.

"Of course they won't go to bed. It's still daylight."

"Your stepmom said eight P.M. sharp."

"Becca hasn't put those kids to bed herself in years. Probably ever."

There was some noise in the background.

"Where are you?" I asked.

"At the Club. With Dad and Becca. The annual welcome dinner."

Chippy jumped off his bed and hit me with a pillow. "I thought you were supposed to switch off your phone inside hoity-toity clubs," I said.

"I might have kept mine on vibrate, just in case. Have you pulled down those magical blackout shades?"

"Yes. Bathed and combed, jammies on, teeth brushed. Read the books. Ow!" Pillows from both sides this time.

"What about *Toy Story*?"

"Becca said no TV before bed."

"Pinks, for God's sake. Let the poor kids watch a fucking movie. I do it all the time. I promise you, they won't tell on you."

"Not on the first *night*, Monk. I have a little pride."

He sighed into the phone. "All right. Give me fifteen minutes. I know a trick."

"What? You can't just leave in the middle of *dinner*!"

"I *so can*, Pinks."

"Forget it. I can handle it."

Chippy let out a whoop and banged the pillow against his sister's head. Blue started to howl.

"Yeah, sure. You got it all under control. I'll be right over."

"What about your parents? Dinner?"

Monk let out one of his low, rumbling chuckles. "That's a joke, right?"

Twenty minutes later, Monk appeared at the door to the twins' bedroom, wearing tan slacks, a navy blazer, a white shirt unbuttoned at the collar, and a guitar slung over his shoulder.

"You're late," I said.

"Had to see a man about a six-string." He unslung the guitar from his shoulder and plopped onto a beanbag upholstered in sage-colored plush. Already the kids were crawling over him, begging for a song. "All right, all right. Geez Louise, you two. Aren't you supposed to be asleep by now?"

"But we're not *tired*!" said Chippy, bouncing on the other beanbag. He wore a pair of short Tom Brady pajamas and his eyes looked a little manic. Blue curled up on Monk's lap like she owned it.

Monk looked sternly at Chippy. "Bro. What about our little talk yesterday? What did I tell you guys?"

Blue yelled from his lap, "Do as Mallory says and don't give her any sass!"

"Right. So what am I doing here?"

"Playing us a lullaby?"

"Cute." He strummed a few chords. "What I meant is I'm not supposed to be here, right? I'm supposed to be having a nice lobster dinner with Mom and Dad at the Club. *You're* supposed to be asleep so Mallory can put her feet up."

"Play that one about the cat," said Blue.

"You're gonna have to be more specific, cupcake."

"'Don Gato,'" she said, in a surprisingly accurate Spanish accent.

The random chords lapsed into melody, first in major key and then slipping mysteriously into minor. I plopped cross-legged on the other beanbag. To my surprise, Chippy plopped onto my lap.

"Oof," I said.

"Take it easy there, bro," said Monk.

Chippy wriggled around until he'd made himself comfortable. "Proceed," he said grandly.

Monk plucked a few strings like a Spanish guitar solo.

Oh, Señor Don Gato was a cat
On a high red roof Don Gato sat
He was there to read a letter . . .
(MEOW MEOW MEOW! sing-shouted Blue.)
Where the reading light was better
(MEOW MEOW MEOW! sing-shouted Chippy.)
'Twas a love note for Don Gato

The kids belted out a chorus of meows. Monk waved them quiet like a conductor.

I adore you, wrote the lady cat
Who was fluffy, white, and nice and fat
There was not a sweeter kitty
(MEOW MEOW MEOW!)
In the country or the city
(MEOW MEOW MEOW!)
And she said she'd wed Don Gato

Again, the chorus of meows. Monk winked at me and cut them off.

As they proceeded through the verses—Don Gato so excited he falls off the roof (*¡Ay caramba!* the kids sing-shouted together), the doctors hold a consultation, poor Señor Don Gato up and dies—Chippy's limbs relaxed against mine, one by one. His little-boy sharpness softened at the corners. I circled my arms around him and he leaned his head against the hollow of my shoulder.

As the funeral passed the market square
Such a smell of fish was in the air
Though the burial was slated
(Meow meow meow, less shouty now)
He became reanimated
(Meow meow meow)
He came back to life, Don Gato

Slowly Monk spun out the final line. As his buttery voice hung the last note on the air, he turned to me and lifted an eyebrow.

I clapped my hands together. "Bravo!"

"Encore!" murmured Blue, from the crook between Monk's guitar and his lap.

"Encore?" Monk pretended to be outraged. "I'm not singing *that* again. Forget it. I don't even *like* cats."

"Then play something else. Please, Monk?"

Monk held up a finger. The kids went quiet and attentive, watching his finger like a pair of dogs concentrating on a treat. "All right. But only if the two of you get in bed first."

"So is it true?" I asked. "You don't like cats?"

"Like it's a crime?"

"Kind of, it is."

We sat side by side in the Wagoneer, driving down West Cliff Road toward the village, such as it was. Mr. and Mrs. Adams had returned home half an hour ago and Monk had buzzed my cellphone.

Meet me at the end of the drive in 10 min

What why, I texted back.

Surprise

When I reached the end of the drive ten minutes later, Monk was waiting inside Bessie, engine rumbling. The clouds had dried up and the sun had set, leaving the air damp and cool. Monk had reached over the seat to open the door for me. He'd changed out of his blazer and button-down shirt into a plain blue tee underneath a casual shirt in a retro print, unbuttoned. The chinos remained, only more rumpled. I'd asked where we were going.

The Mo, he'd said.

Mo?

The Mohegan Inn. It's where all the nannies and the Club staff hang out in the evening. The only public bar on the island. It's pretty chill, you'll like it.

Okay, I'd said. Then I'd asked about cats.

"Actually," he said, "if you want to know the truth, I'm kind of a sucker for cats. I just didn't want to play that damn song again."

"It's a favorite, huh?"

He propped his elbow on the door. The cool air blew through

the window and ruffled his hair. "The thing about kids, they don't mind hearing the same song over and over again. Drives a man insane."

I sang—not very well—"You broke my will."

"But what a thrill."

Together, howling—"Goodness, gracious, great balls of fire!"

When we were done laughing, I said, "Someone's a little giddy tonight."

"Pinko," he said, "you ain't seen nothing."

It wasn't until he'd parked Bessie along one of the damp, winding streets in the village and reached his long arm over the back of the seat that I realized he had his guitar with him.

"Holy shit," I said. "Are you going to *play* something?"

"Don't tell Dad, but I started playing sets here last summer."

I turned to face him, there in the front seat of Bessie. There were no streetlights and he'd turned off the engine, so I couldn't see much of him. Just his outline. The warmth of his body. The two of us, Monk and me, in the middle of the quiet dusk. Sharing a secret.

"So your dad doesn't know you're here?" I asked.

"Nope." He checked his watch. "Shit, we're late. Come on."

We climbed out of the car. I followed Monk downhill and around a corner to a large, rambling clapboard house of the type that suggested George Washington had slept there. Several cars were parked outside, none of them newer than ten years old. Light burst from the windows. I felt that I knew this place; I'd been inside a hundred buildings like this one. The ceilings would be low, the floors stained by generations of beer. The walls would have been knocked out to create a single large room around the center chimney, which would be boarded up. A dull wood bar would stretch across one wall; a bunch of mismatched junk-sale chairs and tables would clutter the open space. The air would smell like the inside of a barrel of ale.

As we crossed the threshold, Monk grasped my fingers. Only for a few seconds, only until we'd chiseled through the crowd and reached the bar. The bartender caught sight of Monk and his face relaxed in relief. "Thought you were a no-show, bro," he said.

"Sorry, had some parental complications. Mike, this is Mallory. Friend of mine. She's nannying for my dad and stepmom this summer."

Mike wiped his hand on a bar cloth and held it out to me. He was about thirty, a redhead, affable wide face and a brogue on command. "Mallory! You wouldn't be a fellow Irish, now, would you?"

"All the way through," I said.

"Then you're always welcome at my bar, Mallory friend of Monk. What'll it be?"

"Pretty good local IPA on tap," Monk suggested.

"Local IPA it is," I said.

Mike looked at Monk. "Make it two?"

Monk shook his head. "Nah, I'll hold off until the break. Mallory? You okay here?"

"I'll keep an eye on her for you," said Mike, pulling the beer from the tap into a pint glass. "Mic's all set up."

Monk looked down and for an instant it seemed like he was going to kiss me. That was how it felt, the way he'd taken my hand as we walked inside, the way he'd introduced me to Mike. I could see Mike assumed we were a couple. *Keep an eye on her for you.* I waited for the kiss, a little dizzy. A flash of guilt because of Dillon.

But the kiss didn't come. He lifted his hand and gave my hair a ruffle, like you'd pet a dog or something, and disappeared into the crowd.

"Hey, bro," said Mike to the man perched on the stool next to me. "Give the lady a seat, all right? She's with the band."

The man shrugged and slid off the stool. I climbed on and reached for the glass. Monk was right, the beer was perfect. Not too hoppy, like some IPAs. Mike stood across from me, arms folded, bar cloth hanging from one hand, scowling thoughtfully in the direction in which Monk had disappeared. I felt a stir in the crowd.

"Kind of a roomful you've got here," I said. "Is it usually this packed on a Thursday night?"

"Not usually, no. First live music of the season."

I had to raise my voice because a round of cheering had touched off. "Sorry we were late!"

"No worries."

From the other side of the room came some noise from the microphone, some laughter, Monk's familiar chuckle. "Sorry, guys. Got held up en route."

Someone yelled, *I'll bet you did.* Another one made a shrill wolf whistle. Mike looked at me and winked, grinning, and my cheeks turned hot. I wanted to lean forward and explain to Mike that, okay, yes, Monk and I came here together, but we weren't, like, *together.* I had a serious boyfriend! Monk probably had a girlfriend; he always had girlfriends. We were just really good friends, that was all, really good friends who happened to be of the opposite—

A strum of chords interrupted this interior monologue, amplified by the microphone. A climb up a ladder of notes, a swift descent. Then Monk's voice, easy and rumbly, like Bessie's engine idling at the end of the drive. "How's everyone been? Kind of a rocky winter, amiright?" Some laughter. "Hope nobody's trading any mortgage-backed securities for a living."

A few shouts laced the air. I couldn't hear the words.

"Anyway, we made it, right? Back on the island. Summer's around the corner. Even the rain's stopped raining out there." The strumming took on a pattern, the start of a melody. "So I been working on a few new tunes over the winter. Hope you like this one. It's about . . ." A delicate, intricate play of guitar strings filled the pause. "Well, I'll let you figure out what it's about."

A few more mellow chords and Monk's voice came in, melancholy.

I hadn't heard Monk sing onstage for years. Not since *Guys and Dolls* senior year, when (in a move that sent shock waves through the rigid Nobles caste system) he opted out of lacrosse and instead brought down the house as Sky Masterson. As we streamed out of the auditorium opening night, I remember hearing someone say that Monk Adams kid had a killer set of pipes, he could go on Broadway. It wasn't just that buttery voice or the way he spoke Sky's lines like he himself had been raised in the middle of Brooklyn, a block away from Ebbets Field. It was the way he filled the stage. It was the way he made you believe in the story. This energy he had.

I couldn't see Monk from my position on the barstool at the other end of the Mohegan Inn bar. I couldn't even glimpse the top of his head, gleaming in the lights, a few shades darker than it was when I met him in the ninth grade.

All I had was that voice, pouring over the tops of all these heads, the working class of Winthrop Island.

You know the voice. It's more burnished now, a decade and a half older and wiser, but the instrument's the same. Floats a top note all the way into next week, like it's nothing, then dives back gracefully into the chest, where it melts into liquid gold. Where would you be without that voice on your frayed nerves, your hurt soul?

You know the song too. *"Winter Tale"*—it was the lead single on his debut album. Remember how it starts off slow and soft, like he's just musing to himself in front of that old portrait of the man with the *fox-sharp eyes and the triangle beard, the collar of lies and the cross of fear,* how he imagines a whole life for this man, some girl this man wanted to marry and didn't, how she married someone else *on a midwinter night, a midwinter night,* and the man's soul turned into midwinter bone and midwinter blight. The man grows rich and pretends to be happy, until his old sweetheart sickens and dies *on a midwinter night, a midwinter night*—the quiet, controlled anguish Monk packs into those notes, just tell me you haven't cried when you're driving by yourself, late at night, and this song melts through the speakers. And then back to the portrait, which transforms for an instant into an old man *on a midwinter night, a midwinter night,* his fine face wrecked by bone and by blight, but his fox-sharp eyes are young and bright, because he's flying home to his sweetheart in the midsummer light, the midsummer light.

On the way back up West Cliff Road, Monk wanted to know what I thought.

"Not bad," I said. "You might just have a future there, kid."

He reached for the radio dial. Bessie's sound system was pretty basic, just an old-school AM/FM band, and you couldn't pick up a lot of stations on Winthrop anyway. Monk flipped around a little and gave up. "That midwinter one," he said. "You don't think it was too downbeat?"

"What? No! It was gorgeous. The music, those lines of melody, that was unreal. I've never heard anything like it. It sounds so simple, until you realize it's not."

"Not too cheesy?"

"It could have been cheesy, I guess. In the wrong hands."

He laughed—not the usual wide-throated Monk chuckle but something more bashful. "Maine winters, right? It's a mood."

"Seriously, I don't know how you survived them."

"I wrote a bunch of songs. I don't know, sometimes you get this flood of music in you, right?"

"Um, not really?"

"Okay, like your artwork. Don't you get this . . . like a gush of inspiration sometimes? Some idea, something in your heart, right, and you wake up in the middle of the night and it all comes pouring out in the only language you really know. You can't sleep, you can't think about anything else. You're just holding the bucket, trying to catch all the rain pouring over you before it's gone."

I looked out the window, though it was dark and there was nothing to see except some distant lights, sparkling through the ink. "Yeah, I know."

"I know you know," he said.

He was coming off the high now. The euphoria ebbed from his skin. I wanted to say something, to reach out and pull him to safety, but I couldn't make the words take shape.

"So," he said, "how's the boyfriend these days?"

"Dillon? Oh, fine. He took a job at Dunkin' Donuts. The corporate management program?" I added quickly.

"Wow," said Monk. "That sounds . . . that sounds . . ."

"Yeah, I know. But I mean, doughnuts, right? At least? He'll be okay. He's not . . . . he doesn't need . . ."

"Not a wild and crazy type of guy?"

"No."

Monk reached again for the dial. "That's good, Pinks. Nice and steady, someone you can count on."

"No, you're right. He's a good guy." I stared at Monk's fingers, turning the dial. I thought about them strumming the guitar, coaxing music from the strings. "What about you? Anyone special?"

"You mean like a girlfriend? Not at the moment, sadly. There was this girl at Colby, kind of off and on. We're taking a break right now. She's working in Boston over the summer. Some finance shop."

"Really? Which one? My sister's with this guy, he's in private equity. In Boston."

"I don't remember the name. Bunch of Harvard guys, that's all I know. Her dad went to school with my dad? So, the old crowd."

"That's how it works, I guess."

"Nepotism all the way down." He slowed Bessie to turn down a gravel driveway. "I'll just park in our drive and walk you over. Is that okay?"

"You don't need to walk me over. It's not like downtown Providence or anything."

"Humor me, okay? It's dark and you don't know the way."

The lights of his mother's family's house appeared between the trees. The driveway was scarred up and Bessie's vintage suspension hit every pothole like it was a creek bed.

"Sorry," said Monk. "Any teeth left?"

He parked Bessie outside the garage. I hopped out and joined him on the other side. He kept his head down, not looking at me.

We walked side by side across the damp meadow grass. I thought he might take my hand, the way he'd led me to the bar inside the Mo, but he kept his arms to his sides as he loped along. The rain had stopped but the clouds still shrouded the moon, and the wall of old fieldstones came out of nowhere. Monk grabbed my elbow just in time. "Sorry, should have warned you about that," he said, helping me over. "Spaced out a little."

I hopped onto the soft turf on the other side and drew my arm away, so he wouldn't think I was trying to make a move or something. "Spaced out over what?"

"Nothing. It was a trip, that's all. Singing in front of everyone again. Singing in front of you."

I elbowed his ribs. "You did great. Honest. I was . . . I was in awe, actually."

"You're serious?"

"Monk, I mean it," I said. "You're really, *really* good. Your *voice*? Scary good."

He shoved his hands into his pockets and looked the other way. "So, to the left over there, you can't see it, there's a cliff—well, more of a bluff. But kind of steep. Down to this little beach. Just be careful, okay? There's a path, but if you're just stumbling around drunk at night or something—"

"I'm not going to be stumbling around drunk at night. I do have some professional standards."

He laughed. "I know you do. Still. Watch out, okay? My mom broke her ankle once."

"Yes, sir." I saw a light appear ahead of us. "So what brought on this crazy creative manic thing over the winter?"

"Oh, you know. Stuff, I guess. Just thinking about how college is almost over, how . . ." He tilted his head to the night sky. "How you start out with all these paths, all these choices. And then you realize that once you choose one path, you can't go back. You think about all the paths you could have taken and didn't. So I guess that's what all those songs are about, really. Paths not taken."

"That's one way to look at it," I said. "Or you could just enjoy the path you're on. Just be glad you're on whatever crazy path you're given."

Monk stopped. After a couple of steps, I stopped too and turned back to him.

"What?" I said.

He shook his head and started forward again, hands in pockets, until we reached the door of the mudroom.

"That was fun," I said. "Thanks for taking me along. Not that you gave me a choice."

"Hey, you could've said no. You could've said *Fuck off, Monk. It's my first day of work and I'm exhausted.*"

"Monkfish," I said, without thinking, "when have I ever said no to you?"

As soon as the words were out, I thought, *Shit.*

The house was dark. Nobody had thought to leave the porch light on. I couldn't see Monk's face, couldn't tell what he was thinking. As I started to turn for the door, he opened his arms and folded me against his chest.

"Thanks for coming, Pinks," he said.

"Anytime."

"I mean this summer. I'm glad you're here."

The salt breeze rustled around us. I leaned against his sternum and listened to his heart. My arms rested around his middle. I thought, *I don't want to leave. I want to stand like this all night, counting the beats of Monk's heart.*

"You should get some sleep," he said.

I pulled away. "I should."

"All right, then." He leaned down and kissed my lips, the same casual goodbye he'd given me in the driveway of my mother's house on the Cape. "See you around."

CHAPTER SEVEN

Mallory

June 2022
Winthrop Island, New York

Paige pilots the Fjord into the marina in Little Bay, a mile or so away from the bigger harbor where the ferry and the fishing boats take care of business. Little Bay is where you keep your spinnaker or your runabout, where the kids learn to sail on their Optis. There's no drizzle today, just a hazy morning sun that promises hot. The air smells of brine and wet wood. The kids jump onto the dock, one by one, carrying their beach things. They're all decked out with hats and sunscreen and enthusiasm, even Sam. "Feeling okay, buddy?" I ask as he passes by.

He rolls his eyes and says *Yes, Mom.*

I have this picture in my head of Paige's Yale friend, whose family summers on Winthrop Island, and I'm not wrong. She spots us first and squeals. Paige gives forth an answering squeal. I cast about until I find a long-limbed blonde in aviator sunglasses and a polo dress the color of key limes, waving a bracelet-stacked arm. She takes Paige into a delicate embrace of elbows and palms. The kisses vanish into thin air.

"It's so good to *see* you," says Paige.

"Oh my God, you haven't changed a bit," says Lola. She turns to me and raises the sunglasses to the top of her head. She wears no makeup except an apricot tan and a layer of peachy lip balm. "You must be *Mallory*!" She sticks out a hand. The bangles quiver and crash against each other. "Lola Peabody."

* * *

Lola hauls us to her family's place in a gigantic eight-seater Club Car, the Escalade of golf carts. Paige sits up front with Lola, I sit in the middle with Sam and Ollie, and Ida and Maisie cling to the rumble seat in the back while the cart charges up the perilous hill that is Little Bay Road. Ida shrieks with joy. Lola gives us the canned tour, pointing at this and that with so much enthusiasm she sometimes forgets to keep hold of the steering wheel and we veer toward the scrub grass on the shoulder.

"People think Winthrop is so old," she says, "but it was only developed in the 1920s. They bought up the old farmland on the eastern end of the island and turned it into the Winthrop Island Association. I think that was right around the First World War?"

"So that's the private end of the island, right?" asks Paige. "The golf club and everything?"

"Yep. Dave's gran—Dave's my husband—she descends from the last of the Winthrops on the island. Her dad became like the caretaker for the Peabodys? When they first built their place? And then she wound up marrying one of the Peabody boys. Dave's grandfather."

"That's so cool," Paige says. "Are they still around?"

"Oh, Gran's still reigning like the queen she is. She'll be ninety-eight this summer. Like not even Covid could kill her. Dave's grandfather passed when I was in college, sadly."

"I'm so sorry."

"Heart attack. He was this enormous guy. Gentle giant. My family summers here too—the Pinkertons?—and we all like *worshipped* him. Dave remembers how Poppy used to carry him to the harbor on his shoulders during the blessing of the fleet every year. Like being on top of the world."

I lean forward to her shoulder. "Blessing of the fleet?"

"Yeah, it's this old Portuguese tradition. The Catholic priest comes down to the harbor and blesses the fishing fleet every year. Very cool ceremony. Not that we have much of a fleet anymore. They used to trap lobsters but the population's crashed, apparently. Climate change or whatever."

We crest the hill and Lola brakes for the crossing of West Cliff

Road. The familiar scene hits me in the ribs. I shut my eyes and see the chunky burgundy dashboard of a Jeep Wagoneer, my bare feet propped up, ten chips of iridescent mermaid blue against the waving grass horizon. Monk to my left, kids piled like puppies in the back. Air smells of hot car and sunscreen. Katy Perry belting from the radio about kissing a girl. Monk took us sailing and we're driving back home from Little Bay Harbor. My stomach hurts from laughing. We turn left on West Cliff Road. Monk waves to the guard in his shack. For some reason I keep staring at that wide, tanned hand until he turns to me and grins, like he always grins, but for some reason that grin lasts a second or two longer than it should, the gaze holds a second or two longer than it should, and (as you probably know) a gaze that lasts a whole couple seconds might as well last for an hour. It feels the same, like someone lit a torch to your nerves.

"Mom, are you *carsick*?" Sam asks, incredulous.

I open my eyes. We're passing the guard shack now; Lola's waving her hand at the guard, just like Monk used to do.

"I'm fine," I say. "I'm reminiscing."

"Reminiscing about what?" asks Lola, picking up speed.

"Oh, I spent a summer nannying here, back in college."

"Stop it! *Seriously?* Which family?"

I rub Sam's hair. He pulls away. "The Adamses."

"Wait, Buzzy and *Becca*?" Lola smacks the steering wheel with her palm. "I used to babysit those kids! The Hell Twins, my mom called them."

"They weren't so bad," I say. "Once you figured out what to bribe them with."

"They're all grown up now. Chippy played lacrosse at Bowdoin. He's in London now? With Morgan Stanley. Dating some English girl, I heard, like the daughter of a lord or something. Which is like the most Chippy thing *ever*. And Blue's a second-year at Penn Law?" Lola asks, glancing inquisitively at my reflection in the mirror, as if there's some chance we're connected by threads of law school. This is another Winthrop thing—like a pair of sniffing dogs, you establish your bona fides with a new acquaintance. Whom you're related to, and how. She returns her gaze to the road ahead and says, with spectacular nonchalance, "But I'm sure they'll both be back for the wedding."

"Wedding? What wedding?" Paige asks innocently.

Lola hits her. *"What wedding."*

"Oh, I see you. All desperate to spill the tea."

"Tea is for basic bitches like you, honey," Lola says. "I mean, God knows who leaked that story to the *Globe*. Nobody on-island, for sure."

The golf cart bumps painfully over a pothole. From the rumble seat comes a pair of delighted squeals. Sam grabs the metal armrest and pretends to look for the ocean.

"It's such a *trip*," says Lola. "I remember when Monk Adams was just this annoying little tagalong. I mean, cute but annoying? Also he was like an outrageous towhead. By end of summer his hair would be *white*. And his skin would be *nut brown*." She snorted out a chuckle. "I was best friends with his big sister since I can remember. Thayer? We're the same age. She's out in Cali now. Went to Berkeley and never looked back. You know their place is two houses down from ours? I saw the wedding planners heading over there last week."

"He's not around right *now,* is he?" I ask. Attempting to sound as nonchalant as Lola.

"Oh God, no." She glances at the mirror again. "Wait a sec. You must have known him, right? If you were nannying for his dad and the stepmonster."

"We hung out a bit."

Paige swivels her head a few inches and winks at me.

Lola looks again in the mirror at my reflection, a couple of beats longer this time. A flutter of speculation appears and vanishes across her face. "So this must have been, what? The summer of oh-nine? Ten?"

"Oh-eight, actually. Fourteen years ago."

"Oh, right. That's the summer I was working in Paris. You remember that internship I got after college, right?" This was to Paige.

"That fashion thing?"

I turn my head to watch the meadows pass by. You don't see a lot of trees on Winthrop Island, just meadows and ponds and shrubs. Maybe a vestigial orchard or two, missing most of its original members. I remember I asked Monk about it once, and he shrugged and said he heard that the trees were all wiped out in the hurricane of 1815, and they only came back—in the wild, anyway—after the hurricane of 1938 blew in some seeds from the mainland. He said he wasn't sure if that was true, but it was a good story. At the time, we were sitting side by side on a stone wall, watching the leading edge of a squall bend the meadow grass. The wall divided the Adams property from the Monk property, where he spent the summers after his parents' divorce with his mother's family. His mother was a Monk, he told me; that's how he got his name. His parents grew up summering together, Adams property and Monk property side by side. All nice and convenient, until it wasn't. The first drops of the squall fell on our shoulders and Monk took off his jacket to hold over our two heads like a canopy. Just in time. While the rain poured down around us and soaked our legs and feet, he said to me, *You want to know my darkest secret, Pinks?*

I said sure.

He said, *My first name is Barclay.*

Barclay like the bank? I asked.

Like my dad, he said. *Barclay Benjamin Monk Adams. So now you know.*

I remember I tasted the name on my tongue. *That's just between you and me, Pinko,* he told me. *Circle of trust.*

I swore I wouldn't tell a soul. Then I asked about Benjamin, and he told me about how the Monks always named the first boy Benjamin, after his grandfather's brother who was shot down over Germany in the Second World War.

The cart slows. Lola points past Paige's nose. "That's it right there. The Monk place?"

A plain gravel driveway cuts through the wildflower meadow to the right, so exactly like they appear in my memory that for a second or two, I don't know where I am. I don't know who I am. I close my fingers around the armrest and everything returns to me in a bang. The vast, complicated present. I turn my head to find Monk's blue eyes staring back at me in the face of my son.

Paige says, "So, what about the bride? Lennox Lassiter. What's *she* like?"

"I don't even know," says Lola. "She doesn't really *mix* with us?"

* * *

The Peabody estate is right on the water at the end of Serenity Lane—a big, rambling house of shingles and dormers and a single tower overlooking the beach that must be the coolest bedroom ever.

Lola brings the Club Car to a stop next to an ancient clapboard garage. "Here we are," she says. "Summerly."

Paige wants to know when it was built.

"Like 1920, I think?" Lola hops out to unspool the charging cord and plug it into the cart. "I warn you, Gran keeps everything immaculate but she doesn't believe in, like, *renovation,* per se. I think Dave's mom secretly can't wait to get her hands on it after Gran dies. Which like *God forbid.* But it's coming, right? And Gran and Dave's mom are like the best of frenemies. The *passive aggression,* right? Sometimes I'm all, pass the popcorn."

Meanwhile we're extracting ourselves from the Club Car. In the quarter hour since we stepped from the boat to the dock, the temperature has climbed about ten degrees. The sun beats down on my neck. The kids start to clamor about the beach.

Lola puts her hands on her hips. "Tell you what. You guys head right down to the sand. You'll see the cabana, it's got all you need. I'll let Jo know we're back. She'll put the kiddos in their suits and bring them down to hang out, okay? Make yourselves at home! Mi casa es su casa!"

She calls these last words toward their galloping backs as they stampede from the drive to the lawn, past the sea grapes toward the beckoning ocean, Paige in hot pursuit.

We look at each other. Again, that ripple of speculation. Lola Peabody is almost forty, like Paige, and bears a certain similarity to Summerly, in that she keeps herself immaculate but doesn't believe in renovation, per se. There are pleats around the eyes, a touch of sag around the mouth and chin that says *I don't stoop to Botox or dermaplaning, my bloodlines are enough.*

She smiles at me. "What a shame Monk's not around this week. I bet he'd be jazzed to see you again."

I hoist my beach tote to my shoulder and drop my sunglasses over my eyes. "Oh, I doubt he'd even remember little old me. Big famous him and all."

* * *

By two o'clock in the afternoon, the three of us have pulled up to the bar at the Mohegan Inn and ordered cosmos. I don't personally love a cosmo—give me a Manhattan or an old-fashioned, if you must, or a French 75 if you're feeling frisky—but it seems like the sociable thing to do.

Blame Lola. The kids all wound up in the family room after lunch, tapping away on their phones and tablets. She looked at me and at Paige and turned a bright expression to the nanny. *Jo, do you mind keeping an eye on the kiddos while I show these two the village sights?*

The place hasn't changed since the old days. Still murky even in the middle of the day, like a goblin cave; still reeking of decades of spilled beer soaked into the wooden floors. Same low ceilings, same barstools upholstered in peeling avocado-green pleather, same scattering of mismatched tables and chairs, polished with soot. Same cheap ceiling fan turning over the same stale air. Same fucking Babe Ruth bobblehead staring idiotically from the top of the same cash register. Same raised platform, about ten foot square, where they used to set up the live music on Friday and Saturday nights.

Another memory flashes behind my eyes—Monk on his stool, baseball cap, acoustic guitar, microphone. Turning to look at me while he plays this song he wrote.

And there's Mike, behind the bar. Red hair now tarnished and thinning. He takes the drink order and lingers on me for a second or two, speculative frown, before he turns away to mix the cosmos.

"We used to come here in college, to get away from our parents," says Lola. "Everyone would, like, shamelessly hook up with one another. Which was tricky because so many of us are cousins? Although I have to say that once we had enough drinks . . ." She lets the sentence dangle and giggles mischievously.

"That's kind of sick," says Paige, "and yet also weirdly erotic. In a sick way."

"Yeah, well. The Puritans had this kind of low-key tradition of intermarriage, back in the day. I mean, what else could you do? We just don't talk about it. Like everything else." She grabs the stem of a cosmo glass, which Mike has just delivered to the counter in front of us. "Cheers, ladies. To the good old days of kissing your cousin and remembering nothing the next day."

We sip. I have to say, Mike mixes a decent cosmo, even though he probably died a little inside as he measured the Cointreau. Paige waggles an eyebrow at me, the way she used to do when we were kids, on the rare occasion she was about to commit some outrageous act of daring.

She turns to Lola. "So? Did you ever hook up with Monk Adams?"

"Eeeww. He was like my best friend's kid brother."

"So?"

Lola plucks at the curl of lemon on the rim of her glass. "No comment."

"Or don't you remember?" Paige sticks her with an elbow.

"The truth is . . ." Lola gulps down a long drink. She settles the glass back on the bar, swishes the sides, and says to the pink wavelets that remain, "The truth is, Monk was always kind of pure? I mean, he had girlfriends and everything, but he wasn't a hooker-upper. Wouldn't you say, Mallory?"

Lola turns to me. I cough on some liquor and set down my glass. "Say what?"

"Whether Monk Adams liked to hook up on the weekends? I mean, I'll bet you used to hang out here at the Mo. Right? On your evenings off. I remember he played a lot of gigs here in the summer."

"He did. Whenever I see one of his album covers, I always think of him on his stool with that old guitar, right over there." I point to the platform in the corner. "Playing to a bunch of drunk locals."

Lola tilts her glass at me. "That doesn't answer my question, though. Smarty-pants."

"To answer your question," I drawl out, taking my time, "no."

"No, what?"

"No, I don't think Monk was that into the hookup scene."

A few hours and several rounds of cosmos later, I remember to check my phone. "Oh, shit. It's almost dinnertime."

Paige looks at her watch. "Oh, shit. You're right."

"You can't drive home," I say.

"What do you mean? I'm fine. It's a boat. On the water. Not like a highway."

"Drinking and boating is literally illegal. Also stupid. Especially this much drinking."

She wags a finger at me. "Now who's the responsible sister?"

"Ladies," says Lola, "don't worry. I got you. Plenty of spare bedrooms at Casa Peabody."

I look again at my watch, as if that would help the situation. "But Sam has dialysis tomorrow in Barnstaple at nine sharp."

"Not a problem." Paige lurches off her stool and manages, miraculously, to land on her feet. "I'll get you there. Swear. Dawn launch. With the fisherfolk."

"What about Jake?"

"Jake's away at some lov-e-ley golf course in Arizona. No, Palm Springs? No . . . no, definitely Arizona. Scottsdale. Corporate retreat-y thing. Back on Monday."

"While the cat's away," says Lola.

Mike steps over, wiping a glass with a bar cloth. "Ready to close out?"

Paige opens her wallet and pulls out a magnanimous credit card. "I've got it, girls."

Mike shakes his head. "Cash only."

"I'm sorry. Did you say *cash*? *Only*?"

"There's an ATM on Harbor Street."

Lola rummages in her handbag. "Don't be silly. I've got it. I should have warned you about the cash thing. You're just a bunch of old schoolers around here, aren't you, Mike?"

"Aka tax dodgers," Paige mutters.

"Say." Mike points at me. "Now I remember you. You and Monk used to come around here a bunch of years ago. Mallory, right? Nannying for his dad."

Both heads swivel in my direction.

Lola purrs, "You and Monk?"

"That was a while ago," I say.

"Steel trap." Mike wipes his hand on the bar cloth and sticks it out to me. "Nice to see you again, Mallory. You two were a real cute couple. You stay in touch at all?"

"Not really." I take his fingers in a brief clasp. "Not at all, actually."

"That's a shame." He glances to the door and lowers his voice. "You know he's playing a couple sets here tomorrow."

"*What?*" screeches Paige.

I'm feeling a little dizzy. "I thought he was out of town."

"Called me up this morning. He's sailing in tomorrow, on the down-low. I don't know, maybe some kind of wedding surprise for the missus-to-be? Said he'd come around here in the evening and try out some new stuff on the local crowd. That's a secret," Mike adds, pointing a warning finger at each of us.

Paige zips her lips. "In the vault."

For some reason, as we trudge outside to the Club Car, blinking like moles at the high midsummer sun, what socks me in the gut is not the news of Monk's impending arrival nor the notion of him—*literal rock star*—playing sets on the beer-stained microstage of the Mo.

It's the words *missus-to-be*.

Lola spanks me on the bottom. "Dark horse. You held *that* one close to your chest."

"You have no idea," Paige mutters.

"It was nothing," I say. "It lasted about a minute."

"Oh, I hear he lasts a *lot* longer than *that*." Lola struggles into the driver's seat. "Shit. What am I missing?"

"Your sobriety?"

"We'll be okay. It's just a golf cart, right? Can't hurt anybody." She snaps her fingers. "The brake. That's it."

We start forward, up Harbor Street toward West Cliff Road. I sit back in the seat and close my eyes. The sun scorches through my eyelids, not nearly enough to cauterize the memories underneath.

Missus-to-be.

Maybe it would be easier if I didn't know what she looks like. It's impossible *not* to know what she looks like, even if—like me—you turn away from every tabloid photo of Monk Adams on every supermarket checkout line and online news feed on which he flashes his famous grin. In that split second, you get an eyeful.

She's not a bimbo. That would be too easy. No exaggerated Barbie features. She's tall and graceful and looks equally fabulous in an evening gown (posing on Monk's arm at the Grammys) or casual attire (laughing at Monk's side in their engagement photo shoot in *People*—"*Monk's Getting Hitched!*") or, naturally, a bikini (splashing Monk in the ocean on vacation in Fiji). Paige once caught me glancing at one of those magazine covers and said, *You do realize she looks like you, right?* And Paige has a point. You could make a case that we have the same kind of hair, the same type of pretty. But Lennox is the shiny version of me, like somebody ran me through a few Photoshop filters until I came out perfect.

Which somehow makes it worse. I'm the rough draft; she's the finished copy.

The Club Car crawls along. "I could walk faster than this," says Paige. "Do you want me to drive?"

"It's just the hill," Lola says. She does that glancing thing in the rearview, except this time I'm sitting behind Paige so she has to adjust the mirror to get a look at me. "So tell me about it. You and Monk."

"She doesn't like to talk about it," says Paige. "Trust me, I've tried."

"All right, all right. I respect your privacy." She drums her thumbs on the top of the steering wheel. The road flattens out as we reach the summit. The cliffs fall away to the right. Greyfriars swings by on its lonely point.

True to Lola's word, the Club Car picks up a little speed. I close my eyes again and this time the canopy of the golf cart shields my lids from the sun. I hear Bessie's bass rumble, hauling me up West Cliff Road for the first time. The drum of rain on the roof. Monk's right hand on the wheel at twelve o'clock, his left elbow on the door. Window rolled down to let in the fresh, wet air. Monk's reassuring grin, like nothing bad could ever happen to you on his watch.

I open my eyes and straighten my back. The sun must have gotten to me; I'm seeing spots. We pass the guard shack—wave, wave— and my heart starts to pound. My stomach lurches. I reach forward and tap Lola on the shoulder.

"I think I'm going to be sick," I tell her.

The Club Car slams to a stop. I stumble out of my seat and bend over the meadow grass.

Back at the house, the kids are playing pickleball. I'm still a little light-headed, so I ask Lola for directions to the kitchen for a glass of water and find myself, five minutes later, staring into a small room resembling a junk sale.

"Can I help you?" asks a deep, attractive baritone.

I do a startled half-spin to find myself face-to-face with a dark-haired man about my age, wearing a faded green polo shirt untucked over a pair of yellow swim trunks.

"You know, you look exactly like your voice," I tell him.

His eyebrows rise. "Is that good or bad?"

"It's a start. I'm looking for the kitchen?"

He glances over my shoulder. "I don't mean to hurt your feelings, but you're not even close."

"To be fair, the directions were pretty lousy."

"Lola?"

"Drunk Lola."

He nods. "Follow me."

Obediently I trail after him through a series of rooms until we reach the Summerly kitchen, which is like every kitchen on Winthrop—eighty years old, vintage appliances upgraded on an as-needed basis. In the middle of a seventies Formica table sits a seventeenth-century blue-and-white Ming dynasty bowl filled with lemons and limes. My tour guide opens the door of a Frigidaire that might have arrived here from the set of *I Love Lucy* and asks what he can get for me.

"Glass of water is all."

"Rough afternoon?"

"Lola dragged us to the Mo."

"Ouch."

"No kidding. Can you point me to the cups?"

He closes the fridge and steps to one of the cabinets. A jumble of mismatched glass tumblers fills a shelf lined with curling floral paper. He checks a specimen for chips and fills it for me from the sink. "Ice? Lemon?"

"Ice, no thanks. Lemon, yes please."

As he yanks a knife from the block and whacks a lemon into four quarters, I find myself studying the back of his tanned neck. The curl of his dark hair. He's not quite as tall as Monk, but a solid inch over six feet.

"Voilà." He hands me the glass.

"Much obliged, Mr. . . . ?"

"Peabody. Sedge Peabody. Son of the first Sedge Peabody."

"Sedge Peabody the Second. Any relation to the owner of this dive?"

"My granny. I'm just down for a few days to keep an eye on her. You know, make sure she doesn't throw any swinger parties. Drink up all the gin."

"Kind of a wild child, Granny?"

"You have no idea. Lucky for me, she's upstairs finishing up a book this week."

"Big reader, then."

"Not reading. Writing. Ms. . . . ?"

I transfer the water glass to my left hand and hold out my right. "Dunne. Mallory Dunne. The First. Apologies for invading your home and burglarizing your water."

Sedge's clasp is warm and firm. "Mallory Dunne the First. The invasion is a welcome one, trust me. And I don't think it's burglary if your host serves you the item in question? You'll have to confirm that with Lola, though. I dropped out of law school after year one."

"Oh, a screwup! Like me."

"Every family's got one." Sedge Peabody folds his arms over his chest and squints upward at a faint brown stain on the ceiling. He has a thick jaw, a hockey jaw. A slight bump on the bridge of his nose. "So. Are you staying for the weekend, Mallory the First?"

"Just the night. You?"

"About to take Granny back to Boston for a doctor's appointment, sadly. Just when the day was starting to get interesting."

"Ships passing in the night. Story of my life. But I appreciate the pause for refreshment." I knock back the rest of the water and set the glass in the sink. "Sedge the Second. Before you go, would you mind directing me to the pickleball court?"

An hour later, we're lounging on the Summerly terrace, watching the kids run back and forth in the sand. Paige kicks up her feet on a wicker ottoman. "This is the life," she says. "Seriously. I could stay all summer."

"Seriously? I wish you would." Lola cracks open a pink lemonade Spindrift to pour over her vodka. "Relieve the fucking boredom."

I stare across the glistening ocean, the gold light. "*Boredom*?"

She sips her drink and closes her eyes. "Nine years ago I was a law associate in New York. Eighty-, hundred-hour weeks. Asshole boss. Couldn't go on maternity leave fast enough. Now look at me. Just fucking look."

"Looks pretty good from here."

She rolls her head toward me and opens her eyes. "So, I hear you ran into Sedge."

"Thanks to your shitty directions. How did you know?"

"He texted me." She shrugs and turns back to the sun, closing her eyes. A smile bends the edge of her mouth.

Paige reaches out and pokes me with her toe. "You know what you should do, Mal? You should go for a walk."

"A walk?"

"Memory Lane and everything? Go. We'll watch the kids."

"For sure," says Lola. "Enjoy some me time before dinner."

In my head, there's a map of Winthrop Island that doesn't bear much resemblance to the one you find on an atlas, or your iPhone. Take West Cliff Road almost to the village and then veer left toward the airfield and the deserted army base with the bunkers the kids like to explore on cloudy days. Keep walking past the eighth hole at the Winthrop Island Club and pass through the gap in the shrubbery to the Monk estate. Head right out of Seagrapes and follow the bluffs downhill toward the Huxley place and the Pinkertons.

Skirt the inlet that gets a little marshy at high tide and you come to the edge of the Summerly beach, where I stand now, a million years later.

I look back over my shoulder at the terrace. Paige lifts her arm and makes a shooing gesture.

The sun strikes my hair. I forgot to bring a hat, just the oversize Chanel sunglasses I borrowed from Paige. I'm wearing a faded striped T-shirt dress, a pair of flip-flops. My mother's bracelet. No watch or phone. Out to sea, a single white triangular sail arcs toward shore.

I turn to my left and the reeds that line the rim of the inlet. I pick my way around until I reach the firmer ground, where the shore starts its climb to the bluffs.

It's funny, I must have walked this stretch dozens of times that summer. With the twins, with Monk. It hasn't changed. Why would it? The long grass, undulating in the breeze. The shrubs huddled in the sandy soil. The beach rose, spilling almost to the edge of the bluff, so you have to tread with care until the ground curves back out to form a point—the tip of the cove that forms the beach—and the sea roses fall back and break off altogether where the Adams property starts.

Here, the slope reaches its peak and the view from this point grabs your breath from your chest. You can see everything from Rhode Island to Block Island to Long Island, the tide racing past the Fleet Rock lighthouse and the broad, wild Atlantic Ocean. There are tears in my eyes, but it's just the wind. Not because of this feeling in my gut like a sucker punch.

Go back, I tell myself. *Turn around and go back.*

But my eyes can't resist sliding down the side of the bluff to the beach tucked into the cove below.

Nobody there.

If I glance toward the house—hidden by the sea grapes that give the property its name—I can't see a breath of movement, not a sign of human life. Thank God. I wonder if Monk ever goes inside, whether he's still close with Chippy and Blue. Who spends the summers there now. On the other side of Seagrapes lies the Monk estate, which will be bustling tomorrow with staff and security, with entourage. With wedding planners, probably, doing whatever it is that wedding planners do. With Monk. Maybe his fiancée too.

Today, I might be the single person on the island. Only the wind moves.

I find the path and start down the bluff.

The beach is as still and soft as I remember. I kick off my flip-flops and the sand oozes between my toes. The light has just begun to turn gold. With my left hand I turn the bracelet on my wrist.

Like I said, I try to avoid the tabloids, if at all possible. But you know how you're standing there at the supermarket checkout and you've got nothing else to do, nowhere else to look. If I'd opted for the self-checkout that day, eight months ago, I might have missed the headline altogether, and the next week they would have been screaming something else. But I had a lot of vegetables that needed weighing, so I went to the cashier lane and there it was, *In Touch* magazine, this picture of a grief-hung Monk Adams and his girl-friend, wearing tasteful black. *My Father's Son,* the headline read, and underneath it, *Monk Adams Pays Tribute to Father Who Supported His Dreams of Stardom,* which just goes to show you how much truth you get in a tabloid article.

I went into a trance. I stared at Monk's face, stared at the words. *Dead,* I thought. *Mr. Adams had died.*

A hundred questions assaulted me. How did he die? When? Where? How was Monk coping, was he grieving, did he get a chance to say goodbye?

I remember leaving my groceries on the belt and walking out of the Stop and Shop. I got inside my car and stared through the wind-shield until the tears started flowing and turned into sobs. Someone knocked on the window and asked if I was okay. I nodded yes, I was okay. I turned the ignition and drove all the way home before I real-ized I'd left my groceries behind.

On my wrist, the cobra is warm from the sun. The eyes twinkle. I lift my gaze to the sea, rushing against the shore, and figure that if I drew a line along the globe from my eyes out across the ocean, I might reach Ireland. Where my mother was born. Where her mother gave her this bracelet that sits on my wrist, and then gave her away.

For a moment, I imagine I can see her rising from the water, gleaming, this mysterious grandmother and her secrets.

Then I realize it's not my imagination. Someone really is rising from the water, shoulders wide, bare skin gleaming, dark trunks slung from his hips, feet kicking foam from the surf. He shakes the water from his hair and meets my petrified eyes.

His expression turns to shock.

"Holy shit," he says. *"Pinks?"*

CHAPTER EIGHT

Hannah

October 1951
Cairo, Egypt

For some reason, Alistair wanted to travel to Ismailia to see the Suez Canal.

Lucien thought it was a stupid idea, to say nothing of dangerous. "It's not a bloody spa," he said in English, then switched to French. "Has he no idea what's happening in the canal zone at the moment? Have you?"

Hannah blew out some smoke from her cigarette. "The native workers are striking," she said.

"Yes, they're striking. Do you know why?"

"Because they hate the British. They want them out of the canal. Out of Egypt altogether. So they strike. And they attack the shipping. And the Egyptian police do nothing to stop them, because they want the same thing the workers want."

"You should explain all this to your husband."

"He doesn't care. The Egyptian people are just masses to him. Like livestock. No, that's not fair." She took another drag on the cigarette and handed it to him. "*Livestock* is the wrong word. Whatever is the human equivalent of livestock."

"That doesn't exist. You're one or the other, man or livestock."

A pair of horses thundered by. They were at the Gezira polo grounds, watching a match under the usual blaze of sun. The ponies shone with sweat. The white shirts stuck to the backs of the riders. At some point during the third chukka, Hannah had managed to detach herself from Alistair—roaring with laughter over some joke—and maneuver to this spot along the rail that guarded the spectator stand. A moment later, Lucien appeared by her side. *What a charming surprise, Mrs. Ainsworth,* he'd said blandly, and lit this cigarette they now passed between them, by all appearances a pair of acquaintances catching up on conversation amid the atmosphere of hot green grass, the hooves rattling the earth, the sighs and groans of spectators.

Hannah's eyes followed the line of the ball but she was really watching Lucien's hand, clasping the cigarette that was still warm from her lips. He lifted it to his mouth, inhaled, handed it back to her. Their fingertips brushed.

"But you know what I mean," she said. "Masses. Races. Crowds, not individuals."

"Well, the masses in Ismailia don't give a damn what he thinks of them. And the Egyptian police don't give a damn either, not to protect some stupid English tourists who wander into trouble. Your husband can risk his own neck if he wants, but he can't risk yours."

Hannah returned the cigarette. "Are you saying you forbid me to go?"

"As if I could forbid you to do anything."

A pair of riders thundered toward them, mallets swinging. Lucien took her by the elbow and drew her back a step or two. The horses thundered harmlessly past. The smell of hot, torn grass and sweat. The stir of the crowd.

"I mean I'm going with you," he said.

They were on the road at dawn two days later, driving into the sun that rose as a ball of furious orange.

Alistair had invited along the Beverleys. Hannah had gotten to know the two of them pretty well over the last couple of months. Bertie Beverley was some old Foreign Office protégé of her husband, now a press attaché or something, about fifty years old, who sat up front with Lucien. Alistair sat in back with the women, Hannah in the middle, Lillian behind her husband in a white linen dress that strained at the seams. Round face, sloping shoulders. Fair, florid

English skin that must be shielded from the sun at all times. She looked about the same age as her husband but she was probably far younger, Hannah thought. Though of course one didn't ask.

Beverley leaned across the seat. "Ahoy, there! Driver! About how long?"

"His name is Beck," Hannah muttered.

"What? What?"

"Goodness, dear," said Lillian. "Don't you know Monsieur Beck? From Shepheard's?"

"Should I?"

Hannah called forward in English. "Monsieur Beck, could you tell us how many hours to our destination?"

Lucien met her eyes in the mirror. Green sparks. She couldn't breathe.

"About three hours, if the traffic is fair," he said.

Hannah stripped her gaze away. *Shit,* she thought. This would be harder than she'd thought.

They reached Ismailia suddenly—one moment open desert, then you turned your head back to the window to find streets arranged in a European grid, rimmed with palms at orderly intervals.

It's a company town, Lucien informed them, like a tour guide. Built from scratch on wasteland, halfway between Port Said and Suez, for one purpose—to oversee the canal traffic. He turned the car off the main road and rattled down a lane, past a line of vegetation, where he stopped the car. Ahead, the desert sand ended in a line of flat, green-brown water.

"The canal at last," said Alistair.

"Lake Timsah, to be pedantic," said Lucien. "The canal follows the eastern shore."

He climbed out of the car and helped Alistair to his feet, then went around the back to open the door for Hannah and Lillian. Outside, the air was dry, the wind hot. Hannah staggered across the sand toward the water. Behind her, Alistair was saying something pompous about the engineering of the canal, connecting the Bitter Lakes—as if he knew anything about engineering, Hannah thought.

When had he become so tiresome? Or had it grown on him gradually, like the drinking? Her shoes stuck and filled with grit, so she stopped and took them off, then dragged off her stockings from beneath her trousers and continued toward the edge of the lake.

To the right, the water spread over a few flat acres that ended in salt marsh, in docks and warehouses. To the left, maybe half a mile away, a couple of ships glided southward. A horn groaned across the water. *Like toys,* she thought, *toys in a bathtub.* Except there was something massive about them, even from this distance.

A new flavor crept over Hannah's palate—salt and metal and smoke, the scorch of oil.

"There you are." (Lucien's voice.) "The reason for all these rattling swords."

"What's that?" she whispered.

"Fifty years ago it was India. Now it's oil. Half the world's supply, and most of Britain's. They'll fight for this damned stretch of water to the last man. My God, are you all right?"

She gathered herself. "What do you mean?"

"You look like you've seen a ghost."

Hannah turned. He stood a few feet away, wind ruffling the fringe of his dark hair under his hat. His green eyes were large and watchful in his tanned face.

"Don't look at me like that," Lucien said.

"I can't stand this. You shouldn't have come."

"Why not?" Lillian caught up breathlessly and lifted one hand to pin her hat to her head in the breeze off the canal. Her cheeks were pink and bright from the effort of wallowing across the beach. Unlike Hannah, she'd kept her shoes and stockings on. She looked cheerfully back and forth between them. "Why shouldn't poor Monsieur Beck have come with us? A nice outing, I should think."

"Mrs. Ainsworth doesn't like to trouble others," said Lucien.

"Oh! But we *are* paying you, aren't we?" Lillian sounded bemused.

Alistair huffed up, supported by his walking stick. Beverley attentive at his side. "Paying him? I should say so."

Lucien looked at Hannah. "You see? You are not to worry, Mrs. Ainsworth. I'm bought and paid for."

Hannah turned her head eastward. Past the canal, the horizon stretched in a flat dun line. "How strange, we're looking at Asia."

"It looks just the same as Africa," Lillian announced.

"It's an arbitrary distinction, from a geographical standpoint," said Alistair, leaning with both hands on his walking stick, "but one must draw a line somewhere, I suppose."

Beverley twirled his hat on his hand. "I imagine it will all be part of Israel, before long."

"Oh, I wouldn't bet against old Farouk," Alistair said. "Crafty devil."

"I wouldn't bet against Ben-Gurion, either. Eh, Mr. Beck?" Beverley turned to Lucien. "What do you think, Beck? Who wins the Sinai? Do the Arabs hold it against the dirty Jews?"

Lucien removed his handkerchief from his pocket and wiped the face of his watch. "Shall we perhaps move on and see the city?" he said.

Like the rest of Egypt, Ismailia was defiantly French where it wasn't Arab. After an hour or two touring the wide avenues, the elegant buildings, they found a decent restaurant near the canal and ordered the bouillabaisse and the mussels and a nice sole meunière, washed down with a couple of bottles of cold champagne. Lucien waited by the car, smoking a cigarette. Hannah could just see the side of his head through the window when she stretched her neck. He leaned against the bonnet, legs crossed, smoking a cigarette. He'd pulled his hat down low on his forehead and rolled up his sleeves. She was transfixed by his forearms, by the curve of tendon and muscle as he smoked.

"My dear, is something wrong with your neck?" asked Lillian.

"A little stiff. I must have slept on it."

"You ought to try the Oriental massage. I understand it works wonders."

The men were talking about the Free Officers movement. Beverley thought there was going to be a coup, sooner or later. He thought the king was finished and these army officers were the only men who could pull Egypt into the twentieth century. Modernize the economy, fend off the religious fanatics.

"They said the same about Hitler," says Alistair. "Take your pan-Arabic nationalism and substitute *German* for *Arabic*. All these new laws against the Jews."

"It all goes back to this damned business of Israel. Kicking up a hornet's nest. If there's one way to unite the Arabs, why, just hand the bloody Jews a slice of prime real estate on the Med."

"None of whom gave a damn about the Palestinians until now, mind you." Alistair crushed his cigarette into the ashtray.

"I was in Cairo during the war, you know," said Beverley. "I was there when our man Lampson forced his way into the palace and made the king install Nahhas Pasha as prime minister. Damned high-handed. Now, I said to him at the time, I said, 'Lampson, old man—'"

Alistair banged his fist on the table. "No choice! No bloody choice at all. That ass Farouk—"

"Farouk's an ass, all right, but you can't go around installing ministers. The shame of it. Puts their backs up, especially the Egyptian officers." Beverley pointed two fingers at Alistair, the ones holding the stub of his cigarette. "I'll tell you what I think, Ainsie. That's the day we created this Free Officers movement. That's the day we signed off Egypt."

Alistair shrugged and lit himself another cigarette. They were on the last course, dessert and coffee, cognac for the gentlemen. The ceiling fans stirred the hot air. Outside the window, Lucien levered himself away from the car and moved out of Hannah's sight.

Lillian asked her a question.

"I'm sorry, I wasn't paying attention," she said.

A look of irritation flattened Lillian's eyebrows. But she was a diplomat's wife—it was gone in an instant. "You see what you've done, Bertie? All this political talk. You've bored poor Hannah into a stupor."

"I beg your pardon, Hannah," said Beverley. "I'm afraid we got carried away."

Alistair looked at her fondly. "Hannah's never had much interest in politics."

"Why, none at all?" asked Lillian.

"None whatsoever. I remember we were in Nuremberg—she was my translator, you know, that's how we fell in love—long hours, endless ghastly testimony to transcribe and translate. I used to watch her in the middle of the night, at her typewriter, bloody beautiful—come now, you see how beautiful she is, my wife—and I remember I asked her once, it was the middle of the night, naturally I jolly well wanted to go to bed with her instead—"

"Oh, Alistair, *really*—"

"It's only the truth, darling, as you know. I was absolutely mad for her, this little translator of mine, this delectable girl in her dressing gown, charming tits all tucked away—"

Lillian made a faint noise. Beverley stifled a chuckle. Hannah looked at the empty glass next to her husband's plate, the empty wine bottle still in its silver bucket.

Alistair carried on. "So at one point, two o'clock in the morning in my wretched billets, damned shabby room, both of us in our dressing gowns by now, I asked her whether she wanted to perhaps stop for the night, whether the substance of this testimony had become altogether too dire, bloody Nazis ratting each other out to save their own skins, wouldn't she fancy a nice glass of sherry on the sofa, sit together for a bit, and she looked up at me—I'll never forget it, oil lamp, damned electricity was out again, oil lamp casting this delectable glow on her face, she tells me—damnedest thing—she tells me she doesn't pay any attention to the words, she just translates, doesn't give a damn about these chaps and what they've done. The damnedest thing I ever heard. Now, where's that damned waiter with the cognac?"

"Cognac's finished, old man," said Beverley.

Hannah reached to cover her husband's hand. "Alistair. Darling. Perhaps we'd better settle the bill, don't you think? We've a long drive ahead."

"Damn it all, so we do. I'd almost forgot we must drive all the way back to bloody Cairo. Thank goodness we have Beck, eh? Hannah? What would we do without old Beck at our beck and call, ha ha? Sees to our every need, that chap."

Beverley signaled the waiter. Hannah didn't dare look at Lillian. My God, the pity of another woman—was there anything worse? Hannah opened her pocketbook, rummaged out her compact and lipstick, and fixed her lips. Beverley offered a cigarette and lit it for her. She kept her eyes cast down as she murmured some thanks.

* * *

Outside, the sun was high in the west, white and lurid. Now Hannah saw where Lucien had gone—leaning against the other side of the car, facing the street, eyes narrowed, arms crossed.

Alistair called out. "Beck! Beck, I say!"

Lucien straightened and dropped his cigarette on the pavement. "Enjoyed your lunch, I hope?"

"Damned lackadaisical, these fellows," muttered Alistair.

Beverley turned to Alistair. "I say, old boy. What do you say to a stroll and a smoke before we bugger on back to Cairo? Beck can keep an eye on the women."

"Yes, do go," said Lillian. "You'll feel ever so refreshed."

Alistair swung his walking stick in a little arc. "Very well. I shouldn't mind having a look about, after all. It's why we came."

The men struck off, lighting their cigarettes, in the direction of the canal. Alistair had lost the stiffness in his gait but he swung heavily on the walking stick. His voice roared confidently back to them—*The trouble with foreign postings, ha ha, is the bloody foreigners*—followed by Beverley's soothing murmur.

"Had we better sit in the car, do you think?" asked Lilian, a little too bright.

"What, in this hot sun? We'd roast. It's all right, nobody's here. Let's take a stroll down that arcade." Hannah nodded to the building on their right. "Mr. Beck?"

"Yes, Mrs. Ainsworth?"

"Just walking down the arcade."

"Of course, Mrs. Ainsworth."

In the shade, the air was cooler. Lillian linked her arm. "The way he looks at you, my dear!" she said, in a low conspiratorial voice.

"What? Who?"

"Mr. Beck. You do *know*, don't you? About him and Helen?"

Hannah's throat stuck, like she had swallowed something too large. She forced out some words. "Helen Hill?"

"They were lovers. People say. I don't mean to gossip."

Hannah wanted to look back over her shoulder. In her mind she saw him—dressed in white, hat cocked a little to one side, leaning against one of the pillars, watchful. "How do you know?" she asked.

"Nancy told me. They're awfully close. She said Helen's still mad for him."

Hannah thought of the tea salon, when she had first seen Lucien Beck make his rounds from table to table, and how Helen Hill's cheeks had turned the color of a ripe persimmon.

"Are they lovers still?" she asked, in a careless voice.

"Oh, I haven't the faintest. I don't especially care for Helen, do you? One doesn't feel one can properly trust her. Shall we sit?"

They had come almost to the end of the arcade. A bench sat at the edge of the shade, such as you might find lining a path in a European garden, and Hannah and Lillian lowered themselves onto it and crossed their legs.

"When I first came to Egypt," said Lillian, "I was expecting something more . . . oh, I don't know. Primitive? But look at these buildings. You might be in Paris."

Hannah braided her hands in her lap and frowned at the beautiful apartment building across the street. Lillian was right, you might be in Paris. The mansards, the iron railings. But then again, not quite. The colonial whiff. The hot, lazy balconies.

"The snakebite," said Lillian. "Was it awful?"

Hannah dropped her gaze to her hand and the two gleaming pink spots. "I don't remember much about it, really. They tell me it could have been much worse."

"I have a terror of snakes. Bertie teases me. I don't know what I should do if I came face-to-face with one. Faint, probably. It would be the end of me."

"Do you think so?" said Hannah. "I would say it's impossible to know what a person will do when his worst fear looks him in the eye."

Probably she invested a little too much meaning in her voice, because Lillian fell silent. Together they contemplated the Parisian apartment building opposite them.

Lillian re-crossed her legs. "In London, toward the end of the war," she said, "one of those rockets hit the house across the street. The V-2, I expect you've heard of it. Awful. The family there had brought their children back from the country by then, thinking it was safe enough. A little girl and boy, about the age of my own children. They used to play together. There wasn't any warning, not like during the Blitz when you heard the airplanes coming. Just this awful whine, a few seconds before it hit. I felt the blast. Dreadful. I knew something was hit, that it was bad. I could hear them scream-ing. I always thought I should faint at the sight of blood—injuries like that, I mean, such awful wounds. But I didn't. I was rather proud of that afterward, I must say. I just got on with it. Dug them out and first aid and so on. Until the ambulance came to take them away."

"Did they live?"

"I'm afraid not." Lillian smoothed her dress, picked at an imagi-nary speck. "Didn't Alistair say you met at the war trials? How fas-cinating."

"Actually," said Hannah, "we met before that. At a displaced per-sons camp outside Vienna. I had lost everything to the Soviet army. Everybody I loved. I walked from Hungary over the border into Austria on my bare feet. I was starving and mad with grief. When I saw the chance to leave these things behind me, as the wife of a wealthy Englishman, I was happy to do it, believe me."

Lillian turned to Hannah. Her eyes widened and her mouth formed a saucer, rimmed with white teeth. Before she could reply, some shouting drew their attention to the top of the street, where it crossed the main boulevard leading to the canal. A couple of men jostled around the corner.

Like a djinn, Lucien appeared at her side. "Get in the car, please," he said.

His face was narrow and weary. He looked not at her and Lillian but at the two men at the top of the street. Hannah rose from the bench and said to him, "I have a pistol in my pocketbook."

His eyes shifted to hers. "Whatever you do, don't use it."

"Why not, if I have to?"

"If an Englishwoman kills an Egyptian, it will start a revolution. I'll handle it. Get in the car."

They spoke in low, muttered tones. Lillian stood by uncertainly. Hannah studied the green of his eyes and flicked her glance to the two men on the corner, who had stopped at the sight of them and now stood as if waiting.

She nodded at Lucien, took Lillian's arm, and started for the car. Lillian walked in stiff, quick, nervous strides. As they reached the chrome grille, the swooping wheel well, a voice sailed around the corner behind them.

"Heigh ho!"

"Merde," said Lucien.

Lillian called out, "Bertie! There you are."

The two men came to a stop next to the car. Alistair pointed his walking stick toward the men and called to Lucien, "What's this, old man? Trouble with the natives?"

"I wouldn't say that. Only a couple of canal workers, passing the time."

"On strike, I presume," Beverley said.

Alistair muttered, "Bloody wogs." Just loud enough.

Whether or not the men spoke English, they knew the word *wog*. One of them shot a look toward Alistair and banged his elbow into the ribs of the other man. Lucien said something under his breath.

"What was that?" Alistair snapped.

"I said, I think we ought to move along now, sir," said Lucien. "We don't want to start any trouble."

"They wouldn't dare attack a British subject," said Alistair. "In any case, you've got your pistol, I believe."

"I don't wish to be forced to use it."

"There *are* policemen, for God's sake. The rule of law still prevails, does it not?"

"Egyptian policemen," said Lucien.

"Oh, I see. So the wog policemen protect the bloody wogs—"

Beverley grabbed his elbow. "Don't be a fool, Ainsie," he hissed.

Hannah glanced toward the Egyptian men. One of them wore a thick black beard, the other a clipped mustache. They were dressed alike, in short-sleeved shirts and creased pants the color of sand. Wide black belts.

Alistair stamped his walking stick on the paving stones. "Damn it all, Beverley. Where the devil would Egypt be without us, all these years? Corrupt, bankrupt, barbaric."

"Come, now," said Beverley.

"Look around you, for God's sake. Ismailia. Everything here was built with European money. European engineering. The damned democracy they're employing to kick us out is only in place because we bloody well gave it to them."

Had the men edged closer? They didn't seem to be paying attention and yet they must have heard Alistair's words—you couldn't help but hear that carrying voice. One of the men had turned his back but looked over his shoulder at the exact instant of Hannah's attention and caught her gaze. The venom shocked her. She turned back swiftly.

"Alistair, really. If Mr. Beck thinks it isn't wise—"

"Hang Beck. He's been paid to do as he's told."

Hannah looked at Lucien, whose face was grim underneath the brim of his hat. For a second or two his eyes met hers. Then he shook his head and opened the passenger door.

"It's getting late, my friends. Back in Cairo before the sun sets, no?"

Hannah started toward the door. Lillian followed her by an instant. "But it's my turn to sit in the middle," she said cheerfully, nudging Hannah back.

Then Alistair's roar.

"What the *devil*?"

Hannah spun around.

Later, she would remember what happened next as a series of tableaus, a little blurry and not always in order. She would remember Alistair, puce, striding down the arcade. *Say that again, you bloody wog!*

Then Lucien, dropping Lillian's hand to run after Alistair. Beverley puffing behind. The Egyptians shouting back.

Panic.

She would remember running after Lucien. Alistair swinging his walking stick at the man with the mustache.

She would remember how Lucien dove between them and took a blow to the jaw. The walking stick or somebody's fist? She couldn't say.

Nor could she say how she dropped her pocketbook—probably when she reached for Lucien as he staggered back. Whether the pistol fell out of the pocketbook or whether Alistair found the pistol inside when he bent to pick it up—well, did it really matter?

She would remember his cry of triumph.

How she turned just in time to see her husband lift the pistol, cock, aim, shoot.

CHAPTER NINE

Mallory

June 2008
Winthrop Island, New York

It was Monk's idea to hold art class after dinner each night.

Once the kids and I finished our pasta or chicken nuggets or meatballs or teriyaki salmon and cleaned up—I insisted that they rinse off their own plates and put them in the dishwasher—we trooped outside to the terrace that looked out across the lawn to the bluffs and the ocean beyond. Sometimes we set up easels and sometimes we just lay on our stomachs on the paving stones, still warm from the sun, and I'd show them a few basics, suggest a few ideas, let them have at it with colored pencils or watercolors while the air turned gold and the sea rushed against the beach below.

Monk was right. During this hour of tranquility they could pour all their thoughts onto the paper, express everything they'd done and felt during the day. By the time we got up and trooped back into the house, they were rinsed clean. They were ready to bathe and change into their pajamas, brush their teeth, and climb into bed and listen to a single story before falling into a docile sleep.

"Not bad," Mr. Adams said, peering over Blue's shoulder at a watercolor of dolphins and mermaids. "I like that smile on the porpoise's face."

"It's a dolphin," she said.

"Honey, it's a porpoise. Look at his nose."

"*I* painted it and *I* say it's a dolphin."

Mr. Adams made a dry, nervous chuckle. He looked at me, winked, and said, "Okay, honey. Whatever you say. Dolphin it is."

* * *

An hour later, I came downstairs from putting the twins to bed and went into the kitchen, where the housekeeper was putting away the kids' dinner dishes. Grace was a small, dainty woman from one of the Portuguese fishing families on the island, and the top shelf was giving her some trouble.

"Oh gosh, let me help you with that," I said.

"No, no. I'll get the step stool, okay?"

"Please. Just hand me the glasses."

She handed me the glasses. "Thank you, Miss Mallory. Must be nice to be so tall."

"I wish. I'm like, five seven. Not *that* tall."

"To me, that's tall." She laughed. "You and Mr. Monk. You're going to have some *long* babies together, that's for certain."

I spun around. "*What?* What are you talking about?"

"Oh, I have eyes in my head, Miss Mallory. I see the way you two look at each other. You'll make my sweet boy very happy someday."

"That's just—we're just *friends,* Grace. *Totally* just friends."

"The best way to start. Like my Tommy and me." She shooed me to the door. "Go. He's in the sunroom with his father. So you know he could use a little company."

Sure enough, I found Monk in the sunroom with Mr. Adams, deep in conversation next to the french windows. Mr. Adams held a lowball glass of brown stuff, no ice. Monk held a beer. He looked scrubbed, damp. He'd worked all afternoon on the golf course, had showered and changed. It was the end of June and the heat had settled into the earth, into the pores of the floorboards. The two of them turned as I entered.

"Oh, I'm sorry," I said. "I didn't realize—"

"Come in, come in," said Mr. Adams. "Drink?"

"I—well . . ."

"You're off the clock, aren't you? Little monsters all tucked in. Come on, what'll you have?"

"I guess . . . a beer?"

Monk said, "I'll get one for you."

As he passed me on the way to the kitchen, I caught his stony expression. I lifted my eyebrows and he shook his head, just brushing the inside of my elbow with his fingers.

"I hope I didn't interrupt anything," I said to Mr. Adams.

"What? Oh, no. Just trying to pass along a little fatherly advice. Hot day, isn't it?" He hung his hand on the back of his neck and looked out the window to the glistening water. "Shall we go out on the terrace?"

"Um, sure."

I followed him through the door that opened onto the terrace, which ran the entire width of the house. At one end there was a table and chairs, where the family usually ate on those rare occasions when they ate together at home, instead of at the Club or someone else's dinner party. At this end, some wicker furniture formed a seating area, tricked out with a wicker bar cart and wicker coffee table and dainty wicker footrest. Mr. Adams settled himself in a wicker armchair and gestured to the wicker sofa. I perched on the edge. Mr. Adams was on his third wife—the starter marriage with Monk's mother's predecessor didn't take—and somewhere between his fifty-fifth and sixtieth year. He was still handsome in a creased, distinguished way that made you think of boardrooms, like an aging movie star playing a CEO. He wore an impeccable navy blazer and white shirt and silk tie patterned with the Winthrop Island Club crest, and a pair of chinos in a color they called Nantucket red, which you or I would call pink. Party at the Club tonight, I remembered—Club with a capital C, you understand, to convey a subtle prestige over the Little Bay Club on the public side of the island. Mrs. Adams was still upstairs getting ready. Assisted by a vodka bottle, probably.

"I must say, we're extremely pleased with the job you're doing, Mallory," said Mr. Adams. "The kids are thriving."

"Thank you. They're good kids."

"Let's be honest, they're hellions. But you're not afraid to show some discipline. I appreciate that." He sipped his Scotch. "God knows it's an easy habit to slip into, letting children have what they want, when we have so much to give them. It's natural to want to make them happy. The trouble is, you end up with adults who don't understand the responsibility that comes with privilege. Ah, Monk. There you are."

Silently Monk handed me the beer and stood next to me, on the other side of the sofa armrest.

"Sit, sit," said Mr. Adams. "I was just telling our Mallory she's the best nanny we've ever hired. You've got a good nose for talent, son."

Monk tilted his beer bottle—he seemed to have fetched himself a fresh one as well—and drank down two or three long gulps. Touched the back of his hand to his lips. "I told you, Dad. Mallory's the best."

"Well, thanks," I said. "But I can't take all the credit. Monk's been giving me a big hand. The kids really love him."

"This art you've been doing with them every evening. Fantastic. Just fantastic."

"That was Monk's idea."

"You know, you've got real potential, Mallory. Monk's shown me some of your work. Those botanical drawings are exquisite. How long have you been interested in flowers?"

"Gosh. Since the summer after high school? I got this job in a florist shop in Provincetown. Never really paid much attention to flowers before. The color and the . . . the *allure*? How each one draws you to its center. The beauty of biology, you might say. I started trying to figure out how you could paint a scent and ended up . . ." I glanced at Monk, who gripped his beer and stared earnestly at me, "Sorry, don't mean to bore you."

"Not at all, not at all. It's not the most *revolutionary* choice of subject, of course. Particularly for a woman." Mr. Adams jiggled the ice in his drink and smiled. "But well executed."

"Thanks," I said.

"I don't know if Monk's told you, but I happen to sit on the board of the Gardiner museum. MOFA as well. So I do know a bit about art. And some of these flowers you've painted are remarkably well done."

"Gosh, Mr. Adams. I don't know what to say."

"He's only right," said Monk.

I looked at Mr. Adams. "Monk was the one who told me I should study art in college."

"Hey, I didn't *tell* you, Pinks. *You* wanted to apply to art school, remember? I just said you should study what you want to study. Don't worry about what everyone else is doing."

"It was good advice," I said. "Gave me the guts to go for it."

Monk tipped his beer bottle toward me. "Maybe I should have taken it myself."

"You're at RISD, though?" Mr. Adams said to me. "More commercial than fine art, am I correct?"

"Most people say it's probably the best in the country for a career in the visual arts."

"But you never considered training at the conservatory level? Or, say, a liberal arts college?"

I shrugged. "Not really. I mean, I have to make a living, right?"

"Oh, naturally." He spread his hands and smiled. "Call me a geezer. I just worry that in this age of television and computers, we're at risk of failing to nurture the next generation of great artists."

Monk set his empty bottle on the coffee table. "Excuse me. I think I'll go for a walk before dinner."

Mr. Adams sighed and reached into the immaculate pocket of his blazer. One by one he laid out a snack-sized Ziploc baggie, a stack of cigarette papers, and a lighter, and proceeded to roll up a joint. Being a gentleman, he offered it first to me.

I said no thanks. I set down my half-empty beer bottle and rose to follow Monk toward the beach.

Just as Monk had warned me that first night, the lawn at Seagrapes ended in a bluff that fell about thirty or forty feet to a narrow beach of fine sand. You had to pick your way down the path that traversed the side, making a switchback about halfway down. God forbid you should wear flip-flops, like mine. I skidded down the last stretch and staggered into Monk's ribs. He'd taken off his blazer and shoes and socks, rolled up his chinos.

"You're going to wrinkle those," I said. "Frowned upon."

He made a single snort of laughter, just to be polite.

I kicked some sand. "Need a hug?"

Monk stretched out his arm and tucked me against his side. The other hand he kept in his pocket. The air was thick and warm, the breeze had stilled. The water hardly moved, just rustled against the shore in a gentle rhythm. "I'm not sulking, I swear," he said.

"I didn't think you were."

"I just didn't want to punch him."

"Would have been messy."

Something pressed against the top of my head. I thought, *He's kissing me. Kissing my hair.*

Oh, blessed hair.

"I'll tell you what," I said. "That was some seriously impressive passive aggression. Work of art."

Monk released me and sat down in the sand. I sat next to him, knee to knee. My thin cotton sundress stretched between my legs, offering the crabs an eyeful.

"When I was a kid," he said, "Dad pounced on the music thing. Piano lessons, guitar lessons, voice lessons. Summer camps. Sure, son, take that AP Music Theory class! Looks great on those college applications. Shows passion. Commitment to excellence. Well-rounded kid, the whole package. Sports *and* academics *and* the arts. Came to all my recitals. Framed all my awards. He was all in."

"But music turned out to be the means to the end," I said. "Not something you do for a living, anyway."

He lifted his hand and examined the fingertips. "Look at those calluses."

"I love your calluses. Battle scars."

"What kills me," he said, "is the way he presents to the world as this fucking arts patron. Oh, let's encourage young artists. Let's offer scholarships and grants and fellowships. Let's dress in our gowns and fundraise at fancy galas at ten thousand bucks a table. Let's sponsor all those musicians and singers and writers. Just so long as my own kid isn't one of them."

"But *why*? He should be proud as fuck of your talent."

Monk laid on his deep voice. "You see, son, being an Adams is a privilege. It's a burden. We can't do whatever we want in life. We can't indulge ourselves. We work for the greater good." He dredged some sand between his feet. "But you know what? It's all bullshit. It's not the greater good he cares about. It's the prestige of the family."

"Status," I said.

"Not status exactly. Status is kind of a bougie obsession, right?

More like *stature*." Monk lifted his hands and made quote marks around the word. "Musicians. Actors. Artists. The creative arts. That's for people like us to *patronize*. To own. To pass judgment on."

"*What?* I'm sorry, what century is this?"

"He almost killed me when I told him I wasn't applying to Harvard. I mean, what the hell was I supposed to do? Walk around four years with fucking *legacy admit* stamped on my forehead? Or worse, fucking *lacrosse.*"

"Monk, you didn't even *want* to go to Harvard. We used to talk about it, remember? That whole cliché, you hated it."

He deepened his voice again. "If it wasn't for that B plus in AP Chem, son. You should have studied harder. You're the first generation of this family not to go to Harvard."

"Please. They're just a bunch of robots now. Programmed for perfection. Harvard would have squeezed all the juice out of you. Turned you into a nice successful investment banker."

"Yeah, well. I think my dad would have considered that a plus."

I knocked my knee against his. "If you want to know *my* opinion—"

"Pinks," he said, "I swear to God, I swear to *God,* there are times when your opinion is the only damn opinion I care about."

"—in my opinion, or by my logic, I guess, your music brings people joy, right? Which does a lot more for the greater good than moving money around the capital markets."

"Actually, he's thinking Harvard Law now," said Monk. "Redemption or something."

"Do you *want* to be a lawyer?"

"I don't know. I guess, if I can't make a living writing music. Can't . . . you know, support a family on it. I'd rather practice law than finance, anyway. Or tech."

"Those are your only options?"

"Mallory," he said, "Pinks, honey, it's just the world I'm in. That's all. Everyone's reading off this same script. You know what I mean, you saw it everywhere at Nobles, the good life, the money and privilege, and all I want to do is tear this script the fuck up and burn it. I mean, what even *is* the good life? Fuck it, I want to write my *own* script."

"Like what?"

Monk leaned back in the sand and put his arms behind his head. "Like last winter. When I was writing those songs. The way the music and the words came together, I can't explain. It was magic. Like I've always wanted to do. I just did it."

"Why? I mean, what set you off?"

"Because I was so shit miserable." He laughed. "I guess that's irony."

I lay down on my side next to him and stared at the horizon past the sharp, perfect line of his nose. "What made you miserable?"

"I can't even tell you, Pinkie Pie."

"Come on. Don't insult me. We're better friends than that."

Monk closed his eyes. He looked so peaceful, I wanted to cry. His face, his shoulders, his fresh gold skin. A thumbnail of fine metallic stubble he'd missed at the edge of his jaw. The wedge of his cheekbone to the slight hollow underneath. I needed so badly to touch that ridge, just to know what it felt like beneath my finger.

"There was this girl," he said.

"You mean the Colby girlfriend? The on-off?"

Monk opened his eyes and laughed softly. "No, not her. I mean, she's great and all. Smart, pretty, fun. The whole package. Our families are tight. My dad's like, 'She's the one, son.'"

"Wow. She sounds like a dream."

"Maybe. But this girl I'm talking about? She's in a whole other league of special. Someone I used to have a little crush on, back in high school? And then we saw each other again, we spent this amazing few hours, just talking, we connected at this deep, honest level, the way we always had, like drinking from a well when you're dying of thirst, and I realized I was kind of in love with her. That maybe I'd always loved her. I mean, even when she wasn't there, I'd have these conversations with her in my head. If I saw some painting or read some news story, wondering what she'd think about it or how we'd laugh about it together, because she just *got* me, you know? She saw right into me. And now there she was, even better than I imagined her, and all I wanted was to sit there with her forever."

"So why didn't you tell her how you felt?"

"Because I'm a coward, Pinks. Because the way I felt, looking in her eyes, saying goodbye, it was just so fucking *big,* you know? I didn't know how to even begin. I mean, I couldn't even explain it to myself. Drove home in a daze. We went back to our different schools, our regular lives, but we kept in touch, and for a while I had this dream, right? I thought maybe I had a chance with her. I figured I'd work up the nerve to ask her out, once we were back home for the summer. So April rolls around and I'm like, all casual, 'So what are you up to this summer?' And she's like, 'Oh yeah, spending the whole time out west with my dad.'"

"And you didn't think—it didn't occur to you that maybe she was hoping you'd say something to change her mind?"

"It did not, Pinks. I guess I'm not that subtle, you know? I took it all at face value. Figured she just didn't feel the same way as I did. She kept me parked in the friend zone, like she always had. I didn't have a hope. So I got back together with my old girlfriend for a while, tried to move on. But it wasn't the same with her anymore, it wasn't *right.* Lee saw me the way she wanted to see me, the person she wanted me to be, not the person I was. And when I was around her, it was just easier for me to be that person. The old Monk, the face I'd been showing to the world all my life. Swim with the current. And I kind of hated myself for it, but I couldn't see any other way, you know? I couldn't figure out how to be alone."

He knit his fingers together across his chest and stared at the sky. I heard the rush, rush of the tide creeping up the sand. A feather of breeze stirred his hair. I wanted to nudge him, to make him go on, but I couldn't move. Could hardly breathe.

Monk closed his eyes. For a second I thought he was falling asleep to the beat of the ocean, but he opened his mouth and continued.

"Then the leaves fell and the Maine winter blew in. Fucking dark and freezing all the time. And I just couldn't pretend anymore. All I could think about was *her.* This sexy, vibrant, *incredible* girl I was crazy about. This girl who didn't love me back. I'd heard she was seeing some guy, it was pretty serious. I'd write all these texts to her and just delete them. Missing her, it was like a hole in my gut that wouldn't close. I needed her voice, I needed *her.* So I picked up my guitar and started to make some music. That was all I could do. The only way I could deal with this—this shit miserable despair—was to turn it into music." He opened his eyes and turned his head to the side, so we were eye to eye. "Music was the only thing that saved me, Pinks. That's the truth."

By now my throat had wound so tight, I couldn't speak. I was a little dizzy, taking this in. Trying to sip from this fire hose of emotion. *Just don't fuck it up,* I thought. *Just say one right thing. For once.*

I raised my hand.

"Yes, Pinks. I've said my piece. You have the floor."

I cleared the dust from my throat. "So. I just want to say that these past few weeks with you have been hands down the happiest of my life and . . ."

"And?"

We fixed our eyes on each other. Scent of warm sand, scent of Monk's breath.

"Oh, fuck it," Monk said.

He sat up, hauled me into his arms, and kissed me.

CHAPTER TEN

Mallory

June 2022
Winthrop Island, New York

In my dreams, when Monk and I meet again, we're sitting in the booth at the dive in Provincetown, where we sat the night of that long-ago pub crawl.

The reason for this reunion varies.

In the early months, when I was pregnant and miserable, it's because he's been searching for me and finally found me and begs me to let him put things right.

Later, when Sam was little and Monk suddenly famous, it's because he's realized all the fame in the world means nothing without the girl who loved you before you made it big.

Then it's because he's read that article on page 12 of the *Boston Globe* ("Provincetown Woman Dies at Machu Picchu") and wants to comfort me.

Then it's because he's stumbled on that article in the *Daily Mail* ("Boy, 10, Eats DEATH CAP MUSHROOM at Summer Camp, Remains in COMA") and anonymously donated a large sum of money for Sam's care, but I've uncovered our benefactor's identity and written to thank him, and now he's asked, humbly, for this reunion.

All of these scenarios are, of course, impossible. Because in each dream reunion, Monk has already learned the truth. He knows everything I couldn't say in the note I left behind. He understands me and forgives me and wants me to forgive him.

In my dreams, I walk into this dive bar and he's waiting for me at our booth. I stand in the doorway for a second or two, soaking up the sight of him—the slope of his shoulders against the booth's battered wooden back, the way his hands are clasped together as if he's praying. A pitcher of beer sits on the table, next to a stack of Splenda packs, ready to be released into swirls of abstract art. He looks up and sees me and the old grin splits his face. He slides out of his seat and stands—oh, the unconscious grace of him. He opens his arms and I walk into his embrace. I smell his shirt, his skin.

"I'm sorry, Pinks," he says to my hair, my ear. "I'm so sorry."

But this is not a dream. This is real. The real, living Monk Adams stands a few yards away in the ankle-deep water, mouth open, eyes wide. A wave kicks against the backs of his legs. The breeze rattles his swim trunks.

I can't seem to get my feet under me. I stagger upward, totter, catch myself.

Finally I gather enough breath to speak. "I'm so sorry! Oh my God, I thought you were away. I never in a million *years* would have—"

"Mallory, hold on—"

"I only came for the day. Honest, I thought you were gone. My sister's friend. Over at Summerly? We brought our kids to hang out for the day and I went for a walk and I'll just go now, I know the way up."

I've already turned to flee. I flounder a couple of steps in the cushion of sand before a hand grasps my arm.

"Wait. Mallory. Please. It's okay."

"It's not okay, actually. I don't know what I was thinking."

He steps around to face me. Bends a few inches and peers into my face. Holds up his hands, palms out. "Hey. Look at me, okay? Not gonna bite."

I anchor myself on the space between his eyes. "You should. Trespasser and all."

"You're not trespassing. You're always welcome here."

"Well, that's nice of you to say."

The water's starting to dry on his shoulders. A few goosebumps rising. He plants his hands on his lean hips. His abs are like a carton of eggs. Only Monk Adams could reach his middle thirties in even better shape, apparently, than he was in his early twenties. Personal trainer, personal chef, I have no doubt. Kid-free mornings for working out and drinking protein shakes. I have the feeling he's studying me, looking me in the eyes, even though I'm only pretending to look into his. I mean, how could I look right into his eyes, the way he's looking at me? I would scorch to a crisp.

"So how do you know the Peabodys?" he asks.

"Um." I push my hair away from my face. "I don't know the Peabodys. My sister does. She went to Yale with Lola?"

"Oh, that's right. I forgot Paige went to Yale."

"Tale of two sisters, right? Again, my apologies. I just remembered the view from the point, and Mike told me you weren't coming back until tomorrow—"

His mouth splits into a smile. "You saw Mike?"

"Lola dragged us to the Mo for drinks."

"In the middle of the afternoon?" He laughs. "That's our Lola. Come on, come into the house. Call them over, I've got some rosé in the fridge."

"Since when do you drink rosé?"

"It's been growing on me. My—" His voice catches on the word. "My fiancée's into rosé? So I tried a glass and realized, hey—"

"It's not just for chicks?"

"Is that sexist?"

"Kidding. Rosé is great. Love it. But I can't. Super nice of you? But they're waiting for me back at the house. And I have definitely intruded on you enough already. So, you know, I'll be going. Leave you in peace."

"Wait. Mallory. Don't go. It's okay, it really is. I'm—I'm glad to see you." He folds his arms across his chest and heels some sand. "The truth is, I've been wanting to look you up for a while now. See how you're doing."

"Not quite as spectacularly well as you, obviously."

Monk shrugs that off with one luminous shoulder. "Tried looking online, but I couldn't find your socials."

"Yeah, I'm not on any of that stuff."

"Seriously? No social media? Woman of mystery?"

"Crazy, I know."

"No, you're smart. It's a cesspit. Wish I could sign off myself, honestly."

I fidget with my bracelet and shift my gaze past Monk's ear to the flat, hazy horizon. "I'm so happy for your success, Monk. I mean, I always knew. But still, it's been amazing—sort of surreal, honestly, but great—to see all your dreams come—"

"Nice bracelet," he says.

I look down. "My mother left it to me."

"Oh, shit. Pinks, you're kidding me."

"It was a while ago. Freak Machu Picchu accident."

"A *what*?"

"She fell." I stare at my feet in the sand. "That's all. She fell and hit her head."

"*Pinks*. Oh God. Mallory. I am so sorry. I don't know what to say." He makes a motion like he's going to touch me. I step back, the way you step back on the sidewalk when you see a bus barreling down in the bus lane. He drops his hand and says, "She was such a—she was such a *force*. I loved her to death. I really did. She was the one who—after you left, when I was trying to find out what happened, to get some kind of news? I reached out to her. Did she tell you that?"

I nod.

"She was the one who told me you were okay, you'd gone to live with your dad. Said she would let me know if you—if you changed your mind or anything."

"I know," I say.

"She was special, Mallory. You have so much of her in you. I always thought . . ." He palms the back of his head and looks to the side. His eyes blink a few times. "And she left you that bracelet?"

I hold it up. "Yep. Her mother gave it to her, so . . . yeah. She wanted me to have it."

"I've never seen anything like it. A snake?"

"Cobra. See, the hood?"

Monk takes my wrist with a couple of gentle fingers so he can examine the intricate metalwork, the tiny gems. "This is incredible, Mallory. It's a treasure."

I pull my arm away. "You never noticed it on her?"

"I don't remember. But I was just a kid, I guess."

"We were both just kids," I say.

He glances up the bluff and runs a hand through his wet hair, sending the droplets flying. How magnificent he looks. Older, leaner, more honed. All of that. Like a grown lion. "I can't believe I'm standing here, talking to you," he says.

"Weird, huh? You almost gave me a heart attack, coming out of the water like that."

"You gave *me* a heart attack, sitting there on the beach when I came out. I thought you were a hallucination for a second." He grins the old grin. "Come on, Pinks. Let's make it a reunion. Bring everyone over, there's plenty to drink. Be great to see Lola again. She and Thayer used to be tight."

I shake my head firmly. "I can't. Really, really can't. Besides, you must be busy with all the wedding prep. I don't think Lennon—"

"Lennox," he says.

"Lennox. Sorry. I don't—like I said, I live in a cave?"

"Hey, it's okay—"

"But I do know that this is not the right time for an old flame to turn up in your life. It's just bad form."

"No, she'd understand. Seriously. She's pretty centered, you know? She's in the city right now, unfortunately. She won't be here until the weekend." He catches himself. "But what about you? Kids, you said?"

"One." I twist the bracelet. "My son. Sam."

"That's awesome, Mallory. I'd love to meet him. I really would. And your—" Monk glances down to my left hand. "I mean, Sam's dad?"

"Actually, it's just us."

"Ah. Shit. Sorry."

"No worries," I say, a couple of keys higher than my normal voice.

"Still, it'd be great to meet the little guy. Is he going to be around tomorrow evening?"

"For that thing at the Mo, you mean?"

"*What?* How'd you—"

"Mike," I said.

The grin breaks back out. "Oh, *right*. Mike. Loose-lip bastard. He'd better not be telling the whole damn world."

"He's not. He swore us to secrecy." I zipped my lips. "But unfortunately, Sam . . . um, Sam has a doctor's appointment on the Cape tomorrow morning. So we have to leave first thing."

"You're staying on the Cape?"

"My mother's old place. Paige inherited. Fixed it up, you wouldn't recognize it."

Monk looks to the water, looks back to me. A drop of water trickles from his temple; he reaches up and brushes it away. "You look well, Mallory."

"That's nice of you."

"I mean it. It's good to see you. I hope now the ice is broken, we can—"

"No," I say.

"No, what? I didn't even finish."

"No, I don't think that's going to work. Anything that starts with *we*. It's nothing personal. But our lives are so different now. Different worlds. You're—you're who you are, and I'm who I am. Plus you're getting married. You'll have a wife, kids. It's good to see you. I wish you well, I do. So, so well. You can't imagine how well. But no. *We* is not going to work."

I stride past him toward the path at the base of the bluff, and I swear to God it's like someone's dug in a set of claws and ripped a patch of skin from my back. Tears hot in my eyes.

I hear his footsteps behind me, scrambling up the path. "Mallory, wait. Don't be mad."

"I'm not mad."

"That's total bullshit, what you said, by the way. I live a pretty normal life. Under the circumstances."

"I don't care what kind of life you lead, Monk. As long as you're happy."

"Well, maybe I care about *your* life! Maybe I want to know if *you're* happy. If there's anything I can do to—"

I whirl around so fast, he falls back a step. We're standing at the switchback, halfway up. He lifts his hand to shade his eyes from the glare of the sun.

"Don't you dare offer me anything, Monk Adams. Don't you dare. If I wanted a single thing from you, a single cent of yours, I would have asked for it a long time ago."

"I know," he says. "I never expected you to."

"Then what do you want? Closure? Explanations?"

"I just want you to know that it's okay, Mallory. It's all okay. I understand everything. Why you left."

The sun burns the back of my neck, the breeze comes off the bluff in an unruly gust, and for a moment it's all right back in front of me, it's all happening again, the anguish. My limbs are too heavy to move. My thoughts freeze in place.

Monk continues, as if I'm not paralyzed in front of him. "I mean, it took me a while to get there. You left me bleeding in the grass, let's face it. I was a mess for a pretty long time. For years, the only decent thing coming out of me was the music. And then one day I was kind of reflecting and I started writing this song that . . . Look, can we go somewhere? I can't say all this stuff just hanging off the side of a cliff."

I shake my head. I'm coming unclenched, tendon by tendon. My thoughts thaw out. "You don't need to say anything. I'm sorry for hurting you. I was sorry then and I've been sorry since. I can't even tell you how sorry I am."

He steps forward and takes me by the arms. "But, Pinks, I *understand* now. This song. I don't know if you've ever heard it. *Snowbirds Fly*? I was kind of hoping you might. When I sent it out into the world."

I manage a nod.

"See, everyone thought that song was about me, breaking up with some girl. But it was *you*, Mallory. I kind of put myself in your shoes. Started hearing your voice in my head. I got to talking with my dad about it, right before he died, and he worked things out with me, how you had your own art, how you were afraid of living in my shadow and not being yourself, not being able to focus on your own talent, how you needed to be free."

"Your father said that?"

"You were right about him, Mallory. What you said before you left. I mean, in the end, we worked it out."

"Oh, damn it, Monk—"

"Don't feel bad. That's what I'm trying to say. I get it now. I do. Hey. It's okay, I'm in a better place now. Lee's introduced me to all this therapy, this wellness stuff. She's really into all that. I just want you to know that you shouldn't regret what you did. You had to do what was right for you. That's all I wanted to say. I've been wanting to look you up and tell you . . . and then I thought, that's the last thing she needs, the Monk show riding into town . . . and now you just appear on the beach like . . . like . . ."

He frowns. I realize he's looking over my shoulder now, to the top of the bluff. I spin around, lose my balance, crash into Monk behind me. He grabs me by the waist and sets me back on my feet.

"Careful," he says.

A pair of figures stands at the edge of the bluff, looking down. The sun's behind them, so I can't see their faces, but you can tell it's a woman and a teenage boy. The woman waves and calls my name.

"Mom!" calls the boy.

"Wait, is that your kid?" asks Monk.

But I'm already sprinting up the hill. I've left my flip-flops behind on the beach. The pebbles scour the soles of my feet, as I will discover later. I will also reflect, later, that maybe I should have played it cooler. Have waved them away and continued my conversation with Monk on the side of the bluff, where he couldn't see Sam's face.

On the other hand, at this point, it's too late. The die's cast. Nothing left on earth can prevent Monk Adams from coming face-to-face with Sam.

He follows me up the bluff. I call out cheerfully, "Time to head back! Let's *go!*"

But Paige stands her ground. She puts her hand on Sam's shoulder. Her expression, as the two of us thunder toward her, is bemused but also fierce. She's not going to let me get away with it. She's not going to let me run away.

She's getting what she came for.

"Pinks, hold on!" Monk calls behind me.

I arrive at the top of the path. I have time to shoot Paige a single pleading glance before Monk steps next to me. I imagine him grinning, though I can't seem to raise my eyes to his face. He stands there barefoot, wearing nothing but his swim trunks, casual as hell, and holds out his hand.

"Hey, there. Monk Adams. Old friend of Mallory's. You must be her sister."

"Paige Powell." She shakes his hand. "You know, you look kinda familiar. Have we met?"

He laughs. "Nah, I get that all the time. Just one of those faces, I guess."

Then Monk turns to Sam.

"Hey, buddy. Monk Adams."

Sam stands tall. I think he's a little shaken, the way his eyes are blinking, but you would never know just to look at him. I want to put an arm around his shoulder, but he'd just shrug it off. His expression is friendly, determined. "Mr. Adams. I'm Sam. Sam Dunne."

"That's a good Irish name, all right. You can call me Monk. I was just . . . I was just telling your . . ."

You can see when it hits him, bit by bit and then all at once. His voice trails off. His eyes widen and furiously blink, just like Sam's. His jaw wobbles. He looks at me, shocked, then back at Sam.

"Sam," he says, in a voice like he has a bad cold. "Sam Dunne."

"Yes, sir."

Monk turns back to me. The color's fled his skin. He looks as if he might pass out. His eyes beg me for something, I don't know what. Say it's true. Say it's not true.

"Monk, I . . ."

I . . . what? I can explain?

Maybe my grasping silence tells Monk what he needs to know. He looks down at the grass, lays his palm on the back of his neck, exhales. Looks up again, blinking. "Hey. Sam. Can I ask you— I just—Do you mind if I—" Another deep breath. In a calm, controlled voice, he says, "How old are you, buddy?"

Sam is nobody's idiot. He knows what's being asked here. I'm proud and a little annoyed that he doesn't look at me to query how he should reply. He folds his hands behind his back, straightens his shoulders, and says, "Thirteen last month."

The two of them, they just stare at each other. Like you do in the morning when you arrive before the mirror in the bathroom and examine the ravages the night has wrought.

I reach for Sam's shoulder, but he shrugs me off. "Honey, I—"

"Sam," says Monk. "Sam Dunne. Samuel?"

"I go by Sam."

"I am . . . I'm glad to meet you, Sam."

"Yes, sir."

"Monk," I say, "I'm sorry, I didn't mean to—this isn't how I—"

"Mom, stop it," Sam mutters.

Monk keeps on staring at Sam. Staring and blinking. "It's all right, Sam. It's good. It's—I had no idea, that's all. I swear to God. No idea. So—I just need a second to—gather my—I'll be in touch, Sam. Soon. I swear. We'll—speak soon. I promise. After I've had a word with your mom."

"Monk, please—"

He holds up his hand. Keeps his eyes trained on Sam's eyes. On his own face the color starts flooding back. Too much color. His cheeks and nose are red with emotion. The skin of his chest is mottled pink.

"I'm—I'm happy to meet you, Sam. I am. I just need to speak to—I need to *think*—if you'll just give me a second to—gather my thoughts and—please, just excuse me. I'm sorry."

He turns and walks fast across the lawn, in a direct line toward the Monk house, hidden by a profusion of sea grapes. The sun turns his broad, triangular back to gold.

I call out his name.

He holds up his hand again and keeps on walking.

Sam doesn't say anything on the way back to Summerly. Fixes his eyes on the path and marches a few paces ahead of us.

"He just walked away. Can you believe that?" says Paige. "Walked *away.*"

"He's in shock, Paige. Wouldn't you be in shock?"

"I wouldn't walk away from my own *son*."

"He didn't even know he *had* a son until five minutes ago. We're lucky he didn't have a heart attack or something."

"I should have run after him. Asshole. *After I've had a word with your mom.* Yeah, right. He'll probably have his lawyers call or something."

"Paige, do you *mind*?" I angle my head toward Sam's back.

"Sorry." She drops her voice. "But I said what I said."

When we arrive back at Summerly, the sun is shimmering around the peaks of the rooftops and Lola's manning the grill on the terrace. The air smells of hamburgers. The kids are setting the teak table, fighting playfully. I ask Lola if there's anything I can do to help. She says no, everything is under control, have a seat and pour yourself a glass of wine.

I tell Sam to wash his hands for dinner. Find my way to the small white guest bedroom and pull my phone out of my handbag.

After I've had a word with your mom.

I don't know whether I expect to find a message there or not. Monk doesn't have my number, obviously, and I'm not on any socials. Not even a private account. Even my Etsy storefront exists under a brand name. Woman of mystery, Monk called me.

More like a woman who doesn't want to be found.

Whatever I'm expecting, there's nothing from Monk on my phone. Just the usual alerts.

I sit on the bed and close my eyes.

Through the walls of the house comes the laughter of kids. A shrill squeal. Pipes running water somewhere. Everyone going about their business, the world spinning placidly on its axis. A silent howl rises from deep in my chest—the rage, the rage. A hot ball of it, electric with pain and locked in its box until (all the time in the early days, every so often now) the lock explodes and the rage buoys up to choke me.

I know from experience that you can't fight this rage. It's been locked in a box, for God's sake. It wants to get out and make its presence felt. I used to fight back and it only made things worse. Blocked my throat, left me unable to breathe. So I keep my eyes closed and let it rise. Sizzle and boil its way into my head, down my limbs, sparks on my toes and fingers. Breathe it out through my mouth. Counting one, two, three.

Then I swallow the remains back down. Imagine Mom's arms around me, her voice.

It's going to be okay, Mallory.

No, Mom. It's not. I should have reached out, like you said. Long ago. I should have put on my big-girl pants and faced him. For Sam's sake.

We all make mistakes, she tells me. *He'll understand. You just have to explain.*

Every time I try to get a word with Sam, he shrugs me off. At dinner, he eats about three bites of his hamburger and excuses himself for bed. I put down my fork and follow him upstairs to the bunk room Lola's assigned to the kids. He's lying on one of the top bunks, staring at the ceiling.

"Mom, seriously," he says. "Go away. I'm fine."

"Oh, sure. That's why you didn't finish your dinner for the first time in your whole entire life."

"I just want to be alone, okay?"

I climb a couple of rungs on the bunk ladder and wrap my hands around the posts. "Honey, it's a shock, that's all. You heard him. He just needs to get his head around this. He'll reach out. I promise."

"How do you know that?"

"Because I know Monk."

Sam snorts. "Sure you do."

"Okay, fine. It was a long time ago. But people don't change that much. He's a good man. He'll want to be a father to you. He'll want to be a *good* father to you."

Finally Sam turns his head to look at me. "Then why haven't I met him until now?"

The words kick me in the chest. The eyes that meet mine have never looked more like the eyes I abandoned fourteen years ago. A smear of green swirled into that high, clear blue, that's all. For a heartbeat or two I have the strange feeling that it's Monk asking me this question, Monk demanding to know why I kept the two of them so painstakingly apart until now.

Until the inevitable collision.

I let go of the post and reach to lay my hand on Sam's shoulder. "So how do you feel about it? Meeting him for the first time?"

Sam rolls his eyes to let me know he's aware of my redirection. But he answers the question anyway. "Weird, I guess."

"Weird how?"

"Mom, stop."

"Come on, Sam. I know you have feelings stuck inside that head of yours. Talk to me."

Sam heaves a giant adolescent sigh. "Like I don't know. How am I *supposed* to feel? He's my dad, right? But he's a total stranger. So it's like I'm supposed to *love* him, but I don't *know* him. Except that he's, like, *Monk Adams.* Which makes it even weirder. Like, it's *him.* But not the same guy on the magazine covers. A real person."

"*Do* you love him?"

"Mom, *please.*"

"What, then?"

"I don't *know.* I don't know what to call it. It just *is.* I mean, it's *him.* My dad. I've thought about him my whole entire life. Knew he was out there somewhere. Like, felt him in my heart or whatever." Sam turns back to the ceiling and folds his hands together on his chest. "He seems cool, I guess."

"He *is* cool." I turn my hand into a gentle fist and knock Sam's shoulder. "He is one cool dude. But so are you."

"I guess the weirdest thing is, like, he's over there right now. In his house. Thinking about me. I mean, *me.* Probably wondering the same thing I'm wondering."

"Which is?"

Sam shrugs. "What we're supposed to do next."

I lay my hand on top of Sam's hand. His heart thuds underneath. "Honey, I'm sorry. I'm so sorry it had to be this way. I should have done things better. I just—It's just that I couldn't go back. I had my reasons. And maybe there was a point when I could, or maybe *should* have gone back, but I didn't know how. You know how you get stuck in something and you can't figure out how to get out? But I should have tried harder. I should have found a way."

"'Sokay, Mom," he says, about a hundred years wise, sole child of a single mother. "You did the best you could."

"Gosh, thanks, kid." I give his hand a last pat and wrap my palm back around the ladder post. "But seriously. I want you to hold on to one thing, okay? No matter what happens. Good or bad."

"Yeah?"

"I love you more than anything in the world, Sam Dunne. We all do. We've loved you from the moment you were born. And whatever came before, and whatever comes next?" I lean forward to whisper in his ear. "You're worth it."

At dawn the next morning, Lola drives us back to the harbor. She and Paige sit in silence, baring their teeth against the soprano chatter of the kids in back. I'm guessing a couple of bottles of rosé happened last night. I look at Sam's heavy eyes, puffy skin, and reach to pat his knee.

"Mom, stop," he says. "I'm okay."

When the Club Car lurches to a stop at the dock, Paige swings painfully to her feet and shoos the kids out. I gather up my things, check for stray items, and turn to thank Lola for her hospitality. She's on her phone, checking messages. She looks up and raises her eyebrows at me.

"What the hell," she says. "Did I miss something?"

"Excuse me?"

Lola turns the phone toward me. An older iPhone model, single camera lens, giant font.

"Monk Adams. He wants your number."

CHAPTER ELEVEN

Hannah

October 1951
Cairo, Egypt

Over and over, Alistair insisted that he was only defending his wife. The same words, repeated like the chorus of some popular song.

I had no choice, had I? The devil was going to attack her.

They were speeding back toward Cairo in the big black Mercedes-Benz. The setting sun blazed orange before them. Lucien gripped the steering wheel with bone-white hands. Next to him, Beverley lit a trembling cigarette.

"I shall have to report this to the embassy," he said.

"The devil you will."

"Ainsworth, for God's sake."

"Beck won't say anything. Will you, Beck?"

Lucien glanced at the rearview mirror to meet Hannah's gaze. Beverley sucked on his cigarette and looked out the window.

Lillian burst out, "This is ridiculous. Of course we're going to report it. We left a man dead on the streets of Ismailia—"

Alistair pounded his stick. "It was self-defense!"

"He wasn't going to hurt us."

"Wasn't going to hurt you? Did you see how he attacked Beck?"

Hannah glanced at the side of Lucien's face. In the sun's glare, she couldn't see the bruise or the cut very well, but the swollen jaw bulged like an orange.

"In any case," Alistair said, "I have diplomatic immunity."

Beverley turned his head to the back seat, incredulous. "Are you *mad,* man?"

Alistair crushed out his own cigarette and tossed the stub out the window into the desert.

"I don't think that fellow *meant* to hit Mr. Beck," ventured Lillian.

"Damn it, Lillian. It doesn't matter, don't you see? We're in it up to our necks. If the mob finds out that chap was shot by an Englishman, all hell's going to break loose."

"The poor man. The poor fellow."

Hannah turned to stare out the window. In the glare, she saw a field of snow meeting the horizon. "Maybe he didn't die," she said. "Maybe he survived."

A pitying silence filled the car. A hopeless weight.

By the time they reached Cairo, the sun had fallen and Alistair had gone to sleep against the window. Lucien stopped the car outside the Beverleys' handsome house in Garden City and opened the doors without a word. Hannah got out of the car to say goodbye. Under the wash of the streetlight, Lillian's face looked like wax.

Beverley turned to Hannah. The brim of his trilby dug hollows around his eyes and under his cheeks. "Sleep on it, shall we? Tomorrow morning we'll decide what's to be done. Clear heads."

"Whatever you think best. I'll speak to Alistair."

"Good girl." He looked over Hannah's shoulder and back to her face. In an undertone, he said, "What about Beck? Can we trust him?"

"Yes, I think so."

"We can't have any misunderstandings, Hannah. You comprehend my meaning. There is a great deal at stake." He fixed her with his eyes.

"Of course," she replied.

"Good girl," he said again.

Lillian leaned forward and embraced her. "Good night, dear. Do try to get some rest."

"And you."

Lillian pulled back and held Hannah by the shoulders, as if she were inspecting her for disease. Her lips shook. She burst out, "It was the drink."

"Yes, probably," said Hannah.

"The cognac. He's a decent fellow, I'm sure."

"Jolly awful business," muttered Beverley, pulling his wife away.

Lucien helped her get Alistair upstairs to their apartment. She struggled to undress her husband, to slide his pajamas over his limp arms, his limp legs. She made him swallow his pills and drink a glass of water. He stared vacantly across the room as she tucked him in.

"I do have diplomatic immunity, darling," he said. "There's no need to worry."

"Yes, darling."

"You'll be quite safe, I assure you. As my wife, you'll be protected."

She turned off the lamp and walked into the sitting room, where Lucien still stood in the middle of the rug, hat dangling from his hand. How dusty he looked, how exhausted. The cut no longer bled, but his jaw looked as if someone had slid a black ball under the skin.

"How is he?" Lucien asked.

Hannah shut the door behind her. "Something to drink?"

"Whiskey."

She walked to the liquor tray and poured him a glass, neat. "I'm sorry there's no ice," she said.

He took the glass from her fingers. "I don't like ice."

"I mean for your jaw."

"A damp cloth will do."

Hannah slipped back into the bedroom and ran a washcloth under the faucet. When she returned to the sitting room, Lucien stood by the liquor tray, pouring another glass.

She indicated the sofa. "Sit here."

He sat on the middle cushion. Hannah took the bottle of whiskey from the tray and knelt in front of him. Tenderly she cleaned away the dust and dried blood and applied some liquor to the cut. He stared at the wall and winced.

"It's not deep," she said. "But it will probably scar."

Lucien took the washcloth from her hand and examined her fingers. "Tell me about your husband, Hannah."

"Alistair, you mean?"

"No." He looked up. His eyes unsettled her, so green and close. "Your first husband."

Hannah startled. "*What?* How did you know?"

"I guessed, that's all. Some man's ghost in your heart."

Hannah pulled her hand away and sat on the rug. Lucien lowered himself from the sofa cushion to sit facing her, resting his back against the upholstery.

"You don't have to tell me," he said.

She gathered her knees to her chest. "He was Hungarian, like me. We met at university in Vienna. My first year. He was older, a doctoral student. We went to the same coffeehouse each morning. For months, I used to watch him talk to his friends. He was the kind of person who made you want to watch him. Every movement. Every word. But I didn't think he noticed me at all. Then one day he walked to my table and asked if I would go to the opera with him."

"What did he study?"

"Philosophy."

"And you fell in love?"

Hannah allowed her knees to fall to each side, so she sat cross-legged on the rug, between Lucien's spread legs. She stared at the hollow of his throat. It was smooth and perfectly formed so you might place a walnut there. Or you might place your mouth there and lick the warm skin with your tongue.

"Yes," she said. "I fell in love."

They'd wound up on the banks of the Danube at two o'clock in the morning. Somehow they had walked there from the opera house on the Ringstrasse, talking all the way, mostly János asking her questions and Hannah answering them in long, rambling, unguarded sentences. Then the river appeared before them and they stared at the dark, tumbling water, bemused.

"This is terrible," János said to her. "You will get in trouble, coming home so late."

At the time, Hannah lived in a flat with three other students and a housekeeper who was more like a chaperone. Her name was Bernadette and she was very strict. Possibly she had called the police already. Possibly they were out looking for her this very second.

"It doesn't matter," Hannah said. "I'll give them some excuse."

János reached for her hand. "Or we might get married."

"Married? Are you crazy?"

"No. I have wondered for months whether I might be in love with you, and now it's certain."

"But we've only just met. We hardly know each other."

"I don't think I have ever known anyone so intimately. Have you?"

She reflected on the past several hours. "No. But you can't deny we only properly met yesterday."

"I don't deny it. But do you think it's a coincidence I've taken my coffee at the same damned café every morning since September?" He lifted her knuckles to his lips and turned her hand over to examine her palm. "If you don't feel the same, then say so. I'll return you to your flat and trouble you no further."

She stared at the streak of moonlight on his black hair as he bent over her hand, smoothing her glove with his thumbs. He was dressed splendidly in an inky jacket with satin lapels and a shirtfront so stiff it might have stood on its own pleats. He had undone the bow tie but the buttons remained correctly in their buttonholes. When she didn't reply, he looked up and smiled at her, and at that point Hannah's knees gave way. He grabbed her elbows to hold her steady.

"In that case," he said, "I shall wake up this judge who's a friend of mine."

"Just like that?" asked Lucien, incredulous. "You didn't need a license or anything?"

Hannah shrugged. "Apparently not. The judge was an old family friend. He had his wife and butler act as witnesses and married us in his drawing room at four in the morning. By dinnertime we were on our honeymoon in Portofino."

"This can't be true."

"I assure you, it was. János could do anything."

"He must have wanted you very badly."

Again Hannah shrugged.

"Does your husband know about all this?" Lucien asked.

"No. He doesn't even know János's name."

"But he knows you were married before."

"Maybe. I think so, yes."

"You mean to say he never asked?"

"The English don't ask awkward questions, Lucien. It's not good form."

Hannah sat with one hand on each knee, back straight. Lucien slumped a little, so they regarded each other from the same level. He took one of her hands in each of his.

Hannah looked down at her hands tucked into his palms. "Where do you live, Lucien? When you're not in the hotel."

"My dear, that *is* where I live. I keep a few rooms on the top floor of the annex."

"By yourself?"

He laughed softly. "Yes, my dear. By myself."

"What about your mother?"

"There's not much to tell. She lives quietly by the sea. I visit her when I can. I'm all she has left. My older brother was killed in the war, running messages for the Allies. My sister got married and moved away."

"Aren't you a little old to be living in a few rooms at the top of a hotel?"

"It suits me, that's all." He rubbed her knuckles with his thumbs.

Hannah's heart thumped so violently, it made her voice shake. "You should probably see a doctor."

"Doctors ask questions, Hannah. Anyway, I've had worse, believe me."

"But what are we going to do?"

"For now? Nothing."

"You're not going to report what happened?"

He shrugged one shoulder. "What is the point of that? To start a revolution?"

"But I thought you wanted revolution. I thought you were a nationalist."

"What makes you think that? Because my mother is Egyptian?"

"Don't you want this country for yourself?"

Lucien let go of her hands and rose to his feet. She watched him walk across the room to the armchair where he had slung his jacket. His shoes made not a sound on the marble tiles. She wanted to weep at his graceful stride, the symmetry of his shoulders. From a pocket he drew a cigarette case. He made a gesture to her; she shook her head. He took one for himself, lit it, drew in a lungful of smoke so that the end of the cigarette flared like a meteor. Then he exhaled and returned to her. He perched on the edge of the sofa, eyes bright and earnest.

"What about you?" he said.

"I don't know what you mean."

"You are from Hungary, no? Don't you want the Soviets out of your country?"

"I don't think about it. It's in the past. I'm English now."

"Are you, though?"

She stood up. "I don't give a damn about politics. I only care about people. You want to liberate your country from the exploitation of imperialists? Egypt for the Egyptians? Fine, Lucien. Take the country back, I don't care. Just don't get yourself killed, that's all. Don't do anything stupid."

He smiled. "What is this, some kind of love declaration?"

"Don't be flippant," she snapped.

Lucien took a long drag from the cigarette and turned his head to look out the window at the glittering city beyond the glass. The light washed the bruise on his jaw. A pulse beat beneath the skin of his neck. "Hannah," he said, "I do whatever you want. I meet you whenever you ask, on whatever terms. I'll protect this stupid husband of yours from his own idiocy. But don't think for one moment I do these things because of some fucking respectful, bloodless, *spiritual* regard for you. I'm in love with you. This is the truth. This is all I think about. How I want to kiss you. How I want to take you to bed until we're both dead together in each other's arms. Is that serious enough for you?"

Through the wall came Alistair's parched drone, like the engine of an airplane in need of repair. Hannah's heart beat in loud, slow thuds. "Perfectly," she whispered.

Lucien turned his face back to her. His eyes became tender.

"I can't bring you back to life, Hannah," he said. "You can choose to live again, or not. But I can make you remember what it was like to be alive."

By the time Hannah and János reached Portofino, the promise of summer had warmed the air and turned the shadows gold. Her bridegroom stopped the car outside a grand hotel, rich with sunset, and woke her up.

The staff seemed to know him already. At any rate, some obsequious people led them to a suite and brought food under silver domes. Hannah wandered to the balcony and stared in amazement at the sun setting beneath a blue sea. János came up behind her and touched his lips to the spot where her neck met her shoulder.

"Is something the matter?" he said. "You have regrets, maybe? Second thoughts?"

Hannah thought about the long drive over the mountains, the conversations, the sound of his laugh, the shape of his jaw when she looked at him, his hair, his smile.

"No," she said. "The way I loved you yesterday, it's nothing compared to this."

"You're taken aback by all this finery, then?" he said, kissing her cheek, her temple, the soft place behind her ear. "You're wondering what other secrets I'm harboring?"

By now, Hannah was having trouble thinking straight. Up until this moment, they had hardly even kissed, except when the judge in his dressing gown had pronounced them husband and wife, a brief and almost chaste meeting of the lips, and here János's mouth seemed to be setting her skin on fire, licking her alive.

"Well, yes. But I'm looking forward to the surprises, to be honest."

He pulled his lips from her skin and cupped his hands around her face. "Then what is it, Hannah? What's troubling you?"

The last sliver of sun dipped into the sea. Twilight turned the air blue.

János's eyes warmed with understanding.

"Don't be afraid," he said. "It's only me."

* * *

After Lucien left, Hannah went to the bathroom and turned on the taps in the tub. She took off her dressing gown and her underclothes, slid gingerly into the tub, and stared at the water puddling around her belly.

This was not the belly János first uncovered in the hotel suite in Portofino, young and almost concave. It was both skinnier and rounder—less nourished, but more worldly. She traced the curve with her finger, the silver threads that meandered from her pubic hair to her navel. She remembered János's mouth warming the skin of this same belly, his exclamations of wonder and discovery. How this belly had once stuck to the belly of János as they lay joined to each other some hour or so later, trying to comprehend what had occurred, to encompass this emotion that saturated the atmosphere around them. *Love* hadn't seemed like the right word, the right idea. You loved your parents, you loved your dog, you loved the sun on your shoulders, you loved the taste of chocolate and the smell of rain. This was something else. A sense of sacrament.

Her love for him, her absolute confidence in that love, where had it come from? It was faith, that's all. Visceral, stupid. The instinct that you shared some essential element of your composition with this person, whom you had only just met, spent only a few hours in conversation. Yet there it was.

And, of course, he was handsome. He was so handsome she couldn't even quite picture him anymore, like looking into fire, his dark hair and mischievous eyes, the slope of his shoulders, the line of his jaw, the way he could look both rakish (the bow tie undone around his neck) and trustworthy (the buttons perfectly fastened) so your skin melted under the radiance of him.

Now he was dust.

For the past eight years, she had forced the memory of János out of her head. For eight years she had hardly whispered the word *János,* even to herself.

Now here he was again, hovering in front of her, so real she thought she could touch him. She reached into the clouds of steam and cried out in anguish because the air was empty, János was dust, the children were dust, everything was just dust.

* * *

By now, Hannah knew the bones of Shepheard's Hotel. She walked straight through the lobby to the Arab Hall, praying she wouldn't see anybody she knew. That everybody was too drunk or too busy to notice this plain, pale woman flit across the gardens to the annex at the back of the grounds.

Before he left the apartment, dropping a warm, slow kiss on her mouth, Lucien had told her where to find the couple of rooms where he lived. *In case you change your mind,* he'd said. She climbed the stairs, floor by floor. The stairwell was dark, lit only by a single bulb at each floor and a skylight at the top that exposed a square of night sky. At the final landing, bathed in starlight, she found a door. She pushed it open. A short, cramped hallway—some doors. They were labeled. LAVATORY, advised one. ELECTRICS, said another. At the end of the hall, she found the one she was looking for.

HOTEL MANAGER.

She lifted her hand and knocked.

The door opened almost at once. Lucien stood in his shirtsleeves, collar undone, hair falling onto his forehead, bruise more livid than ever. He held a lowball glass filled with ice against his jaw. Before she could say a word, he pulled her into the room and closed the door. He set down the glass on the lamp table and reached for her waist. Unlike her, he hadn't yet bathed, hadn't undressed. The air was thick with smoke, though the window was open. His body sang with heat. When he bent his head to kiss her, she laid a hand against his chest.

"I have to tell you what I'm here for," she said.

"Hannah."

"I want the truth with you. So I have to say this now, before we begin."

He drew back his head a few inches, so he could look her in the eye. His hands were heavy on her waist, so it was hard to think. Hard to get the words out. But it was better to say them, right? So he didn't misunderstand her. She made herself look right back, into the heart of his eyes. She made herself speak.

"I want a child," she said.

CHAPTER TWELVE

Mallory

August 2008
Winthrop Island, New York

I opened my eyes to the crack of sunlight through the curtains. For a moment or two I stared at this line of gold, trying to make sense of it. Trying to shed the remnants of the panicky dream that clung to me—running along a hallway, fire licking at my heels. Something in my chest. Need to find something. Need to find someone.

An arm lay across my ribs. I turned my head and saw a tangle of golden-brown hair on the pillow next to me. Floods of relief. Monk. Winthrop Island. It was true, it was real. He was mine. Then—

"Shit! *Monk!*"

I pushed at his shoulder. He startled, flipped his head over, opened his eyes to half mast, grinned sleepily. "Good morning, Pinkie Pie." Then—

"*Shit!* What time is it?"

He dove for his watch on the nightstand, swore, fell out of bed. Scrambled on the floor for his pants. I leaned over the edge and found my shirt. From somewhere in the house came the thunder of small feet descending a wooden staircase.

We stared at each other and froze.

"Under the bed!" I hissed.

Monk jerked up his pants, grabbed his shirt and boxers, and disappeared below. I let the comforter fall down the side to hide him and pulled my shirt over my head. A second later, a pair of small people burst through the door and jumped on the bed.

"Mallory! Mallory! Mallory! Guess what!"

"What, munchkin?"

Blue held up her fist and opened it. "I lost a tooth!"

Chippy chimed in gleefully. "And there's blood *all over* her pillow!"

"It must have been this morning because the tooth fairy hasn't come yet!"

"I was the one who found the tooth! It was in her hair!"

"It was stuck and he *yanked* it out! Did you hear me scream?"

Chippy picked a scrap of colorful fabric off the comforter and held it up. "Are these your underpants?"

"We have to be more careful," I said to Monk that afternoon, while the kids were upstairs with Carson, the math tutor, a doctoral student in applied mathematics at UMass Amherst who told me (over beers at the Mo, waiting for Monk to start his next set) he made more money tutoring the little scions of Winthrop for the three months of summer than he did the rest of the year teaching undergraduates at the university. (Like, a lot more.)

"Yes and no," said Monk.

"Yes and *no*?"

"I mean yes, obviously, it's not appropriate for my kid brother and sister to come barging in and jump on the bed while I'm trying to have sex with my girlfriend. But no, I'm starting to feel like this whole sneaking around thing is pointless. I mean, give me one good reason why the world shouldn't know we're together?"

"Because I'm the nanny. It's not professional to sleep with the son of the house. Kind of slutty, actually. And worse, it's a cliché. It's a sad, old cliché."

We lay together on the beach below the bluff, tucked out of sight from the main house, where I usually trooped during math time, sketchbook in hand. Monk tried to schedule his afternoon break at the same time and join me here, guitar in hand, and the tranquil hour would unwind to the scent of the ocean and the hot sand, the sounds of the notes plucked from the guitar strings and the scratch of charcoal on the fine, expensive paper Monk had ordered on Amazon and presented to me, bound with a shimmery gold ribbon scrounged from the box of recycled gift wrap that every self-respecting Winthrop resident kept in the attic, exactly one week after our first kiss.

Five weeks and possibly thousands more kisses after that first kiss, I still caught myself daydreaming about it. Returning to the moment of revelation. *Monk Adams loved me!* The shock of Monk's lips on my lips. Monk pulling back to touch my cheek, my jaw, my hair; to look at me with this soft, amazed expression I'd never seen before.

You too? he'd asked, incredulous, and I told him I couldn't believe he had to ask. I couldn't believe he never knew, all this time, that he was the sun to my earth.

He raised both eyebrows and said the sun to your *earth*? I thought I was in the *friend zone.*

I touched his face, the corners of his eyes, the hair at his temples, and told him he was an idiot.

He kissed me again, gently now, because we were trying to wrap our heads around this new idea—the two of us, together, how do we proceed? How do we catch up on lost time? Fall on each other right away, or relish the anticipation?

I'd just pulled Monk's shirt free—had just laid my fingers for the first time on the warm skin of his back—when Mr. Adams's voice drifted down from the bluff above us.

Monk? Son? Come on, we're waiting for you!

Monk swore and lifted his head.

You should go, I whispered. *He's your father. Go have dinner.*

But you, he whispered back. *This.*

Trust me, I'd told him. This *is not going anywhere.*

Now Monk lay on his back next to me, in possibly the same sacred patch of sand. He'd just come in from a swim and the ocean rolled lazily from his skin. I couldn't look away from this one fat drop that balanced on the ball of his shoulder.

"A sad, old *cliché*?" he repeated.

"Banging the nanny, like *where's* your imagination?"

"So you're embarrassed to be seen with me. I get it. It could wreck your whole artist vibe, if word got out."

"There is a certain stigma."

He rolled onto his side and grinned at me. "I mean, I realize I hit the jackpot with you—"

"Oh, the *jackpot,* is it?"

"Mad sexy genius who also happens to be my best friend. Gorgeous *and* talented. I'm punching way above my weight, I realize that."

"I think your dad would beg to differ."

Monk squinted one eye at the hazy sky. "Well, as my remarkably intelligent girlfriend once suggested, fuck him."

"Monk. Seriously, though. Don't break up with your dad because of me. He's your *dad.* He wants the best for you."

"*You're* what's best for me. That's all. Steering us both through the bullshit. Brave as hell." He picked up my hand and kissed the knuckles. The old mischievous glint in his eyes. "Just not brave enough to go public with your preppy boyfriend."

How could I resist him? All wet and gleaming and drenched in sun. I set my sketchbook aside and bent my head to lick the salt water from his shoulder.

You're delicious, I told him.

He leaned forward and kissed the part of my hair. *So are you.*

I looped my arms around his neck. His mouth was warm and soft and tasted of the iced tea we'd drunk at lunch. In no time he'd whipped off my bikini top, rolled me onto my back, had me laughing and gasping and grabbing at his shoulders, pulling impatiently at his trunks.

At which point he rolled away to lie groaning in the sand, arms spread. "We have to stop."

I crawled on top of him and kissed the hollow of his throat. "No, we don't."

"I didn't bring anything with me."

"Well, that wasn't very smart, was it?" I wriggled out of my bikini bottoms and dropped them over the side.

"Sorry if I didn't anticipate my girlfriend getting horny again so soon."

"If you're talking about last night—"

"Hey, there's a reason I passed out cold until seven A.M., oh Insatiable One."

"I'm not insatiable. You satiate me all the time. The more you satiate me—"

He sucked in his breath.

"—the happier I am."

"Whoa . . . Mallory . . ."

"It's okay. My period ended, like, two days ago. We're fine."

"Wow. *Damn*."

I rocked my hips. "Should I stop?"

"I'm gonna die, Pinks. That is all."

His fingers strummed across my breasts, the small of my back, my breasts again. I closed my eyes and stretched for the sun.

"Goddess." He moved his hips to meet mine. "Do you have . . . *any fucking clue* . . . how *good* you look up there. How good you *feel*."

I was full of sunshine, full of Monk. Full of some incandescence I couldn't describe. Like joy, only more. I remember thinking I was going to burst with it.

His hands slid to my waist. "Damn it, damn it."

"Oh my God, keep going—"

"Mallory, *stop* me—"

"Not yet—"

"*Seriously* . . . Pinks, *please* . . . I can't hold on . . ."

"Oh my God, a little longer, *please* Monk."

But it was too good. I couldn't stop; he couldn't stop because I couldn't stop. *I'll pull out,* he gasped. *As soon as you come, I'll pull out.*

I came in long, barreling waves that made me sing. He didn't stand a chance. I felt him jump, heard him shout, heard him swear.

He rolled us over and pulled out hard. Hovered on his elbows, panting, head bowed.

"Shit, my bad. I'm so sorry."

"Honey, relax. Shhh. We're fine. There's no way. Honestly."

"I should've—"

"Hey, it was my bad too. Egging you on." I reached up and speared my hands into his hair. Catching my breath. Sloppy with endorphins. "I couldn't stop, Monk. I *couldn't*."

He eased himself down to rest on top of me, skin to skin. His arms cradled my head, his cheek rubbed mine. He sounded like he'd swallowed a mouthful of sand. "What *happened,* Pinks? What's wrong with me? I'm a responsible guy, I swear. I would *never.*"

"I know you are. I know."

"It's fucking scary, what we have. This. Don't you think? It takes me over sometimes."

"It's nature," I said. "Life force and everything."

"Your damn nakedness. I just lose my *brains.*"

I stroked his hair. "Shh. It's okay."

"Shit. Mallory. I'm such an asshole."

"Seriously, don't worry. Biological impossibility."

"Nothing's *impossible,* Pinko."

"Anyway, it's just this once."

"You remember health class. *The rhythm method is the least reliable form of—*"

"Oh, please. I think I know my own ovaries, okay? Relax."

He levered himself up. The sun streamed down his hair and face and wide, immaculate shoulders, his golden chest. My insides turned over in this convulsion of bliss. I wanted to sing and cry at the same time. Monk looked down at me with his serious face. "You know that if anything happens, I'll stand by you, right? Whatever you decide."

"Nothing will happen."

"Like in my dreams, we're on a desert island with my guitar and maybe a dozen kids running around naked—"

I started laughing. "Stop it."

"Okay, maybe not a dozen. And not naked. That would be weird, right?"

"Plus skin cancer."

He found my hand and kissed the knuckles. "I guess what I'm trying to awkwardly say is I want this to last. Not just for summer. For—you know, as long as you want me. Some place together in the middle of nowhere—I don't know, some cabin in the mountains, beach hut, whatever you like—where you can do your thing and I can do my thing and we just . . . support each other's work and wake up together in the morning and make each other coffee and have sex whenever we want and . . . sorry, I'll stop now."

"Don't stop," I said. "I like this."

"You don't think it's a little—I don't know, co-dependent?"

I sat up on my knees and put my arms around his neck. "But also kind of fun."

The kiss went on and on. I loved the tickle of his chest hair against my breasts, the sun on my bare shoulders, our stomachs colliding. When we stopped for breath, I propped my arms on either side of his neck and crossed my wrists behind him. "Do you know what I wish? I wish I could go back and tell the high school me to chill out. Everything will turn out all right."

"I wish I could go back to my high school self and tell him to man the fuck up and ask you out already," he said.

I shook my head. "No. It would have been too soon. I think we needed to hurt a little, date the wrong people, just so we know when it's right."

"I would never, ever hurt you, Pinks. That I can swear." He frowned. "You think it might help if you got up and, I don't know, swam in the ocean for a bit?"

We climbed the path together. Monk dropped my hand as we came over the top of the bluff and checked his watch. "Gotta head to the course. Working till dinner, then playing at the Mo tonight."

"Pick me up at the end of the drive?"

He started to reach for my hair, then glanced at the house and pulled back. "You're sure you want to watch again? I mean, it's just the same stuff. I can throw in a cover or two to mix things up, but—"

"Ooh, like what? Do you take requests?"

"Whatever you want me to play, Pinko. I'll play it for you." He glanced at the house again. "Fuck it, you know what? They can deal with it."

He cupped my face and kissed me on the lips. Long and slow, like he meant it.

"So, are you and Monk getting *married*?" Blue wanted to know.

My lips froze on her forehead. I'd just put the twins to bed, shades down, covers up. Almost over the goal line. Freedom beckoning.

"Me? And Monk?" I said. "What do you mean?"

From Chippy's bed came a singsong voice. "Monk and Mallory, sittin' in a tree. K-I-S-S-I—"

"*When* did you see us kissing?"

"On the lawn. Right after math."

I stood up from the edge of Blue's bed and put my hands on my hips. "We were *not* kissing."

"Yes, you were," said Blue.

"He was tickling her tonsils with his tongue," said Chippy, right before he burst into maniacal little-boy laughter.

"All right, all right. You two. Fine. That's a secret, okay? Our secret."

"Mom saw it too," said Blue. "She called you a bitch."

I climbed into Bessie and slammed the door shut. "We're busted," I said.

"Busted? Well, that sounds exciting," said a throaty voice from the back, like the ghost of Katharine Hepburn.

I swiveled and jumped at the same time. A woman sat pin-straight on the fraying bench seat, wearing a pink linen blouse and pearls, rusty blond hair, inquisitive blue eyes, cheekbones on loan from a carpenter. A waft of familiarity about her.

Monk said, "Pinks. Meet my aunt Barbara. Mom's big sister."

Aunt Barbara stuck out a slender, bony hand over the top of the seat. "Pleased to meet you, Mallory. My nephew tells me you're his muse." She drew out the word *muse* to its fullest possible extent.

I looked at Monk. "Your *muse*?"

He grinned and shrugged. "Shoe fits, right?" He propped his hand on top of the wheel and leaned in to kiss me as we barreled down West Cliff Road toward the village. "Buckle up, buttercup. We're late."

"You don't care that we're busted?"

"I mean, I'm not surprised, if that's what you're asking. Especially after that fat one I planted on you on the lawn this afternoon. Did the twins give you hell?"

"Your stepmother saw it. Blue says she called me a bitch."

Aunt Barbara leaned forward and spoke above the engine's roar. "That's what the shrinks would call *projection,* I think."

"Barb's not a fan of the third Mrs. Adams," said Monk.

"I think she's a bit of a climber. *And* a drunk. Appalling combination. I can take one or the other, but not both."

"Wait a second," I said to Monk. "You *knew* they were watching, didn't you? You did that on purpose."

A grin appeared at the corner of Monk's mouth, though he kept staring forward at the road ahead. "I kind of *thought* they might be watching. I didn't know for sure."

"You bastard. You *outed* us."

"Look, I'm tired of sneaking around with you, is all. What's there to hide? It's not like we're having some *fling.*"

"We kind of *are.*"

"Maybe *you're* having a fling," he said. "I'm having a full-on affair."

"Children, honestly," said Aunt Barbara. "As long as you're using protection, it's really not that big a scandal. You should have seen what we got up to in the seventies. I remember one summer I came back from college and all the husbands and wives had sort of *swapped places.* Like a game of musical chairs. You needed name cards to keep everyone straight."

"Wow," I said. "Must have been a rough winter."

"No, I really think they were having a ball. Of course, it might have been all the barbiturates. Monk, dear. The Mohegan Inn. Is this one of those places where they serve beer?"

"I'm sure they'll mix you a drink if you ask nicely, Aunt Barbara."

"Good." She sat back against the seat. "I expect I'm going to need it."

The narrow streets around the Mo were packed with parked cars. Monk had to jimmy Bessie into a spot between a house and a tree and lift Barbara out through the back.

"Are all these people here for you, darling?" she asked.

"I doubt it," he said, just as I said, *"Pretty much."*

She looked back and forth between us. "Well? Which is it? Because I'm too old to sit on the bar, like the old days. For one thing, I'm wearing white pants."

"I'm guessing there's a party at the firehouse, that's all," said Monk.

I rolled my eyes. "He's being modest. He's got a real following now. The last show two weeks ago, we had to go in through the kitchen."

She looked aghast. "Are you saying my nephew is a *rock star*?"

Monk threw his arms around his aunt and seized her up into a hug that left her pink Tod's loafers dangling about a foot off the pavement. "I love the way you say that, Aunt Barbara. Like it's cholera."

"Well, there *are* similarities."

I could see Monk was revving up. His eyes crinkled, his skin glowed. He reached into the back of the Wagoneer and pulled out his guitar in its case, stickered over like a vintage suitcase. He grinned at both of us. "Look at you. My two best girls."

Aunt Barbara looped her arm around mine. "Honestly, he gives me a toothache sometimes."

Monk led us around to the kitchen entrance, where Mike waited in a cloud of nervy cigarette smoke. "Fucking fire marshal's going to shut us down." He sucked in the last of the cigarette and tossed the butt on the pavement. "Twice the legal capacity, last I checked. Bunch of kids boating in from Mystic. Some fucker posted it on Facebook."

"Facebook? What on earth is that?" asked Aunt Barbara.

"Like MySpace, only cooler," I told her.

"*That* clears it up nicely," she said. "May I trouble you for a Manhattan, sir? As dry as you can make it."

The kitchen smelled of stale grease and cigarettes, which told you all you needed to know about the standard of cuisine at the Mo. I followed Mike around the stacks of food service boxes that probably should have been taken straight to the refrigerator some time ago—bacon, hamburger patties, iceberg lettuce, French onion dip— and a couple of beleaguered fry cooks. I heard the crowd even before Mike shoved open the swinging door from the kitchen—a dull college roar that rose and fell according to the laws of mob physics. It was probably no more than a couple hundred people, but in an ancient, low-ceilinged tavern like the Mo, it felt like a thousand.

"Good Lord," said Aunt Barbara. "Where am I supposed to sit?"

"I don't think you're supposed to sit, really."

"Don't recommend sitting," Mike agreed.

"What about my Manhattan?"

"I'll mix your fucking Manhattan in a second, lady. I got to get this shit under control before we get shut down."

Behind us, Monk laid a hand on my shoulder. "You'll be okay, Pinks?"

"Don't worry about us. I'll keep your aunt safe from the riffraff."

"Oh, I don't mind a little riffraff," said Barbara. "It's my knees I'm worried about."

Monk looked at me. "Wish me luck."

"Break a leg. Break everything."

"Break it up, you fucking lovebirds," said Mike. "All I need is a riot on my hands. Bro, you want a beer first? Shot of the old firewater?"

Monk shook his head. He stuck his hand into my hair and kissed me. For a second, he rested his forehead against mine. "Pinks. Love you."

Before I could say it back, he was gone. Some whoops ripped through the crowd as people caught sight of him. I felt this instant of terror that I'd never see him again, that he had disappeared between the jaws of some monster, like Jonah and the whale, the way my grandfather used to tell the story to Paige and me when we were kids, in order to terrify us into the faith. Mike's voice came on the microphone, telling the crowd to shut the fuck up so they could hear the music. The crowd shut up so fast, it was eerie. Then Monk's old chuckle, familiar and strange through the mic. He said some words I didn't pick out—my brain had gone into some kind of trance, I think. But I remember hearing his voice say my name.

This first song is for Mallory. Actually—that sheepish chuckle again—*all my songs are for Mallory.*

I reached out and steadied myself against the wall. A few guitar chords—I thought, panicky, shouldn't he warm up or something? Tune the guitar? But this was Monk. He could do anything.

Barbara leaned into my ear.

"Sorry to be a bother," she said, "but I'm afraid I need to use the ladies' room."

As it turned out, Mike didn't need to worry about the fire marshal shutting him down. The fire marshal was in the audience, whooping at every song. He asked for Monk's autograph afterward.

In fact, there were a lot of people who asked for Monk's autograph afterward, most of them women. I stood next to the bar with my arms crossed, trying not to scowl. Aunt Barbara perched on a stool next to me, nursing her second Manhattan. "Are you sure you don't want one, dear?" she asked, in a kind voice. "You look as if you could use it."

I peered at the glass. "What's in a Manhattan?"

"Kids these days," she said. "Rye whiskey, vermouth, bitters. I like mine with a brandied cherry, but that appears to be beyond the scope of Mike's powers. Failing the cherry, a lemon twist will do."

"All right," I said.

Barbara turned and summoned Mike with a flick of her finger. "Another Manhattan for the lady," she said.

"Yes, ma'am," he said obediently.

"I had a word with him about his language," she told me. "For the love of God, how much longer is this supposed to take? I'm going to miss SportsCenter."

I surveyed the lineup of blond blowouts and exposed belly buttons. Monk sat on his stool, using the guitar as a desk while he signed the flyers that had announced the concert, in lieu of anything more official in the way of merch. "Not too much longer, I think. Only a dozen left."

At that instant, Monk raised his head and winked at me over the swoops of glossy hair.

"I did like that one about midwinter," Barbara said. "It brought a tear."

"I'll bet that doesn't happen often."

"Ouch," she said. "Now, who's *that* fellow? He doesn't look much like a music aficionado to me."

"Which fellow?"

"The gentleman over there by the wall. Is he waiting for somebody? I suppose that charming girl is his girlfriend. The one getting her arm signed, who seems to have misplaced her pubic hair."

I craned my neck to find the man she meant. Mike set down the Manhattan next to my elbow. A hum of dread overtook my nerves. I turned to Mike and said, "Is anyone helping him out? If someone gets a little close?"

Mike said, "I wouldn't worry about that, kiddo. He's only got eyes for you."

"No, I mean . . ."

I couldn't say what I meant. The word *bodyguard* seemed wrong—something a real rock star would need, not Monk Adams playing his guitar at the Mo for a bunch of lobstermen and college kids. I picked up the Manhattan and slugged down half of it before my sinuses exploded.

"Jesus Christ," I said.

"It's an acquired taste," said Barbara. "You know, he really has turned out well, under the circumstances."

I wiped the tears from my eyes. "You mean Monk?"

"With Jackie in and out of rehab, and the father—"

"Jackie?"

"My sister. Monk's mother." Barbara sipped the Manhattan. "Our parents divorced when we were in our early teens, after my mother had slept with just about all the other men on the island. Possibly a few of the women too, now that I think about it. Jackie took it harder than I did. Jackie always took everything harder. Then she married a philanderer. Go figure."

"Mr. Adams."

"Mind you, he was more discreet. Took the old-fashioned approach. Strictly secretaries and that sort of person, not someone his wife and children might bump into at a party, God forbid. He was a funny sort of snob that way. Never dipped his pecker in his own inkpot."

I spewed a little Manhattan and reached for the cocktail napkin.

"Poor old Jackie. Buzzy just couldn't comprehend why she was so upset. I don't think he ever imagined he was doing anything wrong. Probably thought he was sparing her, if anything. Drove her nuts."

"What about the kids, though? Didn't it bother them?"

"Well, at the time, they wouldn't have known what Buzzy was up to, would they? His little girlfriends weren't of their world. What hit them hard was Jackie going off her rocker. The divorce. So *she* took all the blame, you see."

I glanced across the room at the top of Monk's head. "Where is she now?"

"Last I heard, she's in Miami with some charming fellow she met in rehab. Buzzy still sends her money—he's a better ex than he ever was a husband—though I sometimes wonder if he should." She pauses to sip from her drink. "I hope I'm not boring you with all this? I don't usually air so much dirty laundry at once."

"No, I appreciate it. Monk and his dad—it's pretty complicated. So it kind of helps to have the backstory."

"Well, I wouldn't say Buzzy's a *bad* father. Compared to some, anyway. Always had time for them, made sure they had the best of everything. But he wouldn't just let them grow on their own. Are you a gardener at all, Mallory?"

"Um, not really."

"Shame. It's better than therapy, gardening, and much cheaper. Anyway, there are two types of gardener, in my experience—the kind that goes for the showy blooms, that knows all these tricks for making them grow the biggest and brightest, in nice orderly rows. Hires in experts, does expensive interventions. And there's the kind that sort of throws in the seeds in a nice sunny spot and waters and feeds them and watches what happens. You do see what I'm saying, don't you?"

"I think so."

She finished the drink and motioned to Mike. "I've always tried to be *present* for Monk, to use the fashionable term. But I really can't claim the credit. I suppose, when your parents fail you, you either go to pieces or you become the grown-up you require. Or maybe our Monk is just that kind of extraordinary boy who would've thrived wherever you planted him. Oh, here's that *man*. He looks as if he knows you, dear."

All this time, I'd been staring at Monk while Barbara's words floated into my ears. The nympho grandmother, the mother in rehab, the philandering father, Aunt Barbara giving him the love he needed, *my two best girls.* Now my gaze moved to the right, to the tall, slender man with the brown hair and the Bruins cap who picked his way toward us, holding a beer.

Staring at me from a pair of familiar, glassy eyes.

"Hello, Mallory," he said. "Thought I might find you here."

Two days after Monk kissed me for the first time, I gathered up my nerve and called Dillon while the twins were upstairs doing math with Carson.

Mallory, babe. What's up? he'd asked me, from his cubicle in the corporate offices of Dunkin' Donuts, across the water in Providence.

I'd plunged right in with the words I'd rehearsed to myself all morning. *So, this is really hard to say, and I want you to know that it has nothing to do with you, I think you're a really terrific person, but I've been doing a lot of thinking and I realized I just don't feel about you the way you deserve to be—*

You're breaking up with me? he'd asked, incredulous.

Sort of. Actually, yes. Yes, I am, Dillon. I think it's best for both of us, under the circumstances.

What circumstances? Is there someone else?

Of course, I'd known he was going to ask that question. Doesn't everybody? Wouldn't you? So I knew exactly how I was going to answer him.

I'm sorry, Dillon. There is. It's someone I've known and cared about for a while, and in the past few days we've both realized that—

I knew it, he said. *I fucking knew it.*

Dillon—

I mean, you don't return my calls. You barely return my texts.

I'm sorry. It's been busy—

Obviously, he said.

I was sitting in the middle of the lawn, in the sweet spot for cell service. Legs up to my chest. I set my chin between my kneecaps and closed my eyes. Last night—the sailboat at sunset, the champagne and the picnic basket Grace had packed for us, Monk leading me across the lawn to the guesthouse, the candles, the hours that followed—I had not remembered Dillon once.

Not once.

It's not you, I told Dillon. *This guy—he and I—we're just—*

Monk, right? The guy who got you the job? Monk Adams?

I said, *Yes. Monk. I've known him since high school. We—*

Look, I get it. Rich prep school guy. That's what I figured. I guess I didn't stand a chance.

Dillon—

I wish you the best, Mallory, he said. And hung up.

Later that evening, after I'd put the twins to bed and found Monk at our meeting spot, on the stone wall that divided the two properties, he asked me what was wrong.

I tried to explain about Dillon, how bad I felt, how much it hurt to hurt someone, even when your whole heart belonged to someone else.

Monk put his arm around me. *I know, Pinks. I know.*

For a while we just sat there on the wall, side by side, paying tribute to the people we could have loved, if we hadn't belonged to each other. The setting sun painted the horizon. I remember thinking how strange it was to feel sad in the middle of so much happiness, how you couldn't just experience joy all by itself without feeling as if you had somehow stolen it from somewhere else. That there was only so much joy in the world.

After a few minutes, Monk stood and turned to stand between my legs, holding my waist gently between his hands. *Last night,* he said. *I just want you to know how much it meant to me.*

Me too, I told him.

I was so damn nervous, Mallory. Naked with you for the first time.

Monk, please. *You're literally a perfect physical specimen.*

His mouth wore this wry, wise smile. *Pinko,* he said, *that's not what I mean.*

Then he kissed me, and I think it's fair to say I never gave poor Dillon another thought.

* * *

Until now. As I looked at Dillon's face, I couldn't quite wrap my head around his presence here, in the warm, woody tavern room at the Mohegan Inn, Monk on his stool on the platform ten yards away. It didn't seem real. Dillon belonged to the mainland, to my past. It felt like a decade since I had slept with Dillon for the last time, kissed him goodbye at the ferry dock in New London. Once, his face had been so familiar to me. I knew every line and color and scar. Now he looked like a stranger whose picture I'd seen before.

"Hey, Dillon," I said. "Good to see you. What brings you here tonight?"

Dillon leaned over to kiss my cheek. "You're looking good, Mallory. Just wanted to see what you were up to. Listen to some tunes." He sipped his beer, angled his head in Monk's direction. "He's pretty good, right?"

"Excuse me, young man," said Aunt Barbara, "but I don't believe we've been introduced."

Dillon turned to her. "I'm Dillon. Mallory's ex-boyfriend?"

"Oh! Like family, then." She held out her hand. "Barbara Huxley. Aunt of Mallory's current boyfriend."

"You must be so proud."

"I am, thank you. I'd like to say he gets his talent from me, but I can really only take credit for his good looks."

A bemused look appeared on Dillon's face, like when I'd tried to explain chicken fried steak. All that time, he thought he'd been eating chicken.

"Well, this is nice," said Barbara. "Monk will be so pleased you've come. In *fact*. Speak of the devil."

I'd been concentrating so hard on Dillon's face, trying to decipher the expression there, that I hadn't noticed Monk walking up to join us at the bar. He slung an arm around me and pulled me in for a kiss that—looking back—might have lasted a second or two longer than it needed to, strictly speaking. He raised his head and said, "Whiskey?"

"Barbara ordered me a Manhattan."

"Good choice, Bar," he said, still looking at me.

"Monk, sweetie," she said, "you'll never *guess* who's here. Such a surprise. It's Mallory's ex-boyfriend, Dillon—I'm sorry, dear. I didn't catch your last name."

"Rooney. Dillon Rooney."

Monk held my gaze another second or two before he turned to Dillon. I had the feeling he'd noticed the whole scene from his stool atop the Mo's foot-high platform of battered wood, ten feet square, signing flyers and tanned, slender arms, and he wasn't surprised at all to hear Dillon's name.

But he didn't show a shred of resentment. Not Monk Adams, drilled from birth in the rules of civilized conduct. He smiled affably and held out his hand. "Rooney. Pleasure. Monk Ad—"

Which was all he had time to say before Dillon pulled back his fist and swung for Monk's jaw.

CHAPTER THIRTEEN

Mallory

June 2022
Cape Cod, Massachusetts

The email arrives in my inbox during the early hours of the morning. I hear the ping but resist the visceral urge to check my phone, which sits on a chair on the other side of the room, just to make checking my phone an effort in the middle of the night. Just so I can get some damn sleep.

Turn off your notifications, Paige tells me. But you can't turn off notifications when your son's kidneys don't work. Trust me, you'll sleep even less. Wondering what you're missing.

So I hear the ping and ride the surge of adrenaline until it subsides. Concentrate on my breathing as I lie in this position, that position, falling occasionally into a brief, shallow unconsciousness—let's not dignify those episodes with the word *sleep*—until the sun breaks the horizon at five, until my alarm goes off at six-thirty.

I trudge across the room and turn off the noise. Open my Gmail and learn that the convent of St. Hilda's in County Galway cannot answer requests for confidential records without presentation of two forms of identification from an official government body, and a copy of the original adoption certificate. Very truly yours.

I toss my phone on the bed and rummage in the chest of drawers for my running clothes. Before I head out, I poke my head inside the door of Sam's bedroom to make sure he's asleep. And breathing.

He has dialysis today at 9 A.M.

* * *

While Sam's in dialysis, I drag out my sketch pad and try to focus my mind on a design I'm working on, this hibiscus motif, but I keep wandering back to the email from the convent. No signature, no human being attached, just this prim legal language.

On my wrist, one emerald eye peers up at me, speculative.

A news alert lights up my phone on the coffee table. I stare at the home screen—a photo of me and Sam, taken two weeks ago on the beach at Summersalt—as it fades and goes dark. Underneath the phone lies a crisp new copy of *Us* magazine, on which a photograph of a woman's face has been retouched to doll-like perfection. My phone rests along the line of her eyes and nose, so it takes a minute or two of staring to realize who this is.

Then I notice the headline. *Wedding Joy! Lennox Talks Monk, Marriage & Starting a Family with the Sexiest Man in Music.*

A new message alert pops up. I snatch the phone.

Hey girl, got your email. Just landed in ptown for 4th. Lunch?

On the ride home, Sam puts in his AirPods and stares out the window. I hear the faint noise leaking from his ears and realize it's one of Monk's songs, an old one.

"So, have you heard from the big guy today?" I ask.

The sound of my voice registers somewhere in the cortex. He turns to me and lifts out one AirPod. "Yah?"

It's been a week now since Monk's first message arrived on my phone, while we were sitting right here in the waiting room at the kidney center in Barnstaple. I recognized the number as the same one he had fourteen years ago, which astounded me. All this time, he was just a single drunk text away.

Can I have your permission to communicate with Sam via text? Of course you are welcome to review all messages. Thx M

While I was typing my reply, another message arrived.

Hope it was ok to ask Lola for your info, not sure how much she knows?

I replied—

Lola radar has picked up vibes but still in dark. Thx for your discretion. Sam would love to hear from you. Contact card below.

Then—

Before you reach out I need to tell you about something. lmk when you can talk

My phone rang immediately. Monk's familiar voice, like a sock to the gut. "It's me. What's up?"

I stepped outside the waiting room into the warm, muggy morning and stood at the edge of the parking lot while I told Monk about the mushroom.

I remember he was quiet while I explained the story. Did not interrupt once. When I finished, there was this silence. I asked if he was okay, if he was still there. I thought maybe the call had dropped.

"I'm here." His voice was so calm it frightened me. "What about his medical bills?"

"Mostly covered by insurance. Paige helps with deductibles and stuff."

"Okay. Kidney donation?"

"He's on the waiting list. We don't have a lot of relatives, unfortunately. And neither of us are matches."

"What about me?" he asked.

"I can't ask—"

"How does the testing work? Can I just set up an appointment? Like, today?"

"Monk," I said, "let's not talk about this right now. Donating a kidney is not something you do on a whim."

"It's not a *whim,* Mallory. He's my *son.* He's my son and he's dying."

"He's not *dying.* It's a managed condition for now. And you're in shock—"

"I'm not in *shock.*"

"Monk, you are. I know your voice, okay? So think it over. Talk it over with him. Plus, there's no guarantee you're a match. Trust me."

"Where is he? Can I talk to him now?"

"He's in dialysis right now."

"Dialysis," he said. "Shit. *Fuck.*"

I heard a loud noise, like something slamming.

"Monk, it's okay. He goes three times a week. He's used to it. It sucks, but you see how well he's doing. We have to watch his diet, obviously . . ."

"Fuck," he said. *"Fuck."*

"Monk, I'm so sorry. I'm so sorry it has to be this way. I did the best I could. I tried so hard to protect him and—"

"Mallory—"

"I mean, I just thought summer camp would be good for him. You know, get him away from the mom bubble for a bit, learn some independence. I just . . . I didn't want to be one of those hothouse parents. Like Barbara said. And look what I did to him. So, I'm sorry. It's a mess."

"Stop, Mallory," he said. "Just stop. I have a lot of bones to pick with you right now, believe me, but not this. You didn't *do* this to him. What happened at fucking summer camp was not your fault. I might be pissed as hell with you right now, but I have no doubt at all in my heart that you've been the best mom you could be."

I sat down hard on the curb and stared at the shrubs across the parking lot, trying to breathe.

Because while he meant the words to comfort me, an unsaid truth teemed between us—that if Monk had been in the picture, if Monk had been part of Sam's life, Sam never would have eaten that mushroom. He wouldn't have gone to that summer camp. Monk would have had him stay at Winthrop, swimming and playing tennis and learning to sail. Not sleepaway camp in New Hampshire.

The original sin was still mine. Would always be mine.

Monk said, "Look, I'm just sorry you've had to shoulder this on your own. I'm sure it's been hell. But I'm here now. We'll figure it out together. First things first, we'll make him better. We'll deal with the rest of it later. From now on, he's going to have the best care in the world, I promise you."

I felt an urge to snap something back, like what the hell do you think I've been giving him, the past three years?

But the words died in my throat. He was right. Paige was right.

With all the love and hustle and medical insurance in the world, I couldn't give Sam the outcome that Monk's money and influence could. Hell, one Instagram post and his entire fandom would be lining up for the honor of donating a kidney to Monk Adams's kid.

"Thanks," I said. "That means a lot."

When Sam came out of dialysis that morning, there was a message on his phone from Monk. Sam's eyes widened and shone. He offered to show it to me, but I shook my head and said, *That's between you and him, I don't want to get in the way between you two. Just let me know if you want to talk anything over.*

Since then, the messages have been passing regularly between Sam and Monk. *Ping ping ping.* I'm dying to know what's in them. But I don't ask. Sam doesn't tell. He's not telling me now, that's for sure.

He sticks the AirPod in his ear and turns back to the window. "Yeah, we texted this morning."

"Good," I say, to nobody in particular.

When we arrive back at Summersalt, Paige is out on the terrace, talking furiously into her phone. She waves me away. More wallpaper drama, I think. I head into the kitchen to rummage out some lunch. Twice a week, Paige treks to the Whole Foods in Hyannis and fills her fridge with plastic containers of foods like tahini and kale dip, ready to be whipped out at a moment's notice so nobody resorts to breaking out the emergency chicken nuggets.

As I'm pulling the kids' plates from the cupboard, Paige steps in from the terrace and drops her phone on the counter.

"Wallpaper again?" I ask.

"Jake's staying over the weekend in Charlotte."

"Again? I thought he was due back tomorrow."

"He says he can't get away. This new company they've bought, the accounts are all messed up or something. I'm like, isn't that what your junior analysts are for? You know, the ones who don't have wives and kids waiting for them at home for fucking *Fourth of July weekend*? For God's sake, his parents are coming up and everything. Is it too early for wine?"

"I don't know if this is a good time to mention that I'm headed to lunch in Provincetown at twelve-thirty."

"Lunch?"

"A friend."

She reaches for a carrot stick. "Let me guess. Booty call from that bartender guy?"

"Okay, first of all, I object to your terminology. A booty call implies an imbalance of power. I just don't have the bandwidth for a relationship right now, that's all."

"Hey, I'm not judging. We all have needs. At least one of us is having sex once in a while."

I snap my fingers. "Oh, that reminds me! I heard back from that convent."

She chokes up some carrot. *"Convent?"*

"You know, the one in Ireland. Where Mom was born. They can't release any confidential records without two forms of ID and the original adoption form."

"Are you serious? We're talking about an adoption from, like, seventy years ago!"

I shrug. "Rules."

"Forward me the email, all right? I could really pick a fight with some nuns right now."

I pull out my phone and scroll through my emails. "Secondly— and not that it's any of your business—I'm not meeting Craig today."

"What, another one?" asks Paige. "Have you ever thought about making a living this way?"

"Fuck you. It's this guy I knew from RISD who went into jewelry design. Now he appraises stuff for Sotheby's. I reached out to him this morning, and guess what? He's in Provincetown for the Fourth."

"Um, I don't want to spoil the fun here, but you *do* know who comes to P-town for Fourth of July, right?"

I lay down my phone. "Not that kind of date. He's meeting me for lunch to check out Mom's bracelet."

"You're *selling* Mom's *bracelet?*"

"Yeah, why not? I could buy a new car." At Paige's look of horror, I roll my eyes. "Kidding. He's going to take a look and see if we can figure out where it comes from. Where *she* comes from. This, you know, *woman* who gave Mom up for adoption."

For some reason, I can't bring myself to say the word *grandmother.*

I met Luca during freshman orientation at RISD, during one of those intersectionality exercises where everybody makes a list of all the ways they are either marginalized or privileged. I remember thinking, when Luca stood up, that he wore the most gorgeous pair of earrings I'd ever seen in my life. "I am a Black boy adopted by an Italian American family," he announced. "African, gay, Catholic as fuck. Deal with it."

And sat down.

I came up to him afterward and asked where he'd gotten his earrings, and he said he made them himself in metal shop for his senior project, and we've been friends ever since. Not best friends—I couldn't always deal with his drama—but close enough to hold my hair when I accidentally got drunk on some vodka Jell-O shots at a Halloween party, close enough to let me cry on his cashmere sweater when a boy once crushed my romantic illusions, close enough that I returned the favor a few months later (except *my* sweater was acrylic).

Close enough that when I realized I was pregnant with Sam, I called up Luca before I told my own mother. (For the record, he told me not to get an abortion or I would go to hell. I told him thanks for the good word, maybe I'd see him there.)

Close enough that I hunted down his listing in the alumni directory a few days ago and emailed him to ask if he was available for a jewelry provenance consultation.

I turn down his first suggestion for lunch—the Black Sheep—which happens to be the same dive bar slash diner where I once hung out with Monk until closing. We meet instead at a café near the beach. The outrageous feathered earrings have been replaced by tasteful diamond studs the size of quinoa, and he wears a pink polo shirt with the Brooks Brothers sheep embroidered delicately on the left breast. "I'm getting kind of a preppy vibe," I tell him, after we kiss both cheeks. "What's up?"

He shrugs. "Working for the Man now. Gotta look the part."

"So I hear. Sotheby's. Nice. Jewelry appraisals, right? You must see some crazy pieces."

"Girl, the jewelry ain't crazy. The jewelry is sublime. It's the people who own it who are fucking batshit."

We order coffee and sandwiches. Luca orders his without bread; he's avoiding carbs, he says. He asks about Sam, pretends interest in kidneys. All the while he's dropping glances at the cobra on my wrist, until I take it off and hand it to him.

"Here. Stop drooling, okay?"

The tender, reverent way he takes the bracelet from my fingers, you'd think it was his newborn child. "Mary Mother of God," he says. "This is something."

"I know, right? I've always thought it was special somehow. My mom wore it all the time. Hardly ever took it off."

"This workmanship, it's incredible. I haven't seen anything like it. Where'd she get it?"

"So that's the crazy story. My sister, Paige, was going through some old papers in the attic, and long story short it turns out Mom was adopted from an orphanage in Ireland. And this bracelet came with her. The birth mother wanted her to keep it."

"The birth mother." He looks up. "You mean your grand-mother?"

"Yes. Technically. *Biologically.* And because of Sam, you know, needing a kidney and everything, Paige and I have been trying to do some research into where she came from. Paige did a DNA swab, and me, I'm just a girl sitting in a café trying to find out where this woman got her bracelet. And why she gave it to Mom, even though she couldn't keep her. Because . . . well, because I'm hoping that might help point us in the right direction."

"Off the top of my head, I'd say Egypt."

"*Egypt?*"

"The cobra, for starters. That's an Egyptian cobra."

"How do you know that?"

He shrugs. "I have a snake thing. So I'm guessing Egypt, maybe 1930s. I see some art deco influence, some traditional motif—you get a lot of that in Egypt, European mixing with Arab. But that's just an educated guess. And you know she might have picked up the bracelet on a visit, or from somebody who visited there, or who knows what." Luca lifts his gaze to me. "Can I take it with me?"

"Hell, no."

"Then I'll have to take some hi-res photographs." He reaches into his handbag and pulls out a jeweler's monocle. "For a start, I might be able to tell you where the stones come from, though I warn you, geology isn't my gig. And that info won't necessarily tell you where the cuff was made. Jewelers source their gems from all over."

"Can I take a photo of you wearing that monocle?"

"Girl. Only if you want to be dead."

As I pull up the long gravel driveway at Summersalt, I spot another car in the place where I usually park. An old Jeep Wagoneer with vintage wood panels, a bit spiffier than I remember her.

I pull up behind, turn off the ignition, and stare out the windshield at Bessie's familiar ass for a minute or two before I climb out of the car. Around back, I hear some noise and follow my ears.

On the lawn, near the edge where the clipped green grass turns to beach scrub, Monk Adams is playing catch with my son. As you might expect, Monk knows how to throw a baseball. The elbow, the shoulder rotation, the release—all enter the world perfectly formed. The ball goes straight into Sam's mitt. The thwack of leather might be the smack of my heart. I stand a minute or two, not moving. The ocean breeze sifts through my hair.

Sam spots me first. Or maybe Monk saw me all along, who knows.

"Mom! Hey. Where were you?"

I step forward. "In P-town, having lunch with a friend. Would you two like something to drink? Kind of hot out."

"I'll have a beer," says Monk.

"I'll have a Coke," says Sam.

"Nice try, kiddo."

"Fine. Water's good, I guess."

I walk into the kitchen and set my hands on the counter to compose myself.

"Sorry," says Paige. "Didn't you get my text?"

"I was driving, dumbass."

"Forgot that old beater of yours doesn't have CarPlay. You look thirsty. How was Luca? Did he tell you anything about the bracelet?"

"Luca was fine. He took a bunch of photos. They have a couple of in-house experts for historic jewelry. He thinks it might have come from Egypt."

"*Egypt?*"

"Just a guess, though." I head to the drinks fridge and take out two beers. Then a glass from the cabinet, which I fill with water and ice from the dispenser on the fridge. "How long has he been here?"

"Couple of hours."

I walk outside and set the drinks on the table, under the umbrella. Monk catches a final ball from Sam and says, "That's it. Time for a cold one."

I open the beers and hand Sam a glass of ice water.

"Sip slowly, buddy." I turn to Monk. "Can't have too much to drink, because the kidneys don't flush it out."

"Gotcha," Monk says, as if we're discussing math homework instead of the complications of renal failure. He gives Sam a gentle punch to the shoulder, such as guys do. "Kid's got a good arm. You play some ball at school?"

"Sure," says Sam.

Monk sinks back a long, thirsty drink and looks at me. "If you've got a second, could we have a word?"

We sit at the kitchen table. Monk brings in a nylon laptop bag, which he sets on the empty chair next to his.

"So how the heck do you keep Bessie on the road?" I ask.

"A lot of tender loving care, believe me. Treated her to a full engine rebuild a couple of years ago. Still gets me around pretty good."

"I figured you might have upgraded by now. I mean, I assume you can afford it?"

"What? I can't do that to Bessie," he says. "Plus, she's good for driving around incognito, right? Stick on a baseball cap and a pair of sunglasses and nobody gives me a second look. How was Province-town?"

"Good. Already filling up for the Fourth. So what did you want to talk about?"

Monk sips his beer and looks out the window at Sam, who's settled himself on a lounger to scroll through his phone. "I have a favor to ask. I was wondering if you'd let Sam spend the Fourth of July weekend with me. On Winthrop. Just the two of us."

"Just the two of you? What about Lennox?"

"She'll be spending the weekend with her folks in Texas."

"Haven't you told her?"

He makes a jerk of surprise. "Of course I've *told* her. She'll be his stepmother."

The word *stepmother* hits me in the ribs. "And she's okay with it?"

"I think so, once she's had time to process everything. She—" He catches a breath and turns his face back to the window. "We've been trying to get pregnant for a few months now. So, this coming up was not the best timing for her. That's not a you problem, obviously, but full disclosure."

"Gotcha," I said.

"Between you and me."

"Of course."

"So how about it? I know you're worried about his care. I mean, I'm well aware I'm a newbie to all this. So I've gone ahead and sourced a nurse practitioner to be on call, plus a dialysis specialist to come out and give Sam his treatments—"

"You *what*? You're bringing in dialysis?"

"We don't have a lot of time together. Anything I can do to make it easy for him."

I stare at the neck of my beer bottle and peel away a little foil that turns into a lot of foil.

"Mallory," Monk says softly, "I know it's a big ask. I want to get to know him, that's all. We've got a lot to catch up on. My life . . . Look, you may not believe it, but I do work pretty hard to carve out some privacy, keep things as real as I can, but my life is what it is. It's the world I'm in. And I know you want to protect him from that. I realize that's a big reason why you never . . . I mean, I get that. I do. I want to protect him too. For this weekend, I've cleared everything else out. Nothing but me and Sam. I promise, I *swear*, I'm not trying to take him away from you. Drag him into the circus. I just want to know him. Make a start."

"All right," I say. "Of course. If that's what you want."

Monk lays out a long breath and finishes the beer. "Thank you," he says. "And now for the boring stuff."

He reaches for the laptop bag on the chair next to him and extracts a brown portfolio. It's the kind with the flap that folds down like an envelope, held shut with an elastic cord. He slips off the cord and takes out a stack of papers.

"So. Before you freak out, this is not a big deal."

"You've talked to your *lawyers* already? It's been one *week*, Monk."

Monk looks back out the window at Sam on his lounge chair. "Mallory, I think it's important we set aside our personal feelings right now and do what's best for our son."

"It may surprise you to know that I've been pretty damn busy doing what's best for Sam for the past thirteen years."

"Mallory, I know. You've been a good mother. Obviously. You only need to spend a minute with Sam to see what a great kid he is. I'm not trying to sic a bunch of damn lawyers on you." He presses his knuckles against his forehead. "Okay, yes. I have a lot of questions running through my head right now. Why you never told me, why you decided for both of us that Sam should grow up without his father even knowing he *existed*—"

"Monk—"

"But like I said before, I want to set that discussion aside until later. If I stop and think about what's happened, the time that's passed, everything I've missed, I'll—I'll lose it, Mallory. I will. And I can't go back to that angry place again, Mallory, you understand? I can't do that all over again. I just want to focus on what I can do for Sam *right now*. Given the situation we're in. Does that sound fair to you? Postpone the melodrama until we've dealt with the big stuff?"

My hands are knotted together in my lap. The words spear me. I dig my fingernails into my palms to distract myself from the pain of impact.

"Fair enough." I nod to the stack of papers. "I'm sorry, but that *does* look like a big deal."

"I know it looks like a lot, but it's just boilerplate, mostly. They do a lot of these, apparently. Paternity agreements, they're called. You can read it through in detail. You *should* read it, make sure you understand everything. But I promise you there's no tricks, Mallory. You know I wouldn't do that to you. At the end of the day, I'm just grateful he's here. I'm grateful beyond words that I have a son." The word *son* makes his voice crack. He clears his throat and fingers the edge of the papers. "I want to do right by him. I want to have a relationship with him. Most of all, I want to make sure that he's able to access the top level of care for his condition."

"That all sounds reasonable. I mean, yes. I trust you."

"So, first. Financial arrangements." Monk reaches into the pocket of his jacket and pulls out a pair of glasses.

"Oh my God. Are those *reading* glasses? When did you start wearing those?"

"None of your business. And that's circle of trust info, by the way. If this gets into fucking Page Six . . ."

"I would never betray your guilty secret."

He settles the glasses on his nose. "Financial arrangements—"

"Monk, stop. Seriously. I don't want your money."

"Yes, Mallory. I *know*. But I have a moral and legal responsibility to support my child, so just hear me out, okay? I undertake to cover all of Sam's medical, education, travel, and security expenses until he turns twenty-one—obviously we can revisit that when he reaches adulthood—plus child support payments to you in the amount of twenty-five thousand dollars a month—"

"What?"

He looks at me over the top of the reading glasses. The effect is so professorial, a giggle chokes in my throat. "Look, do you have any idea what Kanye's paying? This is peanuts, trust me."

"Peanuts? I barely make fifty thousand a *year*, Monk."

Monk takes off the glasses. "You're kidding, right? You've been raising *my son* on fifty thousand a *year*?"

"News flash. A lot of people raise kids on fifty thousand dollars a year. Less."

"Shit," he says.

"Paige helps. Obviously. She's always sending me clothes and shoes. I mean, shoes are the worst. They go on these growth spurts. But that's taken care of. And we spend our vacations here on the Cape, so . . . you know. It's all good. We're good."

He sits back in the chair and fiddles with his glasses. "Sounds like your sister's really been there for you, hasn't she?"

"She's my guardian angel. When he got sick? Paige—she stepped right in. She took care of everything. Everything."

Monk's eyes blink a few times. He turns away and hooks the glasses back over his ears. "All right. Child support. As of last month, from Sam's date of birth, the arrears come to four point two million, which will be deposited into an escrow account until—"

This time I shoot to my feet. "*Four million dollars?* Are you *insane*? I'm not taking four million dollars from you."

"Chill, Pinks. Jesus. Do you think I didn't already figure you'd hit the roof? If you look at the papers, you can initial this clause here and we'll put that money into a trust for Sam until he's twenty-five. Or later. Or earlier. Whatever you think is best."

"You really do live in a different world, don't you?"

"What am I supposed to do, Mallory? What do you *want* me to do? I've been living in fucking la-la luxury all this time, like an asshole. Am I supposed to sit on my hands and watch my son live with *nothing*?"

"He doesn't have nothing! He has everything he needs. Sam is *surrounded* by love."

"He doesn't have a *dad,* Mallory. You didn't give him that chance. You didn't give *me* that chance."

I look at my hands.

"I have an appointment tomorrow at the kidney center in Barnstaple," he says.

"I already told you, there's no rush—"

Monk's voice rises. "There damn well is a rush. I don't need to think about this, Mallory. Why would I need to think this through for even a minute? He's my son. If he needs my kidney, I'll give it to him. If he needs both goddamn kidneys, he can have them. My liver, my lungs. I would rip my heart out, if I could. Rip my fucking heart out and hand it to him—"

"Would you stop making everything into a fucking *song*, Monk Adams? This is my *life*! This is *me*! And *you,* you're just a vampire sucking everything out of me so you can write a catchy *tune* about it, so everyone can shower you with praise and money and tell you what a musical damn genius you are."

The color washes out of Monk's face. He slides the glasses off his nose, folds them into his pocket, and rises from his chair. "I'll just leave these papers with you, okay? There's a return envelope. You can mail them back when you've had a chance to read them over. I'm not suing for custody, just visitation rights. I hope you'll find it's fair. I've tried to be fair. Respectful. I hope you'll sign so we can get these payments lined up for Sam. So we can set up a visit schedule that works for you both. Okay?"

"Okay," I whisper.

"One more thing. At some point, we're going to have to release some kind of statement. Lee wants to wait until after the wedding—"

"Whatever you want," I say. "Just let me know when to brace myself."

"That being said, the news might get out on its own, before we're ready. It happens. So, regardless of what's going on between us, I want you to know you can call me, at any time of day or night, and ask for whatever you need."

"Like what? Security? PR?"

"Like anything. It's going to be a shit show, I'm warning you. I'm sorry about that. You'll need a detail, plus driver. I'll make sure everything's in place." He raps his knuckles on the papers. "Also, could you ask your sister to draw up a list of any expenses she's covered on Sam's behalf. I don't need receipts or anything, just round numbers."

"You know what she'll tell you to do with that."

"If she doesn't give me a list, I'll have to estimate. I'm just going to say goodbye to Sam before I leave."

Monk turns around and walks out to the terrace. I sink back on the chair and watch while he walks up to Sam on his lounge chair and says something. Sam sits up straight and puts his phone down. The old grin appears on Monk's face, the old loose grace around his shoulders. He holds out his hand and they do that arm-clasping thing, in between a handshake and a hug.

I look down at the stack of papers in front of me.

PATERNITY AGREEMENT BETWEEN BARCLAY BENJAMIN MONK ADAMS ("FATHER") AND MALLORY ROSE DUNNE ("MOTHER") IN REFERENCE TO SAMUEL MICHAEL DUNNE ("MINOR CHILD")

"Hey," says Paige.

I turn my head. My sister stands next to the kitchen counter, nursing the dregs of what I assume is a vodka Spindrift. Her hair's scraped back into a ponytail; her lip gloss has evaporated. Eyes puffy.

"How'd it go? Are you letting Sam stay with his dad?"

"I guess he told you about the Fourth of July thing."

"Yeah, we had a little chat when he turned up. I have to say, he comes across as a decent guy, Mallie. He's not being a dick about this." She sips her drink. "And let's face it, he has grounds. Under the circumstances."

I rise to head for the built-in kitchen desk and the blue-and-white Delft cup full of pens that sits on its immaculate quartz surface. "He told me to ask you to give him a list of expenses you've covered for Sam over the years. So he can reimburse you."

Paige slams the glass down on the counter. "What the actual *fuck*? I hope you told him to fuck off."

"Not in those words. Trying to keep things civil for Sam's sake."

She lifts the glass again and finishes off her drink. "I guess that's just his male rock star way of taking responsibility for his seed."

"Let the money do the talking, right?" I select a pen and stroll back to the kitchen table. "He wants to give me twenty-five thousand a *month* in child support. Like what am I even going to *do* with twenty-five thousand dollars a month?"

"*Twenty-five?* You need to tell his cheap ass to ante up. Kanye pays two hundred."

"How do you people *know* this stuff?"

"Buzzfeed." She disappears under the counter to snatch another can of seltzer from the fridge. "So hear me out. Sam's hanging with his dad and Jake's away in Charlotte all weekend. His parents are coming up anyway to see the grandkids. What do you say the two of us take a little trip together?"

I flip through the papers until I reach the last one, where a red-and-yellow arrow sticker directs me to *sign here*.

"You mean like a boozy girls' trip? Like where? Newport?"

I sign my name on the line atop the words MALLORY ROSE DUNNE ("MOTHER") and add the date.

"Actually," says Paige, "I was thinking of Ireland."

CHAPTER FOURTEEN

Hannah

December 1951
Outside Cairo, Egypt

Inside the car, hurtling down the highway, they might have been traveling at any speed at all. Hannah had to check the dial between the prongs of the steering wheel to see that Lucien was pushing the Mercedes-Benz to nearly a hundred miles an hour.

Lucien glanced at her and smiled. "Afraid?"

"Just curious. Nothing really frightens me anymore. If I die, I die."

"But I would rather you didn't die, sweetheart."

"Don't call me that. I'm not your sweetheart."

Lucien reached in his pocket and drew out a cigarette case. With his thumb he sprang it open and offered the contents to her. She selected a cigarette and stuck it in her mouth while he lit her up, then himself, as he directed the Mercedes-Benz down the strip of asphalt at a hundred miles an hour with one hand on the wheel.

"I have a question for you, Hannah," he said.

"What's that?"

"If you're not *my* sweetheart, then whose sweetheart are you?"

Hannah turned her head to stare at the fields rushing past, the fertile Nile delta that spun outside the window. She thought of János, bending the Daimler around the hairpin curves of Capri. Her heart choked her. She couldn't breathe. She reached across the seat and pulled Lucien's shirt from the waistband of his trousers. He looked at her in shock, then back to the road, then down to her hand, unfastening his trousers. Back to the road while she eased his penis free from the layers of trouser and shirt.

He remained silent as she worked him with her mouth and tongue, except for these little sighs that escaped his lungs, almost of pain. The car roared happily along the road. When his balls tightened, he murmured, *Hannah, I'm going to come,* and pulled to the shoulder of the road. The car skidded to a stop in the gravel and he slid both hands into her hair and shouted her name.

What had surprised Hannah most, as she rode home from that first encounter at Shepheard's Hotel six weeks ago, was how little guilt she felt. Oh, there was *some* guilt, naturally. She wasn't inhuman. A pod of unease lay inside her conscience somewhere, small and humble as a peanut.

But the guilt was nothing compared to the exhilaration.

Three times she had committed adultery with Lucien Beck. First on the bed, amazed at her own audacity, at his nakedness, at the way they remained linked after the act of intercourse itself was over—Lucien lying against her breasts, inside her body, for so long that (in the daze of aftermath) she feared they might have died together at the instant of climax and were now bound for eternity. Then, returning to life, they'd fucked each other all around the room (the wall, the rug, the edge of the bed, the armchair, and so on), goaded each other into acts of shocking indecency, on and on, an orgy of two, until they were both sapped dry, sprawled on the bed, incapable of thought or movement. And finally—this was the exhilarating part, the evidence of kismet—after some rest and a tray of food from the kitchen, they could still summon the vigor for a quick, desperate, half-dressed farewell screw against the bedpost.

Hannah's legs ached, her head rang with fatigue, her womb brimmed over with what she had come for, and all she wanted was more.

When she'd stolen at last into the marital apartment, Alistair was still asleep. He had rolled onto his stomach in bed and the rising sun struck the back of his head, turning the silver hairs a brilliant rosy gold. She went back into the drawing room and rang up the Shepheard's Hotel switchboard. In a minute Lucien came on the line.

Hannah, he said. (Not a question.)

I'll be in the main salon this afternoon at teatime, she told him.

The Cecil Hotel reminded Hannah of a palace. Grand pediments and flourishes of stonework. Nearby, the sea beat against the esplanade. The air was gentle and smelled of brine. She stood by the swooping wheel well of the Mercedes-Benz as Lucien spoke to the porter about their luggage, and in her head there shimmered a grand house of pale stone, a green forest, a long gravel drive, a fountain with nymphs.

What do you think? (János's voice.)

It's like a dream. (Her voice.) *A fairy tale.*

(His laugh.) *Wait until the pipes freeze in winter.*

"Second thoughts?" said Lucien, at her shoulder.

She hooked her arm around his elbow. "Of course not."

Like any respectable couple, they crossed the grand marble lobby arm in arm. Hannah felt some irrational terror that someone would see them, some acquaintance, but who came to the great seaside hotels of Alexandria in December? Nobody she knew, and she knew so few people anyway. Lucien strolled confidently by her side, as if he did this all the time. Probably he did.

What had Mrs. Beverley told her? About Lucien and Helen Hill?

They were lovers. People say.

They reached the front desk and Lucien gave the clerk their names, Mr. and Mrs. Beck, checking in until Wednesday. On Friday Alistair returned from his conference in Rome, and Hannah wanted a little space between her dirty rendezvous with her lover and the arrival of her husband. To wash and to think.

When the clerk turned to select the key from the board behind him, Hannah said, "Are you sleeping with Helen Hill?"

He hesitated only an instant. "Not at present, no."

"Did you ever take her here?"

"Of course not."

"Good," she said.

The clerk stepped forward with the key. As Lucien reached to accept it, Hannah could have sworn he was smiling.

Inside the suite Lucien had reserved for them, a bottle of champagne chilled in a bucket and dinner lay piping under a pair of silver domes. They ate first, talked about German music, undressed piece by piece, bathed in the large tub. Lucien took his time making love to her. Afterward, he cradled her while they passed a cigarette back and forth.

"I think Alistair suspects something," she said.

"I shouldn't be surprised. You look unmistakably like a woman who's having an affair."

"When he left for Rome, he said he imagined I would amuse myself while he was gone."

Lucien laughed. "My God, the English. Does he know it's me?"

"Probably. He doesn't seem to care, however." She sucked on the cigarette and handed it back to him. "You've heard nothing more about Ismailia, have you?"

"No. Have you?"

"Not a word. As if it never happened. Nobody mentions it, not even Alistair. I wonder why."

"Bad form, I suppose."

She rolled onto his chest, belly to belly. "Or someone's found a way to keep things quiet."

"Me?"

"You have your secrets, don't you?" When he opened his mouth to reply, she laid her finger over his lips. "Don't tell me. There's no need. I would rather you said nothing than something that isn't true."

"And yet you lie to me all the time."

"Is that so?"

He reached to crush out the cigarette in the ashtray and gathered her hips in his hands. "You say to me, I'm not your sweetheart, Lucien. I don't give a damn about you, I only want a nice fuck from you, a baby from you."

"That's the truth."

He turned her on her back and slid into her. She sucked in her breath. "Tell me something," he said, in a voice that was halfway to a growl. "What happens when you get what you want from me? Do we stop meeting like this?"

Hannah groaned and wriggled her hips to work him deeper. She slung her arms around his neck and pulled him down to kiss him.

"What happens, Hannah? Do you go to this husband of yours and say, it's a miracle, my pet, you're going to be a father at last? Does he take you in his arms and thank God for giving him an heir?"

As he spoke, he thrust into her—long, imperative strokes that made her shout in the back of her throat. She raised her knees and dug her heels into the backs of his legs.

Lucien lifted himself on his palms. His face was dark and furious. "What about me, Hannah? Do I send you back to him, carrying my child, for him to raise as his own?"

Hannah reached to her sides and grabbed his wrists. Together they rolled like a pair of tigers, fighting and clawing. He flipped her onto her stomach. She reared up behind and he took her by the hips.

"This means nothing, does it?"

"Nothing!"

"Like animals? Mating?"

"Yes!" she said. *"Yes!"*

He pounded her without pity. When release delivered her, she collapsed, a limp doll. They sprawled in a hopeless tangle, panting. He pulled back her hair and bit her neck. *You love me,* he said. He was still inside her. She felt him softening, spent at last. His heart thundered against her spine. The sweat dried into a plaster that stuck her skin to his. His spread hand covered her belly.

She fell asleep thinking, *I would die for this.*

Hannah woke alone in the middle of the morning. The champagne and the supper had been cleared away; the curtains were shut tight, though a finger of vivid light betrayed the hour. On the nightstand lay a note. *Gone for a walk. Order breakfast. L*

She rose from the bed and walked on rubbery legs to the bathroom. It was white and modern, flooded with sunshine. From the window she glimpsed a corner of the sea. In the mirror she stared at her belly, her breasts. She cupped them with her hands. A little sore, a touch swollen. Had he noticed?

She ran the taps in the bathtub and washed herself thoroughly. When she'd dressed, she went downstairs to the restaurant and told the maître d' that her husband would be joining her shortly for breakfast. The waiter brought her some toast and a pot of fragrant coffee. She had just stirred in the sugar when a voice startled her.

"Why, Countess Vécsey!"

The spoon dropped from Hannah's fingers. She looked up, half rising from her chair. Her body had some idea she should flee.

A woman stood before the table—tall, slight, fashionably dressed. Short dark hair curled beneath a chic hat; an expression of shock and delight on her pale face, her red mouth. She continued in Hungarian, "But what are you doing here in Alexandria? Safe and sound? I thought you were dead!"

A movement caught Hannah's eye. She looked to the restaurant entrance, where Lucien Beck had just appeared, scanning the tables in search of her. The light gleamed on his hair.

"I'm sorry," she said to the woman standing before her. "I'm afraid you have mistaken me for somebody else."

"Tell me about this woman at breakfast," said Lucien. "The one you were speaking to when I arrived."

They were walking along the esplanade. To the left, a stiff north wind propelled the sea onto the rocks. A flock of gulls shrieked overhead.

"Just a woman who mistook me for somebody."

Lucien stopped and turned to lean his elbows on the railing. His eyes narrowed against the wind. "You said only truth between us, Hannah."

"But I told you—"

"You were both speaking Hungarian."

She stared at the brim of his gray hat, the clean line of his suit along his shoulder. "Where did you go walking this morning?" she asked him. "How do you find all this money for fancy hotels and champagne to shower on your mistress?"

He turned his head to smile at her. "*Are* you my mistress?"

"I respect your secrets, that's all. I don't ask questions. My dominion extends to your bed and no further."

"So who is this woman?" he asked again.

"Why do you care so much?"

"Because she upset you. Anything that upsets you concerns me."

Hannah sighed and joined him along the rail. "Her name is Irina Esterhazy. She was a friend of my husband's, before he met me. We were in Budapest together at the end of the war."

"And why did you pretend not to know her?"

"Because she's trouble. First she fought the fascists, then she fought the Soviets."

"A true Hungarian patriot, then?"

"Something like that. Do you have a cigarette?"

He lit one for her, then himself. "Now, then. To answer your questions, I went for a long walk this morning—along this very esplanade, in fact—in order to clear my head."

"Clear your head of what?"

He examined the end of his cigarette, as if he might find the words there. "Of you. As for the expense, why, I'm a frugal man. Most of my salary goes straight to the bank to brood by itself. Why not liberate a little of this savings to spend on my mistress? It's the least I can do for her."

"You're too sentimental, Lucien. One would think you'd never done this before."

"I have never done *this* before," he said.

"What do you mean, *this*? Whisk your lover away for the weekend? I find that hard to believe."

Lucien turned toward her and leaned his elbow on the railing, smoking pensively. "How does this end, Hannah?"

"How does any love affair end? Tell me, I'm curious to know."

"You don't give a damn for Ainsworth. Why remain married to him?"

"To give my child a name."

"What about *my* name?"

She laughed. "You can't be serious."

"Am I not rich enough for you? Not important enough?"

She stared at his strained face and swallowed back some pain that was gathering at the back of her throat.

"Exactly," she said. "I simply can't *imagine* divorcing my important husband for the assistant manager of Shepheard's Hotel."

Lucien took a last drag of his cigarette and tossed the stub on the wet rocks. "Tell me something else. What are they discussing in Rome, Hannah?"

"Why do you want to know?"

"Curiosity. Your husband is a personal friend of Eden, isn't that right? He must be privy to some interesting knowledge."

"Do you want me to find out for you?"

"Would you do such a thing?"

She shrugged. "It's the least I can do for my lover. Why shouldn't you Egyptians have your country to yourself?"

"Indeed," he said.

They looked at each other, an exchange of confidence. The cigarette scorched quietly between Hannah's fingers. She thought her heart might shatter her chest.

Lucien lifted his arm and caressed the ridge of her cheekbone with his thumb. "I want you to meet someone," he said.

The apartment was spacious and shabby, on the third floor of a building that wore the dignified air of former grandeur. It was like an apartment you might find in Vienna before the war, Hannah thought, or maybe Paris. A dark-haired woman answered the door and led them through an entrance hall tiled in chipped mosaic to a sitting room where a woman of about fifty sat at a desk near the window, writing on a piece of paper with a fountain pen of black enamel. When she looked up and saw them, her face lifted. She laid down the pen, rose from the chair, and held out both hands.

"Lucien," she said in French, "what a happy surprise."

He took her hands and kissed each cheek. "Mama. How are you feeling?"

"Better, better. The cough is almost gone. But you've brought a guest."

"Yes, Mama." He turned to Hannah and beckoned her closer. "I want to introduce to you a friend of mine. Mrs. Ainsworth."

Lucien's mother extended a spidery hand. "Mrs. Ainsworth. I am enchanted to make your acquaintance."

"And I yours," said Hannah.

A fragile, delicate beauty still clung to her. Her dark hair was shot with silver, cut short to curl around her ears; her eyes were an intriguing green, a little darker than Lucien's, large and hooded. They fixed on Hannah's face with sharp curiosity.

"May I offer you some tea, perhaps?" she asked.

Over tea and marzipan, Madame Suarez (this was the name she gave to Hannah) was frank. "I fell desperately in love at a rash age," she said, shrugging her shoulders in a way that reminded Hannah of a Frenchwoman she had once known, as if to say, *What else can one do, when one falls desperately in love?* "I don't recommend it, except that I had this beautiful boy." She nodded to Lucien.

"What about your family?" asked Hannah. "What did your parents think?"

"My parents disowned me, naturally. A married Swiss, twenty years older than me! I was only just out of school. I was supposed to make a respectable match. Well, I wasn't especially pleased with the respectable match they found for me."

"An arranged marriage? I thought that kind of thing belonged to another age."

Madame Suarez glanced at Lucien and smiled. "My family belonged to a certain tradition. To marry outside this tradition—to have a child outside this tradition—to them, it was the same as if you had died."

"I think Mr. Beck acted badly," said Hannah. "To take advantage of a sheltered girl, when he was already married."

Madame Suarez shrugged this away too. "His marriage was not a happy one. And he took good care of us. Didn't he, my dear? He provided generously. Saw to the children's education."

Hannah looked at Lucien, who nodded toward a framed photograph on the lamp table next to his shoulder.

"My sister," he said. "She lives abroad with her husband and children."

Madame Suarez brushed the crumbs from her lap. "So you see, it has all worked out in the end."

"Are you furious with me?" Lucien asked.

They were walking back to the hotel. The sky had cleared and the Mediterranean sun soaked them with an unexpected warmth.

"It was an infamous ambush," she said, "but a pleasant afternoon nonetheless. I like your mother."

"So do I."

"Did she ever reconcile with her family?"

"I'm afraid not. I understand they don't speak her name, even now."

"Do you mean to say you've never met them?"

"Never." He took her hand. "Her people came to Egypt from Spain, in the sixteenth century. Forced out by the Inquisition."

Hannah stopped and turned to him. "They were heretics?"

"You might say that."

The realization hit her like a blow to the head. "They were Jews."

"Yes. Are you shocked?"

"You never hinted."

"It's not something you go about proclaiming, these days," he said. "Only to people you trust."

"I see."

"Does it matter to you?"

He was studying her now. His brows were drawn over the bridge of his nose, his eyes worried.

"It doesn't matter to me at all," she said.

Lucien captured her hand and kissed it, then he bent to kiss her mouth. His lips were warm and gentle; his tongue tasted of tea. When he lifted his head, his green eyes caressed her. He tugged at her hand. "Come along. Let's return to the hotel."

On the road back to Cairo, two days later, Lucien drove at a stately pace. Hannah curled on the seat and burrowed into his side. From time to time, she dozed. The smell of Lucien's clothes made her drowsy; his fingers idled in her hair.

"What are you thinking, sweetheart?" he asked, above the purr of the engine.

"Nothing," she said. Then—"What a brute you are."

Lucien leaned down and kissed the top of her head.

About a mile from home, he pulled to the side of the road and eased her up to a sitting position. "Time to get in back," he said. That was how she had climbed into the car three days ago, when he'd stopped outside the apartment building—into the back seat, as if he were her chauffeur.

It was dark and the car sat in the void between two streetlights. She saw his brow, the ink of his hair, a tiny dot of reflected light where his right eye should be. She wanted to say, *Take me somewhere else, anywhere else, just take me!* Or else, *Come inside with me instead, Alistair won't be back until tomorrow.*

Or—*I believe I'm carrying your child, let's run away together.*

"Kiss me goodbye, then," she told him.

Obediently he leaned forward and kissed her.

"You'll speak to your husband, remember? About Rome."

"Ah, that."

"If you'd rather not—"

"Don't worry, you'll have what you need."

"It might be dangerous. If he figures out what you're doing."

"I have a pistol."

"You would shoot a man? Your husband?"

She shrugged. "If I had to."

He searched her face through the dark air and cupped her cheek. "When did you learn to shoot a gun, Hannah?"

"There was a war, Lucien. Everybody knew how to shoot a gun."

"Did you ever fire one? Kill a man?"

The words were so gentle, innocent almost. Picking at the seams of her memory. *Kill a man.* She wanted to laugh, she wanted to weep. She took his hand and drew it away.

"Yes," she said. "I have killed men before."

* * *

One morning in the winter of 1941, János came to find Hannah in the study, where she played with little Míklos on the rug before the fire. He was dressed for the outdoors in an old wool jacket and tall leather boots. Míklos shrieked with delight at the sight of his father and scrambled to his feet, arms straining upward. János swept him high in the air and loudly kissed his stomach and each pink cheek. Míklos clung to him like a bug. János met Hannah's gaze over the shoulder of their son.

"Let's go for a walk," he said.

Hannah looked at her old nanny, Sofia, who had raised her after her mother died and who now sat on the sofa with her sewing basket. She had come to the country with them to help with the new baby, due any day. "Go ahead," she said to Hannah. "I'll watch Miko. You two could use some fresh air."

Outside, the weather had finally cleared after a blizzard of two days, and the air was so clear and cold it hurt her lungs when she drew it in. They tramped silently across the meadow toward the narrow strip of woods that rimmed the hayfields. János carried a shotgun in the crook of his arm; across his back hung a rucksack of old green canvas. As they wallowed through the snowdrifts, he caught her elbow from time to time to make sure she had her footing. The clouds of her breath sometimes mingled with the clouds of his breath.

When they reached the woods, János stopped and offered her a drink from a flask that turned out to be coffee, still hot. "Hannah," he said, "have you ever fired a gun?"

"No, never."

"You should learn."

He fixed his eyes on hers when he said this. His cheeks were red; his nose was red. He had rested one boot on a fallen log, and the shotgun in the crook of his arm looked as if it had grown there like another limb.

"Because of the war, you mean," she said. "Because Hungary has joined the Axis."

"Yes," he said.

They spent the rest of the morning in the hayfield, where János taught her the fundamentals of cleaning and loading the shotgun, then how to aim and shoot a target. At first he stood behind her and showed her how to hold the weapon—one hand on her right arm and one hand on her left, instructions murmured into the well of her ear. Once she got the hang of things, he stood back and let her fend for herself. After about an hour he nodded with satisfaction and propped the shotgun against a tree.

"Now we will try the pistol," he said, drawing it from his rucksack.

On the way home, they trudged more slowly. The estate had come to János from his grandmother, who'd died the previous year, and the main house dated back some three hundred years. Sofia complained about the shabby furnishings and primordial plumbing, the miles of road between the family and any neighbors, but Hannah didn't mind. White-gray smoke curled from two of the several chimneys. János paused to light a cigarette.

"Do you want to go to war?" she asked him.

He sucked on the cigarette. "It doesn't matter if I do or not. I don't have a choice."

"What about Hungary? Don't you want to fight for our country?"

"To defend my country, yes. But we are not under attack, are we?"

"We're afraid of Germany," she said. "They say jump, and we jump."

"You'd have the nerve to stand up to the Nazis?"

"If I had to," she said passionately.

János's breath emptied his lungs as he labored through the snow. "Yes," he said, after a moment, "I believe you would."

"Besides, this makes us the enemies of the Soviets."

"Yes, that's the trouble, isn't it? Stuck between the two tyrants. Between the rock of fascism and the hard place of communism. A man is seldom lucky enough to fight for what he believes in. He just fights to stay alive." János stopped and turned to her. He had grown a beard over the Christmas season and his brown eyes stood out from this frame of bristling dark hair and pale skin, a little bloodshot at the corners. He took the cigarette from his mouth. "Listen to me, Hannah. You know why I've taken you out here this day, don't you? When you're so big with child?"

"To learn to shoot a gun."

"To defend yourself. I'm going to have to leave, to fight, and I can't fight a war if I'm worrying about you and the children. I'm counting on you, Hannah. You understand what I mean?"

"Yes."

He nodded. "Good, then."

Together they turned back toward the house and tramped on through the snow. When they reached the kitchen door, Hannah realized that the occasional cramps she had been feeling since the morning had turned hard and fierce. She turned to János and told him he had better telephone the doctor, and by nightfall little Léna had burst into the world—a tiny, exquisite daughter, a perfect fit for the crook of her father's arm.

When Hannah arrived at the front door of her apartment, she discovered it was already unlocked. She walked into the drawing room and set down her suitcase. Alistair rose from the sofa and waved away the curtain of cigarette smoke.

"Hello, darling," he said. "Had a nice trip?"

She took off her right glove, then her left. "Quite nice. You're home early."

"Wasn't feeling at all well. Flew home this morning."

"Oh, dear. Nothing serious, I hope? Have you seen a doctor?"

He raised a glass. "Doctor Scotch. Can I pour you a gin and tonic? You look rather wrecked."

"I *am* rather wrecked, to say the truth. The weather was impossible. It's not the time of year for Alexandria." She watched him bustle about the liquor cabinet. "I did walk along the sea, which was lovely. Bracing. Thank you."

He handed her the gin and tonic and lit a cigarette for her. Together they sat on the sofa. She took a long drink of gin and put her hand on his knee.

"Tell me all about Rome, darling," she said.

The funny thing was, as he grunted away on top of her an hour or so later—*Almost, almost, blast it all, hang on, hang on, blast it, almost got it, almost got it*—she didn't mind. She really didn't. She'd drunk two gin and tonics on an empty stomach; she could do anything. She shut her eyes tight and imagined Lucien—no, it was János—no, it was Lucien, Scotch and cigarettes, and her belly tightened, her nerves gushed. She lifted her knees and dug her heels into the backs of his legs. She arched her back and tilted her hips until she met his determined shoving along the exact nexus she required—*hang on, hang on, blast it all, almost, almost*—and worked and worked until finally she climaxed in floods of relief—*Fuck! Fuck! FUCK!*—and so did he.

Then he fell on her chest, so heavy she couldn't breathe, so senseless she thought for an instant he might be dead. Inside, she felt him shrivel and slip free. She pushed at his shoulders until he groaned and rolled away snoring. For a moment or two she stared at his sagging chest, his soft paunch, the damp, timid penis that languished on the sparse hair at his pubis.

She rose to retrieve her pocketbook from the living room and rooted inside for her cigarettes. Her fingers discovered the squashed cardboard box and the lighter and something else. A piece of paper, folded over twice into a square.

She unfolded it and held it to the light from the window.

For Hungary
111 rue de l'Athénée, Genève

CHAPTER FIFTEEN

Mallory

August 2008
Winthrop Island, New York

I insisted on driving back home. Monk sat in the passenger seat with the steak in his hand. I told him to put it back to his jaw and he obeyed me for about a minute.

The fight hadn't lasted long. The one punch. Monk had stepped in front of me and Barbara and blocked the next one with his forearm, then Mike had jumped over the bar—no stranger to breaking up brawls, I guess—and dragged Dillon out the door.

Cue a few moments of hysteria as the groupies tumbled over to see what was going on, to fuss over Monk until Mike (returning from evicting Dillon) hustled the three of us out through the kitchen, where he found a steak in the freezer for Monk's jaw.

"Well, that was exciting," Barbara said, as I aimed Bessie carefully up West Cliff Road. "We hardly ever get fistfights at the Club."

"Are you sure you're all right?" I asked Monk.

"Fine," he said. "I took worse at lacrosse practice."

"I don't know what got into Dillon. He takes *spiders* outside to set them free."

Barbara leaned forward over Monk's shoulder. "Make sure you save that steak in the icebox when you're done with it."

"This?" He held up the steak. "Come on, Bar. Look at this crap. Leather'd grill better."

"Do you remember that time your grandfather brought those nice rib eyes back from the Costco in Providence—"

"You guys buy your meat from *Costco*?"

"My dear," said Aunt Barbara, "*everyone* on the island buys his meat from Costco."

"The older the money, the cheaper the skate," said Monk.

"Anyway," Aunt Barbara said, "he locked poor Sadie in the house—"

"Who's Sadie?"

"Our dog," said Monk. "Grandpa used to keep kind of a rotating lineup of black Lab bitches. When one started getting on in years, he'd get a new puppy. Older dog'd show her the ropes."

Aunt Barbara rapped him on the shoulder with the back of her hand. "Do you mind if I get on with the story, young man?"

"Sorry. Proceed."

"Well, we were all out on the terrace sipping our drinks and *some*body left a door open—I won't say who—"

"Was it you?" I asked Monk.

"Maybe."

"—*some*body left a door open and Sadie slipped out, naturally. Gobbled down every one of those damned steaks and then—adding insult to injury—the poor bitch vomited them back up all over the lawn. Pa was furious. Do you remember that, darling?"

"Never knew Grandpa could swear like that," Monk said. "Damn creative piece of work."

I parked Bessie carefully under the shelter of the porte cochere. Monk helped Aunt Barbara into the house and walked me back to Seagrapes. We didn't say a word. When we reached the glow of the porch light I tried to get Monk to let me look at his jaw, but he turned his face away and said he was fine. Kissed me goodbye and headed back next door, hands in his pockets, guitar case slung across his back, as if nothing had happened.

By now it was almost midnight. I tried not to make a sound, but Mr. Adams called out from the sunroom, where he was nursing a drink. Not his first, from the look of it. He stood by the french doors, staring out to the sea you couldn't see. From the back, he might have been Monk. Same shape to his shoulders, same height, same stance. A little more stoop, maybe. But he *was* closing in on sixty.

He turned and waved me to a chair. "Can I get you something to drink?"

"No, thanks." I considered. "I'll just get myself a glass of water from the kitchen, if you don't mind."

"Please."

I swallowed down one glassful from the sink—the Seagrapes refrigerator was about forty years old, before they heard of water dispensers—and refilled it before I returned to the sunroom, which was now empty.

"On the terrace," called a voice through the open door.

I carried my glass outside, where Mr. Adams sat on one of the wicker chairs, rolling a joint.

"My wife won't let me smoke indoors," he said. "Sit."

I perched on the edge of the wicker sofa and sipped some water. "What's up?" I asked.

He lit the end of the joint and offered it to me. "I insist this time. You look as if you need it."

"Funny, that's the second time someone's said that to me this evening."

"Then maybe you should take the advice."

I stared at the glowing end of the joint and reached to take it from him. I tried to draw shallow but the effect was immediate.

"I've been buying from the same fellow for years," said Mr. Adams. "Never let me down."

I gave him back the joint. "Did you want to discuss something with me?"

"My wife wants me to fire you," he said.

"Fire me? For what?"

He brushed at his leg. He wore pajamas under a dressing gown, slippers on his feet. Like a page from the Lands' End men's catalog, except he was smoking a reefer instead of a pipe. "I don't know how to put this. I understand from Becca that you and Monk—that you've undertaken a—well, let's call it a romantic relationship," he said.

"With all respect, Mr. Adams, my private life is my own business."

"He's my son, Mallory."

"Then maybe you should speak with him instead?"

"I've left a message."

"Good, then." I started to rise.

"Don't run off, Mallory. I'm not here to judge, believe me. Why shouldn't the two of you enjoy yourselves, while you're here? Perfectly natural. That's what I told Becca, anyway." He held out the joint.

I took another hit and handed it back. "And?"

"Mallory. I want to be candid with you. I want us to be friends, here. On the same team."

"Of course."

"Monk is . . . well, he's remarkable. I knew that from the beginning, when he was just an infant. Rare, gifted. A natural leader. Born to do great things. You saw it at school, I'm sure. Everyone saw it." He finished the joint and crushed it out into the water tray beneath the geranium pot. "This business about Harvard. Stubborn idiot. He should've gone, you know. What's Harvard for, if not to prime a boy like that for greatness? For Christ's sake. I wanted to shake some sense into him. Still do. But he won't listen to *me,* will he?"

I started to speak, but Mr. Adams held up his hand.

"You, though. He likes *you.* I've seen the way he looks at you. Not that I blame him. I think he's got a pretty good eye, if you don't mind an old geezer telling you that."

"Of course not. Um, thank you, Mr. Adams." The weed was making everything seem better. Not so serious.

Mr. Adams sat down to roll another joint. "I mean it, Mallory. I like you very much. Best nanny we've had around here. You're smart, you're pretty, you teach them how to draw. Do you know what I told my wife? She wanted to fire you? Called you all kinds of names? I told Becca to mind her own business and let you continue doing what you do so well."

He lit up the end of the joint and motioned in my direction. I shook my head. He shrugged and took a drag himself.

"Your mother raised you on her own, isn't that right?" he asked.

"Pretty much. My dad left when I was eight."

"I was on the board at Nobles for a time. I remember you well, in fact. Had my eye on you. You were unusual. Not the kind of girl we typically see there."

"No," I said. "I wasn't."

"And you've always had a talent for art."

"I don't know about talent. I've always had a passion for it."

"Well, it's remarkable, what you've been able to accomplish. Given the circumstances. Really remarkable. I hope you don't mind, but I've taken the liberty of showing some of your work to a few of my colleagues at the Gardiner museum. You know the Gardiner, of course. The Isabella Gardiner museum."

"I know the Gardiner. Obviously."

"At my suggestion, one of the board members has referred your portfolio to our scholarship committee. I don't know if you're aware, but we offer a number of fellowships annually to promising young artists."

"Wow. That's . . . I don't know what to say."

"It's become a mission of mine. After watching so many talented female artists get passed over for grants and gallery shows by arrogant sons of bitches like me, who think we know so goddamn much about art. I woke up one day and decided it was time to act. Started pushing this at board level, really getting out there to support women artists. Encourage them to dream big. And you're a perfect example. If you really want to be serious about your work, you shouldn't be at RISD, Mallory. It's a fine school, obviously, but a real artist needs to study at the conservatory level."

"I'm—wow, I'm—that's a lot to take in, actually."

He leaned forward and gave my knee a friendly pat. "I want you to think of me like a godfather, Mallory. When I think of the advantages my own children have been able to enjoy, compared to how you've had to forge your own path. At every step. Without anyone to fight in your corner. A father, I mean."

"My mom's always been pretty supportive."

"Yes, but a kid needs a father too." He smiled, stubbed out the rest of the joint, patted his own knees, and rose from the chair. "Anyway, I'm off to bed. Switch off the lights before you turn in, won't you?"

I sat there for a few minutes after he left, staring across the water. The quarter moon had already set and the sea was black, almost invisible except as a void between the twinkling lights of Orient Point and the outline of the shore before me. I thought about this one time I shared a joint with Dillon. We were sitting on his sofa, I remembered, passing the joint back and forth, and he'd told me that he was named after Bob Dylan.

I'd turned this over in my head. *Are you sure it wasn't Matt Dillon?* I ventured.

I still remembered the way his eyes had screwed up with concentration. *Yeah,* he'd said, after a while. *Maybe it was Matt Dillon.*

To the left, through the gaps in the shrub that separated Seagrapes from the Monk property, I glimpsed a light. Not the main house, but the guesthouse where Monk sometimes went to work on his music, after everyone was asleep.

I finished the water and took the glass into the kitchen. Turned out the lights and slipped out the mudroom door, taking care to leave the knob unlocked behind me.

Not that people ever really locked their doors on Winthrop Island.

Instead of going to bed, it seemed, Monk had gone to the guesthouse. Had taken out his guitar and plucked out some music. I could see him through the window, head bent to watch his own fingers.

I rapped on the glass. He looked up in surprise. I guess he couldn't make me out very well in the darkness, because a few seconds passed before his face relaxed and he motioned me inside. I went around the corner to the door. As I reached for the knob, he opened it.

"Hey," I said. "Couldn't sleep?"

He sniffed. "Are you *stoned,* Pinks?"

"*No,* I am not *stoned,* Monkfish. Your dad was outside rolling joints. I took a couple of hits to be polite."

He raised his eyebrows. "Ah."

"Are you going to invite me in?"

Monk stepped back with a flourish. As the light fell on his jaw, I bit back a gasp. He touched it with his finger and grinned—at least, grinned with the half of his face that wasn't swollen to the size of a baseball.

"That bad?" he said.

"I feel terrible."

"Don't. Seriously. It's nothing. Can't blame him, right?"

"What? Yes, you *can*!"

He shrugged and closed the door behind me. "Stole his girl."

"You didn't *steal* me, Monk. I'm not a *possession.*"

Monk walked back to the sofa and picked up his guitar. "I'm just saying that if you broke up with me and I had to sit around my cubicle at Dunkin' Donuts imagining some asshole having sex with you all summer, then yeah, I'd want to walk into a bar and hit said asshole too. Sorry if that sounds a little primal. Men are Neanderthals, what can I say."

I propped myself on the sofa arm and watched his hands as he picked a gentle melody. The guesthouse was authentic midcentury modern, by which I mean it hadn't been touched since it was built around 1960. All angles and lines, a single studio room with a kitchenette and living area and bed, where Monk and I had slept together for the first time over a month ago. I folded my arms. "You say that like I didn't have to witness a literal parade of girlfriends through your bed in high school."

"A *parade*? Come on. Like who?"

"Like Soccer Sophie."

"Soccer Sophie? You mean Sophie *Sadler*?" He laughed and changed key. "For the record, I didn't have sex with Sophie Sadler. What were we, fourteen? Fifteen?"

"You had at least two other serious girlfriends. Junior and senior year. Like Julia Cooper? Playing opposite you in *Guys and Dolls,* senior year? She was Sarah?"

"Oh, shit. Julia Cooper, that's right."

"Monk, I painted all the sets. I literally saw you two hiding out backstage during rehearsal, eating each other's faces."

He grinned. "Sorry about that. Method acting."

"Stop it. I cried for *days.*"

"Hey, Julia came on to *me*. I was just being a gentleman." He strummed a few notes, which I recognized as a variation on the main theme in *"Winter Tale."* Glanced at me sideways. "And I'm just offering it up that I might, somewhere in my immature, juvenile teenage brain, have been trying to get a certain crush of mine to maybe notice I was good for something more than cracking one-liners during AP Lit."

"Oh, *seriously*? You made out with Julia Cooper to make me *jealous*."

"Just offering it up."

"Come on. You two were into each other for months. You went to prom together, remember?"

"All right, fine. I admit I didn't leave high school a virgin. Who does?"

"I don't know. Me?"

He looked up. "You? What about Max Whatshisname? Math Max."

"Lathrop. Max Lathrop. I dated him for about five minutes and no, we didn't have sex. For the record, Your Honor, I was officially a virgin until spring semester of freshman year. *College,* to be clear."

"No way."

"Yeah way."

He looked back down at his fingers, plucking the guitar strings. "So who was the lucky guy? Dillon?"

"Dillon came later. Just this guy I met. We pretended to be madly in love. The problem was that we were both virgins. So it wasn't the greatest situation."

"Like, how?"

"Like, I don't know. We went to this hotel in Boston to make it *special.*" I put quote marks around the word. "He wanted me to go on top. And I was like, fine, whatever turns you on, but it turns out being on top is kind of a challenging position for a girl's first time. Because, you know, you're doing all the work, right? So I'm trying to get him in and it hurts like hell and he just *comes,* right? Comes like a truck before he's even all the way inside. I'm like, crying in pain. He's howling with pleasure. *Oh my God, Mallory, that was uh-maze-ing.* And I'm just, what the *actual fuck.* Where is my romance-novel version of this? Your first time is supposed to be this—I don't know—this *transcendent experience,* when your lover expertly initiates you into womanhood, and I'm lying there wondering if I'd actually had sex or not. I mean, I honestly wasn't sure until I saw the blood the next day. I was just . . . I was just . . . *crushed* . . . and—and *mad,* right? I mean, you only get one first time and . . . I'm sorry. I'm so sorry, I didn't mean to . . . to just *unload* with all that . . ."

Somewhere in the middle of this, Monk laid down the guitar and pulled me into his lap. "And then what?" he said, stroking my hair.

I waited until I had my breathing back under control. "And then I was so pissed I ghosted the poor guy."

"Goddess."

"And pretty much avoided dating anyone for, like, a year."

"Honey," he said. "Pinks, I'm so sorry. I had no idea."

"It's not a story I go around and regale at parties, believe it or not."

"No," he said. "You wouldn't. But I'm glad you told *me.*"

I sat up. "I'm okay. Really. It was a while ago. I'm over it."

"You shouldn't be over it. It's literally one of the shittiest things I ever heard. I want to punch this guy. I want to . . . I don't know." He urged my head into the hollow of his shoulder. "I guess I just want to go back in time and make it right for you. Make it better."

"He wasn't that bad a person, really. Kind of a romantic. He was just clueless."

"He wasn't clueless, Pinks. He was selfish. He made it all about him. His little personal fantasy of having sex with a hot girl."

"To top it all off," I said, "his credit card was declined. So I ended up paying for the damn room. And breakfast."

"You're kidding, right?"

"He was like, *That's so weird, I thought I paid the minimum last month.*"

Monk's chest heaved.

"Are you *laughing*? Tell me you are not *laughing,* Monk Adams."

"I'm—what?—*no,* of course not. I'm not *laughing.* I'm just—oh Jesus, what a fucking *tool.* I mean, I was all wrong. That is one hundred percent *the* shittiest thing I ever heard. It's not even close."

"And then we got mugged on the way back to campus."

"*What?*"

"Kidding." I turned to straddle him. With my fingertips I brushed the baseball under the skin of his jaw. He winced one eye, a flicker.

"Pinks," he said. "Mallory. I really am so sorry. I'm gutted for you. You deserved so much better."

I bent to softly kiss him.

"Make it right for me, then," I said. "Make it better."

The windows of the guesthouse did not have curtains, for some reason, so I woke up as soon as dawn struck the eastern horizon. Monk sprawled on his stomach next to me. I turned on my side, curled my knees to my stomach, and watched the steady rise and fall of his back, the slopes and shadows of skin, the tangle of hair, the lump on his jaw, until his head stirred. His eyes started to open, he winced, they opened the rest of the way, and he fell on me.

"Hey," he said. "What time is it?"

"Time for me to get on my horse and ride back to the home-stead."

He closed his eye and threw an arm over me. "Stay."

"Can't stay. Sun's coming up. Gotta do the walk of shame before anyone sees me."

"Don't go. Take the day off."

"My day off is Monday."

"So? Call in sick. Let Becca take care of her own damn kids for once."

"I'm a working girl, honey. We don't call in sick for work. Even when we *are* sick."

Monk hunted all over my face for something. He pulled his arm free from the sheet and cradled my cheek with his hand.

"What's wrong?"

"It hurts, Pink. Like a pain in my chest, like it's too much to hold. Like I'm going to lose you."

"You're not going to lose me."

"Stay, Mallory. Another hour. Come on."

"You know I can't stay. So try to stop looking so adorable and help me find my shameful clothes."

We walked across the lawn in the pink light. The air was cooler than yesterday and the dew clung to the grass. From the left came the sleepy beat of the ocean. When we reached the porch, Monk drew me up for a kiss. It was a brief kiss and when he lifted his head he stared at my face, one hand cupping the back of my head.

"Tell me something, Pinks," he said. "What's your last day here? Working for Dad and Becca, I mean."

"The fifteenth? I think that's what we arranged."

"That's what I thought. A week from today, right? So, then what?"

"Well, school starts at the end of the month. So, you know. Get my life back in order. Hang out with my mom for a bit. Paige is in Singapore right now, so . . ." I shrugged a shoulder.

"Yeah, you told me. Working for some bank." His hand fell away from my hair. "I'd like to meet Paige."

"She'll be home at Christmas, I think. So maybe . . . you know, winter break . . ."

My voice faded out. Monk put his hands in his pockets and looked away, toward the sea. He started to speak, cleared his throat, tried again.

"Mallory, the thing is . . ."

I lifted my hand and laid it on his chest, over his heart. "I know. It sucks. I've been trying not to think about it."

"Me too." He reached up to gather my hand under his palm. "But when I do think about it, when I think about driving you down to that fucking ferry and watching you sail away, when I think about heading back to college, like nothing happened, everything back to the way it was, I just . . . it's going to kill me, Pinks. Like the sun's gone out. Winter all the way through." He gathered me close and spoke into my hair while my heart thundered. "This summer with you, Mallory. The way you love me, the way you *see* me, the way you show me how to see *myself*? It's like finally I know for sure, for dead certain, what I was put on this earth for. And I'm just supposed to walk away from that?"

"I know. It's been killing me too," I said.

"There's no way to go back, Mallory. No way I could live without this. Without you."

His chin rested on top of my head. Over the crest of his shoulder I saw the rising sun, the streaks of dawn. I thought, *Don't forget this. Don't ever forget a single detail of this.*

"Sorry if that's a lot to take in," he said. "I don't want to freak you out. But it's true. It's just true. I can't play it cool any longer. I'm sorry."

"You don't have to play it cool with me, ever. Just say what you feel. I won't freak out."

"You should. If you knew how much . . . God, if I could even find the *words*. Just touching you. Your heartbeat, Pinks, your breath. Your hair. Your skin. Your shoulders and ears, they're so fucking beautiful to me. It freaks *me* out."

I lifted my head to look at him. The bruise on his jaw jarred me. I drew the pad of my thumb over the swelling. "Are you sure it's not broken?"

"Nah. If it were broken I couldn't move it. Don't worry, I'm good. We'll just turn the lights off. Problem solved."

"Does it hurt? When I touch it like this?"

"Trust me, Pinko, *nothing* hurts when you touch it like that."

I sank my cheek back into the cozy hollow where his shoulder met his breastbone. "Are we crazy, though?"

"Crazy how?"

"I mean, how can this be real? We've only been together a few weeks."

"I don't think that's true at all," he said. "We've been *sleeping* together for a few weeks, sure. Which has been amazing, don't get me wrong. Best month of my entire life. But we've been *together* for years. All the way back to high school. Do you remember the first time we talked? In the dorm, after your mom dropped you off?"

"Of course I remember."

"This new girl with the crazy hair and the green eyes that saw through everything. Kept trying to find an excuse to talk to you and losing my nerve. I mean, I'm just some shallow preppy asshole, right? Why would she waste her time? And then it was October, I remember it like a movie, Dad dropping me off Sunday night, I hear this voice calling out. Your mom."

"Literally the most embarrassing moment of my life."

He laughed softly. "I was like, *finally*. This is it, Adams. Don't fuck this up. And it was the greatest. Talking to you. For hours, like we already knew each other. Remember that? How it felt? Because that's love. To me. That's what love is. And this physical thing we have, this insane *combustion* that happens with us, the bonfire last night? It's *because* of that. Because the connection goes right down to the bones of us. Am I making any sense? Do you get what I mean?"

I looked back up. "Monk. Wait a second. What's all this about? Are you worried about me *leaving*? You think I'm just going to walk away next week and that's it?"

"No, of course not. I just—"

"Because I need you to know—I'm sorry, I'm not good at this, I don't have all the words like you do. I draw, that's my language. But what I *feel* . . . Monk, even *thinking* about leaving you, being apart from you, it's so bleak, it's like . . . it's like . . . So I tell myself . . . I remember it's just for a couple of months, right? We'll have breaks. Weekends. And it'll be May again before we know it. Graduation. So you don't need to worry. No matter how far apart we are. You understand that, right?"

He stroked my hair a few times, like he was gathering his thoughts. "Listen, Pinks," he said. "I was thinking about all this last night, after you fell asleep. And I was thinking, next week? We don't *have* to go our separate ways, do we? Not right away. We could maybe go somewhere together."

"You mean like a vacation?"

"Sure, a vacation. Take a break from all this noise. Just the two of us, for once. You and me, hit the road, see the sights. Bessie'll take us wherever we want to go."

"Until school starts?"

"Right, until school starts. What do you think?"

"I think that sounds . . ." I choked back an unexpected flood of relief, of joy, of sunshine. I thought I might float to the sky if Monk weren't holding me so close. "I think that sounds amazing."

"No more sneaking around. Fall asleep together, wake up together. Make out on top of a mountain somewhere and figure everything out. Where we go from here."

"I'm in," I said. "Oh my God. *Totally* in."

"Seriously? That's a yes?"

"Of *course* it's a yes! What did you *think* I'd say?"

He pulled back and held me by the shoulders. Looked into my

eyes, grinning. "Jesus, you're the best. You know that? You're so *game,* Pinks. You're fearless."

I laughed. "Two weeks road-tripping with you? What's not to love about *that*? I mean, you had me at making out on a mountain-top."

"You don't need to worry about anything. I have a little money my grandfather left me last year. Plus what I've earned this summer. Not a ton, but we'll be able to get around okay. No sketchy motels, I promise."

"What are you talking about? The sketchier the better."

Monk lifted me up and swung me in a circle. "You're my dream girl, you know that? You're not even real."

"And you haven't even *seen* me wash underwear in a sink."

"Tell you what," he said, "the laundromat is on me."

"Shallow preppy asshole. I bet you've never even gone camping."

He cupped my face with his hands. His expression turned serious. "Mallory, listen. I want to speak to your mom before we go. I think that's the right thing to do. And my dad, I guess. He'll hit the roof, but fuck him."

"Really? You think he'll be mad? It's just a road trip."

"Nothing's just anything to Dad. But don't worry, I'll handle him. I'll make it happen." Monk leaned his forehead against mine. Already the sky was lighter, the morning had come. The new sun glowed around the edges of his ears. "One week. How does that sound?"

"One week. Got it."

"One week from this moment, right here. August fifteenth, we pack up Bessie and blow this joint." He pulled apart from me and held out his little finger. "Pinkie promise, right?"

I curled my little finger around his. I remember thinking how strong he felt, his musician's finger. How this finger would do great things.

"Pinkie promise," I said.

CHAPTER SIXTEEN

Mallory

July 2022
County Galway, Ireland

Paige pokes her head inside the rental car and turns her head to address the agent, a nice-looking lad with thick dark hair and a thick dark beard and eyes the color of this morning's sky before the airplane descended into the drizzle. I hear my grandmother's voice in my head—*Black Irish*.

"But it's a stick shift," she says. "I requested an automatic transmission."

To his credit, the agent maintains his professional face. "I'm afraid we won't be having any automatic cars left on the lot, miss. Are ye not trained to drive a manual transmission?"

"Well, yeah. I mean, in high school. Once."

"I'll drive," I say. "Just tell me where to point the nose."

"Where the hell did you learn how to drive a stick?" Paige wants to know.

"That summer I spent with Dad out at Ruidoso."

"You were, like, thirteen."

"It was New Mexico. And he was drunk." I keep looking for the rearview mirror in the wrong spot. It was a little hairy getting out of the rental lot onto the motorway, what with all the other cars traveling down the wrong side of the road, but here we are, intact, flying north toward this village with the unpronounceable Gaelic name where our mother was born.

Paige scrolls her phone. "You know, I'm dreading the day when your guardian angel goes on strike to protest the inhumane working conditions."

"Paige, will you quit with the phone? Unplug. We're on a girls' trip. Everyone's fine. My kid has literal renal failure and he's staying with a childless musician who's known him for five minutes, and do you see me checking for messages?"

She sighs and slips the phone into her bag. "He's not childless, Mallie. He's Sam's dad."

"I was referring to his work experience. You did bring the adoption certificate, right?"

"Oh my God, Mallie, I forgot the adoption certificate! I'm such a screwup."

"Fuck you, Paige. At least I can drive a stick shift."

Paige looks out the window at the wet green landscape rolling past, dotted with miserable white sheep. "I swear to God, if those nuns give us any trouble."

"Hey," I say gently. "What's up?"

"Me? Nothing."

"Me? Nothing," I sing back to her.

She reaches reflexively for her phone, then pulls back. Dips into her handbag again and pulls out a tube of lip gloss. She unscrews the wand and strokes it over her lips.

"Do you think Jake's having an affair?" she asks.

"*What?* No! *Jake?* Come on. Mr. Nice Guy?" I reach for a knob that might be the radio dial. "What makes you say that?"

"I'm just being paranoid, I guess. He's always spent a lot of time on the road, right? Working all the time. It's just the nature of the job."

"True."

"And everyone's growing a beard these days. Even in finance."

"Oh, we're at peak beard right now, for sure. Maybe even past peak."

"And this rowing kick he's on, that fancy erg he bought, it's super trendy right now. Getting rid of the dad bod. It's a thing. Would you stop fiddling with that fucking dial and just drive? I'll find us something."

I put both hands on the wheel. "Can't you get CarPlay to do your Spotify or something?"

"This is Ireland. We should listen to the local music."

Under her fingers, a song comes into focus.

"Oh, fuck," she says. "Et tu, Ireland?"

"No, leave it. I like this one."

The car bends around a curve in the motorway and a foggy gray sea comes into view to the left. The drizzle drums on the windshield. Monk's voice croons in our ears, his guitar plucks at our throats.

Paige says, "I found a charge on his personal AmEx at Cartier. Seven thousand dollars."

I flip on the turn signal and bravely shoot past a trundling minibus full of schoolchildren, staring at us through the windows with dull eyes.

"Seven thousand six hundred and twenty, to be exact."

"Maybe he's shopping early for your birthday?"

"My birthday's in November," Paige says. She zips up her makeup bag, tucks it back in her handbag, and stares back out the window at the smoky sea.

"If you need me to swing by with a pair of shovels and a bottle of bleach," I tell her, "just say the word."

The Convent of St. Hilda lies in the cleavage between two bleak hills, about thirty miles northwest of Galway, on a landscape of grass and sheep, pockmarked by lakes. When we pull through the gates at a few minutes before noon, the car park is deserted. The drizzle hangs over the roof.

I stop the car and gaze up at the stark stone walls. "It looks like a Victorian prison. They're expecting us, right?"

"Sort of. I mean, I *told* them we were coming today. Around midday."

I switch off the ignition and step out of the car. "I'll bet this is where they used to flog all the pregnant teenagers."

"Our grandmother wasn't a teenager, though."

"Can you not call her that? It's confusing. I keep thinking of Granny. The last person in the world who'd end up here. I mean, these women were like indentured servants. The nuns had the girls do laundry all day long in exchange for room and board—like old school, with scrub boards and wringers and lye soap and boiling fucking water. They gave away the babies. Sold them, basically. To say nothing of the hunger and abuse and disease and everything. It was horrible."

"You are a font of uplifting information, Pollyanna."

"I did some research. Not to shock you or anything."

We walk up to the door, a wooden monster. There is a tarnished plaque that says CONVENT OF ST. HILDA. Paige pushes open the door. I follow her into a wide stone hall, staircase at the opposite end. A young woman wearing a literal wimple looks up in surprise from a desk at one side. "I'm afraid we don't do tours for the general public," she tells us, in a brogue so thick I need to squint my ears to pick out the words.

"We're not here for a tour," Paige says. "We're looking for your adoption records."

"Oh, ye'll be wanting the Mother Superior, then."

Paige says, "I emailed her to let her know we'd be arriving around noon today. We just flew in from Boston?"

"Our mother was adopted from this place in 1952," I say. "We only found out a few weeks ago. And we have a—a medical issue that makes it really important we find out who she was. Who her biological parents were."

"Is your mother here with you, then?"

"She passed away a few years ago. We don't think she even knew about this."

The nun's face softens. She looks from me to Paige and back again. "I'm sorry to hear it. I'll just run and see if Mother Bernadette will be taking visitors."

She steps from behind her desk and glides across the hall to disappear into a corridor. Paige crosses her arms and casts a look around. "Not exactly inviting, is it?"

The walls are plastered white; the floor is made of bare, worn flagstones. On the wall above the first landing of the staircase, before it makes a sharp right turn to continue up to the next floor, a plain wooden cross hangs at a tilt, like it's staring down at you and finds you vain. After the heat of New England summer, the cool, damp air makes me shiver.

"Not a place I'd choose to have a baby, anyway," I say.

"I don't think these girls had a choice."

"But *she* did. She wasn't a girl. She was a married woman. I don't get it."

"Maybe they were poor. Couldn't afford another kid. Or maybe her husband died."

"Erm, sorry to interrupt."

The two of us spin to the wall, where the nun's reappeared in the passageway. She looks like she's about twelve years old. Her cheeks are round, her eyes small and dark, her face plain except for her skin, which is like the inside of a seashell, almost pearlescent.

"The Mother Superior says she will see ye in an hour. Will ye be wanting to have a bit of a look around, while ye're waiting?"

"I thought you said no tours."

"To the general public, no. But we do have a wee old saying inside these walls, that the babes of our lost girls carry with them a special dispensation."

I don't want to go all woo-woo on you, but when we step outside to cross the courtyard, the drizzle stops and the mist no longer sticks to your skin. There might even be a sun hanging up there somewhere. Sister Kate walks at a brisk pace, wimple fluttering in the draft. She keeps up a tour-guide patter over her shoulder, of which I understand about one word in five. Paige even less. Something about the origins of the convent in the days of St. Patrick (*She did not just say St. Patrick, did she?* whispers Paige) on the site of some Druid something-or-other (*She did not just say Druid, did she?* I whisper) and this stone *here* (Sister Kate stops, we pile to a halt just in time) being laid by King Brión himself (*Who?* whispers Paige)—"Or so it's said," Kate adds, resuming her pace.

I stare at the stone in question, a few shades darker than its neighbors, worn to silk.

"This is all bullshit, right?" says Paige.

I turn to jog after Sister Kate's fluttering wimple. "Like I'm the Irish history expert?"

We reach the other side of the courtyard and a long, gaunt building of stone, embellished by two rows of small windows such as you might find in a prison block.

Sister Kate halts at the door. "This'll be the dormitory, where they kept the girls. The laundry used to be below, washing and hanging both. But Mother Bernadette's turned it into a wee chapel now, where we come to light the candles for the souls of the girls and the babes that died here. Would ye care to see inside?"

Paige and I look at each other. "*I* would," I say.

Paige shrugs. Sister Kate opens the door to a large, low-ceilinged room, bone clean except for a cross on the far wall, hanging above a table covered with a white altar cloth, on which several candles flicker patiently. A nun sits on one of the two wooden benches before the altar, head bowed.

Sister Kate leans to my ear and whispers, "We can finish here if ye like. Go on upstairs to see the dormitory and the birthing room."

She leads us out of the chapel to a narrow hallway and up a flight of stairs to the second floor. A long hall stretches before us, windows to one side and doorways to the other. The light sneaks in through the glass. "The girls slept here during their confinements," says Sister Kate. "Four to a room, it was. There was no heating, as ye see, just the heat that came up from the laundry. It was part of their penitence, do ye see, for they hadn't just fallen into sin but leapt. According to the sisters, in those days."

I stand for a minute or so, staring through one of the doorways into the tiny room beyond. "Did you say four girls?"

"Two sets of bunks," says Sister Kate. "The ones that were earliest along had the top. Then once the labor came on, the nursing sisters would take them down the hall to the birthing room to have the baby. Dosed the poor lasses with the chloroform so they wouldn't scream. Then the wee babes would be taken away to the nursery in the convent proper, for the families to choose from. When the girl woke up after, they told her the babe had died."

"My God, it's barbaric," says Paige.

"*If* the girl woke up, mind ye. Should there be any sort of complication, the sisters would save the babe, not the mother. The families, do ye see. The families from America paid a lot of money for a nice fat healthy baby. And the girls—well, the poor girls were but sinners, after all."

I turn to Sister Kate. "I want to see the birthing room."

* * *

I went into labor with Sam just after lunchtime on the day before Mother's Day. I was staying with my dad out in California, because I didn't want to run any risk of bumping into someone I knew. The pregnancy was pretty straightforward, thank God. The morning sickness lasted a few rough weeks. I got a job as a barista at a coffee shop in Pomona and worked right up until the last week, when I couldn't tie the apron over my stomach.

I called up Mom. "I think the baby's coming," I told her.

"But the baby's not due until next week," she said.

"Mom, the baby was due three days ago."

"I could swear you said the seventeenth."

"I said the seventh, Mom. The seventh of May."

"But my plane tickets are for the fifteenth."

"Mom," I said, "if you fly out here on the fifteenth, you'll get to meet an adorable little week-old grandchild, I'm just saying."

There was a short pause, then—"I'm leaving for the airport in five minutes. Just keep your legs closed, all right?"

Dad was at the track, so I drove myself to the hospital. As I passed through the various stages of reception and check-in and examination, as they settled me into a bed in labor and delivery and hooked me up to the machines, gave me the epidural, the nurses kept asking if the father was on his way.

The father is not in the picture, I told them. Over and over.

Dad finally arrived around nine o'clock. He'd been drinking, but not enough to cause any trouble. At first the nurses assumed he was the father of the baby, kind of a sketchy situation but to each his own, so I had to repeat this line all over again. *The father is not in the picture.* By this time I was progressing quickly. Around midnight I was five centimeters dilated. At one o'clock I was eight centimeters. The doctor looked up from my vagina and said it was going to be any minute now, was I ready to push.

No, I'm not ready to push, I said. *My mother's not here yet.*

The doctor said she didn't think the baby cared one way or another. Could my father maybe lend a hand?

I said my dad went on a cigarette break an hour ago and hadn't come back.

Just then a massive contraction walloped me, blasting through the epidural meds like a red-hot knife through a pound of cold buttercream frosting. After it subsided, I felt an overwhelming urge to empty my bowels and mentioned this desire to the doctor, since after all she'd had her nose up my vagina for a good part of the evening.

She turned her head and called for a nurse.

I started pushing. Forty-five minutes into the pushing, I started screaming for a Caesarean, for God's sake, could someone just slice me open and get this damn baby out of me. And as I'm yelling at the doctor, and the doctor barks at the nurse, my mom runs into the room and yells, *Over my dead body you'll cut my daughter open, so help me!*

Ma'am, said the doctor, *if this baby isn't out in ten minutes, I'm wheeling her into the operating room* right over *your dead body, so help me.*

Mom turned to me and grabbed my hand. She said, *Look in my eyes, Mallory, do as I say, you feel that contraction coming on and you just think about the asshole who did this to you.*

She's crowning, yelled the doctor from my vagina.

Two more pushes and Sam gushed into the world, eight and a half pounds, red and loud as hell. They put him right on my chest, all slippery and beautiful. I looked into his squashed face and started to cry. Mom cradled us both and said, *Look what you made, you made me a grandson.* Then the nurse said they needed to take him for a minute, do the tests, and I remember I looked up at her and thought, *Nobody is taking my son away from me, nobody ever.*

At which point my dad strolled in, reeking of cigarettes and booze, and asked if he'd missed anything.

As I stand in the middle of the cold stone birthing room at St. Hilda's, maybe ten feet by eight feet—not enough room to swing a cat, my grandfather would have said—and stare at its walls of white plaster, the single small window, I think of the mayhem of Sam's birth, the doctor barking between my legs, my mother galloping in, even my dad eventually present and accounted for; Paige (though I didn't know it at the time) in the air on her way from Singapore, where she'd been working on some currency trading desk.

I remember something I said to Monk, one true thing in the middle of that lonely scene in Paige's kitchen, the two of us bent over a stack of legal documents—Monk who had held me in his arms and loved me once.

Sam is surrounded by love.

He has that, if nothing else. From the moment of his birth, we were gathered together in love for him.

Paige leans against the doorframe, watching me. Her eyes glisten.

"Isn't it weird?" she says. "Mom was born in this room."

When the Mother Superior opens her mouth to welcome us, I'm a little taken aback to hear a Brooklyn accent.

Paige leans forward. "Excuse me, are you American?"

"I sure am," says Mother Bernadette. "Came overseas to nurse in '44. Fell in love with a bomber pilot, like the young idiot I was. He got killed, of course. When the war ended I didn't want to go home and get married, like everybody else. I felt the calling. Wound up here as a novitiate in '46. Been here ever since."

I stare at the woman's smooth, sagging face and try to run the numbers. Paige is better at math than me and speaks first.

"So you must be, what? Ninety-six at least."

"Ninety-seven in September." She taps her forehead. "Still have all my marbles, thanks be to God."

"And your complexion," says Paige.

"Well, that's this Irish weather. Haven't seen the sun in weeks." She looks down at a curling caramel-colored folder on her desk, which looks like it was once manila. "While you were off with Sister Kate, I rooted around the archives and found the file on your mother's adoption."

Paige reached for her handbag. "I have the identification and the original certificate right here—"

"Never mind all that. I can see who you are. That." She nods to the bracelet on my wrist. "That's all the identification I need."

I look down at my wrist, then back up at Mother Bernadette. She's staring at me with these small, nut-brown eyes, as if she's waiting for something.

"You were there," I say. "You were there when she was born."

Mother Bernadette spreads her small palms across the folder and stares at the backs of her hands. "I remember your grandmother like it was yesterday. She wasn't like the other girls who came here. She was a woman, for one thing. She was lovely, or I guess you might say she had once been lovely. A man brought her here in a big black car. Said he was her husband. There had been a fire, he told us, a terrible fire. Her hair was burned short." Mother Bernadette held up her hands to her wimple. "Her face was bandaged. Her hands were bandaged. Her right leg was broken."

I leaned forward. "Did you say a *fire*? What kind of fire?"

"The man didn't say. He spent about an hour with the Mother Superior, in her office. Oh, she was an old bag, that woman. You give some people an ounce of moral authority and they turn into tyrants, you see. They become despots because they know they're right. He spent an hour with her and got in his car and left. I took charge of the poor woman, because I was a trained nurse, you see."

"What did she say?" Paige asks. "Did she tell you anything about herself?"

Mother Bernadette shakes her head. "Not a word. She hardly spoke, poor thing. Her wounds healed up and her hair grew in. She had scars on her face and her hands but everywhere else she was lovely, just the loveliest thing. But she wouldn't speak. When she was well enough she worked in the laundry, like the other girls. Then her time came. Oh, it was terrible. Everything went wrong from the beginning. The baby was turned around, the doctor was late and stone drunk. He wanted to do a Caesarean but I wouldn't let him, not in his condition. I saved that baby myself. Got her turned around at last and out she came. Beautiful little girl. A bit squashed after what she went through, but beautiful like her mother."

"That was Mom," I say. "That was our mother."

"When she woke up from the chloroform," says Mother Bernadette, "I gave her the baby to hold. The other sisters said we should take her to the nursery, but I said over my dead body, that child has a father and a mother, married and everything, she's not born in sin, she's not going anywhere but her mother's arms. And Mrs. Ainsworth—"

"Ainsworth! Was that her name?"

"Mrs. Ainsworth. Hannah Ainsworth. It's been in my head ever since. She looks down at her darling wee babe and puts her to nurse, just like that, like she knows what she's doing. And she looks up at me and says—not the first words I ever heard her say, but the first words I remember her to say—she says, *She has his eyes.*"

Paige looks at me. "*You* have Mom's eyes. Her green eyes."

"Have you, now?" Mother Bernadette finds a pair of glasses at the side of her desk and puts them on to peer at me. "Well, I wouldn't know. New mothers will say such things. But I do recall I felt a shiver at that. I remember I thought that this man who brought her in, who said he was her husband—well, I was pretty sure his eyes were blue. Not green."

"Hold on a second," says Paige. "What are you saying?"

"I'm saying I had a funny feeling about the whole affair, that's what. That it was the husband who wanted to give up the baby, not her."

"So how did Mom end up getting adopted?" I ask.

"Well, I did my best. But the Mother Superior was furious. She came up and said in that voice of hers, I'll never forget her voice as long as I live, she said, *What do you think you're doing, letting that baby nurse with its mother. We've got a nice American family right here that wants to adopt the child.* And there was nothing I could do, really. They got their hands on the baby and took her away. Oh, you should have heard that poor mother screaming for her child. Like one of those banshees. I had to give her something to make her sleep. When she woke up, she gave me that bracelet. She said to find the family that had taken her baby and give them that bracelet to give to her daughter. Of course, they'd left for their ship by then. I had to take the bus to Galway. I made it to the docks just in time. Found the parents with the baby and told them this was the mother's dying wish. I'm sure the Lord forgives a wee white lie such as that. I'm glad to see the parents kept the promise. They seemed like a nice couple. Here, love."

She hands me a Kleenex. Paige reaches for the box on the desk and takes one too.

"I hope you murdered that husband when he came to fetch her," says Paige.

"Well, that's the funny thing. He came to fetch her, all right, about a week after the birth, but she was already gone."

"Gone! You mean she ran away?"

Mother Bernadette shakes her head. "A woman drove up the day before and asked to see Mrs. Ainsworth. Of course the Mother Superior said no, there was no Mrs. Ainsworth in the convent, never heard of her. But after this woman walked out, I ran to her car—it was raining fit to drown—and said to come with me. Between the two of us, we got Mrs. Ainsworth down the stairs and out to that car, and that was the last I saw of her." She lifts the folder from her desk and holds it out to us with her short, knobbled fingers. "You can take that with you, if you like. I'm only glad to see the pair of you with my own old eyes before I die. I always did wonder what became of that poor woman's child."

The sun burns through the mist as we wind between the hills on our way back to Galway, where Paige has booked us a room at some luxury hotel. A sky of preposterous blue appears patch by patch, then spreads out like a sheet from horizon to horizon. Against the green hills, it breaks your heart.

"So what do you think?" I said. "Do you think she had an affair? Mom wasn't the husband's child?"

Paige stares straight ahead. "I don't know what to think. I guess we'll find out more when the DNA stuff comes in."

I reach out to turn on the radio. "At least we have a name now. Hannah Ainsworth. That gives us something to go on."

Paige lets me have the bathroom first. I don't know if she's taking some kind of revenge on Jake or whether this is how they usually travel, but the suite she's booked is larger than my house. After a long, hot shower, I stand in front of the lighted mirror and examine my eyes.

I remember going sailing with Monk and the twins one afternoon. I guess he must have had the day off or something. Like all the Winthrop kids, he'd learned to sail around the time he learned to walk, or maybe shortly after. It was a gorgeous day but humid, and I

gathered up my hair in a knot at the back of my head and complained about how frizzy it got in weather like this; how I should
move to the desert. This was in June, before Monk and I got together, and he didn't say anything for a minute or two. Just busied
himself with the tiller and the sheets. Out of the blue, he said, "You
have the greatest eyes, though." I laughed it off. He said it was true,
they made him think of King Arthur's castle. (I remember those
exact words, *King Arthur's castle,* because they could mean anything,
because they warmed me from my belly outward.) *That green color,*
he told me. *Nobody has eyes like yours.*

Naturally I blushed and turned away to pull Blue back from the
water—she had leaned over the edge to look for fish—and Monk
said quickly, *Not that there's anything wrong with your hair. Your hair is
great too.* And we laughed, because my hair is the color of poop, let's
face it, and regularly defies the laws of physics.

But that night, I stood in front of the bathroom mirror and stared
at my green eyes, the way I'm doing now. My mother's eyes. I remember I had this strange feeling that they weren't really mine, or
even hers.

That they belonged to somebody else who had given them to me
for safekeeping.

When I emerge from the bathroom, swathed in a towel made of
clouds, Paige is sitting on the sofa in the living area. She's spread out
the papers from the manila folder on the coffee table and bends over
them with that look of superhuman concentration she gets, the look
that got her into Yale.

"Bathroom's free," I tell her.

She looks up as if I've woken her from a trance. "I guess I could
use a shower."

"I wasn't going to say anything, but yeah."

Paige disappears into the bathroom. I head for my suitcase and
pull out some fresh clothes. My phone buzzes from inside my handbag. I pull it out and find a message alert from Monk Adams.

Shit, I think.

I click on the alert and the message comes up.

Sam is fine don't worry. Has your sister been checking her messages

I stand there in my towel of clouds and type back, *idk, whats up*

The gray dots appear (so gratifying, those gray dots, so validating) then—

I think her husband is on the news.

CHAPTER SEVENTEEN

Hannah

January 1952
Cairo, Egypt

The day János came back from the dead, seven or eight weeks after the defeat at Stalingrad, Hannah had gone out hunting. It was the end of March and she hadn't expected to find anything worth eating, but eventually she spotted a skinny brown rabbit bounding across a meadow of wet snow and raised the rifle János had left for her. The shot rang out; the rabbit fell. She carried it back to the house in the dying light. The snow had begun to freeze and her boots crunched into it as she trudged along. The seams had split long ago, so she had tied the leather together with pieces of string. Her feet squished inside the sodden wool socks.

Numb and exhausted, she didn't notice the scent of woodsmoke until she reached the kitchen door. She stopped and tasted the air. She'd let the fire go out in the cookstove before she left, so as not to waste fuel, yet here was this tang of smoke. At her feet, she saw the prints of a pair of large men's boots on the half-frozen slush.

Hannah set the rabbit by the doorstep and raised the rifle. Carefully she turned the handle and kicked open the door. A man stood up from the chair next to the stove. He had draped his clothes over the hot metal to dry and wrapped a blanket around his cadaverous body. Some dirty bandages covered his right arm and shoulder. His boots tumbled in a pool of melted snow on the stone hearth. His eyes met hers—a glassy, febrile brown.

She did not quite recognize him at first. In her mind, she had laid him to rest in the mud of the Volga riverbank. Nothing had been heard from him since November, when the Hungarian Second Army was dug in to the north of Stalingrad, shredded to pieces by Soviet artillery. Now here was this ghost in her kitchen, this cadaver from whose feverish skull gleamed János's eyes.

"Hannah," it said. "Hannah, wife, don't you know me?"

Friday night at the Mena House. Somebody's birthday; the usual crowd. Hannah and Alistair sat with the Beverleys at a table in the corner of the ballroom. The air was full of cigarette smoke and dance music from an orchestra at the other end. The men leaned close and spoke in hushed voices about an attack on the Egyptian police barracks in Ismailia. As the embassy's military attaché, Beverley had the latest news.

"Exham assures me they've surrendered," he said. "Forty or fifty dead."

Alistair swore. "Stubborn bastards."

"Brought it on themselves." Beverley rattled the ice in his empty glass. "Do you know, the bloody Egyptians just sat on their hands while the *fedayeen* harassed our soldiers, harassed the legitimate shipping—"

Alistair's fist hit the table. "We've got a right to defend the bloody treaty, by God, to uphold the rule of law. They signed the damn thing, didn't they? If a sovereign nation can simply walk away from its legal contracts . . . look here!" He gestured with his empty glass to a passing waiter. "Another one of these. Bertie? You? Yes? Make it two. Scotch."

Lillian Beverley looked at Hannah. "You're looking so *well*, darling. That lovely frock you're wearing."

Hannah wore the dress she had bought from Circurel the week before, made of crepe the color of palm leaves, draped around her waist to disguise the way her belly had begun to round out from her hip bones. Her breasts strained against the low bodice, suspended by a pair of precarious jeweled straps. Not a dress to hide in. She tapped some ash from her cigarette. "This old thing? Thanks."

"No, really. Simply ravishing. I do wish I had your figure."

The orchestra swung into a waltz. Lillian lifted the martini glass at her elbow. A sip caught her the wrong way; she began to cough, waved Hannah away, sipped again. Her husband turned to her and lifted an eyebrow. She waved him off too, and he returned to his conversation with Alistair. What that ass Farouk should have done, what he ought to do now.

"This awful business at the barracks," Hannah said.

"*Jolly* awful. It's been building for weeks. It's all Bertie will talk about."

Hannah leaned forward. "You don't think it has anything to do with . . . ?"

"*Do* you? It's so long ago. October, wasn't it?" Lillian reached for her cigarette in the ashtray. Her movements were quick, nervous. She sent a glance around the room and sucked on the cigarette. "Bertie thinks something's brewing."

"Something's always brewing."

"I mean trouble *here*. In Cairo."

"What kind of trouble?" Hannah asked.

Lillian fiddled with the olive at the bottom of her empty glass. "I can't say any more. He made me promise."

"Why, we're not in danger, are we?"

Lillian glanced at her husband, leaned toward Hannah, lowered her voice. "They want to burn it all down, you know. To make us leave."

"Who does?"

"The Free Officers, I suppose." Lillian shrugged. "The nationalists. You know. It's all very . . . it's all so . . . oh, what's the world coming to? Everything's falling apart, isn't it? It's all so jolly *awful*."

Across the room, on the other side of the orchestra, a man came into view near the tall french doors, dressed in a tuxedo, hair combed into sleek dark waves. He caught Hannah's eye and slipped outside to the terrace.

Hannah stubbed out her cigarette and rose. "If you'll excuse me, I'm going to get a breath of air."

The Mena House was famous for its gardens—its luxurious lawns and exotic plantings, its paths and fountains and benches. Over the past few months, Hannah and Lucien had often taken advantage of the way you could find some private space among the various features, the pyramids to one side and the magnificent hotel to the other. She caught up with him now under the shadow of a stand of palm trees. The air was cool and dry; the breeze came off the desert and smelled of dust. Lucien's kiss was short and hard.

"You're well?" he asked.

"*Well?* You've been gone for a week, not a word."

"Business."

She grabbed his elbows. "What's wrong? What's the matter?"

"Nothing. You have something for me, I understand?"

Hannah exhaled a long breath. The smell of him made her giddy with relief. "The police barracks in Ismailia. They've surrendered. Forty or fifty dead, Alistair said."

"Bloody idiots," he said in English.

"Lillian thinks there'll be trouble here in Cairo. Something her husband told her."

"Lillian?"

"Beverley. Her husband's a military attaché, remember?"

"I remember."

He grazed her cheek with his hand. Hannah closed her eyes and leaned into his palm.

"Listen to me, Hannah," he said gently. "You must leave."

She opened her eyes. "Leave the hotel?"

"Leave Cairo. Leave Egypt."

Beyond the palm trees, Hannah glimpsed the three large pyramids on the Giza plain, soaked in moonlight. The smaller ones clustered nearby. She felt a movement in her chest, like her heart was shriveling. She pushed his hand away from her cheek.

"Don't be ridiculous," she said. "I can't simply leave the country. Not unless my husband's ordered out."

"It's not safe for you."

"It was never *safe*, Lucien. But if you want to end things, I quite understand. You've had what you needed from me, haven't you? And I've had what I needed from you."

He glanced briefly downward. "I was wondering if you meant to tell me."

Hannah folded her arms and thought about the last time they

met, a week ago—the hurried, furtive coupling in his office at Shep-heard's, straightening her dress, touching up her lipstick in the re-flection from her compact mirror. When she'd looked up, she'd caught him gazing at her middle. She'd clicked the compact shut.

"Let me fix your tie," she'd said. She had taken the knot of his necktie and tenderly straightened it for him. Had laid her forearms against his chest and kissed him. He had returned the kiss, of course. But she remembered thinking his lips held something back from her. She remembered thinking his eyes didn't quite touch hers, that they seemed to have caught on something in the distance, like Já-nos's eyes when he'd returned from Stalingrad.

"Well, now you know for certain," Hannah said.

She turned to leave. He caught her elbow.

"Hannah. Wait a moment."

At the back, Hannah's gown swooped irresistibly low, almost to her bottom. A slope of spotless, luxurious flesh. János had always worshipped the shape of her back—like the curve of a violin, he said once, kissing his way down her spine. She heard Lucien's breath catch. She closed her eyes and waited for him to speak. A hoarse whisper.

"I'll find you again, Hannah. When this is over. I promise you."

His lips touched her throat, her shoulder. His hand brushed the bare skin of her back, the way a child can't help running his finger through the cream inside of an éclair.

The electric lights blazed through the ballroom windows. A peal of laughter rang above the lilting orchestra, the pitch of conversa-tion. Everybody having such a jolly time.

"About the child—" he began.

Hannah shrugged off his hand from her arm.

"It's getting chilly," she said. "I'm going indoors."

She found Alistair near the bar, ordering another drink.

"I want to dance," she said.

Obediently he took her hand and led her to the ballroom floor, where everybody was drunk and dancing. Between the lurching bodies Hannah glimpsed the birthday boy, whatever his name was, wearing a paper crown. Lipstick on both cheeks. *Blotto,* she thought. The English had so many expressive words for the concept of drunkenness.

Alistair was an experienced, graceful dancer. Sometimes Hannah wondered how a man could dance so beautifully and yet fuck you like a marionette. The orchestra played a foxtrot that kept the two of them busy and breathless, so they didn't have to talk. Then the foxtrot ended and a waltz picked up.

"Darling," said Alistair, "I've been thinking perhaps we ought to return home to England. Egypt's turned rather hot, if you've noticed."

"But it's only January," she said.

"I mean the social situation, darling."

"I was only joking. I know what you meant."

Alistair frowned and executed an elegant turn.

"Where have the Beverleys gone?" asked Hannah. "You and Bertie have been thick as thieves tonight."

"Beverley's been called back to the office, I'm afraid. This damned situation in Ismailia."

"Darling," said Hannah, "I've been meaning to ask. I don't know if I ought. You don't think—what happened in October—"

"Good God. Of course not."

"I didn't mean—"

"Then don't open your silly mouth. You don't know a bloody thing about it. Keep to your bloody gossip and frocks and—"

"Alistair, please. People are staring."

"They're staring because of that bloody indecent frock you're wearing. Tits spilling out. Arse spilling out. Only a—"

Hannah pulled out of his arms. "I think you've had quite enough to drink tonight, Alistair. I'll get my coat."

But she did not get her coat. She stalked out of the ballroom and through the french doors to the terrace. To the stand of palms, where she could stare at the moonlit pyramids and fall to pieces. She leaned against a slender trunk and slid downward, inch by careful inch, until she was sitting on the damp grass, trying to get a decent breath to sob with. This silly frock. What had she been thinking? To entice Lucien, of course. Stupid. When men were getting massacred in Ismailia. Well, the dew would ruin the crepe, so that was that.

Lucien's voice echoed in her ear—*About the child.*

She laid her hand on her belly. She had that, anyway. She was not alone. Nobody could take this child from her, at least; she had what she came for. *I want a child,* she had told Lucien, right at the start, and he had given her that, without question, so who was she to want more?

I'll find you again, Hannah. I promise you.

The words a man said to the lover he was discarding. The toll he paid to his own conscience.

Hannah closed her eyes and listened to the small, delicate noises around her. Wouldn't it be funny, she thought, if an Egyptian cobra happened to slither up just now. Would Lucien appear again like a djinn to save her?

Or was she on her own again, no one to save her except herself?

A hiccup escaped her. Her head weighed so much. She leaned it against the palm and closed her eyes.

A fine May morning in the ancient kitchen of János's grandmother. A morning for miracles.

Hannah had been scraping the last speck of dough out of the bowl and into the pan when she heard a noise behind her.

János! she gasped.

I'm feeling a little better today, he said. *I thought I might get out of bed.*

Since arriving home, János had lain ill with some combination of influenza and the infection in his wounded arm, and in his emaciated state he had hovered on the brink of death for weeks. Hannah had spent most nights in the armchair in the living room—she had brought down a mattress for János to sleep on, because there was no fuel to heat the bedrooms upstairs—and had lived each day in the expectation that it would be his last on earth, that he had returned home like this simply to die in her arms.

Then about a week ago, the fever had receded. The wound had begun to heal at last. He ate some bread with his broth, a little cheese from the wheel that Hannah had so carefully husbanded in the larder.

Now he stood like a skeleton in her kitchen. A gust of breeze through the window might blow him over. Hannah had rushed to settle him in a chair inside a patch of fragile sunlight, to heat some broth and brew some feeble coffee from the few beans remaining, mixed with acorns she had roasted and ground in the mill.

When she'd handed him the cup, he had closed his fingers around her fingers. The steam curled between his gaunt face and hers. Even today, she remembered the smell of the ersatz coffee, of woodsmoke, of promising spring air rushing through the window. She remembered the way the sun pitied his cheek and the anguished stare with which he regarded her. The way he lifted his hand and touched the ends of her hair, which had grown out a few inches and stood around her head like the hair of a shaggy dog.

"The children," he said.

She sank to her knees between his legs and laid her head in his lap. "Sometimes I think, if I had only found more to eat. They would have been stronger, they would have survived it."

For some time, he stroked her hair. "I nearly gave up. Every minute I wanted to lie down in the mud and go to sleep. So fucking cold, so hungry. My wounds wouldn't heal. I thought, I should just die."

"I thought you were dead. That's what people were saying. Everybody said the entire army was dead or captured. When I saw you in the kitchen I thought you were a ghost. I thought I was dreaming."

"I looked up and saw you standing there in my old coat. Muddy boots held together with string. Your hair all short."

"Because of the fever."

"And I knew why I had kept walking through the snow and the mud, when I wanted to lie down and sleep. When I wanted to die."

Hannah lifted her head. His face was streaked with tears. The ersatz coffee cooled in the cup he had rested on the arm of the chair.

"It wasn't your fault, Hannah," he said. "You tried to save them."

She shook her head. He took her face between his hands.

"You did all you could. It was typhoid."

"*I* survived it."

"That was God's will. He took away everything else. But he left you. He spared us both."

"God didn't spare us," she said. "We survived, that's all."

"Yes, because you willed it. You willed me back to life."

"Then why has God spared us, János?" she asked him. "Tell me."

He stared at her with his eyes that seemed to rest beyond her, on some distant object. His thumbs felt along the ridge of her cheekbones. She slid her fingers to the fastening on his trousers and his hand moved to stop her.

"Hannah, wait." His face filled with shame.

"Don't tell me," she said. "It doesn't matter."

She rose to her feet and unbuttoned her shirt, unbuckled her belt and let her trousers fall to the floor. One leg she swung over his lap, then the other. His hands reached for her waist. He sank his face between her soft breasts. The groan he made when she settled him inside her, it was like all the misery in the world, released from his chest into the delicate spring air.

Hannah must have dozed off for a minute or two, because she came alert to some noise in the foliage to her right.

An animal, she thought. *Don't move.*

She forced herself to hold still. Her heart felt as if it were beating from her skin.

A voice. A human voice. Another one—female. Pleading.

Softly Hannah rose to her feet, holding the palm trunk to steady herself. On the damp grass, she made no noise. The heels of her slippers sank into the turf. The man and the woman spoke in low tones, urgent ones, packed with meaning. The woman a little louder than the man, as if she couldn't help herself. She made a little groan of pain or pleasure, and it was funny that this noise—not the words preceding them—identified her to Hannah as Lillian Beverley.

The pair of them could not be more than a few yards away, just inside the rim of foliage. By now, Hannah's eyes had tuned to the darkness. She stared at the fronds until the moonlight picked out some movement. Lillian's dress flashed into view—strapless, the color of apricots, not especially flattering. The man wore a black tuxedo, as most did, so she couldn't see him clearly. He had his arms around Lillian. He was murmuring to her. The scene was so intimate, Hannah wanted to flee. But she did not. She remained planted in the grass by the heels of her shoes, until she was absolutely certain the man—as he bent his face toward Lillian's—was Lucien Beck.

CHAPTER EIGHTEEN

Mallory

July 2022
Winthrop Island, New York

Paige is on the phone with the lawyers again. I give her a wide berth as I shepherd the kids back to the house from the beach, but snatches of conversation still find my ears as she paces up and down the lawn.

. . . not going to stand in front of the cameras like the loyal fucking Stepford wife and . . .

. . . suing for how *much? Is that a fucking* joke*? . . .*

. . . don't care if she's lying or not, he shouldn't have been sticking his dick *. . .*

. . . understand why I'm supposed to defend the indefensible here . . .

. . . well, someone's *gotta show a little dignity . . .*

We pass by the guest house, from which you can hear the notes of a piano meander faintly behind the walls. In the days since I knew the old Monk estate, the pool house has been rebuilt with changing rooms and an outdoor shower, where I frog-march the kids to rinse off all the sand before proceeding to the side entrance of the main house.

Grace calls out from the kitchen. "There you are, Miss Mallory! Could you tell Mr. Monk the steaks are ready for the barbecue?"

"Will do! Kids, go get a snack from Grace and run upstairs to change for dinner."

Six days after landing at Logan Airport to be bustled into a black Escalade and delivered to the ancestral Monk estate on Winthrop

Island, I'm well aware that Monk Adams will have his cellphone switched off while he's working. I strike off back across the lawn and knock on the door of the guesthouse that's now his studio. The notes pause on the piano.

It's open, calls Monk's voice.

I push the door wide. "Hey."

"Hey." He gives me this quizzical look, then takes off his readers and glances to the clock on the wall. "Oh, shit. I'm supposed to turn the grill on, right?"

"You got it."

I turn to leave and check myself.

"Hey, Monk?"

He's gathering up the pages of music manuscript scattered over the grand piano, which sits at the side of the room where the bed used to be. "What's up, Pinks?"

"I just want to say thanks. I hope we're not getting in your way or anything. I mean, trust me, I realize kids can be pretty chaotic."

"Are you kidding? You guys are great. The place needs a little chaos, if you want to know the truth. Just like the old days. Except now I'm the patriarch holding the barbecue fork instead of my grandpa."

"Well, it's incredibly generous and I want you to know we appreciate it. I promise we'll be out of your hair as soon as the . . . the thing dies down a little. The TV trucks parked outside Paige's house."

Monk motions me out the door ahead of him. "It'll blow over soon if you lie low. The general public's got the attention span of a gnat, trust me."

"I still can't wrap my head around it. I can't even imagine what he was thinking. Having an affair with a junior associate, that's just so *basic.*"

"I'm guessing the thinking part didn't really enter into the decision-making."

"But *Jake!* Seriously, the nicest guy you could ever meet. If even half the stuff she's saying is true, he must have a serious dark side."

"Everyone's got a dark side, Pinks. I'll bet even you have a dark side hidden in there somewhere."

Across the lawn, Paige rips her AirPods out of her ears and stomps toward the house.

"I should go change," I say. "Grace has everything ready in the kitchen. I'll send the kids down to set the table."

"Pinks, wait."

I turn back.

"Sorry, that came out a little wrong."

"It's okay. I know what you meant."

"It's just my awkward way of telling you that you have the most integrity of anyone I know. That's all."

I push back my wind-tangled hair and look beyond his ear at the ocean, rolling in past the tip of Long Island. "I don't know about that."

"Also my way of saying that whenever you're ready to talk, I'm ready to listen. No anger, no judgments. I feel like the past few days, it's been good for us. Right? To see each other as human beings again. The same human beings who cared about each other before. So I really—I just want to understand this. I want to hear you."

Shit, I think. Shit. Here it comes, out of nowhere. Soft, expensive therapy words. Who can resist them? Who doesn't want to be heard? Understood?

I shift my weight from one foot to the other and imagine Monk in the office of some therapist, some stranger who knows all the details of our summer together, the secrets that were supposed to remain inside the sacred space between Monk and me.

From a second-story window floats the shriek of Ida's voice— *That's* mine! *Give it* back!

"Although," Monk says, in his old voice, the voice I know, "before you go thinking I'm some kind of hero, the real reason I invited everyone here is so I can keep spending time with Sam. Selfish jerk that I am."

I gather myself. "It's not selfish. It means the world to Sam. You're . . . you're terrific with him. You are. When I saw you showing him a few chords this morning, I kind of . . ."

He raises his eyebrows and waits for me to finish the sentence.

Fell in love with you all over again, I think. *Melted into a pathetic puddle of infatuation.*

He's wearing a worn orange T-shirt over a pair of crumpled chinos. The falling sun shines in his eyes. The breeze riffs his hair. I force out a smile. "Anyway. Go start that grill, okay? Everyone's starving."

What you probably don't know about Monk Adams—multiple Grammy winner, chart-topping whisperer of the nation's soul, the Sexiest Man in Music—is he can grill the best damn steak you've ever eaten, with one hand holding a bottle of beer.

"There's no secret," he tells me, when I bring him the plate of steamed asparagus to finish off above the flames. "Little salt and pepper, high heat. And a timer. I learned at the feet of an old grill master."

"Your grandfather?"

"Every time I stand here, I picture him. This cheesy red apron we got him one year. World's Best Grandpa. He wore it every time. He was a real character. Wish you could have met him, Pinks. You'd have loved him."

"I would expect nothing less from the father of Aunt Barbara."

"Yeah, she was his favorite. I mean, he would never admit it. But they just had this thing, you know?" Monk tilts the bottle to his mouth and drinks. "I think that was a big part of my mom's issues. Feeling like a third wheel."

"How's your mom doing these days? She must be so proud of you."

"A lot better, thanks. Finally got her into some treatment that really worked for her. We're closer now, it's good. She's got this place in Maine, she loves it. Right on the water, plenty of space. A— uh, you know, female friend. They're together. Kind of a surprise, but not really, right? Awesome woman. Treats her well. Everyone's happy."

"I'm so glad to hear that, Monk. I really am."

"Yeah, I'm kind of looking forward to taking Sam to meet her. When the time is right. If that's okay with you."

"Of course it's okay with me. I think that would be terrific. He could use a grandma."

Monk checks his watch and flips the steaks, one by one, with a pair of silicone-tipped tongs. When he turns to me, there is a watery gleam to his eyes. "Thanks, Pinks," he says. "I appreciate the trust."

We eat outside on the teak dining table, to which Monk has added an extra leaf. The kids have set the places somewhat haphazardly with old plates and a bewildering mismatch of forks and knives, along with side dishes of red potato salad and roasted corn succotash and green salad tossed with fresh strawberries and walnuts, all whipped up by Grace during the afternoon. Monk uncorks a bottle of red wine and sets out the platter of sizzling rib eyes and tells us to dig in.

Grace joins us. She nearly passed out in a pile of laundry when she first saw me the other day. *Miss Mallory!* she exclaimed. I asked her what she was doing here, and she said Monk hired her over here when his father died, since the twins hardly ever stayed at Seagrapes anymore. We had a good gossip until Grace put her hand on my arm and her eyes filled with tears.

Why did you leave him, Miss Mallory? Why did you break my boy's heart?

What could I say? I just opened my arms and gave her a hug and said it broke my heart to go.

I pour some wine into Grace's glass. She protests, then gives in. The steak disappears; the air turns gold. Monk shows Ida how to balance a spoon on her nose. Even Paige starts to crack a smile, once she's had a couple glasses of wine. Maisie forces us to start a game of telephone, and pretty soon everyone is laughing from their bellies, so hard and so loud that I guess nobody hears the car in the driveway, nobody hears the slam of doors and the voice calling out, until a woman steps through the french doors and comes to stand near the table.

I spot her first. She has tumbling, sun-streaked brown hair and her skin glows like a lightbulb. A shrunken green T-shirt clings to her breasts and her ribless waist, ending an inch or two above the waistband of a pair of satiny blue wide-leg pants. The conversation stops. Monk is the last one to turn in her direction. He almost spills his wine.

"Holy shit. I thought you were in Texas!"

Lennox Lassiter opens her arms. A million suns catch the facets of the rock on her finger. "Well, darn it. I realized how much I missed you, sweetie!"

Monk jumps out of his chair and rounds the corner of the table to return her embrace. They kiss tenderly. My throat shrivels into sand and blows away in the wind. Lennox makes this laugh from somewhere near her esophagus and turns to face all the goggle eyes. Her smile lands on Sam. She puts her hands over her mouth.

"Oh my goodness! It's *you*!" she says, like she's been waiting for him all her life. She looks at Monk, at Sam, at Monk again, and tears fill her eyes. "Sweetie! He's like *you*! Oh, honey. Come *here* and let me meet you. I'm going to be your *stepmom*!"

Sam shoots me this terrified look. He's due for dialysis tomorrow morning and his face is flushed and a little bloated. I give him a smile and what I hope is an encouraging nod—believe me, this takes everything I have, a total focus of maternal will—and he rises from his chair and walks toward Monk and Lennox and holds out his hand, like I've taught him.

"Oh, no, honey," she says. "I'm a hugger."

She opens her arms and folds him in. Across the table from me, Paige makes a noise like somebody's strangling her. Sam looks at me from Lennox's shoulder like he's being filmed in a hostage video. Monk clears his throat.

"Hey, everyone. I'd like you to meet my fiancée. Lee Lassiter."

Probably you know more about Lennox Lassiter than I do. For me, what happens on social media is like a tree falling in a forest on the other side of the world. Besides, ignorance is bliss. I don't need to read all the breathless accounts of Monk and Lennox, in print and on the internet. So I don't.

But thanks to Paige, thanks to the atmosphere of celebrity gossip our modern culture breathes, I know her story in outline form. Quit her Wall Street career in her late twenties to found a beauty and wellness empire that—tell me if I get this wrong—curates the New England lifestyle, whatever that means. Probably you already follow her on Instagram or (more recently) TikTok. You've traveled along on her mother's sobriety journey, her best friend's endometriosis journey, her college roommate's transgender journey. You know her tear-streaked no-makeup face and her no-makeup makeup face. You realize, as a sophisticated internet consumer, that the real Lennox (*call me Lee,* she instructs me) is not the same as the social media Lennox.

Still, when you sit next to her on a beach, it's hard to separate the two in your head. To know so much about a person you hardly know.

Lennox—*Lee,* I remind myself, and for some reason this is a difficult mental transition—lounges on her stomach in a Barbie-pink bikini the size of a Kleenex and flips through her phone. A paperback copy of *Where the Crawdads Sing* sits in the sand next to her beach towel.

"You know what sucks about this gig?" she's telling me. "I can't take a single day off."

"Why not?"

"Analytics," she says. "Engagement."

She swings her legs and curls her toes. Her thumbs are a blur. I'm on my laptop trying to tweak a bamboo trellis pattern for next spring's collection and the umbrella's shade keeps moving as the sun climbs in the sky, making it difficult to see the screen. When I glance in Lee's direction to think of some reply, I realize she's unhooked her bikini top. Tan lines, I guess. Thank God Sam's indoors for his dialysis right now.

I avert my eyes from the obvious and say, "I honestly don't know how you think of all these posts. I would have run out of ideas in a week."

"Oh, it's not just me, trust me. I have a team back in Austin, where I'm from? We do a big brainstorm every Monday morning, come up with all our content for the week, what we're obsessing over. What eats up all my time are the videos. Thank you, TikTok." She sighs. "So, every day I have to shoot tons of footage and send it to Austin so the team can edit everything into a literal one-minute reel. It's insane. I mean, today's easy, at least? The wedding planners are coming over? My followers love all the wedding shit. Can't get enough." She sets down the phone and turns her head to me. "So, what are you up to? Monk says you design fabrics and things?"

"That is correct. I'm kind of semi-freelance. I do some stuff for a clothing retailer and also for a home design company. This one's for a new collection of coordinated wallpaper and curtains." I turn the laptop screen in her direction.

"Oh, neat. You're so talented, Mallory. I can barely draw stick figures. I mean, I have an *eye,* obviously. I love design. I just can't *do* design."

"Well, there's a lot of technique involved. Pattern is geometry as much as art. It's not just raw talent, trust me."

She lays her head in the cradle of her elbow. "I'd love to feature some of your designs on my channels. That's right in our sweet spot. I don't know if you've checked us out at all? But the platform is all about my passion for body positivity and wellness and empowerment. Help women find their joy, you know? I mean, look at you. Maybe you're not what the world considers a *success*"—her fingers make quotes around the word *success*—"but you're following your passion and bringing joy and that's just *so inspiring.*"

"I'm not really trying to inspire anyone," I say. "I'm just trying to make a living."

"So let me help you. Send me some of your designs and kind of a few lines about what inspires you and your craft and all that? My team can turn it into a cool reel. Boom, millions of eyeballs on your work."

"That's—that's generous of you."

"Mallory, I feel so passionately about this. I do. I feel like women should just be out there helping one another out. Lifting one another up?"

"Oh, totally."

She reaches out one hand and squeezes my wrist. "I'm so happy to meet you. I really am. You're such an important part of Monk's past. His story. And I feel like we should embrace all of that, the good and the tragic, right? It's what makes us who we are. I mean, do you think we can be friends, Mallory?"

"I would love to be friends."

"Because . . . can I be honest? I feel like you're a little wary of me, right? And I totally understand. But we share this beautiful thing. We both care about this incredible man. And I know Monk wouldn't have loved you if you weren't an amazing person. So I want you to open yourself to me, Mallory. Trust me."

She's lying on her side, effortlessly graceful, long-limbed. In three dimensions, she's even more compelling than when you see her in a photograph. Maybe it's the light beneath her skin, this illumination she wears like it's the natural state of all women to glow like that.

I close my laptop and turn a little to face her. "I'm sorry if I seem a little standoffish. It's kind of an East Coast thing, maybe?"

She laughs. "Oh, I know. These women here on Winthrop! All this passive-aggressive bullshit. I mean, you're not like *that*, obviously. But you know what I mean."

"It's a culture," I say.

"We're just so *open* out west. I have to remember sometimes that I can come across as a little pushy over here. I mean, even Monk took a long time to really open up, you know? He just held everything in, everything he was feeling. I nearly broke up with him a million times. Probably I should have broken up with him for my own sanity, but—oh my goodness, you know how adorable he is. You loved him too. But I'm an *empath*. You know what that is? It's like you feel everyone's pain." She presses a hand to her chest. "And I felt his pain in my bones and I couldn't do anything about it, and it was killing me."

Her hazel eyes fix this earnest look on me. The long, sun-streaked hair swings down to veil her boobs. She's wearing a tiny gold cross on a tiny gold chain, and the cross nestles right in the hollow of her throat, tilted a few degrees like it's taking a nap.

"So what happened?" I ask.

"The trigger, you mean? When his dad passed away. He was devastated. I mean, so was I. Buzzy was always so kind to me. But they had such a complicated relationship, you know? So the whole cancer diagnosis was a roller coaster. I remember coming to visit with my dad—that's how we reconnected, Monk and me—and it was like trying to get two stray cats in the same room. And then he went into remission, and then it came back a year later, and the end came pretty quickly after that. Really awful. Monk was just a wreck. So I got him into therapy. At last. And it was like a drain coming unplugged. He finally told me about you. And I was like, oh, *babe.* That explains *everything.* The trust issues and the intimacy issues. Not that I'm *blaming* you." She reaches out for another wrist squeeze. "Honey, I understand. I'd have bolted too, if I was in your shoes. The *toxicity* of this family. You know about his mother, right? His bratty brother. And the sister? Blue? Cold as ice."

Something's hammering at the back of my head.

Texas, I think. *Lee. Lee and her dad and Monk's dad.*

I glance down at her hand on my wrist, which happens to be her left hand, ring glittering. "So, Lee—and this is not to be critical or anything, I'm just curious—if you're from Texas, and you have this whole Western sensibility and everything, which is awesome, what sort of prompted you to found your business around the New England lifestyle?"

She withdraws the hand and laughs. "Oh, I love the vibe, don't get me wrong. I went to college in Maine, got a job in Boston. This old-school finance shop. So all my friends were New Englanders, I was spending weekends on the Cape and Kennebunk and everything—"

"Hold on a second." My mind is reeling fast, like a video on fast-forward. "*Where* did you say you went to college?"

"Colby." She smiles. "Didn't you know? That's how Monk and I got together. Our dads were friends from Harvard?"

"Oh," I say. "Right. Of course. Harvard."

"We first met when we were ten years old, can you believe it? Class reunion. They put you in the kid camp so the parents can get wasted together. And I show up at this thing and it turns out all the other kids knew each other from school or summers or whatever—it's like this whole Cosa Nostra thing, this fucking Harvard mafia, you're so lucky not to have to deal with this shit—and I was the brat from Texas with the wrong clothes and the wrong accent. The wrong everything. Little bitches were so mean to me. So then Monk swoops in, right? Like my own personal Lancelot. Literally takes me by the hand and drags me in to join in all the fucking reindeer games. And of course they all turned sweet on me after that. Punks."

"That sounds like Monk."

"Oh, he claims he doesn't remember, but I knew right then he was the one. I knew from the bottom of my heart we were meant to be together. I spent the next eight years dreaming about him, and yeah, I might have made a hurry-up red zone drive to get into Colby once I heard he was going there." She winks and lays a finger over her lips. "Then our dads took over. Kind of low-key set us up, freshman year. Buzzy made Monk call me up and ask me out for coffee, you know how it works, and this time I made sure he wouldn't forget me, right? We hit it off right away. So many good times."

"So what happened?" I ask.

"Oh, you know, it was college. He was still figuring stuff out. He wasn't ready. And I had to let him go. Broke my heart, but if the time isn't right, it's not right. So he did his thing and I did mine, just kind of biding along until Buzzy got sick and it brought us back together. The way it was meant to be, right? The love of my life. And finally it hits him too. The love of *his* life."

In the ocean before me, Paige and the girls are bodysurfing atop the lazy water. It's nearly eleven and the air's already turning hot. I realize my laptop screen is back in the sun again and I stand up to adjust the umbrella. My legs are a little wobbly, my brain's numb. A voice calls down from the bluff above us.

"Hey, hon! Wedding planners are here."

Lee turns forward and props herself on her elbows. "Hi, sweetie! What's up?"

Monk cups his hands around his mouth. "Wedding planners!"

"But they're early!"

Monk shrugs and squints at the umbrella, behind which I'm hiding in my retro-style granny-panty swimsuit. "Hey, Pinks! That you? How's the trellis coming along?"

I stick up my thumb over the top of the umbrella.

"Why does he call you that?" Lee asks. "It seems kind of like, demeaning."

"Oh, it's just a high school thing. My mom once said something embarrassing about how I used to draw My Little Ponies when I was little, and Pinkie Pie was my favorite. I guess the nickname was our way of owning the humiliation? Just kind of a stupid joke that wouldn't die, I guess."

"Are you serious? Pinkie Pie?" She laughs. "You're like
kids, you two."

Monk calls down again, a note of exasperation. "Hon?
ing? They're waiting."

Lee sits up and reaches back to gracefully rehook her
over her nipples. "What do you think of this one?"

"Excuse me?"

"This bikini. This designer sent me their stuff to try ou
it's a little too sexy, don't you think? Not my vibe at all."

"Oh gosh. I think you look beautiful whatever you're

She stands, brushes off the sand, and reaches for her
"Diplomatic answer, Mallie. You'll go far in this world."

The wedding planners stay a few hours. When I head insid
for lunch, Monk and Lee are nibbling sandwiches on th
photographs and fabric samples spread out on the teak tabl
encing earnestly with three women and a stylish man.
quickly and dart inside the kitchen, where Grace sits at th
She jumps up and wipes her eyes.

"Grace, what's wrong? Are you okay?"

"It's nothing." She turns to the sink and rests her wri
edge. "Miss Mallory, you don't think my cooking is
fashioned, do you?"

"Of course not! You're the best cook I know. Who says

She picks up a pair of glasses from the sink and puts th
dishwasher and doesn't say a word.

For some reason, I can't settle to work. I wander around
and grounds, trying to find a quiet corner to set up my la
everything distracts me. At half past two, the wedding
leave. Lee hurries inside to send all the footage to her tear
tin. Monk vanishes somewhere. At some point I find mys
ing in front of the pool house fridge, in search of a cold d
rows of cans and bottles blur into a psychedelic collage.

A noise startles me. I turn to the doorway, where Monk
a pair of board shorts and T-shirt, silhouetted by the sun.

"Mallory. There you—" He breaks off and takes a step forward. "Hey, are you okay?"

I realize there are tears in my eyes and blink them away. "Just getting a drink. What's up?"

"Thought I'd take the kids down to the old bunkers for some exploring. You okay with that?"

"Oh, totally. Sounds like fun. Wish I could join you."

He smiles. "Why can't you?"

Something in that smile reminds me of the last time I visited those bunkers, with Monk. I push back a loose curl over my ear. "Work to do. And it's good for you guys to hang out without me."

"Are you sure? We'd love to have you."

"Totes."

Monk holds my gaze another second or two, grin still stuck on his mouth like he doesn't know what else to do with it. "Okay, then. See you later."

"Have a great time."

He turns away and swings through the doorway, into a pile of sunbeams.

"Wait!" I burst out.

"Yeah? On second thought?"

"No. No, not that. Just something I—I don't know, I feel kind of stupid. I didn't realize Lee was your old girlfriend? At Colby?"

My voice comes out a few notes higher than usual. Monk steps back inside the doorway. The sunbeam falls from his face.

"Um, yeah. Yeah, she was." He puts a hand on the doorframe. "Sorry. I guess—I guess I thought you already knew that? Under the incredibly arrogant assumption that the whole world knows my business these days."

"*I* didn't know. I don't—I try to stay off the internet, mostly."

"Well, you're smart. Keep doing that." He looks at his thumb, worrying the edge of the doorframe. "So I guess Lee mentioned it?"

"Oh, I put a few facts together. While we were talking on the beach. You hooked back up when your dad got sick, right?"

"Yep. That's right. She and her dad came to visit him in the hospital. It was a pretty low moment for me. I was kind of beside myself, to be honest. Dad and I didn't get along. As you know. And

it got worse after you left. For the longest time, I blamed him for that."

I feel a draft of cold air on my back and realize the fridge door is still open. As I turn to shut it, I say, "Wow. Why?"

"I figured he'd stuck his finger in, that's all. Maybe talked you out of it or something. Anyway, it was easier than blaming myself."

I turn back to face him. He's still staring at his hand, braced against the doorframe.

"But Lee worked her magic," I say. "Brought you back together."

Monk sighs and lifts his head. "You have to understand, Pinks. Seeing her again, it was like coming home. She'd cared about me before—you know, before all the music shit happened. So I knew I could trust her. I was safe with her. I could settle down, finally. And my dad. My dad thought the world of her. It just—it felt right."

Inside my head, I'm screaming some nonsense. Some shit I've apparently locked deep in that box of mine, the one I don't open. The one that will burst open, from time to time, all on its own, for its own reasons.

No! NO! This was supposed to be our *story! You and me. I was supposed to be the old girlfriend you found again. I was supposed to be your happy ever after. Lovers reunited.*

Not her. Not Lennox Lassiter. Lee.

"Well, you chose well," I say. "She's pretty incredible. Building that business from scratch. And healing the rift with your dad. She's a keeper."

"My dad." Monk clears his throat. "My dad, right before he died? He said I should pop the question. So I did. We got engaged. He'd come home at that point, we had a hospice nurse for him. She showed him the ring. He was over the moon. Died the next day."

"That's—wow. I'm so sorry. But at least—you know. You're happy now. And wherever you dad is, he's smiling. The girl he always wanted for you."

Monk looks at the floor. Lifts his hand from the doorframe and sets it on the back of his neck.

"Pinko," he says.

A voice calls from the doorway. "Babe? Is that you?"

Monk spins around. Lee Lassiter blocks the sun, slim and long-legged. Her bikini winks beneath a kaftan of white linen. She looks from Monk to me to Monk again.

"Oh! Hey, honey," says Monk. "Just checking in with Mallory about the bunker plan."

Lee's face screws up. "About that. Bad news. Kevin called me? He's been trying to reach you. Emergency conference with the lawyers about that copyright thing. He says they're waiting for you."

"Shit," says Monk.

While Paige supervises the kids at the pool, I find a quiet sofa, open my internet browser, and type into the search field.

Fire egypt 1952

I click on the top result, a Wikipedia entry—*Cairo fire.*

The Cairo fire (Arabic: حريق القاهرة), also known as Black Saturday, was a series of riots that took place on 26 January 1952, marked by the burning and looting of some 750 buildings— retail shops, cafés, cinemas, hotels, restaurants, theaters, nightclubs, and the city's Casino Opera—in downtown Cairo.

I dig between the sofa cushions for my phone and send a text to Paige. *Wikipedia says there was huge fire in Cairo in Jan 1952!!!!*

PAIGE: *So???*
ME: *Remember nuns said Hannah arrived at convent with burns. Early 1952*
PAIGE: *Wait why Egypt?*
ME: *Bc Luca thinks bracelet is from Egypt*
ME: *Dates fit*
PAIGE: *Idk seems tenuous*
PAIGE: *Probably coincidence. Correlation does not mean causation*
ME: 😌

I look again at the cobra on my wrist, resting atop the laptop keyboard. *An Egyptian cobra,* Luca said confidently. *I know snakes.*

From another room comes the sound of Lee's voice. She's on the phone, I think. Talking to her team. Wouldn't it be nice to have a team. Instead, I *am* the team, or part of it. That's what the head of design calls us, her team. Lee's voice takes on an edge. I hear the words clearly now.

But that's not the direction I gave you, Kayla. This is all wrong. We talked about this, the evolution of the brand.

I turn the bracelet so the eyes look toward the doorway, so the tiny ruby tongue tastes the air breezing in from the hall.

Believe me, if there was literally anyone else I could ask to do this, I'd ask. But I'm stuck with you for now, honey, so can we pull on our big-girl pants and get this shit done exactly the way I told you to do it? Thank you.

Before I have time to react, Lee storms into the room. When she catches sight of me, she makes a start of surprise. "Oh, my gosh. I'm so sorry you had to hear that."

"No, it's okay. I wasn't really paying attention."

She plops on the sofa next to me. "Managing people is just the hardest thing. I mean, I admit. I'm a perfectionist. I have high standards. Is that wrong?"

"Of course not. You should never apologize for having high standards."

"Thank you. That's exactly how I feel." She glances at the laptop screen. "Ooh, Cairo. Looking for design inspo?"

"Not really. Just some genealogical research."

"Oh, cool. I did that a couple of years ago. Sent in my DNA just to see what turned up. It was lockdown, I was bored. You know."

"Anything interesting?"

"Ha. You might say that. So, I'm part Scandinavian and part British Isles, which I knew. But then I started getting all these pings from random people and, long story short, my dad was a sperm donor in college, before he met my mom." She shakes her head. "Can you believe it? Apparently Scandinavian is super popular. Height and coloring and everything?"

"Okay, that's kind of creepy."

"*Kind* of? And that's not even the craziest part."

"Yeah? What's the craziest part?"

"My sweet, lovely grandpa who I loved more than anything on earth? Fucking cheated on Grandma. Had a whole other family on the other side of the state."

"Are you kidding me?"

"Nope. My therapist was like, honey, it happens way more than you think. She's dealing with this all the time now. DNA results turning up all this crazy shit. Apparently the official term is *paternity incident*." Lee makes her quote marks around the words.

"Paternity incident?"

"When the guy on the family tree isn't the biological dad. Is that what you're researching? One of your grannies had an affair with an Egyptian guy?"

"Maybe. I don't know. We don't have the DNA results back yet? But this bracelet my mom left me . . ."

Lee takes my wrist and looks at the bracelet. "Holy shit. That's the coolest piece I've ever seen. Your mom gave that to you?"

"When she died. Her mother left it to her. Her biological mother. She was adopted."

Lee lets go of my wrist and fixes that earnest look back on my face. "And how are you dealing with all that?"

"Me? Oh, fine. I'm just fascinated, that's all."

"I mean, believe me, I know it can be crazy as fuck, finding out all this shit about people you thought you knew. But then you start to realize it can be kind of cool too. When I went to go meet with all my new aunts and cousins in El Paso, it was the most amazing thing. I felt this bond, right away. I could literally see my grandpa's gestures and—I don't know—the way he looked at you? Surreal. We talked all night." She reaches for my hand and squeezes it. "I'm so glad we're talking like this, Mallie. I'm so glad you're opening up to me."

"Well, I mean—"

"Seriously. This is like our *one peaceful moment* to get to know each other. Before all the wedding craziness. I want us to be like sisters. I mean, we're going to be co-parenting this beautiful kid together. Isn't that amazing?"

"It's wonderful. Sam is really . . . really happy to meet you. Develop a relationship."

"He's so cute. I'm in love, I really am. He's so much like Monk, it's scary. He's almost enough to make me want to get pregnant."

I turn my head to her in surprise. "But Monk said . . ."

"What?"

"Nothing."

"No, tell me." She reaches out for another squeeze. "Honey, talk to me. We're sisters, right? Sisters in spirit."

"Nothing. I was just, you know, under the impression you were already trying? For kids?"

"Did Monk say that?" She smiles. "I mean, sure. He's super eager to start a family. I'm just . . . I don't know, one thing at a time, right? We'll get pregnant when the moment is right." Her head falls back on the sofa. She holds up her phone and flips around her apps with lightning thumbs. "Look at me, obsessively scrolling. I'm going to find Monk. Sex always de-stresses me."

She jumps up from the sofa and swings out of the room.

At one o'clock in the morning, someone knocks on my door.

"It's me," Paige whispers. "You awake?"

I sit up and turn on the lamp. "Come on in and join the party."

My room is on the first floor, a study that was converted into a bedroom when Monk's grandfather grew too old to climb the stairs. There's a bathroom attached with grab bars in the tub. For some reason, this makes me feel ancient.

Paige wears a tank top and lounge pants that hang from her hips. In her hand, she's clutching her phone. She climbs into the bed next to me and pulls up the covers.

"Paige, you need to eat something," I say.

"What's that supposed to mean?"

"I feel like I'm lying next to a skeleton."

Paige lifts her phone. "So I've been texting Lola. She says she'd love to have us over at Summerly."

"You mean for the day?"

"I mean move over there. Don't you think that's a good solution? Sam's just a few houses down from his dad. We get a little space."

"What makes you think—"

"Mallie, for God's sake. This isn't fair to you. This is the literal shittiest thing in the world and it's my fault. Okay, Jake's fault. Since he was the one fucking his junior. But also my fault for marrying him."

"Paige, this is not your fault. This is all on him."

"Yeah, well. My drama shouldn't be your problem, so—"

"Fuck you, Paige. Your drama is always my problem. What are you saying, I can't come to *your* rescue once in a while?"

"No," she says. "That's not our dynamic. *You're* the screwup, I'm the big shining success. I'm the one who—who—"

I drag her crumpling face into my shoulder. Her back heaves a few times. "Paige, it's okay. We'll find our way through. Just sticking together, you and me."

Paige heaves another sob. "Do you want to know the latest?"

"What's the latest?"

"She's pregnant. Of course."

"Pregnant? Are you kidding me?"

"She's pregnant and she told him about the baby in Charlotte— you know, when he was fucking her brains out over Fourth of July?—and he said he wanted her to get an abortion, and she said no, and they had a big fight where she threatened to go public if he didn't leave me and marry her, and he said you're bluffing, sweetie, and booked a flight home to surprise me."

"Asshole," I say.

"Asshole. So whatever. They deserve each other. But you know what kills me the most? There's no clean break. He's always going to be the father of my girls. He's going to stand there at graduations, he's going to walk them down the aisle when they get married, and I'll have to grit my teeth. I'll have to make nice with his new wife and his new kids."

"Oh, Paige—"

"And then I think—I can't help *imagining* him with her. I try to stop myself, but I can't. Naked with her. Having sex with her. Having an *orgasm* inside her, Mallie. *My* Jake. And I just—I just—"

"I know, honey," I say quietly. "I know."

We lie there next to each other, listening to the noise of our breathing.

"So that's why I texted Lola," Paige says. "I thought, I can't put you through this any longer. I mean, the look on your face when they go upstairs together."

"What look?"

"Like you're giving yourself a root canal without anesthetic, just to prove how tough you are."

"Shit. Has anyone else noticed?"

"You mean Monk? He's clueless. Plus he's getting laid by a literal swimsuit model, so what the fuck does he care?"

"She's not a swimsuit model. She's actually pretty smart. She's a businesswoman. You know she went to Colby with Monk?"

"Wait, *what*?"

"She was his old girlfriend. They broke up junior year, right before—you know, the summer I was here. So—"

"Jesus, Mal. You never told me this."

"I just found out. Today. She told me the whole story. She's been in love with him since she was ten years old, Paige. He's the love of her life."

Paige stares at me. "So, she's been stalking him since she was *ten*?"

"Paige, come on. She wasn't *stalking* him. It was meant to be, that's all. She's a good person. She's good for him."

"*Good* for him? Have you scrolled her Instagram? She's *drunk* on herself. She's selling this fake version of herself, this manufactured perfection, this fucking curated lifestyle crap, and she's mining her private life, she's mining *him* to promote all that shit—"

"She's a businesswoman, that's all. Everyone understands that. *You* used to understand it, remember?"

Paige straightens against the pillow. "Oh, fuck you, Mallory. Stop being so fucking *understanding*. I mean, I'm sure you've seen the stats on depression and suicide. Teenage girls. Which will be *my* girls in a few years, by the way. *My* girls scrolling through Instagram and Tik-Tok and seeing her fucking aspirational photoshopped body and her crazy-ass narcissist wellness routines and makeup tutorials on how to make yourself look like a flawless little sex doll. So, yeah, I do take this shit personally. And I don't see her treating you with even a grain of sensitivity. All that flexing with the itsy-bitsy bikinis and the PDAs. So fuck her."

I pick at the duvet. "Are you finished?"

"For now."

"Look, she's going to be Sam's stepmom, okay? She's going to be part of his life. She wants him to be in the wedding. So I have to get along with her. I have to find a way to . . . to deal with this . . . to see them together without . . ."

258 • BEATRIZ WILLIAMS

"Oh, honey." She yanks me into her lap and pats my back. "To-morrow morning we pack up and move to Lola's house. She's com-ing over to pick us up. It'll be cool. She has this awesome guesthouse, two bedrooms plus an attic for the kids to mess around in on rainy days. She says we can stay as long as we like."

I stare across the whipped peaks of duvet at the bookshelves along the opposite wall, a relic of Monk's grandfather. Filled with masculine midcentury bestsellers in peeling dustcovers. Norman Mailer, Graham Greene. Herman Wouk, James Michener. Leon Uris, Sloan Wilson.

"Paige, seriously. If you want to talk about it."

"What, about Jake? We already did, right?"

"I mean how you're feeling. Your beautiful life blowing up. Your fuckface husband. Any time you want to vent, I'm here."

"Look, I'm fine, okay? It's under control." She nudges me back up and pulls out her phone. "I came downstairs for something else, believe it or not. Something kind of incredible. Check this out."

She clicks through a link or two and hands me the phone.

"What am I looking at?"

"My DNA profile. Well, our DNA profile. The results came back. There's a bunch of stuff to pick through, I'm already getting pings from cousin matches. But this is what blew me away."

I squint at the lines of type. "Can't this wait until tomorrow? I cannot do science right now."

"You don't need to do science. Here." She snatches the phone and scrolls down until she comes to a pie chart. "Look. Look at that. It's our geographical slash ethnic heritage."

I take back the phone and use my thumbs to enlarge the image. Examine the pie wedges and the numbers and words. My jaw falls open.

"Stop it." I swivel my head to take in Paige's grinning face. "We're *Jewish*?"

"One quarter Jewish, sister. Mazel tov."

CHAPTER NINETEEN

Hannah

January 1952
Cairo, Egypt

When the taxi pulled up at her apartment building a half-hour later, Salah stepped forward from the awning to open the door for Hannah. His face was hung with grief. She took his hand to help her out of the seat and held it between both of her own.

"Have you heard anything from Ismailia?" she asked. "Your son?"

He shook his head. "There is no news yet. It is the will of Allah."

"Salah, I might be able to find something out for you. My husband might be able to learn some news."

She was trying to meet his gaze, but he wouldn't look at her. He pulled his hand away and turned to open the front door for her. "Mr. Ainsworth arrived home an hour ago," he said.

"Thank you, Salah."

She started to cross the foyer toward the staircase.

"Ah! I almost forgot. A package arrived for you this afternoon, Mrs. Ainsworth."

"A package?"

Salah stepped behind the porter's desk and disappeared for an instant. He emerged with a box wrapped in brown paper, about the size of a paperback novel. Her name and address were penciled in charcoal in precise block letters.

She shoved it into the pocket of her coat.

"Thank you, Salah," she said again.

* * *

Hannah found Alistair in the bath, smoking a cigarette. The ashtray was full and a half-empty bottle of Scotch rested on the tiles next to the tub. She dragged the stool across the floor and sat down near his feet.

"I have wonderful news," she said. "Our marriage has borne fruit at last."

He stared at her. "A miracle."

"Yes. The baby will be born in June, I think. Aren't you pleased?"

Her husband settled his head back on the rim of the tub and closed his eyes. "I'll tell you who *won't* be pleased. My sister Vera and her wretched spawn."

"You're an ass, Alistair."

"I believe," said her husband, "the word you mean is *cuckold.*"

Under her coat, Hannah still wore the dress of green crepe, stained with dew. In the steamy air of the bathroom, it had now begun to wilt like a lettuce leaf. It had cost fifty pounds and Alistair hadn't said a word. Unlike most husbands—even rich ones—he never complained when she spent money on herself.

"Do you care?" she asked.

"Care? I owe the chap a debt. Stepping in where I failed. So long as he doesn't come along later and cause trouble."

"I don't think there's much danger of that."

"No, I rather think not."

There was something about his voice as he said this. Some smug note. He took a last drag on the cigarette and reached over the side of the tub to stub it out in the ashtray.

"Why do you say that?" she asked.

"My dear, I may be a cuckold, but I'm not a fool. I *do* know who it is you've been fucking all autumn. I confess, I didn't imagine he was your sort."

"You don't have the slightest idea what *my sort* is."

"Hannah, for God's sake, the fellow's fucked his way through half the British and American diplomatic staff, to say nothing of the officers' wives. Obviously sets his sights on a particular woman. The kind of woman who's privy to interesting information." Alistair lifted the bottle and the empty glass from the tiles and poured himself a drink. "Naturally I had him investigated."

Hannah felt as if she were looking down a long tunnel. "Did you find anything interesting?"

"*Should* I have, Hannah? Tell me."

"I don't know. I suppose he's a nationalist of some kind. Most Egyptians want the British out. We didn't talk about such things."

"No, of course not. A man of his training, he'd have got the information out of you without your even realizing it."

"I don't have the least idea what you mean."

"Mind you," he said, lighting another cigarette, gazing at the ceiling, "it's a jolly good joke. I'd have paid in proper gold to see the expression on my father's face. Blame me for it, of course."

"A joke?" she said.

He blew out some smoke. "Jew blood in the ancient family line. Dreadful bigot, my father. My elder sister wanted to marry a Jew once. Handsome fellow. She was eighteen. Put a stop to *that*. She died not long after. Consumption. Dreadful."

Hannah stared at the fold of skin that wobbled from her husband's throat. "Jew blood?"

"A taint of Hebrew." He dropped his gaze to meet hers. "Or didn't you know?"

"I—he might have mentioned it—"

"Did he mention he's working for the intelligence agency of the state of bloody Israel? I daresay he didn't mention *that*." Alistair sipped his Scotch and reached over the side of the tub to tap a long crumb of ash into the ashtray. The ash missed and landed on the floor in a small puddle of water. He smiled at her shock. "The report's on my desk if you wish. Typed up just this afternoon."

Hannah found herself standing before the liquor cabinet, pouring a glass of gin. Her hand was shaking and the gin kept splashing over the side to land on the tray. She set down the bottle and drank the gin in a gulp or two. For some reason she glanced at the clock and saw it was nearly one o'clock in the morning.

A scene sprang from her memory. A July morning, in a world that no longer existed.

She remembered how she had been nursing the baby on the stool at the corner of the kitchen. She had just put the kettle on to boil water for tea. There was no more coffee, real or ersatz, and for tea she brewed the herbs and roots she'd grown in the garden— mint, chamomile, ginger.

The baby had been born in May, a year almost to the day since János's fever broke. They had named their new son Károly after her father, and like Hannah's father he had blue eyes and fair hair. On János's mother's side he was Austrian, so he liked to joke that Károly was their little Aryan baby, so colored in order to make himself safe from the Nazis. He was a strapping baby, wanted constantly to nurse. His appetite exhausted her, but she didn't care. Each time her son reached for her she grew a little more in love with him. At night, Hannah tucked him in a cradle next to the bed, and even though he slept well (for an infant, anyway) she would wake up all the time to make sure he was alive, to touch his satin cheek with her finger and marvel at the way his mouth worked while he slept, as if he were dreaming of milk.

The kettle had just begun to whistle when the door flew open. Hannah looked up in surprise to see János stride into the kitchen. Early that morning he had kissed her on the forehead and left to work in the fields all day. He had promised to bring back some river trout for supper. Now it was only the middle of the morning and his hands were empty, except for this piece of paper, folded over twice into a square.

She remembered how he had dragged a chair from the table to sit beside her. How he put a hand on her knee and bowed his head to kiss their son's fair hair.

What is it? she'd asked János. *What's the matter?*

He had unfolded the paper and stared at it. *From Irina,* he'd said. *Your father was deported last week.*

Because her son was suckling his life's milk from her, she couldn't scream or rail at God or otherwise fall to pieces. Anyway, the news was not unexpected. Since German troops had moved in to occupy Hungary in March, Jews had rattled away by the train-load, northward to Poland and the infamous death camps, of which everybody knew but no one spoke. Time and again she had pleaded with her father to join her and János in the countryside, but he had always refused. Budapest was his home, he said. Among the highest reaches of Hungarian government, his former students held sway. Surely they would protect him in his hour of need. He would stay where he was.

So Hannah had known for months that her father's fate was sealed. Now she simply closed her eyes and asked János to read the note aloud to her. Was Irina certain of her information? Had any attempt been made to rescue him from his fate?

The note was short. Irina had done all she could. Had strained every nerve to obtain a safe conduct pass from the Swedish embassy—the diplomats there were handing them out by the thousands—but it arrived too late.

By the time János read out the last sentence, Hannah was weeping. *What are we going to do?* she'd asked him. *What if they come for me and the baby?*

They won't come for you, he'd said. *So far east, the middle of nowhere. And you're my wife. The Countess Vécsey. You're safe here. You're safe with me.*

She remembered how she had stared at János's stark face. How she'd shaken her head and said to her husband, *Don't you understand, there is nowhere safe on this earth. No square inch of ground where I can rest.*

Hannah turned her head toward the window. Alistair had left the curtains open and the view looked east, toward downtown Cairo, alight and teeming. All the nightclubs and the department stores, the Auberge des Pyramides and Circurel and Groppi's and Shepheard's Hotel.

Hannah lifted her arm and hurled the empty glass against the panes.

Then she went to the writing desk in her bedroom and pulled out a piece of paper. Not the engraved stationery with her married name, their address in Cairo, but a plain sheet. She wrote hurriedly and stuffed the note in an envelope. In the back of the bottom desk drawer she felt along the side until she found the scrap of paper that had appeared in her pocket upon her return from Alexandria. She copied the address onto the back of the envelope and sealed it.

Then she rose from the desk and went downstairs, where she gave Salah the envelope to be posted in the morning.

* * *

In the taxi, she stuck her hand in the pocket of her coat to search for a handkerchief and discovered the parcel that Salah had delivered to her an hour ago.

Though her name was written in block letters, she recognized the writing. She clawed apart the string and unfolded the brown paper to reveal an ordinary cardboard box. Inside the box, wrapped in cotton wool, was a gold bracelet in the shape of a striking cobra.

There was no note. She ran her finger along the inside of the box, examined the cotton wool, the other side of the brown paper in which the box had been wrapped. Not a word. Only her name and address in those sterile block letters.

She lifted the bracelet to the glow from the passing streetlamps. A pair of tiny emerald eyes stared back at her; a tiny ruby tongue tasted the air. The hood exquisitely flared. The tail wound around the wearer's wrist in a delicate spiral. In the artificial noon, surging and falling as the lamps went by, Hannah could have sworn it was alive. She meant to wrap it back in its cotton wool and stuff it inside the box.

Instead she found herself sliding the bracelet over her right hand to clasp her wrist.

A perfect fit.

At the front desk, the clerk told Hannah that Mr. Beck was not on duty that evening. He asked whether he could be of assistance instead.

Hannah still wore her dress of green crepe, stained by the dew and wilted by the steam of her husband's bath, under her coat of dark blue cashmere wool. Her hair was still gathered on one side in its diamante clip; her pearl earrings still dangled from her earlobes. She suspected her lipstick had faded to a disgraceful pink line at the rim of her lips.

She smiled at the clerk. "Perhaps I could leave a message?"

The clerk gave her a pen and a piece of paper and moved tactfully to the other end of the desk. Hannah wrote, *Please see me upstairs at once on a matter of great importance. H.* She folded the paper twice into a square and wrote *J. Beck* on the back. From her pocketbook she extracted a pound note, which she also folded into a square. The clerk's eyes lit with interest. She handed him both notes.

"Please see to it that Mr. Beck receives this as soon as he arrives."

Lucien's room was locked, but Hannah had expected that. She unfastened the diamante clip from her hair and knelt before the lock. It was an easy mechanism; hotel locks usually were. The door swung open. Everything tidy, the bed made, not a scrap of paper out of place. In the bathroom, the towels would be hung neatly on the rails. She had always appreciated the pristine surroundings. When you were committing sordid acts, you felt less sordid doing so on an unimpeachable bed. That was how she'd felt, anyway.

And yet. As she roamed around the room, touching the familiar, sacred objects—the lamp, the chair, the bedpost, the mirror atop the chest of drawers—it seemed to her that the room was *too* tidy. Where were the books stacked on the nightstand and the desk? The gentlemanly silver-backed hairbrush before the mirror? She opened the closet and found it empty. The drawers—vacant. In the bathroom, not so much as a flake of soap, a toothbrush, a stray hair.

Hannah sank onto the chair before the desk and started to laugh.

How heroic she'd felt. A character in a novel, racing to warn her lover of his impending arrest, *before it was too late*! But some earlier bird had chirped in his ear. He had already fled. Never mind.

The hysteria in her chest soon ebbed. She laid her head on her arms and stared at the dark, glittering eyes of the cobra wound around her wrist. The only trace of Lucien that remained in the room. That, and the smell of him.

On a golden afternoon in late September, Hannah sat on a blanket in the meadow with her son, smiling at his attempts to lift himself up on his hands. The air smelled of warm, ripe hay. She had gathered the last of the potatoes that morning and stored them in the baskets in the cellar, and though her hands were chapped she now worked a pair of knitting needles, trying to rescue one of János's moth-eaten woolen vests before the cold set in. She was just admiring the glow cast by the sun on Károly's fine hair when a shadow appeared to extinguish it.

She looked up. "János? What's the matter?"

He crouched next to her. His face was heavy with grief. "The Soviets have crossed the frontier, fifty miles away."

Hannah made an exclamation and gathered up the baby in her arms.

"Pack whatever you can," said János. "We have a little petrol. I'll drive you as far as I can."

"But what about you?"

He looked to the eastern horizon, which had already started to dim. "I'm going to have to fight," he said.

A hand on her shoulder. A gentle, urgent voice next to her ear, calling her name.

Hannah startled upright. "János?"

"Shhh. It's me. Lucien."

For a moment, she was lost. This peculiar, antiseptic room. The polished furniture. The air that smelled of whiskey and cigarettes. The golden snake wound around her wrist. The trim, white-shirted man who stood next to her, who possessed the whiplike body of János but not his eyes, his smile, his emaciation, his hair that had turned abruptly gray and begun to thin at the temples.

This one was robust and well fed. His hair made thick waves you could sink your fingers into.

"Lucien," she said.

He crouched next to the chair, so they were eye to eye. Like János in the meadow. But now her arms were empty. Károly was gone.

"What's the matter, Hannah? Why are you here?" the man demanded.

She leaned forward against his chest and sobbed.

Lucien let her weep all over his fine white shirt. He closed his arms around her and murmured soothing noises into her ear. At some point, when the leading edge of the squall had blown itself out, he lifted her in his arms and carried her to the armchair, where she curled into a ball on his lap. She remembered who she was, who he was. Where they were and why.

"You have to leave," she said.

"Yes, I know."

"It's my fault. I should have realized—Alistair—"

"It makes no difference."

She lifted her head. "You were going to leave anyway?"

"Yes," he said.

"Without telling me?"

"I did tell you." He touched the cobra with his finger. "I also told you I would find you again, afterward."

"After what?"

He tried to stir from the chair, but she held him down by the shoulders. "You should have told me what you were doing. That you were spying for Israel."

"But I did, Hannah. Didn't I?"

Lucien held her gaze. Steady green eyes, the color of hope. Hannah thought back to the afternoon in Alexandria, in the apartment like an apartment you might find in Paris, the tea and marzipan, the sunshine dreaming through the enormous windows. Lucien's mother, slight and exquisite. Her gentle voice.

And Lucien, as they ambled back to the hotel. *It's not something you go about advertising, these days. Only to people you trust.*

What an idiot she was. Thinking only of their destination—the hotel room, the bed, the hours of passion until supper. He had split himself open for her and she hadn't noticed. A pair of bodies, that's all they were to each other.

"It's all right," he said to her. As if she had spoken the words aloud. For an instant she thought she had.

But of course she hadn't. Hannah had never given him her thoughts. Had never split herself open for him. A body, that was all. A field to sow.

She laid her head against his chest and listened to his heart.

"When the Soviets came," she said, "I was living with János at his family's estate in the east. We had lost a girl and a boy to typhoid while he was fighting at Stalingrad. By some miracle he came home and we had another son. Károly. My boy."

Lucien's heart thumped in her ear. It seemed to her that she had melted into him somehow, that the beat of his heart had become her own. That she didn't need to speak this terrible thing out loud, because he would see her memory in his own head.

Still, she went on.

"János had word that the Red Army had crossed the frontier. After Stalingrad, everyone thought he had been killed, and he was happy to pretend to be dead and live quietly with me in the country. But the Soviets in Hungary, that was another matter. We packed our things. I was supposed to go to Budapest, to stay with friends. János was going to rejoin the army and defend the country. We were so stupid, we thought we had until the morning. One last night in our home together. One last night in our bed together. Just before dawn, some Soviet soldiers broke into the house."

Lucien made some small noise in his chest, as if he had taken a blow that knocked him senseless.

"I don't know how many there were," she said. "Six or seven, I think. They took turns beating me while the others held János down and made him watch. I remember I called out to him to close his eyes but he wouldn't do it. He wouldn't let me suffer without him. When they tired of this they shot János through the head. This Soviet rifle. A single shot in the middle of the forehead. I don't remember the sound of the gun, or the bullet hitting his head. Just the sight of his brains on the bedroom wall. They left me on the floor cradling his body. I was frantic, I was out of my mind. I remember thinking, this is how it ends? Like this? I heard them outside, these soldiers. They were laughing. To them it was all a big joke, a jolly time. I thought, why didn't they just shoot me? Then I smelled the smoke. Smoke everywhere. They had set fire to the house in order to burn me alive. To burn me with the body of my dead husband. And I thought, *Károly.* I remembered Károly in his cradle next to the bed. He had slept through it all. He was always a sound sleeper, we used to joke about it. How the house could burn down around him and he wouldn't wake up. Somehow I got up on my hands and knees. I don't know how. There was all this blood. Mine and János's. On the floor, the rug. I crawled around the bed to the cradle. And I saw it was empty. They had taken him. When I was holding the body of my dead husband. They had taken my son."

The word *son* was a whisper. Lucien held her with both arms. If he had said something she would have dissolved. A word of pity would have destroyed her. But he did not. His heart thumped in the same steady rhythm against her ear. His white tuxedo shirt smelled of cigarettes, of laundry starch. Of a woman's perfume.

"Somehow I got outside. I don't remember how. I must have taken the back stairs. I was screaming for him. My baby. He had the most beautiful curls, like God had spun sunshine into silk for his hair. János used to play this game with him, he would hide an apple under the table and then pretend to find it behind Károly's head. And he would laugh. The sound of his laugh, I hear it all the time. I hear it in my sleep. In the street, always just around the corner. I got outside, through the smoke, screaming for my son, but they had already driven away. I ran around the house, looking for them. Down the drive. These Soviet soldiers. They had driven away with him. Or killed him, I don't know. I could smell the exhaust from their damn trucks. Smoke and exhaust and gasoline. This terrible stench. So I thought, *I will go back into the house and burn to death in my husband's arms,* but I didn't have the strength. I just fell where I stood. When I woke up, the house was gone. It was just a pile of ash and stone. I need some water."

Without a word, Lucien lifted them both from the chair. He settled her on the bed, against the pillows, and walked into the bathroom. She heard the taps swish. He came out again bearing a glass of water and sat on the edge of the bed while she drank it. She tried to steady her hands but they shook anyway. Gently he drew the glass from her fingers and set it on the nightstand.

"Anyway," she said, "that's how I wound up in Budapest during the siege. With my husband's old lover Irina. To kill as many of them as I could. Nazis and Soviets, I didn't care. I learned how to fire a rifle from the window of an apartment building and smack a man's forehead with a bullet. It was so satisfying to watch his body make this jerk when the bullet hit him. When the city surrendered, I was arrested. SMERSH, you know what that was? The Soviet counterintelligence squad. They interrogated me for weeks, I think. I lost track of time. You know their methods."

"Yes," he said.

"For women it's even worse. These barbarians. You have to

separate your mind from your body, your soul from your body. You have to think of your body as some sack that doesn't belong to you. I only escaped when they got so drunk one night, the night Berlin fell, they left the door of the interrogation cell unlocked. Stupid brutes. I walked right out. I walked all the way to Austria. You know the rest."

Lucien lit a cigarette for her. Side by side they sat on the bed, passing the cigarette back and forth. In the crack between the curtains, dawn poked a finger.

"You must go," she said. "Alistair will have passed on his information to the authorities. You'll be arrested any moment."

He stubbed out the cigarette and reached for her. Hannah still wore her coat of dark blue cashmere over her dress from the party. He pushed the coat over her right shoulder and kissed the bare skin, then covered it again.

"I have to drive to Alexandria to put my mother on a ship," he said.

"To Israel?"

"Yes. For years, she wouldn't go. She thought Egypt was her home, the way Jews used to think Germany was their home. I told her she had to leave now, while she could still take her money with her. Finally she agreed. But I must put her on that ship myself. I have to be sure. You understand?"

His eyes were green and steady. The whites a little bloodshot. She said, "You should go with her. You should board that ship."

"I can't leave you behind."

"Nonsense. You had already planned to leave."

He took her by the shoulders. "Come with me, Hannah."

"Because you feel sorry for me now?"

"Because I'm in love with you."

Hannah removed his hands from her shoulders. "There's no need for that kind of talk anymore."

"Hannah, stop it. A moment ago you were telling me the truth."

"That doesn't mean I intend to leave my husband and go off with you—where? Israel? You must be joking."

"Wherever you want. Anywhere in the world. We have a child, Hannah."

"*I* have a child. You're free, Lucien. Go. You're not cut out for fatherhood."

He flinched. In the instant before he turned his face away, she glimpsed the anguish in his eyes.

"You were right to leave," she said. "It's best for both of us. You know it is."

He rose from the bed and went to the window. "Do you love me, Hannah?"

"Whether I love you or not, it's not the point."

"It's a simple question."

She looked at her lap, stained and wrinkled. The thickness at her belly. "It's stupid of me—"

He turned to face her. "Say it, Hannah. You love me. Admit it, for God's sake."

"Don't be an idiot. Of course I do."

"Then it's simple, isn't it? We go together."

She stared at the hand he held out to her.

"Go," she said. "Just go."

His hand fell to his side. He walked to the bed and dropped to his knees. Hannah touched his hair, cradled his head and kissed it. She could smell the peppermint tang of his hair oil. His hands slid up her thighs to cover her belly. Through the thin green crepe he kissed her. She closed her eyes so there was nothing else but his warm lips on her womb, his hands, his head between her palms, his hair against her face.

He lifted his head and closed his hand over the bracelet on her wrist.

"I need to show you something," he said.

CHAPTER TWENTY

Mallory

July 2022
Winthrop Island, New York

I wait until about half past five, when the sun is halfway up above the horizon and the air is made of pink light, before I get out of bed and dress in my running clothes. My head's heavy; my arms and legs feel as if I was hit by a truck in the middle of the night.

A metaphorical truck, you might say.

To go running on Winthrop Island at dawn is about as close to heaven as I can imagine, at least anymore. I start off down Club Road at a gentle jog. Houses to my left, fairways to the right. The still air tastes of salt and memory. The landscape is peopled with ghosts. There I fly on an old bicycle, chasing the twins toward sailing lessons in Little Bay Harbor, passing Monk and his golfer at the eighth tee. He spots us and lifts his hand to wave.

I run past the silent guard hut, where I usually turn down Little Bay Road and loop back at the harbor. But the endorphins have kicked in early. A sleepless night will do that to me. I keep on running down West Cliff Road, past the old Longfellow meadow and Monk leading me over the grass toward the path down to Horseshoe Cove, where we light a fire and roast the marshmallows we feed to each other, one after another, exchanging marshmallow kisses in the velvet night until a downpour douses the fire and sends us racing back up the hill and across the meadow to make love, soaked and laughing, on the dog blanket in the back of Bessie.

Past the old Fisher estate, a glimpse of the Fleet Rock lighthouse, the cliffs, the sharp plunge downhill to the village, where I veer left and circle the airfield to the path leading over the old bunkers to the dunes and back again along the other side of the airfield. Then back up the sharp pitch of West Cliff Road with all that I have, all the breath left in my body, until I crest the ridge and cruise back high as a kite the way I came, houses stirring now, golfers and caddies appearing on the fairways. Past Serenity Lane and Summerly at the end of it. I avert my gaze from the Seagrapes driveway and turn down the gravel strip toward the Monk house, where a couple of voices reach me from the kitchen.

I drop to a walk, panting, dripping, hands on hips. I can't help but hear them.

But, Miss Lennox, you said—

A simple sorry, Grace. That's all I'm asking for. Is that too much to ask? A simple sorry and maybe, just maybe, *follow my directions next time?*

But I thought—

I mean, do you seriously not know the difference between oatmeal and overnight oats? You told me you did, Grace. I trusted you. So what is this shit? Fucking instant Quaker? *Filled with fucking pesticides and GMOs? Am I supposed to put that into my body?* Monk's *body?*

I'm sorry, Miss Lennox.

If you don't know what I'm asking for, look it up on the fucking internet. If you can't remember, write it down. I assume you can write, *can't you? So make a list. You know what? I'll do it. I'll type it up with every last fucking detail highlighted so you won't screw up next time. Okay?*

I'm sorry, Miss Lennox.

Sorry really doesn't cut it here, Grace.

By now I'm storming through the mudroom on the way to the kitchen, where a bowl of oatmeal sits on the wooden counter, studded with fresh blueberries. Lee stands next to the oatmeal, wearing a pair of black capri leggings and a cropped black camisole, yoga-ready. Her hair tumbles down her back like it's been through a wind tunnel.

"What in the hell is going on here?"

Lee tucks her hair behind one ear. "This is between me and Grace, Mallory."

"Grace is a friend of mine."

"I'm sure she is," says Lee, "but she *works* for me."

"She works for Monk."

Lee smiles. "Honey. I think we understand that means she works for me too?"

"Well, I'm sorry, but I can't just stand here and listen to you *berate* someone who's been working for the family since before you were born. I don't care if she smashed all the crystal. You might be sleeping with the boss, but you still owe her respect, okay? Don't act like a toddler. Grace, I'll clean that up for you. Go take a minute to yourself."

Lee and I stare at each other for a few seconds. The tears stream soundlessly down her cheeks.

"Look," I say. "I didn't mean to hurt your feelings. That's just not the way we speak to people around here."

She turns and walks out of the kitchen. I hear the quick thump of her feet as she climbs the stairs to the master bedroom.

Monk finds me an hour later, as I'm helping Sam pack up his things.

"Hey, buddy. Can I talk to your mom a minute?"

Sam looks at me, eyebrows raised.

"Go ahead," I tell him.

Once Sam passes out the door, Monk says, "What's going on here? Are you packing?"

"Lola's invited us to stay with her at Summerly."

"When did this happen?"

"Last night. You and Lee went to bed early, remember?"

I hear him sigh behind me. "Mallory. Look at me."

I turn. He's dressed in a T-shirt and gray jersey joggers. His hair's a jumble, his face heavy. He frowns at me. "Look, I realize the situation is a little awkward—"

"It's okay. It really is. Staying here was a mistake to begin with."

"Was it, Pinks? Was it that bad?"

I turn back to Sam's drawer and pull out a tangle of shirts, which I dump on the bed to fold. "It's just awkward, like you said."

"Can you tell me what happened downstairs just now? Lee's been on the floor sobbing."

"She was disrespectful to Grace, that's all. So I called her out on it."

"What did you say to her?"

"I said just because she was sleeping with the boss didn't give her the right to act like a toddler."

"Jesus, Mallory. You said that?"

"Monk, even your alcoholic stepmother treated Grace like a human being."

A groan slides from his throat. "So, what happened down there, exactly?"

"Why don't you ask your fiancée?" I set one neat, folded shirt in Sam's duffel bag and pick up another. "You know what, forget it. I'm not here to bring the household drama. We'll be out of your hair in an hour, and I think things will go much better for everyone."

Monk sits on the edge of the bed, a few feet away, and tries to capture my gaze. "I know Lee can be a little exacting."

"That's one way of putting it."

"But she's a good person, Mallory. She's been there for me. I was in a pretty shitty place a few years ago, when we got back together. I'd been avoiding commitment, avoiding adult relationships for a decade. And she led me back. Pulled me outside of my own head. Made me start some therapy, wouldn't take any shit from me. I needed that. I needed her."

"Monk, that's a nice story. I'm sure she's wonderful for you. I'm sure you'll be fantastically happy together. I want you to be happy together."

"Pinks, will you stop it?"

"Stop what?"

He crosses the room, stares at himself in the mirror that hangs on the bathroom door, and turns around. "You know what? Let's have that talk. I think we need to have that talk."

"What talk?"

"I don't think you get it. I don't think you really understand how you destroyed me when you left. I didn't just lose my girlfriend, the love of my fucking life. I lost my best friend. I lost the one person on this earth I knew I could trust. You broke that trust, Mallory, and you broke me, and now it turns out you broke way more than I even imagined. That boy out there. My *son*. You kept my son away from me for *thirteen years*. Who does that, Mallory? Who does that to the guy she's supposed to love?"

"I thought you had all that figured out. You know, I needed to pursue my art and everything. Be free."

"Was I wrong? What did I miss, Mallory? What am I missing?"

"Nothing."

Monk reaches out and takes my hand, just below the bracelet. "Am I the asshole, then? Is that what you're trying to say?"

"No."

"What did I do, Mallory? Just tell me what I did to you. For God's sake. I need some fucking closure here."

A voice breaks in from the doorway. "Hey, you two. Mallie, could you lend me a hand with the girls' stuff? Lola's going to be here in like, ten minutes."

Monk drops my hand. "Paige, do you mind giving us another second, here?"

I gather up the rest of the shirts and dump them in Sam's duffel bag. "Hold on, Paige. I'm coming."

It turns out Lola's grandmother-in-law celebrates her ninety-sixth birthday in a week, and the entire Peabody clan has gathered to pre-game. Lola apologizes for the chaos.

"Dave has seven aunts and uncles, including the steps, and . . ." She pauses to count. "Nineteen first cousins. I mean, not all of them are here this year, obviously. The hundredth, that's going to be the rager."

Mrs. Peabody is a small-boned, shrunken woman with sharp, hooded eyes and coral lips. Her white hair fluffs around her face. She walks right up to me to introduce herself.

"Dunne," she says. "So you're Irish."

"Actually, I'm Jewish," I tell her. "I love your dress."

"Don't patronize me. You should have seen me when I was young. I was really something then."

"I'll bet. I understand you're a writer?"

She cups her ear. "A what?"

"A WRITER!"

"Hell, no. I'm a historian. But I'm required to write it all down so people will remember." She looks me up and down. "*I* understand a certain somebody's got the hots for you."

"I'm sorry, *what*? *Who*?"

"Oh, he gave me an earful on the way to the doctor a couple of weeks ago. I guess I can't blame him." She hands me her empty glass. "Fetch me a gin and tonic with lime, will you, please."

At the liquor table, a dark-haired man expertly rattles a cocktail shaker and strains it into a glass. He looks up from his work and his mouth breaks into a grin.

"Mallory the First," he says, in a deep, attractive baritone. "What can I do for you?"

Mrs. Peabody looks pleased with herself. She takes her glass and says, "I see you've found my favorite grandson."

"Don't be too impressed. We're all her favorites," Sedge tells me.

"Sedge recently broke up with the girlfriend everybody hated, and he's terrifically handsome—well, you can see *that* for yourself—*and* I understand he makes a lot of money on the internet. Isn't that right, Sedge?"

"It's not as sketchy as she makes it sound, I promise," says Sedge.

"Did Miss Dunne tell you she's a Jew?"

"It's Mallory to my friends," I say. "And I'm only one-quarter Jewish. Sorry to disappoint."

"It'll have to do," says Mrs. Peabody. "We've only got one Jew in the family these days, and he could use someone to help him celebrate the high holidays. Sedge, take Mallory out on the beach and see if she'll go on a date with you. Just keep an eye out for the KGB."

"What did your grandmother mean by that?" I ask Sedge, once we've kicked off our shoes to enjoy the squelch of sand between our toes.

"Apologies. Don't mind Granny, she's a meddler."

"No, I mean about the KGB."

"Oh, that?" He laughs. "Just an old family legend. They say

Summerly was a hotbed for Soviet spies after the war. Kept some kind of secret radio in the guest cottage."

"Intriguing. I happen to be staying in the guest cottage."

"Then you should check out the attic some evening." He sips his beer and stares out to sea. Cheekbones stained pink. "I could help. If you need a local to show you around."

I kick a little sand and sip my gin and tonic. "Before you make any more irresistible offers, I think you should know I have a thirteen-year-old son who needs a new kidney."

"Well," he says slowly, "I didn't see *that* coming."

"On the plus side, I'm not looking for anything serious."

"That's supposed to be a plus?"

"You tell me, Sedge the Second."

Sedge has one hand in his pocket, one hand on his beer. The falling sun hits the side of his face and turns it gold. He examines the neck of the beer bottle and glances toward the house and the generations of Peabodys mingling around, paying us no attention. With his head, he inclines me to the right, where a tangle of beach roses shields us from view. He puts his arm around me and kisses me. His mouth tastes of beer, of comfort. My crushed, bent emotions uncurl and stretch out to warm in the sun. When he lifts his head, he says, "I'm sorry about your son. That must be tough."

"Yeah, it's been real."

He makes gentle, nibbling kisses along my jaw to my ear. "So you're looking for a little escape from reality, is that what I'm hearing?"

"You're a good listener, Sedge."

"I've been well trained by my former owners." Sedge sets the beer in the sand and unfastens the top button of my shirt, then the next. He kisses my neck, my chin, my mouth. "Thirteen, huh? What were you, a child bride?"

"Sweet of you. Not a bride at all, actually. Just a dumb kid who made a mistake."

A noise to the left springs us apart. Before I can turn to see who's there, Sedge steps in front of me. "Buddy. Can I help you?"

Around the corner of Sedge's shoulder, I spot a familiar head of hair.

"Sorry, man. My mistake."

Sedge says, "Oh, shit. Monk *Adams*?"

I leap to one side of Sedge. "Wait! Monk! Is something wrong?"

Monk's already turned away to walk up the beach. A bunch of meadow flowers dangles from one hand. He stops and makes a quarter-turn, so he speaks to me without quite looking at me. "Sorry, Pinks. They said you were down on the beach, I didn't realize—"

"But everything's okay, right?"

He looks at the flowers in his hand. "I just wanted to apologize, that's all. You were right, I was the asshole."

"Wait, what happened?"

"Another time. When you're free." He turns his back to stride up the beach, not toward Summerly but along the water, toward his own house. I stand there staring after him.

"You should probably get that," Sedge says softly.

"Shit." I hand him my gin and button up my shirt. "I probably should."

I catch up with Monk on the other side of the inlet, just as the ground starts climbing upward to form the bluff. "Wait! Monk!" I call out.

He stops and turns. He's dropped the meadow flowers somewhere along the way.

"Pinks, it's all right. It can wait."

"Well, I'm here, aren't I? So you might as well tell me."

Monk runs a hand through his hair, a gesture so familiar I think for an instant that I'm twenty-one years old again, that we've rewound this movie to the beginning.

"Grace quit," he says.

"What? No!"

"She spoke to me after you left. She was kind of a mess. I tried to salvage the situation but she—she was too upset. About what happened. About what's apparently been happening all along, and I never figured it out. Because Grace was too . . . because she . . ."

He turns his head away and puts his fists on his hips. The ocean sends a gust of wind to fly around his hair. He lifts one hand to brush a knuckle beneath his eye.

"Because she was too ashamed to tell me, Pinks. She didn't want to *hurt my feelings.*"

"It's not your fault."

He snorts out a laugh and lifts his head to face me. "It kind of *is,* Pinks. Right? I'm responsible for what happens in my own house. And I turned a blind eye. Because I didn't want to see it. I needed this relationship to work. I needed something in my life to last. And then *you* come along, Miss Integrity. You're not having any of *that* bullshit, are you? Three days is all it takes for you to set my house in order."

"That's not really—"

"Look, I've taken up enough of your time." He checks his watch. "I have an early flight out tomorrow. I need to get home and pack."

"You're leaving?"

"Something came up. Business."

"What about . . . ?"

"Lee? She left this afternoon. We had a little discussion. About not abusing the people who've cared for me all my life. She says she's been misrepresented and she's the injured party. I'm sure we'll work it out."

I can't tell if he's laid some irony on that last sentence or not. Fourteen years ago, I would have known. I could have sensed every nuance of meaning in his voice and face.

"Go back to Summerly, Pinks," he says. "Enjoy the party. You deserve a little fun."

"Well, I happen to think this is more important."

"*This?* What do you mean, *this?*"

"I mean you're upset. You're unhappy."

"Oh, so *now* it matters?"

"I never wanted to make you unhappy, Monk. That's the absolute last thing in the world I wanted."

Monk sighs and hangs his hand on the back of his neck. He looks out to sea. "So, you know that shit they used to drink, during the Second World War? When the real coffee ran out, they drank this ersatz coffee. Fake coffee. It wasn't real. It was made from whatever they could get their hands on. Acorns or chicory. I don't know what. My grandfather used to tell me about it. He was shot down in France, went down one of those Resistance escape lines to Spain. It tasted like shit, he said, but they drank it anyway because they didn't have any real coffee and they needed *something,* right? Something to keep them warm? They pretended it was real, but it wasn't. And when the war ended and they tasted real coffee again, they wondered how the hell they'd made themselves drink that ersatz shit. How they even got it down. How they survived so long pretending it tasted all right. But it was all they had. And it got them through the war, like I said."

I cross my arms over my chest and stare down at my flip-flops.

"I'm not *unhappy,* Pinks. Trust me, this right here? Is not *me unhappy.* I have a son. You and me, we have a son together. And I am grateful beyond words for that, Mallory. I'm so grateful for Sam, I can't explain. Just to know something good came out of that summer, something real. So now it's my turn. My job to take care of him. Keep him around for us to love."

I tell my toes, "I realize I should have found a way to inform you sooner."

"Hey. You were a dumb kid. You made a mistake."

I look up. "Oh, shit, Monk. I'm sorry. I didn't mean that."

"'Sokay." He steps forward, takes me by the elbows, and kisses me gently on the lips. "Good night, Pinko."

As I walk back to Summerly, my chest feels as if it's being crushed by a refrigerator. I reach the edge of the beach and hear some shouts. The mother-instinct geysers up. I run to find Sam and discover him right away, watching the other kids play volleyball. No dialysis today, so his energy's low. He sits in the sand, forearms propped on his knees, fingers linked. He follows the ball with such intense concentration that when it arcs his way on a wild shot, it's like he manifested it. He lifts one spindly arm and palms the ball. Hurls it back into play. The kids turn around and carry on and something chokes me, a wad of helpless rage.

For God's sake, Monk, he needs you. He needs his dad.

But as I start toward Sam, a girl about his age drops into the sand next to him. Cute girl. She says something to him, he says something back. I change course mid-stride and walk on, crossing the beach to the terrace, where Paige spots me and waves.

"Did I fuck up?" she asks. "I didn't realize you had company out there."

"No worries. I seem to have lost my drink, though."

"Everything okay?"

"Yes. No. Shit." I pull the glass from her hand and gulp down about half, while Paige watches attentively. "I think I might need a few more of these."

"So, what did he want?"

I stare into the glass. A couple of ice cubes have melted into chips. "You know, for a minute there, I was almost happy. All of us hanging out together, like a real family. Beach and sunshine and wine and the rib eyes on the grill."

"Until Lee came on the scene, you mean?"

"It's not just Lee. It's everything." I hand back the drink. "I need to stand back from his life. I'm in the way."

"You can't stand *back*. You have a son with him."

"I can't do this. I don't fit into his life. *We* don't fit into his life. And Sam's the one who's going to get hurt."

"Oh, *Sam's* going to get hurt? Is that what you're telling yourself? Listen to me, Mallie." She takes my arm. "Look at yourself. All these years, have I ever met a guy you're dating? Not once. Because you refuse to open yourself up again. You have fuck buddies, that's all. And now that I'm here, seeing you with him, I finally figured out why."

"Oh? Why?"

"Because a piece of you keeps hoping it's going to work out with you and Monk. A piece of you is still in love with him."

I shrug off her arm. "Fuck off, Paige."

"It's true. Whenever he's in the room, you light up. You get all glowy. And I'm telling you, Mallie, you have to find a way to put out that fucking candle, okay? Put out that candle so you can stand in the same room with him without burning up. You need to move on from him. For your sake and for Sam's."

I meet her gaze and think how hard her eyes look, how little she's slept. "Paige, you know what? You have your own shit to deal with. Don't worry about mine, okay? For once?"

"Mallie, I'm trying to *help,* here. Just hear me out. You don't have to learn to live *without* him. You can't, that's the shitty part. You're stuck, because of Sam. So, you just have to learn to live *with* him. You know, like the wise man sang? If you can't be with the one you love—"

"Incredibly helpful, Paige. Thank you."

"—love the one you're with." She looks past me, toward the beach. "Did I ever tell you how I ran into Sedge Peabody a few times in Boston? Party circuit. Super guy."

"Paige."

"Seriously. You know he started this internet company, right? Some kind of boring back-office finance shit. I can't remember what. He sold it last year for just under a billion dollars."

"Paige, I—"

"A *billion dollars,* Mallie. *And* he's hot. *And* he's single. And—"

"Paige, *please* shut the fuck up."

"—*and* his ex-girlfriend is a friend of this mom in Ida's class, and the mom says the ex told her it was the best sex she ever had—with Sedge, I mean, and—"

"Hate to interrupt," says Sedge Peabody, at Paige's elbow. "Thought I'd bring this woman a fresh drink? But I can come back later if you're not finished."

Paige's eyes open wide at the space between my eyebrows. She lifts her glass and drains what's in there. "Nope. I think I'm finished here."

I watch her walk off across the terrace. "I think this is the moment when the earth is supposed to open up and swallow me?"

"For the record," Sedge says, "it wasn't even close to a billion dollars."

"But the sex thing?"

"Oh, definitely true. Here, you might as well drink this. Good for dousing the flames of awkwardness." He hands me the glass in his left hand. We clink. "Seems like it's been a pretty rough afternoon for you, Mallory the First. Is there anything I can do to cheer you up?"

I eyeball him over the rim of the glass. The breeze ruffles his dark hair. His hazel eyes are soft with kindness. "For starters," I say, "you can tell me what Sedge is short for."

"That's easy." He smiles. "Sedgewick."

Just after dawn the next morning, a phone starts to ring. At first, I think it's inside my head. Ringing violently. Bouncing off the rocks. *Make it stop,* I think.

Someone stirs nearby. "Yours or mine?"

The words make no sense. My head hurts like hell.

The ringing stops. "Hey," says a deep, attractive baritone. "How are you feeling?"

My eyes fly open. I turn my head. Sedge Peabody's upside-down face grins sleepily at me below the edge of the bed above me. I'm lying on the bottom bunk; a patterned Shaker quilt tangles around my legs.

"Oh, *shit.*" I jump to a sitting position, back hunched. Heart jagging in my chest. Panic rising to choke my throat. "What—did we—"

"Hey. Relax. Nothing happened." He grins. "Well, not much."

I look down at my crumpled shirt. All buttoned up, small stain on the sleeve. The collar of a chaste white undershirt rims the bottom of Sedge's neck. My heartbeat slows, the panic recedes. I ask, "Where's Sam?"

"Your sister took him back to the cottage last night with her kids."

"Oh, fuck. *You* were going to cheer me up."

"So? Did I succeed?"

"Maybe a little too well?"

"Like I said." He reaches down for my hand and kisses the fingertips. "Well trained by former owners."

"I'll say." My gaze snakes along the length of his arm. "Are you sure we didn't . . . ?"

"What kind of a jerk do you think I am? We fooled around a little, that's all. Remember?"

I can't help smiling. "I remember some foolery, yes."

"All above the waist, I swear. I would've tucked you up in a room of your own, but the beds are fully occupied at the moment. And you were—um, unwilling to part, I guess?"

"Oh my God. I'm so sorry."

Sedge swings himself off the top bunk and sits on the edge of mine, a couple of feet away. Even puffy with sleep, he's attractive. Dark, tousled hair. Hazel eyes. A reassuring, responsible, grown-up handsomeness. He rubs his thumb along the joints of my fingers. "Hey, what's up? Buyer's remorse?"

"I don't know. Do you come with a money-back guarantee if I'm not completely satisfied?"

"Mallory Dunne," he says, "you are something else."

"That's what they tell me."

With his other hand, he brushes at some hair that's falling over my forehead. His expression is so kind, it hurts my chest. "So, Mallory. Do you get nightmares often?"

"What do you mean?"

"Last night. I shook you awake, and I guess it stopped. But it seemed pretty intense."

I close my eyes to the clash of cymbals inside my head. "I'm sorry. I just get this dream sometimes. When I'm upset about something."

"Like, a recurring thing?"

"I guess so. It's pretty much the same dream, every time. I'm running down a burning hallway. Trying to find something. Someone. But there's fire everywhere and I can't find whatever it is I'm looking for. The dream always ends before—" My eyes fly open. I clutch my wrist and find the reassuring curve of the bracelet. "Oh my God. Fire. Oh my *God*."

"What? What's wrong?"

"Nothing." I pull my hand away. "You know what? I feel like shit. I should go home and make myself some coffee."

"Not on your life. You rest. I'll get the coffee." Sedge presses a kiss on my forehead and hoists himself off the bed. "Be right back, sweetheart. Don't go anywhere."

As he picks his way toward the door, the phone starts ringing again. Mine, definitely. Sedge scoops it from the floor and glances at the screen. "Boston Children's?" he says.

I spring up. "Give me that."

Five minutes later, I'm running down the Summerly drive in the predawn fog. The guest cottage dozes in its rhododendron shawl. I throw open the front door and pound across the hall to the kids' room, where Sam's asleep on the bottom bunk.

"Wake up," I tell him. "Pack your things."

He props himself up on an elbow and cracks his eyes open. "What? What's going on?"

"They found you a kidney."

CHAPTER TWENTY-ONE

Lucien

January 1952
The highway outside Cairo, Egypt

The dust billowed from the Fiat's tires. He glanced at the speedometer—eighty, and his foot was flat on the accelerator. He should have borrowed the damn Mercedes. He should have done a lot of things. He should have made Hannah come with him.

Now the damn ship was steaming for Tel Aviv without him. "Some unfinished business," he told his mother. He gave her an envelope containing money and a list of names. She was philosophical. "On ne badine pas avec l'amour," she said. "Find her, if you must."

He checked his watch. Half past noon, and he was still twenty minutes from the outskirts of Cairo. Along the horizon, he could see not a sign of rising smoke. Yet.

He had already changed his mind by the time the message reached him in Alexandria. A man brushed past him on the dock; the note, tucked into his palm, only added to his urgency.

He should not have left Hannah behind in Cairo. What was he thinking? You did not leave your arm behind, your liver or your ribs or lungs; you could not exist without these vital parts. He was going to turn back anyway. He had already decided he was going to find Hannah, to fall on his knees and pledge his life to her; he would find some respectable position in a bank or an import-export firm; he would go anywhere, do anything in order to live by her side, to sleep in her bed each night, to hold their child in his arms. To protect her from any further evil, the rest of her life.

Now he had to hurry.

But where to find her?

According to the message, the crowd was already on its way from Fuad University to the parliament buildings downtown. But this was almost two hours ago. Once downtown, there was nothing to stop them from starting the riots that Lucien's sources had predicted for weeks now. Last night, Lillian said she had taken down a telephone message for her husband from the airport, that the workers there were refusing to service the BOAC planes. She'd said the army was going to intervene. She was almost hysterical with fear; he'd had to comfort her, in the usual way—the kind of thing he used to regard as simply a part of his job and now filled him with self-loathing.

Maybe that was why he hadn't pressed Hannah in the hotel this morning. *You're not cut out for fatherhood,* she'd told him, and the words were like a knife in his gut. In that moment, he could have taken her in his arms and loved her into compliance, the way he'd loved Lillian into compliance a couple of hours earlier. When he drew her coat away from her beautiful shoulder and kissed it, he could have then taken off the coat altogether, could have taken off that green dress she was wearing that made him want to devour her whole, could have taken her out of her mind with pleasure so she would have followed him anywhere.

And what had he done, like an idiot? Put the coat back on her damn shoulder.

Instead, he should have been ruthless.

Now, a few miles outside of Cairo, he saw the first thin line of black smoke threading its way from the center of town.

Before getting back into his car, he had telephoned Shepheard's and dictated a short sentence of a note to Tarek, a man he trusted—*Stay in the room until I return for you.*

Push the note under the door and knock twice, he'd told Tarek, and Tarek had assured him the note would be delivered.

But what if she disobeyed him? What if she had already left?

You're not cut out for fatherhood, she'd said. *It's best for both of us. You know it is.*

Because Gezira lay on his route to downtown Cairo, he drove there first, to the apartment building where Hannah lived with her husband. He looked for the porter Salah, but Salah was nowhere to be seen, so he ran up the stairs—elevators were a waste of time, and anyway he had energy to burn right now, he wanted action—and pounded on the door of the Ainsworths' apartment. The door swung open. Hannah's husband stood unsteadily in his shirtsleeves, his tie loose around his neck.

"Where's Hannah? Is she home?" asked Lucien.

"None of your bloody business."

Lucien seized him by the shirt. "Listen to me. There is a fucking riot taking place downtown, do you know that? I need to know where she is."

"Let go of me, you damned Jew."

Lucien drew back his fist and connected to Ainsworth's jaw with a satisfactory crunch. The bastard gave him a stunned look and dropped to the floor. Lucien stepped over him and raced around the apartment, calling Hannah's name.

No answer.

Back in the drawing room, he lifted the receiver of the telephone and asked to be connected to the switchboard at Shepheard's Hotel. The operator connected him. The switchboard rang and rang; there was no answer.

He slammed down the receiver and stepped over Ainsworth's body again, on his way to the stairs.

He had hardly crossed the bridge when he had to abandon the Fiat and continue on foot. The streets swarmed with shouting men; the air reeked of smoke, of anger. He saw no policemen. He stopped a man on the sidewalk, an Egyptian, hurrying in the other direction, and asked what was going on.

"The opera house is in flames," the man said, in a shocked voice. "They're going to burn everything, all the foreign buildings, all the British shops."

"Shepheard's, what about Shepheard's?" Lucien demanded.

"I saw with my own eyes, the shawish on duty, he let the rioters right in!"

"You mean it's on fire?"

"I don't know! But I wouldn't go there if I were you!"

The man tore away from Lucien's grip and disappeared into the crowd.

Lucien broke into a run.

Had she stayed in the room, then? She'd been up all night, she was strung on her last nerve. Had she gone to sleep? Had she seen the note pushed under the door? Had she started for home anyway and been caught up in the mob?

If there was no answer at the Shepheard's switchboard, what did that mean? Was it already on fire?

As he ran down Fuad el Awal, the air filled with smoke. Without breaking stride, he lifted the collar of his jacket over his face. In his pocket he held a small pistol. Not much use in a crowd, but it was something. He elbowed his way along the street. To his right someone swung a café chair through a window. Between the buildings on Sharia Aly Pasha he saw the Turf Club, where Ainsworth and his colleagues liked to get away from their wives. Smoke poured from the window; he heard shouts, yelling. The bang of a gunshot. A lorry full of policemen drove by without stopping. He ran up Sharia el-Kamel, pushing past men, left and right. Someone tried to grab his arm; he shrugged it violently off. Smoke everywhere. Ahead of him on the left, where Shepheard's Hotel stood, had stood for decades, he saw a lick of orange fire amid the billows of charcoal smoke. Fear seized his throat. A crowd had gathered on the street, just outside the reach of the flames. The porch collapsed; a cheer went up.

Hannah, he thought. *The child.*

He fought his way between the men, threw his jacket over his head, and ran inside.

* * *

He had been sitting right here at Shepheard's, in fact, ordering a fourth whiskey and soda at the Long Bar when he spotted an old friend from his days in the desert, blowing up German staff cars. By then, the war had been over for a year and he was trying to pretend interest in his job as the Egyptian agent of an import-export firm owned by one of his Swiss cousins, without much success. He started most of his evenings here at Shepheard's, followed by the Auberge, followed by some woman's bedroom, followed by his own, until the hot sun poked around the blinds and his day began over again. He was in a bad mood, a destructive mood. The sight of his old friend Shiloah perked him up. They ordered some more drinks, talked about this and that. The subject of Palestine came up.

"It's going to happen, you know," Shiloah said, lighting a cigarette. "We have assurances from the British, the Americans."

"What's going to happen?" Lucien asked, though he was pretty sure he knew already. Shiloah had been born in Jerusalem, the son of a rabbi; he was a Zionist, as he had made clear to Lucien over a bottle of Scotch after the euphoria of El-Alamein.

Shiloah looked him in the eye. "Statehood."

"All right," said Lucien, "but how are you going to keep this state once you've got it? You know how the Arabs feel about Jews. It's the one damn thing they agree on, other than turfing out the British."

"In the first place, we're going to need some eyes and ears on the ground," said Shiloah, and long story short Lucien wound up with his job as an assistant manager at Shepheard's Hotel, eyes and ears on the ground, at the bar, in the dining room, in the beds of the wives of British diplomats. What were the British going to do, what were the Egyptians going to do. In the heady days of 1948, when the Long Bar became the unofficial headquarters of a certain group of diplomats and army officers subverting official British policy to encourage Farouk's involvement in the Arab League, Ben-Gurion had learned every shift and nuance in time for his morning coffee. Now it was this revolution, as inevitable as the summoning to prayer. How much longer could Farouk hold on? Who would replace him? How hard might the British fight for the canal zone? Noiselessly he extracted all these pellets of information and spirited them to Shiloah. It was a job that suited him far better than the import-export firm, at least until Hannah Ainsworth had sat down to tea with some ladies in the Moorish salon and shattered his equilibrium with a glance.

But at least his years here had not gone to waste. He knew every rug of Shepheard's, every corner and crevice, every groove in every palmiform column, even though they were falling down around him in smoke and flame and rubble and ash. He pounded down the length of the lobby to the Arab Hall. The glazing in the dome had shattered; glass crunched under his shoes. He could scarcely see through the billowing smoke. He could scarcely breathe. The wool jacket covered his mouth and nose, the smoke stung his eyes. In his ears was the roar of the fire, the debris crashing to the ground. The heat was so intense, his skin seemed to be splitting like the skin of a ripe plum.

He burst free from the Arab Hall to the garden and pulled down the jacket from his face. With all the air he could muster, he shouted Hannah's name. The noise vanished into the din.

Don't be stupid, he thought. *She's not here, she's gone. If she's here, she's already dead.*

But his legs moved forward anyway.

The fire hadn't fully engulfed the annex building yet. A door stood open; he ran through it, down the hall to the stairs, up the stairs, flight by flight. The smoke grew thicker. He stopped counting the floors; he couldn't look up to see the numbers. When he got to the top floor, he staggered along the hall to his room, his old room, where he had taken a parade of women during the course of the past five years, women of all kinds, and made love to them in all ways, and finally Hannah. Since Hannah had first come to his bed with her request that staggered him, he had brought no other woman back to these rooms. He was faithful in that respect, anyway.

Had God taken note?

He reached the door and kicked it open.

The room was empty.

He checked the bed, the bathroom. No sign of her. He allowed himself an instant to sag in relief, one hand on the back of the chair. *Thank God,* he thought. *Thank God.*

She was safe. She'd escaped. She would live.

The child. His child would live.

He turned and ran down the hall, back down the stairs. The flames had reached the annex now, licking over the roof and walls. The heat came in gusts, like when you opened an oven. He held his breath down the long flights of steps until he reached the bottom and dashed across the vestibule to the open door.

He couldn't say what made him turn back one last time to look across the smoke to the staircase. There was nothing to see, nothing to make out through the soot. He couldn't even say what he noticed in the small alcove where the stairs met the wall—a sense of movement, maybe? A feeling in his gut, such as he had been trained never to ignore?

He found himself plunging back to the stairs, to the space between stair and wall. He reached out and felt something warm, soft. He heard his name groaned softly.

Hannah, he shouted. *Hannah.*

She lifted her head. *Go, go! My leg.*

He didn't bother to ask what had happened. Fallen down the stairs, stumbled, overcome by smoke? It didn't matter. He bent and lifted her in his arms. She screamed with pain. Tried to pull away.

Go! she yelled. *You can't carry me, you'll die!*

He ignored the fist that struck his collarbone and carried her across the vestibule and out the door, into the garden.

The pavilion was alight, the pavilion where he had flung the cobra from Hannah's arm. Fire everywhere, all around them. To the right, where the long wing of guest rooms should have stood, there was only orange light, rubble, smoke, except for a single mansard window engulfed in flame.

He stood for a second or two, mesmerized by the tongues that licked the roof tiles, the explosion of glass from the window. He heard the crash an instant later. Then the whole structure toppled in a slow, graceful crumbling, like a sand castle felled by a wave. Whatever piece of debris struck him, he never knew. Just a blow to the head, a white streak that blinded him.

* * *

He came to when a pair of arms shook him violently awake. A voice screamed in his ear.

"Lucien, get up! Get up!"

Hannah.

He tried to speak, but his throat was stripped. Her fist slammed again against his chest; he managed to prop his knees underneath him, to suck in a searing lungful of breath. Pain, everything was pain. The whole world was built of it.

"Go!" she yelled. "Run! Get out of here!"

She lay on her stomach, covered in white dust and streaks of dark blood. Somehow he got his arms under her. She tried to wriggle out, to push him away, but she was like a kitten now, a new kitten, there was no strength in her. He forced his feet into place and heaved them both upward. Hannah made a noise of agony and went limp. He staggered forward. Ahead, the only thing standing, the only recognizable structure, was the Arab Hall. He fixed it with his eyes, his mind, and his legs followed. The waves of hot air, the crunch of glass. He faltered. Too much. No breath. Pain like a fire inside his marrow.

Memories billowed in front of him. Like mirages. Like ghosts. Now he's seated next to Hannah on the pyramid, talking about opera, sand and sun, sweat. He wants to kiss her. Full, warm lips. He's driving a car into the sunset, Hannah beside him. He's in bed with her the first time, she writhes and calls his name, he can't hold back, he's going to come. Ecstasy and anguish, he can't tell the difference, shattering his nerves, both at once.

Was he dying? Was this what death was like?

A fist gathered the fabric of his shirt. She writhed; she called his name.

Hannah. The child.

They barreled through the smoke, the falling walls. To breathe was to swallow hot ash. They were in the lobby now, what was left of it. Ahead was the open street. Only yards to go. The floor burned through his shoes. Still she pulled his shirt, she yelled in his ear. His legs, his stupid legs, keep them moving. If he stopped she would die. They would burn together, he and Hannah and the child. So he had to go on. They reached the doorway that used to be, the porch where everybody used to sip a gin and tonic, smoke a cigarette. He plunged with her through the inferno, across the street, debris raining around them, men running, the curb, collapse.

When Lucien was thirteen and a bit of a hellion, his mother—at her wit's end—had shipped him to Switzerland to spend the summer near his father.

Of course, even in an open-minded European country such as Switzerland, you couldn't just flaunt your bastard son in front of everybody. So Lucien had gone to work at a farm in the mountains outside Salzburg, owned by some friends of Beck. The work was hard and dirty, exactly what Lucien needed, and when his father came to visit they would go climbing in the nearby mountains and eat their sandwiches on the summit of some peak, sometimes talking and sometimes not. As they lay in the grass, staring at the immaculate blue sky, listening to the burr and rustle of insects, Lucien often fell asleep from mountain air and sheer exhaustion.

When he opened his eyes again, there was always a moment of disorientation, of amnesia almost—a feeling that he had just been reborn in a new body after a spell in the heavens. His amused father would say something like, *Ah, returned to earth at last,* which only heightened the sense of otherworldliness.

Eventually they would descend to the valley and Beck would deposit him back in the sweat and routine of the farm. But sometimes when the sky was clear, Lucien would pause in his work and contemplate the distant mountainside against this field of immaculate, eternal blue, and for that instant the feeling shimmered back, that he had died and come to life in a new body, inside a fresh new skin, to try his luck again.

Together they lay on the sidewalk. The noise, the chaos receded to the outer limits of the universe. Here with Hannah, there was peace. He stared at a patch of blue sky that appeared and vanished between the clouds of smoke and thought of the blue sky at Giza, the first touch of her mouth. In Switzerland, the sky would be blue. He would take her there, to the top of some mountain, touching the heavens. Lie with his head in her lap, her hand in his hair, the cool, fresh air cradling his skin. She would say she loved him. Over and over, he heard her gentle voice. *Lucien, I love you.* The curve of her belly on his cheek, the child they had made together.

The pain was gone now, he realized. Maybe he wasn't hurt so badly as he thought. Maybe he would live, after all. Maybe he would live to lie with Hannah on a mountaintop, to hold his child in his arms.

He had to tell her something. He moved his lips.

I will build you a throne next to the sun.

Her voice, from a distance. "We're safe now, darling. Nothing will part us."

CHAPTER TWENTY-TWO

Mallory

July 2022
Boston, Massachusetts

I'm sitting in a chair in a hospital room, watching my son's urine drip into a plastic bag, and it's the most beautiful sight in the world.

Paige has dropped off to sleep in the chair next to me, curled into an awkward ball. The morning sun lights the metal blinds in the window, casting long, slanting stripes on the opposite wall. Some sports highlight show flickers soundlessly on the television mounted to the wall. Sam's also fallen back asleep. The machines beep next to him. I rise to adjust the pillow at his back and a nurse opens the door behind me.

"Mrs. Dunne?"

I'm too tired to correct her. I notice the lines between her eyebrows and ask, "Yes? Is something wrong?"

"There's a Mr. Peabody asking for you at the desk? I told him visiting hours don't start until ten, but he's . . ."

"Persistent?"

"Very. And he brought coffee."

"Ah." I look at Sam, sleeping peacefully. Paige, her head crooked at an angle that makes me wince. The urine bag at the side of the bed, filling with beautiful yellow pee.

"If you want to step out for a few minutes," says the nurse, "we'll keep an eye on him."

* * *

Sedge Peabody rises from a chair in the waiting room and holds out a bouquet of fragrant blush-pink roses. "You look like shit," he says, kissing the bare patch of skin between the mask and my ear.

"I haven't slept since I woke up in your bunk bed yesterday morning. Sorry if I smell."

He nods to the hallway. "How's the kid?"

"He's doing great. The surgery was textbook. His vitals are superb, doc says. And he's peeing! Into the catheter, I mean. It's like a miracle."

"I will never take pee for granted again."

"You shouldn't. Trust me." I look at the flowers. "I'm not sure these are Sam's color."

"They're for you. For the other night." He reaches for a Starbucks cup on the coffee table. "And this is for this morning. I guessed caramel macchiato. I figured you could use the double whammy. Sugar *and* caffeine."

I unloop the mask from one ear and roll the first sip over my tongue. "You are an angel of mercy, Sedge Peabody."

"That's how I like to think of myself. Sit?"

We settle down on a pair of plastic chairs. The fluorescent hospital light bathes us in a sickly glow.

"So, I won't keep you," Sedge says. "I know you have more important stuff to do. I just wanted to check in and make sure you were okay."

"I'm definitely okay, thank you. More than okay. Can't-wrap-my-head-around-it-yet okay. I mean, it's a long road ahead. He's going to be on immunosuppressants basically all his life. Anything could go wrong at any time. But the kidney was a perfect tissue match, so that's a start. Six out of six."

"Sorry, that means nothing to me. But I'm eager to learn."

"Basically, it's good news. Great news. I've been trying to get hold of his dad, but he's away on business, so . . ."

"How's that going? With the dad?"

"Good." I sip my coffee. "We're friends now. It's good."

"Good," he says.

We stare together at my coffee cup. The flowers on my lap.

"I guess that was kind of a dumb idea," he says. "Flowers are the last thing you need right now."

"They're beautiful. And sweet of you. I'm sure they have plenty of vases around here. I'll get them in some water and put them in Sam's room to remind me I'm a human being. Not just a mom."

"And maybe, when you're out of the hospital, life getting back to normal again . . ."

I meet Sedge's gaze over the top of the coffee cup. He gives me a sheepish smile, looks at the fake potted palm across the room, meets my gaze again.

"I was thinking maybe I could take you out to dinner or something," he says. "Get to know each other a little better."

I lift my eyebrows. He laughs.

"All right," he says. "Get to know each other in a different way. But also the same way. Well, not *exactly* the same way. Maybe just forget the whole thing and start all over? Sorry, I seem to have lost my legendary charm. What I'm trying to say is, I'm having a little trouble getting over what happened between us, or I guess you could say what didn't happen between us, and I'm starting to think that, no, it's not a plus for me at all."

"What's not a plus?"

"That you're not looking for anything more serious."

I lift the roses from my lap and hold them to my face. The scent is delicious. Expensive.

"From my grandmother's garden," he says. "She let me have them. But I had to beg."

I reach out to squeeze his hand, where it rests on his knee. "Mr. Peabody. I would be delighted to have dinner with you at some unspecified future date."

When I return to the hospital room a few minutes later, Sam's eyes are open and fixed on the television screen.

"Hey, bud. How are you feeling?"

"Weird."

"That would be the painkillers." I brush his hair with my fingers. "Doctors say everything is going great. You're peeing again! Can you believe it? No more dialysis."

"I think I might barf."

"So, that's pretty normal. Bowl's right here if you need it. And your water bottle. If you need anything else, I'm right here."

"Nice flowers."

"You like them? They're for me, believe it or not." I wink. "An admirer."

"Nice. Where's Dad?"

The word *Dad* jars me. In my head, Monk is—well, *Monk.* Not *Dad,* the way parents sometimes call each other Mom and Dad even when the kids aren't around, out of habit. So I pause for a second or two, run my hand over the blanket, and say, "You know what? I'll just see if he's responded to my messages yet. He's been on a business trip. I'm sure he's on his way. He's going to be over the freaking moon about this."

My phone's buried deep in my handbag. Paige has been handling communications with the few family members and close friends who need to know, so I can concentrate on Sam. I burrow for it now and pull it free.

"No wonder," I say. "It's out of battery. Let me see if I can find a charger."

"A charger for what?" Paige says sleepily from her chair. She tries to lift her head and grimaces. "I think I broke my neck."

I reach over and massage the base of her skull. "My phone."

"I should have one in my handbag."

"Of course you do."

I plug the phone into the wall. While I'm waiting for it to revive, I smile across the room at Sam. He's pale and kind of bleary-looking. But alive. Well. Whole. My heart swells generously. "Your dad's probably in a car from the airport right now. He wouldn't miss this for the world."

"Sure," says Sam.

"Buddy. I mean it. Maybe he's only known you for a few weeks, but already he loves you more than anything."

Sam manages a half-smile. "Mom, that's you. He loves *you* more than anything."

"What? Why do you say that?"

"Because he told me."

Paige stands up. "I'm going to go see about some coffee. Mallie? Coffee for you?"

"I just had some. Sam? When did he tell you that?"

"I don't know. While you were in Ireland, I guess. We talked a lot. I asked him why things didn't work out with you and stuff, and he said he wasn't sure, but he loved you more than anything in the world and he still does."

"Oh." I thump down on the chair. "Well, that's nice of him to say."

"Mom. Like, he meant it."

"Not the way you're thinking, honey. I promise. That was so many years ago. We're both different people now. He's engaged to Lee, remember? They're going to get married and have their own family. Plus, like I said, *You're* the light of his life now. I promise you *that* for sure."

My phone comes to life in a never-ending pulse of beeps and buzzes. The alerts flash and pile on one another—texts, phone calls, news, a bank deposit from my Etsy storefront.

"Hold on a second, buddy. Everything's loading."

Sam's attention shifts back to the television. I give up waiting for the alerts to end and click on my text messages. Scroll down to Monk's number.

Nothing. No reply to my last message, sent late last night, right after Sam came out of surgery.

I check my phone log. Nothing.

I look up at Sam and smile. "Nothing yet, bud. I think his phone might be off or something."

"Okay," Sam says.

I drop my gaze back to my phone. The euphoria bleeds out of me, replaced by the old unsettled feeling I've grown used to, ever since Sam ate that fucking mushroom three years ago. That edge of dread. Something terrible lurks offstage, waiting for a cue.

By themselves, my thumbs flip from app to app, searching for something to land on. Back to my text messages, of which there are dozens unread. I scroll until one catches my eye—Luca. Five new messages, the most recent sent just this morning in shouty caps.

GIRL PLEASE I AM DYING HERE

I blink a few times and open at the oldest message.

Check this out girl. In house expert says look at the tail of the cobra and see if you can unscrew the tip

Beneath the text, Luca attached a photo enlargement of the bracelet that showed a fiber-thin line circling the snake's tail, about a quarter-inch up from the tip.

The next message said—

This was a typical device for SPIES to carry messages!!!!

Then, a couple of hours later—

hurry up girl, am in SUSPENSE

At midnight—

going to bed now but expect reply manana!!!!!!

I set down the phone and work the bracelet off my wrist. All these years, all my life, the head of the cobra has mesmerized me. The tiny emerald eyes, the flickering ruby tongue. The intricate decorative engraving of the hood. The way it seems alive, the way the face captures you. I don't think I've ever glanced at the tip.

But that's what snakes do, don't they? They mesmerize their prey, so you can't look away. Even to save yourself.

I turn the cobra upside down and peer at the tail. I don't see a line, but even in the photograph, magnified several times, you can hardly tell it's there. I try to loosen the tip with my thumb and finger, but it doesn't budge.

I move to the window and hold the bracelet to the mid-morning sun. *There!* You can just see it. The thinnest possible fiber, a delicate ring almost at the tip.

I fix my thumb and finger securely to the end. Lefty-loosey.

Stuck fast.

Well, it's been seventy years, right? I wipe my fingers on my sweatpants and try again.

Paige sweeps through the doorway, carrying two cups of coffee. "What the hell are *you* doing?" she demands.

"Luca texted me. His jewelry guy at Sotheby's thinks the tip is hollow. For carrying spy messages or something."

"What?"

Sam looks over from the television. "What did you say, Mom? Your bracelet is, like, a spy gadget?"

I realize my heart is thumping against my ribs. My palms are sweating. I hold out the bracelet to Paige. "Here, you try. I'm too nervous."

She rolls her eyes and sets down the coffee cup. Wipes her fingers and applies them to the tip of the snake. Her face turns pink with effort.

"We need pliers," she says.

"You're not touching my bracelet with pliers! You'll dent it!"

"Please. My jeweler can fix the dents. If there are any."

Sam says, "Can I try?"

I shoot Paige a look and carry the bracelet to Sam. He turns it over in his hands, gets a grip on body and tail, and strains to loosen the tip. With a grunt of frustration, he bends over to put some weight into it.

"Stop that! You'll burst your stitches."

I snatch the bracelet back. Paige hands me a set of folding pliers. At my look of surprise, she shrugs her shoulders. "I keep a pair in my handbag."

"Of course you do."

I carry the bracelet back to the window and carefully apply the prongs of the pliers to the tip. Bit by bit, I increase the pressure.

"Is it coming?" Paige asks.

"Almost," I gasp.

The tip gives way.

With shaking fingers I unscrew it the rest of the way and turn the hollow tail over. A small piece of rolled paper drops into my palm.

"I think I'm gonna puke," says Paige.

"Open it!" says Sam.

"I can't. My fingers are shaking too hard."

Paige takes the paper and hands it to Sam, who unrolls it on his lap.

"What does it say? What does it say?" Paige begs.

Sam holds up the paper between the thumb and forefinger of each hand and reads:

> *I named you Lucile for your father, Lucien Suarez Beck, who gave his life to save you.*
> *Hannah Countess Vécsey (Ainsworth)*

"That's in parentheses." Sam looks up. "*Ainsworth* is in parentheses."

"Holy *shit*," says Paige. "She was a *countess*?"

"Don't swear in front of the kid," I tell her.

My phone rings. In shock, I answer the call without looking at the screen. Without thinking.

A firm, businesslike male voice replies to my greeting. "Good morning. Am I speaking to Mallory Dunne?"

"Yes. Speaking. You are."

"Mrs. Dunne, this is Dr. Grenardo at Massachusetts General. I understand you hold medical power of attorney for Benjamin Monk Adams?"

The blood drains out of me. I crash down on the seat of Paige's chair, the nearest one. "I *what*?"

"According to his registration forms, he's granted you medical POA in the event of incapacitation during surgery and recovery. We've been trying to reach you since yesterday."

"Oh my God," I whisper. "Oh my God."

"What?" Paige turns in my direction. "What's going on?"

The voice continues in my ear, as dulcet as a newscaster. "I need you to remain calm, Mrs. Dunne. Listen to me carefully. I regret to inform you that Mr. Adams went into cardiac arrest on the operating table yesterday afternoon, due to a previously undiagnosed heart condition. He's currently receiving treatment in the ICU here at Mass General, under strict security. I'm afraid we're going to need you to transport yourself to this hospital as soon as possible in order for you to make informed decisions regarding his care."

In the Uber, staring dazedly ahead.

"He'll be fine," says Paige. "The operating table is the absolute best place in the world to have a heart attack. The doctors and the lifesaving equipment are right there."

The Uber lurches to a stop. Traffic. I gaze at all these cars, all these fucking cars. Who are they? Don't they understand? Can't they get out of our way?

Paige scrolls her phone. I glance at the screen.

"You're on the 'Gram, Paige? Seriously?"

"Sorry. Nerves." She turns the phone facedown on her lap and looks out the window. "Who the fuck are all these people? Can't we get them out of our way?"

"Boston traffic."

"How are you so *calm,* Mallie? Jesus."

"I'm not calm." I look at my hands in my lap, my white knuckles, like they belong to someone else. The bracelet catches a flash of sunlight from between a couple of buildings. The words return to me—*I named you Lucile for your father, Lucien Suarez Beck, who gave his life to save you.*

Your father. Gave his life to save you.

I grab the edge of the seat and swallow hard to shove back a wave of dizziness. "Has Jake texted?" I ask Paige.

She picks up her phone. "He's there with Sam. Sam's fine. Jake's parents have the kids. Everything's covered, don't worry. Just—we can just focus on this."

The Uber hurtles forward again. Paige scrolls her phone.

"What the fuck," she says. "What the *actual fuck.*"

"Honestly, Paige—"

She turns the screen toward me. "You have to see this."

Because of security, we've been given detailed instructions regarding our arrival. Already the news seems to be spreading. People are milling around Cambridge Street, checking their phones, dazed faces. Traffic is at a standstill.

The Uber driver turns down the talk radio. "Sorry, ladies. Some rumor going around about that singer being here. Monk Adams? Like he OD'd or something."

"I heard he had a heart attack on the operating table, donating a kidney to save his love child," says Paige. I drive an elbow into her side.

The driver laughs. "Or *some* shit like that, right? You said around back?"

"Blossom Street," I tell him. "There's a side entrance. Someone's meeting us there."

"Good plan. Avoid all this crap."

Finally we break free of the gridlock around the emergency entrance on Cambridge Street and whip around the corner to Charles Street, then right on Blossom. I scan the side of the building until I spot a pair of men in security uniforms, standing next to a small metal door.

"Right here," I tell the driver.

When we arrive at the ICU, the first person I see is Lennox Lassiter.

She sits in a small waiting area, otherwise empty except for a pair of security guards like the ones who've accompanied Paige and me and the doctor. Her thumbs fly away on the phone she holds before her face. (She told me once that she always keeps her phone at eye level to avoid neck wrinkles.) Her hair is gathered back in an uneven, sun-streaked ponytail; the lightbulb beneath her skin is switched off.

"Hold me back," mutters Paige.

I grab her arm. "Later, okay?"

"It's her *fault* all these people are here."

The movement catches Lee's attention. She shifts her glance from her screen to us, and the look of concentration transforms into shock. She jumps to her feet. "Where are you going?"

But the security men are already whisking us down the hall to the last room, where another pair of officers stands before the door. The doctor nods; the guards stand aside. One of them opens the door.

You think you're prepared for a sight like this. The doctor meets you upon arrival for a briefing—heart arrhythmia, previously undiagnosed; full cardiac arrest on the operating table; heart restarted; heavily sedated; three units of blood; next twenty-four hours critical—and there is all this time to tell yourself you will be calm, they will open the door and you will see Monk in a hospital gown, in a hospital bed; his eyes will be closed; he will be surrounded by machines that make alarming noises, by tubes hooked up to his arms that once held you, his mouth that once kissed you.

But then the door opens and you see him like this.

Paige grabs me around the waist just in time. I turn my head into her shoulder, just for a second or two. Just to gather myself. When I look up, a man and a woman rise from the chairs near the bed.

"Mallory?" says the woman, slight and honey-haired, shadows beneath both eyes.

"Yes?"

"Thank God you're here," she says. "Remember me?"

I cover my mouth with my hands. "Blue!"

The young man walks forward and folds me up in a hug.

"Chippy," I sob.

"Is that bitch still out there?" asks Blue. "Did you see what she posted?"

"The hashtags were the worst," says Paige. "Hashtag stepmom? Really?"

Blue leans forward and whispers to me, "We stopped visiting because she drove us nuts. But Monk was, like, devoted. He wouldn't hear a word."

Dr. Grenardo says, "I'm sorry. I understand everyone's upset, but could we keep this kind of conversation outside the room? Mrs. Dunne, when you've had a moment to assess Mr. Adams's condition, I'd like to have a few words with you."

Chippy looks at me. "Hey, how's the kid?"

"Sam is great," I tell him. "He's got one hell of a new kidney."

He looks like wax. I imagine if I touch his skin, he will be cold and hard, like a candle. So I stand there and tell him about that time we were on the beach together with the twins, before we had even kissed, when I was sketching a seashell. Do you remember that, Monk? Something hooked me about the grooves of the shell, the way they mimicked the waves on the ocean's surface. The patterns of nature, the way they repeat themselves elsewhere, the way they repeat themselves into eternity.

And you asked me what was it about patterns that I loved, and I said it was the rhythm, like we all shared this fundamental living beat, plants and animals and people and everything else, the earth and the stars, physics, radiation, electromagnetic waves, and you nodded and said, *Like music.*

And all along, your heart was hiding this secret. Arrhythmia. Out of sync with the beat of the universe.

It hurts, Pink. Like a pain in my chest, like it's too much to hold.

I reach out and touch his forehead, the only patch of skin that's bare of tubing and bandages. It's warm, of course. Flesh, not wax.

I'm sitting in the chair next to Monk's bed, watching the steady drip of urine down the catheter. The afternoon sun rims the edges of the blinds. The machines beep on, keeping him alive.

The door creaks. Paige walks in with a pair of coffee cups. She hands one to me and sits in the other chair.

"Chippy and Blue are taking one for the team," she says. "Told Lee she needed to get some rest and dragged her to a hotel."

"They're not wrong. She could definitely use some rest."

"So could you, honey."

I shake my head. I'm beyond sleep.

"She does love him, though." I lift my gaze to Monk's nose, outlined against the wall. "She does."

Paige makes a noise. "She walked right out the front entrance, Mallie. Right into the crowd of paps, one pretty tear streaking down her left cheek. But at least she took down that selfie of her and Sam. She said it was all a big misunderstanding."

I sip the coffee. Thin and bland. Keurig, probably. *But at least it's hot,* I think.

It gets you through the night.

I glance down at the hand on my lap. The snake coiled around my wrist. One tiny, watchful emerald eye. "I keep thinking . . ."

"What's that, honey?"

"If I had told him earlier. I mean, he was a perfect tissue match. I could have told him earlier and Sam wouldn't have spent three years on dialysis. I don't know, maybe this wouldn't have happened."

"You don't know that. His heart might have stopped on an operating table three years ago."

"But if Monk were in the picture, Sam wouldn't have gone to summer camp at all. He never would have eaten the mushroom to begin with."

"So he might have fallen off a sailboat aged five. Hit in the eye by a lacrosse stick. You just don't know."

I stick my face in the hollow of my two hands. "I ran away, Paige.

I ran away and hid. I should have been braver. Monk's suffering, I made him suffer. Maybe even killed him. And for what."

"Exactly," says Paige. "For what. I know you walked away for a reason. I know you, Mallory. You wouldn't hurt a fly."

"I was just a dumb kid, Paige." I lift my head to stare at the machines keeping Monk alive. "A dumb, scared kid who made a stupid mistake."

Paige sets her coffee cup on the floor and picks up my hand.

"So explain. Tell him about it."

"What, *now*? It's too late. He can't even hear me."

"How do you know that? He's on medication, he's not asleep. Anyway, it's not for *him,* is it? Not really. You know how confession works. This is for you."

The door rustles. A nurse comes in. We sit quietly while she checks the machines, the tubes. Changes the IV bag. She nods to us as she leaves.

"Here's the deal," I say. "The catch-22."

"What are you talking about? What catch?"

"If I tell him, if I get this off my chest, give him his fucking closure, he'll never—I mean, that's it. Whatever chance we still had, it's gone."

Paige makes a noise of exasperation. "Jesus, Mal. Will you just wake *up*? There are only two outcomes here. *Two.* Do you understand that? And the best of those two outcomes is, he pulls through and marries his fiancée and lives happily ever after. The *you* train? The you and Monk train? That left the station a long time ago. And you don't even want to be on it. Where that train is headed, you don't want to live there."

I pull my hand from Paige's hand and rise from the chair. The reassuring beep of Monk's heartbeat on the monitor draws me forward to the edge of the bed. When I find his hand on the soft ecru blanket, I could swear the fingers twitch against mine.

Or maybe that's my imagination. Wishful thinking.

"Hey, Monk." With my other hand I push at a curl of hair that threatens to droop on his forehead. "It's me. Mallory. I'm here. Not going anywhere this time, I promise."

There is no sign that he hears me. Not a flicker of eyelids or fingers or anything. The machine beeps on in the same steady rhythm. I put my other hand around Monk's hand, so I'm clasping his fingers between my palms, like when you pray.

There was this time. I think it must have been the night before the afternoon Monk kissed me for the first time. The end of June. Warm, muggy day. I'd just put the kids to bed and a text arrived from Monk. *Bike ride?*

Five minutes later we were coasting down West Cliff Road, draft coursing through our hair. Flying past the golf course, the guard shack, the fields, the houses, the village. Gleefully I followed the white flash of Monk's T-shirt, all the way to the airfield at the other end of the island. The old bunkers set into the dunes, left over from the war. We tossed the bikes into the grass and staggered to the beach, where we threw ourselves into the sand. Monk produced a bottle of champagne he'd smuggled out of his dad's cellar. We passed it back and forth and talked about . . . I don't remember. It doesn't matter. We talked ourselves to sleep, so that I opened my eyes to some unknown hour, to the bruised night, the stars, the warm sand under my skin, my hand clasped in Monk's hand. I don't know how I knew he was awake, just that he was. Just that I knew he knew I was awake.

We didn't look at each other. That would have wrecked it. We stared at the sky together, breathed the damp air together, floated together on our champagne cloud.

Hand in hand. Each of us pretending that the other one was asleep.

Now I look down at Monk's hand between mine. The same old hand. The same Monk.

"Monk," I say. Soft voice. "I need to tell you something."

CHAPTER TWENTY-THREE

Mallory

August 2008
Winthrop Island, New York

It's a funny thing about human nature. Once you break the rules, it's so much easier to break them again.

I couldn't really tell you why neither Monk nor I even brought up the subject of condoms during the course of that night in the guesthouse, after Dillon punched him. I was just a teeny bit stoned, for one thing, and we'd had that incredible sex on the beach earlier that afternoon, fresh in our memories, which made it not just possible but irresistible to continue riding bareback, *just this one night*. Besides, in the backs of our minds we knew it was practically impossible for me to get pregnant at that point in my cycle.

Practically.

Just the one night, right? Two days after my period? The risk was so tiny, and the bonfire between us so fierce.

But as the week went on, and the risk grew bigger, we kept breaking the rules. I don't have any excuse. We were young and foolish and invulnerable. We were madly in love, crazy with our plans, losing our minds on the total certainty of our life together. It felt so natural to make love without any barriers—so primal, so *right*. And a little bit dangerous, to tell the truth. A little exciting, to lie there afterward, buzzing with pleasure, nothing between us. The thrilling little rush when he pulled out at last.

"Pinks," he said, two nights before our planned departure, in the middle of sex in the middle of a sweltering evening in the middle of the bed in the guesthouse, "we're playing with fire."

"It's okay," I said. Not very convincing.

"No, it's not." He pulled out and lifted himself up.

"What are you doing?"

"I'm getting a condom."

He came back from the bathroom a moment later and we finished off. Afterward, I rolled on my side to face him and said maybe I should go on the Pill or something.

"But the hormones," he said. "I don't want to put you through that."

"The coil isn't great, I've heard. Complications."

"Nah, we'll just keep on using the condoms for now, Pinko. I don't mind."

He lay on his back, one arm around my shoulders, one arm behind his head, staring at the ceiling. I leaned forward and kissed him. "Hey, handsome. What are you thinking?"

"One more day," he said. "One more day until we're free. That's what I'm thinking."

August fourteenth. Monk had signed up to caddy all day. *We need the money, honey,* he told me as he kissed me goodbye at dawn and crept back to his bedroom in the house next door.

I couldn't go back to sleep, so I got up and showered in the attached bathroom. I had this unsettled feeling in the pit of my stomach. Not *doubt*—I knew to the ends of my bones that I loved Monk and he loved me, and it was right and perfect for us to be together. This felt more like foreboding. Everything was *too* right, too perfect. Life wasn't like that. Life was messy, life abhorred perfection. Something was going to go wrong.

The hot water coursed down my limbs. I cupped my breasts, ran my hand over my stomach, slipped my fingers between my legs. Closed my eyes and focused on Monk.

Two weeks together on the road. Like a honeymoon, almost. All good vibes.

Everything would turn out all right, I told myself.

* * *

When I brought the twins indoors from the beach for their math lessons, Mr. Adams was waiting for me in the sunroom. He wore the usual summer uniform of pale chinos and a polo shirt in mint green. A crest of some kind was embroidered discreetly on the left breast.

"Mallory," he said, "would you care to have lunch with me at the Club?"

My mind scrambled for an excuse. I could only think, *But I'm going on vacation with your son tomorrow morning and need to pack.*

"Um, of course." I looked down at my beach dress, sprinkled with sand. "I think I should probably change?"

"Nothing too fancy. The dress code is fairly relaxed during the day."

At the time, it didn't occur to me that there was anything inappropriate about going to lunch with Mr. Adams at the Club. He was on the boards of several important institutions! His distinguished family! His impeccable credentials! I was a college kid. Mr. Adams was three times my age. I was sleeping with his son, for God's sake. It all seemed so avuncular. He helped me into his car—a low-slung vintage convertible that was probably handed down from his father—and off we zoomed down the drive.

I'd visited the Club countless times already. The twins had swimming lessons there on Tuesdays and Thursdays, and we often came to the beach so they could scoop sand and catch waves with the other young princes and princesses. There were parties and playdates. During the big Fourth of July party, I might or might not have snuck off to the gazebo with Monk while Chippy and Blue competed in the children's limbo contest.

But I had never arrived there as a guest, rather than the help.

I remember being surprised the first time I saw that clubhouse, Memorial Day weekend. I'd imagined some grand, historic building, or at least a majestic modern reconstruction. Instead, it reminded me of my mother's house on Cape Cod, only bigger. The walls were shingled in cedar, the rooflines peaked, the trim white. Inside it smelled of lemon polish and intractable damp, laced with a hint of mothball. According to Monk, the original clubhouse was grander—built in the 1920s—but it was impossible to maintain and a little embarrassing by the 1960s, so they decided to knock it down and rebuild on a more modest scale. The cost of demolition being what it was, though, nobody raised much fuss when a mysterious fire tore through the old barn late one night, just before the wrecking balls were supposed to swing.

Monk told me all this with a shrug. *The older the money, the cheaper the skate,* he said.

Nobody raised an eyebrow as Mr. Adams escorted me through the foyer to the dining room, where wicker tables and chairs spilled through the open french doors to the stone terrace overlooking the sixth-hole fairway. He spoke to the manager (the trim, immaculate Mr. Irwin), who led us to a table at the very edge of the terrace, so I could almost lean over the wall and touch the grass. He handed us menus.

"May I offer you anything to drink?" Mr. Irwin asked me, entirely without judgment.

"Just the water, thank you."

"No, no," said Mr. Adams. "It's your last day with us, isn't it? Might as well celebrate with a glass of bubbly. Irwin? Two glasses of Bollinger. No. Why not the bottle."

"A bottle of Bollinger it is," said Mr. Irwin.

When he left, I laid my napkin on my lap and asked cheerfully, "I assume Monk's told you about our plans?"

"He telephoned me on the way to the golf course this morning." Mr. Adams steepled his hands. "I must say, I was hoping you'd stay on until the end of the month. This puts us in a bit of a childcare bind. My wife is . . ."

He reached for his water glass and sipped.

"Mrs. Adams?"

"We'll manage, of course. When Monk and his sister were small, all the teenagers around here used to babysit. Now the teenagers are off to orphanages in Haiti and immersion language programs in Argentina and that kind of thing. Nor are they interested in earning pocket money. I guess they don't feel they need it. Thank goodness for girls like you."

"I'm sorry about that. I thought we were clear about the fifteenth. Monk and I—"

Mr. Adams waved a hand. "It doesn't matter. The important

thing is the two of you and your plans for the future. I've been doing some thinking, to tell you the truth. I mean, it's fair to say this development wasn't unexpected, hmm?" He smiled. "I'll come right out and say that you haven't exactly hidden what you've been up to. An old house like ours, the noise carries."

My cheeks turned hot. I snatched the menu and pretended to study it.

Mr. Adams laughed. "Don't worry, Mallory. I'm not here to scold you. Of course Monk's attracted to you at this moment in his life. That's all well and good. Enjoy yourselves. You're young and free. Nothing more poisonous to happiness than regrets, believe me. My concern is that—"

The arrival of the champagne cut him short.

"Ah," he said. "Here we are."

Mr. Irwin unwrapped the foil and eased out the cork with barely a hiss. Once the glasses were poured, he melted away with a promise to return momentarily for our lunch order.

"To art," said Mr. Adams, "and young love."

I didn't know how to reply to that, so I clinked my glass against his without a word. I was nervous enough to drink deeply, maybe too deeply. The champagne was cold and dry, delicious.

Mr. Adams set down his glass. "Mallory, I'm going to do you the favor of speaking frankly. And I want you not to take offense. I know that doesn't come easily to your generation. But I *have* seen something more of life than you have, can't we agree?"

"I agree," I said coldly.

"You're young, like I said. You're in love. You're full of dreams. At your age, you can't imagine an end to any of this. You can't imagine these powerful feelings between you could ever fade. Believe me, when I married my first wife, I thought we'd feel that way about each other forever."

"Mr. Adams," I said, "I have to say that I think you're being incredibly presumptuous here."

Mr. Adams leaned back in his chair and raised his eyebrows. "Do you?"

"I mean, honestly, you have no idea how we feel about each other. And if you're trying to *warn me away* or something—"

He held up one hand. "That's not what I'm saying at all."

"What, then? What's this *concern* of yours?"

"Mallory, honey. Look. I admire your pluck. I do. Your determination to choose your own path. It's just that a young woman from your background—well, you have a certain freedom. The world's your oyster. Whereas Monk's lived to a certain standard all his life. He takes certain things for granted. He doesn't understand the sacrifices necessary to achieve and maintain this life to which he's accustomed." Mr. Adams turned his head to idle his gaze over the nearby tables. "Do you see that man over there? In the seersucker suit?"

I squinted to my left, into the sunshine. "That guy over there by himself?"

Mr. Adams turned back to me with such an intense gaze, from those blue eyes that looked so much like Monk's eyes, I felt a little sick.

"His name is Cooper," he said. "Bud Cooper. His family made a fortune in textiles, I think, over a hundred years ago. Bought some land and built a house here around the same time my grandfather did. Good man, Bud. Couple of years ahead of me at Harvard. Loved books, you know, loved literature. I think he had some idea he was going to be a writer. The next Fitzgerald or Hemingway or something. Did a little of this, little of that. Never settled into what you might call a career. And his father—good man, Mr. Cooper—he figured, why not indulge him? There was plenty of money, right?" He made a motion with his hand; Mr. Irwin swooped in to refill our glasses. "Bud's broke now, Mallory. That big summer house his grandfather built, over on Plum Lane? He lives there year-round. It's all he's got. Falling apart. The Club stopped sending him any bills about a decade ago. The membership covers his dues and charges. Nobody says anything about it—I mean, he's an old friend. A good man."

I glanced again at the man sitting at the small square table at the edge of the terrace, all by himself in a suit of yellowing blue seersucker, spooning some soup in careful, well-bred strokes. "That's nice of you," I said.

"We have this idea among us, Mallory, that it's vulgar to mention money. That it's vulgar even to think about money. And I agree.

Money isn't the object of life. *Life* is the object of life. But the un-mentionable fact is, money is what sustains that life. *Our* life. These beautiful houses, these nice families, this lifestyle, you think they last forever. But they don't. You have to take care of your legacy, or it vanishes into nothing. And the world isn't like it used to be. Taxes and inflation and everything else. There's no such thing as old money anymore. Old *families,* maybe, but if you don't replenish the well, then—you know the saying? Shirtsleeves to shirtsleeves in three generations. And you end up like poor old Bud. Good man, never accomplished a damn thing. Kids are living in New Hampshire somewhere, doing God knows what. He's got nothing left." He signaled again to Mr. Irwin. "I think we're ready to order now. Mallory?"

I raised the menu again. "Um, the crab cakes? Please?"

"Certainly. For you, Mr. Adams? The usual?"

"Yes, Irwin. Thank you."

Mr. Irwin took our menus and Mr. Adams leaned forward. Returned the full force of his attention to me. "Do you understand what I'm trying to tell you, Mallory?"

"Mr. Adams," I said, "I get what you're saying, and I appreciate the concern, but aren't you kind of jumping ahead a little here? We're still in college. We're just going on a vacation. Not . . . you know, making any life-changing decisions here."

Mr. Adams set down his glass and furrowed his eyebrows at me. "You don't think dropping out of college is a life-changing decision?"

"Dropping out of *college*?"

"I'm sorry, but isn't that what we're talking about, Mallory? About Monk quitting college to start his so-called music career? In Providence, with you?"

The Club chattered pleasantly around me. The champagne bubbles rose in lazy threads between my fingers. Mr. Adams's face turned blurry against the backdrop of modest midcentury architecture, the trim green links to his right.

"I . . . I don't . . . Is that what he told you?"

"Mallory," said Mr. Adams, in a slow voice, "he's already disenrolled from Colby."

"He's *what*?"

"I assumed you'd already spoken about it." Mr. Adams waved a hand at the champagne bucket. "I hope I haven't put my foot in it."

"I—I think maybe you've misunderstood, Mr. Adams."

"I don't think I have, Mallory. Monk was very clear with me. Very sure of himself."

I squared my knife and fork alongside my plate. Reached for my glass and gulped down the icy champagne. When I set the glass back, I said, "In that case, I support his decision."

Mr. Adams reached out and touched the fingers of my left hand. "Look, Mallory. I want you to be happy. I do. But I want you to know that if things don't quite work out as planned, I'll be here to offer you a helping hand."

"I don't think that's necessary. Really."

"All the same." Mr. Adams released my hand and reached into the pocket of his jacket. "I want you to take my card. Monk doesn't have to know. He has his pride, God knows, stubborn as hell, and I respect that. But if you find yourself in a tough spot, here's where to find me. You can count on me, Mallory. I mean that."

I looked at the card, not really reading it. "Thanks," I said, and slipped it into my wallet.

A waiter arrived with our food. Mr. Adams's usual turned out to be a turkey club with bacon on whole wheat, toasted, with french fries. The crab cakes went very well with the champagne.

In fact, we finished the bottle.

My cellphone rang inside my handbag during the drive back to Seagrapes. I turned to Mr. Adams and said apologetically, "It's Monk."

Mr. Adams made a courtly gesture.

"Hey, Monkfish," I said. "What's up?"

"Hey. How was the lunch date?"

I gulped. "*Lunch* date?"

"Pinks, come on. I saw you. I was caddying the sixth hole and I happen to look at the clubhouse, and there's my dad having lunch with my girlfriend. Champagne in a bucket and everything."

"Monk." I turned my face to the side, where the draft could carry my words away. "Don't be weird. He's right here. We're driving back to the house. He just wanted to talk about our plans. What you told him."

"*What?* What did he say I told him?"

"Like, about how you'd dropped out of *college*?"

Monk swore under his breath. "Mallory, look. Honey, I'm so sorry. I just wanted to talk to my dad about it first, okay? I wanted his blessing. Which he didn't give. But I thought I should square it with him before I sprang it on you. Are you mad?"

"Not *mad*. Just—I don't know. He was under the impression we were basically eloping. He kind of put me on the spot, like it was somehow my fault. That I'd led you astray."

"Oh, Jesus, Pinks. He didn't."

"He did."

"So what did you tell him?"

"I told him I supported your decision. What else was I going to say?"

Monk heaved a sigh that rustled in my ear. "Pinks, you're the best. Seriously. I don't even deserve what a fucking clutch hitter you are, you know that? I'm just sorry about the ambush. I am. That was all supposed to stay between him and me."

"But why? Why didn't you tell me? Don't you trust me?"

"Mallory, what are you talking about? I trust you more than anyone else in the world. You're literally the only human being I *do* trust. Look. Is he still there?"

"Yes. Driving. We're almost at the house now."

"Gotcha. I'll be quick. So the real reason I called was actually *not* to pull your chain about the champagne lunch with Dad. Believe it or not."

"Oh?"

"Mike called," said Monk. "He had a band coming in that was supposed to play tonight and they bailed. Wants to know if I can step in."

"Are you going to do it?"

"It's four hundred bucks, Pinks. That's a lot of gas money. And Bessie drinks a lot of gas."

"Then do it."

"Are you sure?"

"Of course. I'll take the first driving shift tomorrow. It'll be fine."

"So you're still in? Not too pissed off to share a car with me?"

"I told you, I'm not pissed off. Just kind of—I don't know, blown up a little."

"I'm sorry, Pinks. I am. I wasn't trying to keep any of this from you, I swear. I just wanted to surprise you. That's all. Do the romantic thing on the mountaintop. And I fucked it up, apparently, and I'm sorry. I didn't realize Dad would—shit, you know what? I'm an idiot. I *should* have known. Fucking Machiavelli. What was I thinking?"

We turned from the main road onto the Seagrapes driveway. The car began to fetch in the potholes. I felt Mr. Adams's ears straining for our conversation. I glanced at him and smiled. He lifted his eyebrows and shrugged his shoulder.

"What do you mean, Machiavelli?" I asked.

"Look," said Monk, "can we unpack all this later? While we're driving through Pennsylvania? It's a big state. Goes on fucking forever. Plenty of time to psychoanalyze Dad's manipulative ways. Just don't let him get to you, okay? Don't let him set up house in your head."

I stared across the meadow grass to the crumbling stone wall that separated Seagrapes from the Monk property. The spot where I'd once sat with Monk, and a squall caught us, and Monk held his jacket over our heads while the rain drummed around us.

"I've been kind of thinking New Mexico lately," I said. "What do you think of New Mexico?"

"Never been to New Mexico. I hear Santa Fe's a great spot."

"Georgia O'Keeffe lived in Santa Fe."

"No shit, that's right. That's a sign, Pinks. An omen. I'll see you in the morning. Bring you coffee, how's that? Grace promised she'd pack some sandwiches for us."

"Oh my God. We're really doing this."

"Pinko," he said, "we really are. Get some sleep."

"You too."

"It's going to be okay, I swear. I love you, all right? I'm all yours."

"Same," I said.

I hung up the phone and slipped it into my handbag. My head was still spinning from the champagne. Mr. Adams eased the car to a stop in front of the garage and cut the engine. "Everything all right?" he asked.

I stared through the windshield at the cedar shingles in front of us.

"You're wrong about Monk," I said. "He's a great artist. Maybe it's not your kind of art. Not your kind of music. But it's special, it is. He writes these songs that dig into your soul. And he can sing, Mr. Adams, he can really sing."

"I know that, Mallory. He's always had a terrific singing voice."

I turned in my seat and looked at Mr. Adams. He concentrated on the garage door facing the car, like he was trying to use Jedi mind tricks to open it. Not listening to me at all.

"You should know something," I said. "You should know that he's been playing gigs at the Mohegan Inn all summer, and he's killing it, Mr. Adams. Killing it. They're boating in from the mainland to hear him. They're lining up for autographs. You have to see it to believe it. You have to hear him, Mr. Adams, you have to understand. This is what he was born to do."

"Then perhaps he should have told me about all this. Don't you think?"

"Because he didn't want to disappoint you." I reached out and put my hand on his arm. "Look. Listen to me, Mr. Adams. Please listen. He's going to kill me for telling you this. But I think you should know he's playing tonight. He's stepping in last minute to earn some extra money. You should go. It starts around nine o'clock. Just go. I mean, don't let him see you there. But just watch. Please, Mr. Adams. You have to watch him play. Before he leaves."

Mr. Adams turned to look at me. His face was tired and full of compassion.

"You care about him very much, don't you?" he said.

"I love him, Mr. Adams. I'd do anything for him."

"Then he's a very lucky boy." Monk's father gave me this kind, wistful smile and reached out to pat my knee. "All right, then, Mallory. If you want me to go, I'll go."

* * *

Even though Mr. Adams assured me I was now officially off the clock, I went upstairs to tuck the twins into bed when evening fell. We'd been reading from Harry Potter, and it seemed somehow wrong to finish up the chapter and slide in the bookmark, without any intention of continuing to the end. Deceitful, almost.

"So," I told them. "You know how you asked if Monk and I were getting married?"

Blue sat up in bed. "You're getting *married*? Can I be *bridesmaid*?"

"Gross," said Chippy.

"No, silly. We're not getting married. Sheesh. But we are—you know, boyfriend and girlfriend. And we decided we would take the rest of the summer off and go on a little vacation together, before college starts."

Blue sighed. "I know *that*. Mom said."

"Oh."

"She called you a slut," said Chippy.

"Well, that's nice. You know that in olden times, a slut was a woman who was really messy. Like an artist sometimes gets when she's in the middle of creating something wonderful. So maybe your mom was right. Now lie back down so I can tuck you in."

Blue lay back and stared at me with her moon eyes while I kissed her forehead. A little unnerving, but whatever. "Are you coming back?" she asked.

"Of course we're coming back, sweetheart. Monk's your big brother, he loves you more than anything."

"Do *you* love me?"

"Oh, sweetheart." I pushed her fine hair back from her forehead. "Of course I do. Maybe you and Chippy can come and stay with us sometime. Would that be fun?"

"Yes," she said. But her eyes were still moons.

When I turned to Chippy, he pretended to be asleep. Curled on his side, eyes shut tight. I ruffled his hair and kissed his smooth, damp cheek.

"Good night, sweet boy," I whispered. "Love you always."

* * *

Get some sleep, Monk had told me.

I tried. I lay in bed for the longest time, rolling to one side and the other. The champagne buzz had worn off a while ago. I tried to concentrate on my breathing, to concentrate on childhood memories, TV shows, go through the to-do lists, but the things Mr. Adams had said to me over lunch kept dropping into my head.

Isn't that what we're talking about, Mallory? About Monk quitting college to start his so-called music career?

There's no such thing as old money anymore.

And: *Believe me, when I married my first wife, I thought we'd feel that way about each other forever.*

I glanced at the clock. Nearly eleven. Monk would be finishing up by now, signing autographs. Signing arms. All those belly buttons tucked in their sleek, tanned bellies. Fun-loving, music-loving girls. Girls who didn't spend an hour staring at a seashell, mesmerized by the pattern of ridges that resembled the ripples in an ocean.

I love you, all right? I'm all yours.

I rose from the bed and changed into pajamas. Belted my dressing gown over them. I'd bought the robe at Marshalls before I left for college, imagining long midnight conversations in the dorm hallway. It was getting a bit tatty by now, as my grandmother would have said. The teal satin was fraying at the seams. I tiptoed to the liquor tray in the sunroom and poured a splash of vodka into a glass to numb my anxious nerves a little. Some lemon seltzer.

"Mallory. Good evening."

I spun to the french doors. Mr. Adams stood there in a dressing gown of his own, much richer than mine. Smoking his evening joint.

"I—I thought you were at the Mo."

"I came home after the first set. You reach my age, you can't stay out the way you once did. And Becca called." He examined the joint, inhaled, examined the result. "She was under the weather."

"I'm sorry."

He waved his hand. "Join me?"

"I really—I was just going to bed—"

"Come along. It's a lovely night."

I followed him to the terrace. He sat in his usual wicker chair; I perched on the edge of my usual wicker sofa. He offered me the joint. I hesitated, then took it. It would help me sleep, I thought.

"You know, I once had aspirations to be an artist," Mr. Adams said.

"Did you really? Doing what?"

"Oh, I painted. Oils. Back at school, they thought I had some talent. That was some time ago." He picked up the glass of brown liquid sitting on the wicker coffee table and swirled the sides. "In fact, I took a minor in fine art at Harvard. My father thought it was a good idea. Everyone needs a hobby, he told me."

"Do you ever wish you'd pursued it more?"

"Oh, not really. Not to any great extent. I married early. Divorced and married again. Monk's sister came along, and Monk. Duties, you know? God gives us habit in place of happiness. As Pushkin tells us." He drank the Scotch, set it back on the coffee table, and picked up his joint. "But nothing goes to waste, Mallory. Remember that. Instead of indulging my creative ambitions at my family's expense, I poured all my energy into supporting young artists."

"So what did you think of Monk's show?" I asked.

"I thought it was very good. He's a natural performer." He chuckled and shook his head. "All those women, my God. I don't know where they came from. The mainland, I guess."

"Mike must have sent the word out. He's got kind of a following now. Monk, I mean."

"I thought I recognized one of them. Daughter of an old friend of mine. Harvard. Oil family, out in Texas? We used to tease him about it. Called him Tex. Tex Lassiter. Good man. Now the girl's at Colby with Monk." He smiled. "*Was*, I guess."

"Oh?"

"He joined her at the bar during the break. They seemed to be having a nice chat together. Catching up, I guess. Lovely young thing, Lee. You know, I always imagined—well. Never mind that." He sucked on the joint and shook his head. "Girls these days, their figures. All these sports they're doing. Can I get you another drink?"

I looked at my glass and realized it was empty.

"I really shouldn't. I couldn't sleep, that's all. I thought it might help."

He rose and took the glass. "A second will put you right out, trust me."

I heard him step through the door behind me. I stared at the joint burning in the ashtray. Thought about Monk, putting his guitar into the case. Walking out the kitchen door of the Mo, down the street by himself, into Bessie by himself. Followed, possibly, by a fan or two. Maybe the one who'd joined him at the bar, according to Mr. Adams. The old girlfriend from Colby, catching up.

I reached for the joint and dragged in a lungful of weed.

"Mallory?"

I realized my eyes were closed. I opened them and there was Mr. Adams, holding out a drink. "Thanks," I said.

He had refilled his own drink too. He sat down, picked up the joint, and said, "Have I put my foot in it again?"

"What? No."

"Monk's a loyal boy, Mallory. You have nothing to worry about."

"I'm not worried."

"I'm sure he's on his way home now." With his drink, he gestured in the direction of the Monk estate. "If you'd like to go over there and wait for him, instead of sitting around here with a doddering old man like me, I understand."

I picked up the glass and sipped. A little strong on the vodka. "That would be silly."

"That's my girl." Mr. Adams sucked on the joint and set it back on the edge of the ashtray. "So, tell me a bit more about your drawings, Mallory. I want to know everything about you."

When I think of what happened next, which is not often, I think of it from a distance. I watch it happening like it's some other girl, some actress playing me in a scene. Even at the time, it didn't seem real. I felt like a puppet. Like something else had taken over the action of my arms and legs and thoughts. My emotions sandpapered away to a dull matte. So I don't remember every detail. Every word. They alter a little in my memory, every time I think about that night. Which is not often.

But this is the gist.

I remember I talked to Mr. Adams about my drawings, about the repeating patterns in nature and how I'd taken this course in textile design and started weaving those ideas into my work. He found it fascinating. He asked me about my father, my relationship with my father, how old I was when he left. He asked how close my father and I had been. How often I see him now.

I heard myself say, "I think I'd better head for bed now."

"I think you'd better," said Mr. Adams.

He helped me rise from the chair. Held me around the shoulders as we crossed the sunroom to the hall. "I'm feeling a little strange," I told him.

"Yes, you probably do," he said. "I might have given you something to help you sleep. You seemed a bit on edge. Don't worry, I'll take care of you. This way, honey."

I wanted to tell him that I didn't need help, that I could get to bed by myself. But my limbs were heavy and my head seemed to lack any will of its own. He guided me around the corner and down the hall to my room. Turned on the lamp next to the bed and untied the sash of my dressing gown.

"I can take it from here," I said.

"Now, Mallory. Just let me help you. I don't think you can get these buttons by yourself, can you?"

"But I don't . . . I need my pajamas . . ."

"Mallory, honey. Let's be honest. You've been wanting me to do this. I've seen the way you look at me. Those dirty little glances. And your paintings, my God, those flowers. Don't think I don't know what you were trying to tell me with *those*."

"I think . . . I think you misun . . . mister . . ."

"Nobody has to know, Mallory. Our secret."

I was falling. He caught me and sat me on the bed. The pajama top came apart in his hands.

"That's right. Here we are," he said, in that soothing baritone. "Well, now. Look at these little devils. Even prettier than I imagined."

He laid his hands on my breasts. I remember looking down in shock at his fingers, raising my nipples to points. *You need to panic now,* I thought. *You need to do something.*

"You see?" he said. "You want this, Mallory."

"No."

He laughed softly. "But I *know* how much you enjoy a good screw. Right, Mallory? I've listened to you at night. You're just one of those girls. One of those girls that needs it."

I tried to lift my hands to stop him, but they were so heavy, like they were filled with iron. "I can't," I said.

"I'm going to take care of you, Mallory. Everything will be fine, I promise. Nobody will know. Just lie down for me. Let it happen."

He pushed me gently back on the bed and took hold of my pajama bottoms. I stared at the ceiling as he worked them down my legs. When I summoned my arms to rise against him, they wouldn't move. *This must be a dream,* I thought. *That's it. A dream. Hallucination. Nightmare. This is not my body. This is not real. This can't be real.*

This isn't really happening.

But it did. It happened. It happens to a lot of women, more women than you think. Women who never imagine it could happen to them, women who trusted the wrong person, women who dropped their guard at the wrong moment. Women who think it was maybe their fault. Women who are too ashamed to talk about it afterward. Women who try to forget, to move on with their lives, to block the whole thing out, to stuff it in a box and close the lid. Go on living and loving, don't let it define you. Don't let it beat you.

But it did happen. That night, it happened to me.

CHAPTER TWENTY-FOUR

Monk

September 2022
Mystic, Connecticut

The house is larger than he expected. In his head—in his fears—she's been bringing up Sam in some kind of run-down rural shack with a single, frayed Depression-era power line running in from a battered pole on the edge of a dirt road roamed by feral dogs.

As usual, he's an idiot when it comes to Mallory.

He turns Bessie into the neat-edged gravel driveway, shifts her into park, and shuts off the engine. A clapboard New England farmhouse sits before him, painted pale yellow with dark green shutters, window boxes overflowing with late-summer blooms. There is a porch with a pair of sky-blue Adirondack chairs and a small wooden table between them for your coffee or beer or lemonade. Looks about an acre or two. Plenty of room for a boy to roam, climbing trees and kicking a ball around, catch some fireflies on a June evening.

He grips the steering wheel and thinks, *Don't fuck this up, Adams.* Don't. Fuck. This. Up.

He grabs the flowers and laptop bag and climbs out of the car. As he approaches the porch steps, a voice calls out behind him, "You're early."

He swings around. The old familiar punch to the gut, the longing that shuts off his breath for a second. She's wearing faded jeans and a sleeveless shirt, rubber gardening clogs and an apron and a straw hat over her wild dark hair, knotted up behind her head. A trowel hangs from one hand. A smudge of dirt along one cheekbone just about begs for his thumb.

"Hey," he says. "The drive took less time than I thought. I like your place."

She gestures with the trowel. "I was just finishing up in the garden. Are those for me?"

He holds up the flowers like he's never seen them before. *Idiot,* he thinks. "Last of the summer from Aunt Barbara's rose garden. Thought she'd want you to have them."

Mallory's face transforms into joy. "Oh! That's—Monk, I'm so touched. I loved her so much. Thank you. Go make yourself comfortable out back and I'll put these in water."

She hurries past him to spring up the porch steps and disappear through the front door. He watches it close and sets off around the side of the house, through an open gate in a crumbling stone wall, to the most profuse garden he's ever seen in his life. Containers everywhere, tumbling vines, rioting beds, flowers upon flowers, vegetables. Couple of pear trees beyond, fruit hanging ripe. There's a pattern to all this, but he can't quite grasp it. Against the house is a patio paved with old red bricks. He sets his laptop bag on the table and walks down the center path until he comes to a row of sunflowers. He imagines Sam as a young kid, playing here.

The air is warm and drowsy, drenched in September gold. The sun bakes his head. He's shoved both hands in his pockets but he takes one out now to touch the perfect yellow petals of the sunflower.

You can do this, he thinks.

With his thumb and forefinger, he rubs the sunflower petal for good luck. He runs through his lines in his head, the things he must say. He rehearsed it all again in the shower this morning, during the drive down from Boston after his checkup. How he'll start the conversation, the questions he should ask her, what she might say, what he should reply to this or that. He's run through several versions of this conversation in his head, but they all end the same way.

Over the phone the other day, he told Mallory he needs to go over some legal documents with her before it's time to pick up Sam from soccer practice and take him to Winthrop for the weekend.

330 • BEATRIZ WILLIAMS

Discuss the visitation schedule for the fall, some ongoing security arrangements now that the world is officially aware of Sam's existence ("we ask for respect and privacy as we heal physically and as a family," like *that* would send the paps and the trolls back to their caves). This is all true. He wants to make additional provisions for Sam and for Mallory, to recognize Sam as his legal heir; he wants to make Mallory a shareholder and board member on the production company, as Sam's trustee; he's got some ideas about combining the Adams and Monk properties on Winthrop into a single compound and he wants her input. All of that. Plans for the future. Now that he has a future.

But everything depends on *not fucking up this conversation first.*

He spots a flash of movement between the sunflowers. Mallory's quick step down the path.

"There you are," she says. "I got you a beer."

He takes the bottle from her hand. "Nice flowers. Is this where you get your inspiration?"

Oh, for fuck's sake, you idiot. Is this where you get your inspiration?

She smiles. "You know my stuff better than anyone, I guess. Should we sit?"

"Sure."

Monk follows her back down the path to the patio table. She takes a chair in the shade. She pulls off her hat and her hair frizzes from its knot. The table is round and Monk sits in the chair next to hers, a quarter-hour away. He points himself in her direction and sips his beer. She smooths back her hair with one hand. He nods to the sketchbook lying on the table, next to his laptop bag.

"Drawing much lately?"

He loves the way the blush crawls along that satin skin of hers, her pale olive skin you want to feel under your lips to find out how warm it is, how it tastes.

"When I can," she says.

"Can I see?"

"Right now?"

"Sure."

She looks at him, at the sketchbook. "I guess so. It's pretty raw, I warn you. I copy the best ones into my portfolio. This is like—

I don't know, like you scribbling down a melody that comes into your head."

She hands him the sketchbook. He takes his readers out of his chest pocket and flips the book open to a drawing of a pear, so beautifully shaped, so luscious and obviously ripe, the stem poised at an expectant angle at the top, like a question mark, that he wants to reach into the page and eat the juicy, sun-warmed flesh. Even though it's in charcoal.

"Tell me something, Pinks." He takes off the readers and looks up. "What do you want to do with this? I mean, in an ideal world, what does your work look like?"

She looks surprised. She takes a sip from her beer and looks to one side, at her garden. "In an ideal world? I guess I'd quit my freelancing contracts and start my own design house. Drawing on themes from nature, you know, the patterns in the natural world. Remember how we used to talk about that?"

"I remember."

"Your father—" She falters and glances at Monk. He nods at her to continue. "Your father used to tell me that I should study fine art, that I was shunted into commercial art because I'm a woman, and I guess I only recently realized how fucked up that was. How it fucked up my perception of myself, like I was just doing second-rate art somehow, that commercial art was selling out. But to me . . . you know, I don't *want* to see my drawings hanging on the wall of some museum. Some art gallery for people to stare at. I want to surround people with art. I want people to touch my designs, to sleep with them, to sit on them, to eat off them. That's how art began, to make everyday things beautiful, to make meaning out of use. I don't know where we got this idea that art should be worshipped. That artists should be worshipped. Do you know what I mean?"

"I get you," he says.

"I'd rather be an artisan than an artist. Bring beauty and meaning and joy right into people's lives. Their homes. And it took me a while to get there and kind of own it for myself, you know? But anyway, that's what I would do. In an ideal world, of course."

Monk looks at her finger tapping next to her beer bottle and thinks, *Don't fuck this up.*

He raises his gaze to her face. Her green eyes that warm him. "How's your sister doing, Pinks?"

"Paige? Oh, she's fine. Doing much better. They've moved on to the boring part, the lawyer stuff. Custody and financial agreements and all that . . ." She trails off, blushing again. "She keeps herself busy with all this ancestry research. Tracking down what happened to our grandmother—you remember how we went to Ireland to look up the adoption records? She keeps finding out all this amazing stuff."

He could sit here listening to her voice forever. "Like what?"

"Oh, gosh. So this guy Lucien Beck—that's our grandfather—it turns out he was some kind of Israeli intelligence operative."

"You mean like Mossad?"

"Exactly. And he was in Egypt after the war, gathering intelligence, and that's where we think he met Hannah. Our grandmother. She was married to this British diplomat, and Paige thinks she was passing on info to this Mossad guy, Lucien Beck, because this bracelet"—Mallory holds up her arm, her graceful arm—"holds secret messages. . . . I'm sorry, I'm being as boring as Paige."

"No, no. This is seriously cool. Your roots."

"Anyway, it turns out there were these massive riots in downtown Cairo in January of 1952. The protesters ended up setting fire to hundreds of buildings. And the mother superior at the convent in Ireland said Hannah arrived about a month after that, with all these burns, right? So it fits. Paige's theory is that she fell in love with this Mossad guy and got pregnant, and then something happened. They were caught up in the riots or something and Lucien died trying to save her. And her husband took her to Ireland to have the baby and give it up for adoption."

"That's just completely fucked up. I don't understand how a man could do that."

She's been working the bracelet around her wrist. Now she looks up and meets his gaze, just for a second or two. Long enough that he forgets how to breathe.

She drops her gaze back down to the bracelet. "But apparently Lucien also had a sister, and the sister had kids. So Paige started getting these pings from new cousins. That's how she found out about the Mossad thing. She's trying to find out more about this guy, about what happened in Cairo. It's like an obsession with her now. She wants to take the kids to Israel. She's literally learning Hebrew on Duolingo, it's crazy."

"That's how she copes, though. Isn't it? Copes with all the shit."

Mallory looks up, a little surprised. "Yes. That's exactly how she copes."

He's relaxing a little now, thanks to the beer and the sound of Mallory's voice, the hum of bees, the drunken perfume of the flowers. "What about your grandmother? Hannah, right?"

"This is the cool part." Mallory leans forward, animated. "The mother superior in Ireland told us she was rescued by a woman in a car who arrived right after my grandparents adopted Mom, right? And it turns out Hannah was *Hungarian*. She returned to Hungary and got involved in the Hungarian independence movement. You know, behind the Iron Curtain, trying to kick out the Soviets? We've been finding all kinds of records. She ended up spending about a decade in prison, but she lived to see the last Soviet tanks roll out. She died in Budapest in 1992."

"Are you serious? That's amazing."

"Yeah, our minds are pretty blown. Like, this was our grandmother. Kicking ass."

"It makes sense. I mean, look at you. Her granddaughter. Following your own road. Standing up for what you believe in."

Another blush. She lifts her hand and works the cobra bracelet on her wrist. Jiggles the rubber clog from the ends of her toes. "We spent our whole lives thinking we were one thing. Irish Catholic, Boston, working class. My grandfather, he worked in construction and ended up owning his own business, which is what put us through Nobles. So, the American dream, right? But it turns out we're something else. A whole different story."

"But you're still the same person. I mean, do you *feel* any different?"

"Grateful. I feel grateful. I think every day about how we're all here because of a series of little miracles we know nothing about. The miracles that brought me right here, sitting in this chair beside you. What they sacrificed so I could live." She looks at him with gentle eyes. "What you sacrificed for Sam."

Now, he thinks. *Time to rip off the Band-Aid. Take one end and pull.*

334 • BEATRIZ WILLIAMS

Just don't fuck it up.

He sets the empty beer bottle on the table. "So, I guess I should tell you. I went to visit Paige about a week ago."

"Oh?" Her voice goes up about an octave. "What did you talk about?"

"I needed to ask her about something. Been kind of bothering me since I got out of the hospital. I had this memory. Like the memory of a dream. Couldn't get it out of my head. I'm lying on the bed, right? Can't move, can't open my eyes. But I can hear your voice."

"And what did I say?"

"You told me this story. This crazy story about something that happened with you and Dad. Something so terrible I—I didn't think it could be true. Or maybe I just didn't want to think it was true. But that's what I remembered. So, I went to ask Paige if it *was* true. What I remembered you telling me. And she said that it was."

The blood whooshes from her face. "*What?* She said—she told me she wouldn't—"

"Pinks."

(Don't fuck this up, Adams. Do not fuck this up.)

He reaches out and touches his fingertips to hers. "I just want to say how sorry I am. I know that's beyond inadequate. Honestly, I'm devastated. That he did that to you. That I never saw it, never knew. All this time. Just thinking about it now, I'm sick. I didn't sleep for days. I—"

The words jam up in his throat. She stares down at his fingers intersecting with her fingers and he tries to force something out, anything.

"But forget that. It doesn't matter how I feel about it. What matters is you, Pinks. What matters is that you went through this alone, that we failed you. That I failed you. So, I'm just here apologizing to you for what he did, from the bottom of my heart. And I understand why you left. I support whatever decision you felt you had to make. And I wish to God I knew how to make it better for you. Make it go away for you."

She pulls her hand away. "I know I should have come to you sooner."

"Mallory, I understand."

"No one needs to know that about his own father. No one should have to carry that."

"Pinks, for fuck's sake. Did you think I wouldn't understand? Not believe you?"

"Of course I knew you'd believe me. That's the point. It would've *wrecked* you, like it's wrecking you now."

"Jesus, Mallory. *Losing* you wrecked me."

"Monk, *I* was wrecked. I was so fucked up afterward. He made me think I'd asked for it, like I'd wanted it somehow. That it was my fault. All this shame. I wasn't worthy of you anymore."

He tries to remember the words he had ready for this. Something about loving her no matter what, nothing in the world more important than her. *Just say* something, he thinks. *Idiot. Say anything.*

"All by yourself, on that fucking ferry." (*Idiot,* he thinks.) "All by yourself."

"My mom picked me up at the terminal. Took me home."

"Did you tell her what happened?"

"Sort of. Eventually. I mean, she knew something was wrong. And then, you know. Pregnant."

"Pinks," he says, scratchy voice, "I told you I would take care of you. Remember?"

"Not like this. Everything would've changed between us. You'd never want to touch me again, you'd be *revolted—*"

"Oh, Mallory. *Revolted?*"

"You would. It's true. Your own *father.*" She looks down at her hands, knotting the apron in her lap. "And, to be honest, vice versa. I think, deep down, I was kind of scared it would have ruined you for me too. I would have looked at you and seen your dad, and I couldn't stand that."

"Do you? Now? See my dad?"

"No," she says. "I can't even picture him anymore, to be honest. And you're nothing like him, nothing. You're . . . well, you're *you.* You gave Sam your kidney, for God's sake."

He rubs a thumb against his forehead. "But that's the thing, Mallory. What's so fucked up. My dad would've given *me* a kidney, if I needed it."

She takes the corner of her apron and wipes at her eyes, leaving a few more streaks of dirt on her face. "Well, by the time I figured out what a fuckup he was—forgave myself, basically—you were this *celebrity*. You were Monk fucking Adams. You'd moved on. I couldn't just turn up with Sam. Like the dumb mistake from your past."

Careful, Adams. Watch your step. Don't break anything.

He says, "Do you remember what I told you, when I picked you up that first day, at the ferry? I said I was going to look out for you. Not to worry. And I failed. I failed you. If I hadn't taken that gig at the Mo that night—"

"Please don't."

"I never imagined he'd—I swear to God, if I'd had any idea he was capable of that shit, I never would have asked you to Winthrop, never would have left you alone with him for a second. It makes me sick, Pinks. All that time—*all that time*—I swear to God, I would kill him now. If he wasn't dead already."

"I know," she says. "That's why I couldn't tell you."

"Mallory," he says. "Mallory."

She spreads out the apron on her lap and smooths the wrinkles. Some sunlight plays in her hair. In his head, he hears the notes of a piano, a series of cascades like the fall of rain. He wants to cup his hands, to capture it, but like rain it slips between the cracks of his fingers. Maybe he'll remember it later. Sometimes it works that way.

She says softly, "He sent me a letter, you know."

"A *letter*? When?"

"A couple of weeks after he died. It came from his lawyer's office, in Boston. But it was from him. In the event of my death kind of thing."

"What did it say?"

"He used the word *remorse*. How recent events—I assumed he was talking about the whole MeToo thing?—made him reassess his past actions. Made him realize the imbalance of power and consent and blah blah. Made all these excuses about his marriage being on the rocks, his age catching up to him, all this bullshit, nothing about his issues with you—"

"With me?"

She looks at him with an expression you might call pity. "Monk, he was jealous of you. Of his own son. Didn't you see that? I mean, of course he was proud. But you were also the man he wanted to be.

Everything he could have been and wasn't. And me, I was the help. I wasn't the girl you were supposed to marry. The girl who would set you on the right track. So he had to put me in my place. To put me out of your reach."

"Jesus, Pinks. You were not the *help*. You were my *friend*. My best friend. The love of my fucking *life*. He *knew* that."

"Exactly," she says. "And he wanted you back."

He stands up and walks to the edge of the bricks. Shoves his hands into his pockets and turns his face up to the sky.

"There was a check inside," she says. "Enclosed with the letter. For—get this—for twenty-five thousand dollars. I guess that's the going rate?"

He turns. "Oh, shit, Pinks."

"I ripped it up, obviously."

For fuck's sake, say something, he tells himself. *Don't be the asshole.*

She speaks in a gentle voice. "Look, I made my choices. I thought I was doing the right thing for everyone. And now here we are. We have Sam. I'm sorry it took so long to get here. And if you want to take a DNA test—"

"A what?"

She meets his gaze. "To see if he's really yours."

Somewhere in his throat, there are words. He can't get them out, though.

"Shit," she says. "Think about it, Monk. You mean you haven't even *considered* that—"

He sits back down and grabs her elbows. "Mallory, he's mine. I didn't *consider* because I already *knew*. Are you saying—"

"*How* did you know?"

"—all these years, you *weren't sure*? You thought you might have had *Dad's* baby? *That's* why you didn't tell me?"

"*How do you know for sure, Monk?*"

He lets go of her arms. "The DNA test, Pinks. The contract, re-member? It was in the contract. Standard boilerplate for paternity agreements. Pending DNA confirmation. Don't you remember?"

Her green eyes open wide.

"Pinks," he says, "tell me you read that agreement before you signed it."

"Well, I trusted you."

"That's beside the point! I don't care if you're signing a contract with God, you read the fucking contract first! Trust me on that. I'm in the music business."

Mallory looks down at her lap and brushes at some dirt on her apron. "I might have been a little mad at the whole situation. At the time."

"Whatever. You can set your mind at ease. You're not—Jesus— I mean, it doesn't even matter to me, you know that? He's got my kidney. He's mine. But also, he happens to be biologically mine. Not that I would even care. If he weren't. Because he's yours, and we . . . you and me, that summer, we . . . Look, Pinks—"

She stands and swipes up the empty beer bottles. "I'm just going to go inside and put these in the recycling, okay?"

Monk stares at the row of sunflowers across the garden and slowly, deliberately bangs his head against the wooden table.

What did we talk about, Adams? What did we talk about?

Don't. Fuck. This. Up.

He finds her in the kitchen, rinsing out the beer bottles with maniacal thoroughness. On the table next to the window, Aunt Barbara's roses sit in a glass vase.

"Hey," he says. *Idiot.*

"Hey," she says.

He takes a deep breath and forces his voice into the cheerful range. "So. You and Sedge Peabody, huh?"

She aims some side eye at him. "Mmm-hmm."

"He's a good guy. I'm happy for you."

"We're taking it slow at the moment," she says. "I've been pretty focused on Sam's recovery the past couple months."

"He's a lot richer than me. Be nice for you."

"Oh, you know me. It's my dream to fly private and buy those shoes with the red soles. Limousines or whatever they're called."

"Louboutins, Mallory. Personally, I think you look hot in flip-flops, but sure. Whatever makes you happy." He leans back against the kitchen counter and folds his arms. "And hey, at least one of us is getting laid, right?"

"Oh? Haven't the doctors cleared you yet?"

"Pinks, it's not just a question of having a doctor's note."

Another sideways glance.

"So . . . you and Lee . . . ?"

He shrugs. "She kept the ring."

"I'm sorry," she says.

"Are you, Pinks? Sorry?"

She turns off the faucet and stares at the bottle in her hands. Her thumb runs around the rim. "I know that she loves you. That you're the love of her life. So, yes. I'm sorry."

He stares at her thumb and thinks, *Careful*.

"I was sorry to hurt her," he says, examining each word before it leaves his mouth, "but I couldn't pretend any longer. Either to myself or to her. Which brings me to something else. I want to apologize to you personally, Mallory, for what Lee posted on Instagram—the way she violated your privacy and Sam's—"

She waves a hand. "Everyone makes mistakes."

"Yeah, well, my dad made a mistake too. And I would argue that mistake revealed more about him than thirty years of thinking I saw the full man, warts and all." He turns to face her, leaning his hip against the counter. "I'll tell you what, Pinks. How about I give you veto control over the next one, okay? Any girl I get involved with has to pass the Mallory test."

"I don't know if I can handle that kind of power."

"Well, we're co-parenting, right? So you have a stake in whoever I'm seeing. And vice versa."

"Oh, *vice versa*. I knew there was a catch."

Finally, a smile turns up the corner of her mouth. He uncrosses his arms and sets one hand on the edge of the counter, not far from hers.

"I guess I should tell you, Peabody came to see me," he says. "Kind of decent of him, I have to admit. This was about the middle of August, when I was back home recuperating. He laid out his feelings for you. Asked how things stood between you and me."

"And what did you tell him?"

The kitchen faces the patio and garden. Mallory won't look at him; she's looking at her pear trees in the distance. Like she's trying to make them come alive or something. Drop all their pears and dance for her.

It's go time, Adams. Like we rehearsed in the shower. In the car on the way down.

"I told him," Monk says, reaching up to brush at one of the dirt streaks on her face, "that I was still crazy in love with you, pretty much, that I loved you more than anything in the world except Sam, obviously, this beautiful kid that we made together, and even then it's more like a dead heat, like the two equal pieces of my heart, and if he ever hurt a hair on your head I'd knock his nuts clear into Long Island Sound."

And there it is. Out there in the open. *Your ball, Pinks.*

She sets down the beer bottle she's been holding. Sits her palms on the edge of the big farmhouse sink and stares at the drain.

Okay. Still his ball.

"Mallory," he says, "it's fair to say I've had a lot of time alone with my thoughts, the last couple of months. Probably too much time. I've been thinking about how, a while back, I got my heart broke in a million pieces, so I wrote some sad songs and turned on this fire hose that became my life, that filled the hole you left behind. And now I maybe need to turn that hose down. For Sam's sake. For yours."

At last, she turns to him. "*What?* You can't quit music!"

"I'm not talking about quitting music, Pinks. Music, it's what I am. It's how I say what's in my head. My heart. And I guess I love the high of performing, I'm not gonna lie. But to record another album right now, do another tour—what does *that* do for me? Nothing I need. Nothing I even want. More money? More of this celebrity shit, so I can't even have a basic fucking heart attack in peace and quiet? So I can't get caught in a bad parallel parking situation without the whole world pissing its pants laughing?"

She looks away to stare out the window. "All right. What *do* you want, Monk?"

He edges closer, so his fingers brush hers, there on the edge of the sink. What is it about her, he needs to touch her? Like magnets or something. He can't be without her touch.

"I already told you what I wanted. Fourteen years ago, I told you all about it. Honestly, none of that has changed. I want the same things. Maybe even more than I did then. But I was just a dumb kid. Everything was all about me. I never asked what you wanted."

"Yes, you did. You asked me if I wanted it too."

"That's not the same thing. At all. So tell me, Pinks. What do you want? What can I carry to your table?"

"I already have what I want. I have Sam. I have a healthy son again. You already gave me that. And I can never, ever thank you enough. And I have my house that I love, my garden. My work." She brushes back her hair. "I have you standing here in my kitchen. Alive. What more could I ask for?"

"Pinks, you're killing me. Come on."

"I guess, you know, what I said before. I want to be able to start my own design house, someday."

"That's better," he says. "Keep going."

She takes a deep breath. "Are you sure you're ready for this?"

"Bring it, Pinko. I'm here for all of it."

In a rush, she says, "I want Sam to have a sibling. Or two. Okay? Before he gets any older, before I get any older. And I want someone to share all that with me, because it's pretty damn lonely feeding a newborn at three o'clock in the morning, trust me. And the diapers and the tantrums and the endless fucking Saturday-morning soccer."

"What are you talking about, girl? Saturday-morning soccer is the *best*. Earlier the better. Hangover a plus, I'll bet."

"And I want a dog."

"Dog. Check. Anything else?"

"If I ever get married," she says to the garden outside the window, "which is not necessarily on the wish list, but if it happens, I want it to be small and quiet and perfect, without any wedding planners or social media. And then I want to go to Europe and see the museums."

"But you just said—"

"I know what I said. After Europe I want to take some road trips. I want to go to Santa Fe, to see the O'Keeffes. And all the Native American art."

"You have a lot on your list, Pinks. You think Sedge Peabody is up for all that?"

Finally, she turns back to face him. "I like Sedge Peabody a lot. He's a great guy. He's funny. We have a lot of chemistry."

"You can stop now."

"And he lives a normal life. Nobody wants his autograph. Nobody wants to sleep with him. I mean, not *nobody*, obviously. But not *everybody*."

"Everybody does *not* want to sleep with me, Pinks. And even if everybody did . . ."

He wipes at another streak of dirt.

"Don't stop," she says. "I need to know how that sentence ends."

Monk turns to the sink and picks up the dishcloth hanging from the faucet arm. He wets it with a short blast of water and turns back to wipe gently along her cheekbones, that spot on her chin. At her temple.

"All right, Pinko. This is important, okay? Are you listening?"

"All ears."

"Since the exact second I staggered back to shore from my nice little quiet swim in the sea and found *you* sitting there on our old beach, like a fucking *cosmic hallucination,* like a miracle, like Venus in her goddamn *shell,* except with clothes on, unfortunately, Pinks, I have looked at nobody but you. Nobody." He makes a last wipe and turns her face this way and that. All clean. "Is that clear?"

Her brow furrows. "What about . . . ?"

"No, Pinks. We didn't. Not even once. Not while you were under my roof, okay? I couldn't do that to you. And I think Lee realized that. She saw how it was. She wasn't her best self. And, you know, it was for the best. At least I don't have that damn phone in my face all the time."

Mallory lets out a laugh and leans her forehead into his chest. He puts his arms around her to keep her there. Her hair smells like applesauce.

"Also, Grace came back. I had to play the heart attack card. Go on my knees and beg. But she came back."

"Are you going to go on your knees for me?"

"You want me on my knees, I'll go on my knees."

She reaches around her back and takes his hands. "I kind of like it when you go on your knees," she says.

* * *

Afterward, she makes him turn on his stomach and draws her finger along the scar on his lower back. He rests his head on his arm and stares at the dreamy gold light slanting from the window. Feels her touch like it's the sun on his skin.

"Why didn't you tell me you were going to do this?" she asks.

"Because you had Sam's surgery to worry about. I didn't want you to have to worry about me too," he says. "That backfired, obviously."

She turns on her side next to him and tucks her hands under her cheek. "Your heart, Monk. It *stopped*."

"That's what they tell me."

"Don't ever do that again."

"Not planning on it."

"What was it like?"

"I just remember kind of coming to—not exactly conscious, just low-level aware—and thinking this is bad, this is not the way it was supposed to go."

"Did it hurt? Were you in pain?"

He thinks back. "I don't remember pain, exactly. Just feeling like I'd been kicked by a whole stable of horses. But also knowing you were there. Somehow I knew you were with me. And I knew that if you were with me, then Sam must have come through okay, because you wouldn't leave Sam alone if he wasn't okay. So I just hoped *you* were okay. I just thought, please God, take care of them for me. If I have to go."

Mallory lifts her arm and drapes it around the back of his head. Her eyes are wet.

"I sat there next to your bed and thought, how *stupid* was I? What kind of a scared dumbfuck *kid* was I? I should have trusted you. We could have had all this time. We could have shared so much. And I was afraid your time was up, and Sam would lose you, and I would lose you. And until that second I thought that the worst thing in the world had already happened to me, but this was a million times worse. You gone."

"Pinks, I know. I heard you."

"You were asleep."

"I remember your voice. Like a thread, you know? Holding me

to the world. And I thought, if I get out of here alive, I can't let her go."

She leans forward and kisses him. He turns on his side and draws her close. She burrows deep, like she's trying to get inside his skin. Like she's not already there.

"I think we should get married," he says.

"We can't just have a nice fling?"

"No, Pinks. Not this time. Sorry. We have to do it right. For the kid. For the kids."

"Kids?"

"Maybe I missed something back there, but it seems to me like we're already trying?" He gives her a kiss, because she's right there and he's allowed to kiss her now. "I'm thinking kind of a Columbus Day weekend thing. Winthrop's a ghost town in October; we'd have the place to ourselves. Nice and easy. Sam. Paige and the girls. Mom and Vicky. Chippy and Blue and whoever else can make it. Your dad, obviously, if he's into it. My manager, Kevin—you remember meeting Kevin, right? That little all-clear party at the hospital? The one who called you Rosebud?"

She laughs into the hollow of his throat.

"Kevin and his husband. Kevin's a good guy, he's been there for me. Grace'll bake us one of her cakes. She'll be stoked, she adores you. What do you think, Pinko? Tie the knot? Columbus weekend?"

"Monk. That's like, three weeks away."

"Sam's thirteen, Pinks. He's not getting any younger. Neither are we."

"Speak for yourself. I'm not the one with a damn *pacemaker* in my chest."

She says it like a joke, except the word *pacemaker* catches in her throat.

Monk strokes her arm and stares across the room at the old brown chest of drawers, the mirror that stands on top of it. He thinks of her climbing out of this bed in this room, morning after morning, opening the drawers, getting dressed, getting Sam ready for school, and how all that time he had no idea they were living right here under his nose, in this little farmhouse across the water in Mystic. Her reflection in the mirror, morning after morning.

"What are you thinking?" she asks.

"It wasn't because you were the nanny," he says. "Maybe a little. But mostly because you're immaculate."

She laughs. "Immaculate? Me?"

"Incorruptible. He had no power over you. All these assholes, it's about power."

"Hey." She lays her hand on his cheek and turns his head. "Look at me."

He looks. She stares earnestly through his eyeballs into his dreams.

"It's important to know where you came from," she says. "It's a part of you. But it doesn't have to define you. They give you the paper and ink, but you write the story yourself."

Those eyes. The color of spring, he thinks.

"Tell me something, Pinks," he says softly. "Do you think we would have made it? If my dad hadn't done what he did. If we'd taken off together on that road trip, like we planned."

"Do you?"

"Look, all I know is the way I feel now. And if fourteen years later you're more beautiful to me than ever, inside and out, then yes. I think we could have survived whatever life threw at us. What do you think?"

"I think it would have been hard. I do. We were a couple of kids, Monk. We would have been a couple of kids with a baby, really struggling, and the music thing wouldn't have happened for you right away. It would have happened eventually—I mean, your talent, it's just too big—but even that would have been hard, because of Sam. Because of all the pressure."

"Life's supposed to be hard. You have to fight for what you love. And I would have fought for you and Sam. I would have fought so hard for this."

"Would you? With all the bright, shiny things thrown your way?"

He picks his words. "Pinks, do you remember when we were lying on that beach together, and I finally worked up the guts to tell you how I felt about you? And you said you couldn't believe I didn't already know I was the sun to your earth?"

"Oh God, you remember that? I can't believe I said something so corny."

"Not corny. It was just wrong. It's the other way around. You're the sun. I'm just here soaking you up, Pinks. So yes, I would have fought for us. I would have fought like hell. Because I happen to know how dark and basically fucked up my world is when you're not in it."

She looks away and lays her head back down against his chest.

"Listen," he says. "I'm so sorry you're going to have to put up with all this shit to be with me. I understand, I do. I know you love your house, your garden, this beautiful life you've made for yourself. I'm not asking you or Sam to leave all that for me. We can do this however you want. Just maybe clear out a couple of drawers for me and—"

"Oh, Monk." She laughs and lifts her head again, so he can see the tears there. "A couple of *drawers*?"

"I mean, we can't move Sam, right? He's got his school here."

"Well, since you brought it up, I should probably tell you that I've already put you down to play the PTA carnival in May."

"The *what*?"

Mallory kisses the tip of his nose. "Kidding."

"Pinko," he says, "sign me up. I honestly can't think of a better gig than my kid's school carnival."

She rolls away and laughs at the ceiling. The sound of her laugh, it's like the whole world turns gold. "Monk. Oh my God, Monk. Yes. You are absolutely right. I love my little bitty house and my little bitty garden. But you know what? I love you more."

"So, what I'm hearing is you'll let me buy us a bigger house? Like, your dream house?"

"I'm saying my dream house is the one you're in."

For that, he kisses her mouth, kisses her neck. Just touching his mouth to her skin makes him horny again. Less than half an hour ago they were mating like wildcats, desperate to get back to where they'd been, to plant their flags back on each other.

Cathartic as hell. But not enough.

Now he takes some time to savor her. The undersides of her breasts; the curve of her belly, where Sam grew. The backs of her knees, between her legs. She tastes the same, it's a miracle, she drugs him. She pulls at his hair and sings as she comes. He lifts his head and sinks his face into the sweetness of her stomach. Kisses his way across her belly button, her ribs, between her breasts. She cups her palms around his cheeks and smiles at him with her whole face, her green eyes, *incorruptible,* and he thinks with raw, sudden shame of the other hands that have touched his body, the other bodies he has touched with his hands. The guilt of it drenches him. He can't stand it, her faith. He opens his mouth to explain, to confess. *The first time I slept with someone else, it was twenty-two months and eleven days after you left. I threw up afterward and then poured myself a drink and went back to bed and we did it again. I remember the hotel room but I don't remember her name.*

Before he can speak, she turns his head a few inches to the side and touches her thumb to the scar on his jaw. "Lacrosse stick, eleven years old," she says.

So he pushes back inside her and loses his mind.

Maybe they fall asleep, who knows. He's not sure whether the noise of voices outside the window startles him out of a daydream or a real one. He looks down at the woman tucked under his arm, blinking her eyes open.

"Expecting someone?" he asks.

She looks at the clock on the bedside table. "Sam's not done with soccer practice until four. And he knows you're supposed to pick him up."

He kisses her forehead and swings out of bed. "I'll check it out. Stay here."

He pulls on his shirt and pants and peers out the window. Mallory's bedroom is above the porch; he can't see anyone, but there's a black Mercedes SUV parked outside that looks like the one Paige drives.

"I think it's your sister," he says.

Mallory sits up, flushed and tousled, clutching the sheets to her chest like some kind of Victorian maiden. "Paige?" she whispers. "What's she doing here?"

And it hits him again. The soft, sweet punch to the gut. Like that morning she stood shivering outside her mom's house on Cape

Cod to see him off and he had to kiss her lips, kiss her goodbye. Like that morning he cracked open his eyes in the guesthouse bed, after making love to her most of the night, and saw the blush of dawn on her skin. Like that June afternoon he stepped ashore, shook out his hair, and saw her sitting there on his beach, their beach, knees tucked under her chin.

She owns you, man. That's it, that's all. Lights out.

The front door creaks open. Paige's voice calls up from the hallway. "Maaaaalloreeee? Are you in here? Isn't that Monk's car in the driveway?"

"Busted," he says.

"What are you doing?"

"I'm going downstairs, what else?"

"Monk, wait!"

He walks out of the bedroom, around the landing, and down the stairs. Paige stands with her back to the front door, looking into the kitchen. She swivels as she hears Monk on the steps and takes him in with wide, startled eyes—his rumpled clothes, his bare feet, his disorderly hair.

"Hey, Paige," he says. "Can I help you?"

"*Monk?* Hi. Hello. I was . . . you know, looking for Mallory?"

"She's upstairs," he says. "In bed."

"Coming!" Mallory calls down.

Paige folds her arms. "*Please* tell me you were wearing protection this time."

"It's okay, honest. We're engaged."

"I didn't actually say yes, you know!" calls Mallory.

"Still working out a few kinks," Monk says. "But she'll come around, I promise. What's up?"

Paige looks bewildered, like she can't remember her own name. She gathers herself and turns to the living room, which Monk can't quite see because of the angle of the stairs. She holds out her hand and beckons. "I brought someone to meet my sister."

Into the hall steps an elderly man, wearing a flat cap and a white beard and a brown corduroy jacket over a blue knit shirt and a pair of worn tan pants. He offers a hand to Monk.

"Sir. Monk Adams," says Monk, shaking the hand, the way he was taught.

The man nods and glances up the stairs, where Mallory's just appeared on the landing in her jeans and her sleeveless gingham shirt, hair gathered back up in its knot. Cheeks still pink. Green eyes luminous, brows cocked inquisitively upward.

Monk lifts his arm and holds out his hand for her.

"Mallory," says Paige, like she's unwrapping a present for a small child. "I want to introduce you to somebody. This man was born in Hungary. He was kidnapped by Soviet soldiers as a baby during the Second World War and raised outside of Leningrad. After the Berlin Wall came down, he traveled back to Hungary and tracked down his birth mother."

The man says, "Hannah Vécsey."

By now Mallory's reached the bottom of the stairs and put her left hand into Monk's right hand. He knits his fingers with hers and thinks of Aunt Barbara's ring, tucked into the inside pocket of the laptop bag. How it will look on her finger, what she'll say when she sees it.

Mallory turns to the old man, a little bemused.

Paige's words fall into Monk's head on a time delay. "Wait a second," he says. "*Birth* mother? Are you saying . . ."

The man steps forward and reaches for Mallory's other hand. He folds it between a pair of kindly, callused palms.

"My dear," he says, in a heavy Slavic accent, "I promised your grandmother I would find you. My name is Károly. Count Vécsey."

Author's Note

I first came across the term *paternity incident* several years ago while reading an article about using DNA research to resolve a few rumors deep in the lineage of the British royal family. It turns out they're pretty common—in the general population, up to 30 percent of "official" dads turned out not to be the biological fathers of their offspring. We are shocked, shocked. But it also explains our deep cultural fascination with adultery, with a good father quest. It's all anthropology . . . which happens to have been my major in college.

While Hannah Vécsey and her story are fictional, a true event (as often happens) planted the seed in the soil of my brain, via an article in the *Wall Street Journal* some years ago about the rise of commercial DNA kits, and how sequencing companies are starting to hire therapists to help customers deal with the fallout when results uncover shocking family secrets—that is to say, paternity incidents. One woman interviewed for the article described a long path of research that led back from one of the notorious Irish Magdalene homes for unwed mothers to an affair by a married woman with the manager of some overseas hotel or club during the postwar disassembly of the British empire. This last bit especially intrigued me, since my own father was born in Calcutta to British parents in 1946 (though without, I'm pretty sure, any question of his paternity).

Still, this particular seed took some time to germinate. Because of the DNA element, I needed a contemporary narrative to go along with the postwar one, so it wasn't until I came across another story about a death cap mushroom and a kidney transplant (full disclosure, I'm not a fan of mushrooms) that I sat down with my notebook and started sketching out a plot. As it happened, I'd just been doing some research on early Cold War politics and the Suez crisis—it's no coincidence that the short-lived Hungarian revolution, so brutally put down by the Soviets, coincided with the crisis's climax in October–November 1956—so I set my love triangle in Cairo as the first sparks of the Egyptian revolution began to fly.

While my characters are fictional, Shepheard's Hotel and the Cairo fires, as well as the other events and locations described in the book, all existed inside a tangle of colonial, geographical, and postwar politics. My research stack for this book was extensive and occasionally obscure, but for those of you interested in exploring this subject further, I recommend Artemis Cooper's *Cairo in the War: 1939–1945* for a vivid picture of Egyptian politics and the adrenaline-packed maneuverings of the British military and diplomatic communities in Cairo. For background on the Egyptian Jewish community and its precarious postwar experience, you can turn to Lucette Lagnado's brilliant *The Man in the White Sharkskin Suit* and Viviane Bowell's touching self-published memoir *To Egypt with Love*. Keith Kyle's *Suez: Britain's End of Empire in the Middle East* is a dense and somewhat daunting but comprehensive account of the Suez crisis, from the building of the canal in the late nineteenth century to the geopolitical fallout afterward.

This is my third book set on fictional Winthrop Island (loosely inspired by the real-life Fishers Island off the southeastern Connecticut shore) and the first that takes place in the present day. Those of you who have read *The Summer Wives* and *The Beach at Summerly* will recognize a few of the families and their houses—Monk Adams, of course, is the grandson of Clay Monk, who spends most of *The Summer Wives* pining for Isobel Fisher. They say you should write what you know, so I don't quite understand why Monk popped fully formed into my head during the summer of 2022 as a contemporary musician. (My kids will be in therapy forever because of the permanent state of opera around our house, and the copy editor had to correct my spelling of Katy Perry—sorry, Katy! My daughters love your work!) But Monk is who he is, and if I don't know a lot about what he sings, I do know how he sings it, thanks to the terrific interviews and commentary on vocal technique on Met Opera Radio. For details on Monk's medical emergency, I turned to my old Stanford Football teammate Ozzie Grenardo—excuse me, Dr. Oswaldo Grenardo of Centura Health in Colorado—who patiently walked me through conditions that might lead to a near-fatal operating-table experience. Needless to say, any medical errors or misunderstandings in this book have nothing to do with Oz, who is a brilliant doc and a superb human.

More thanks! First and hugest, to my marvelous new editor, Kara Cesare, practically perfect in every way, for welcoming me to Ballantine and back into the Penguin Random House family, and for lavishing *Husbands & Lovers* with so much devotion and attention to detail. I feel especially fortunate that my new publishing home is packed with talented professionals who also happen to be fans (and even superfans) of my novels—when no less than Random House publicity director Susan Corcoran cornered me at our first meeting and told me that *Her Last Flight* was her favorite, I knew this union was meant to be. To the rest of the team—Kara Welsh, Jennifer Hershey, Kim Hovey, and Jesse Shuman on the editorial side; Jennifer Garza and Karen Fink in publicity; Quinne Rogers, Taylor Noel, and Megan Whalen in marketing; production editor Cindy Berman; art director Belinda Huey; plus all those book pushers and sales reps I have yet to meet—my gratitude for all your hard work, sung and unsung.

If my writing career has kept one constant, it's the guidance of my literary agent, Alexandra Machinist of CAA, who snagged my first manuscript from the slush pile when we were both just babies in the business and stuck with me ever since. Thanks to Alexandra's keen judgment and dogged commitment, I've been able to convert the contents of my imagination into a living for my family for over a decade, and I've come to treasure her friendship as much as her boundless professional energy.

I'm so grateful for all the bookish people this job has brought into my life. Kathie Bennett of Magic Time Literary wove her wand to connect me with so many bookstores and literary organizations as I've traveled around the country to speak about my novels, and I can't thank her enough for her enthusiasm and endless support. And it goes without saying that my writing sisters Karen White and Lauren Willig have propped me up daily in the writing of this book, enduring months of mushroom links ("THEY'RE EVERYWHERE!") in our ongoing group chat, with all the appropriate emojis.

Finally, to all my darling writer friends who have shared their encouragement and commiseration in this crazy business, the book bloggers and reviewers who have championed my stories, and especially the readers who have loved my novels and the people in them—thank you. Your kind words mean more than I can say.

About the Author

BEATRIZ WILLIAMS is the *New York Times* bestselling author of *The Beach at Summerly, Our Woman in Moscow, The Summer Wives, Her Last Flight, The Golden Hour, The Secret Life of Violet Grant, A Hundred Summers,* and several other works of historical fiction, including four novels in collaboration with fellow bestselling authors Karen White and Lauren Willig. A native of Seattle, she graduated from Stanford University and earned an MBA in finance from Columbia University. She lives with her husband and four children near the Connecticut shore, where she divides her time between writing and laundry.

beatrizwilliams.com
Facebook.com/authorbeatriz
X: @authorbeatriz
Instagram: @authorbeatriz